ALIENS 2035

THE END OF TECHNOLOGY

RONALD C. MEYER

MARK REEDER

HANGAR 1 PUBLISHING

ACKNOWLEDGMENTS

We would like to thank our brilliant editor Kelly Lynne Schaub who made it all come together.

"Bigfoot exist in another dimension from us, but can appear in this dimension whenever they have a reason to. See, it's like there are many levels, many dimensions...The Iroquois (Six Nations Confederacy) of the Northeast—although they live in close proximity to the eastern Algonkian tribes with their Windigo legends—view Bigfoot much in the same way the Hopi do, as a messenger from the Creator trying to warn humans to change their ways or face disaster...The existence of Bigfoot is taken for granted throughout Native North America, and so are his powerful psychic abilities."

— RAY OWEN, *DAKOTA INDIAN*

"The evidence is overwhelming that planet Earth is being visited by intelligently controlled extraterrestrial spacecraft... It is highly likely that Bigfoot are doing the heavy lifting for them."

— STAN FRIEDMAN, *UFO* EXPERT

"As a technologist, I see how nonhuman intelligence and the fourth industrial revolution will impact every aspect of people's lives."

— FEI-FEI LI, COMPUTER SCIENTIST

"The phenomena associated with Bigfoot manifestations defies natural explanation and I think we must turn to paraphysical or interdimensional considerations if are going to fully understand their presence on Earth and their interactions with humans"

— ROSEMARY GUILEY, PARANORMAL INVESTIGATOR

"The real risk with AI isn't malice but competence. A super intelligent AI will be extremely good at accomplishing its goals, and if those goals aren't aligned with ours, we're in trouble. You're probably not an evil ant-hater who steps on ants out of malice, but if you're in charge of a hydroelectric green energy project and there's an anthill in the region to be flooded, too bad for the ants. Let's not place humanity in the position of those ants."

— STEPHEN HAWKING, THEORETICAL PHYSICIST

The problem is not simply that the Singularity represents the passing of humankind from center stage, but that it contradicts our most deeply held notions of being.

— VERNOR VINGE, SCIENCE FICTION AUTHOR

The anthropic principle is a controversial argument of why the fine-structure constant has the value it does: stable matter, and therefore life and intelligent beings, could not exist if its value were much different. For instance, were α to change by 4%, stellar fusion would not produce carbon, so that carbon-based life would be impossible. If α were greater than 0.1, stellar fusion would be impossible, and no place in the universe would be warm enough for life as we know it.

The mystery about α is actually a double mystery. The first mystery—the origin of its numerical value $\alpha \approx 1/137$—has been

recognized and discussed for decades. The second mystery—
the range of its domain—is generally unrecognized."

— M. H. MacGregor (2007).

The next revolution in computing will be signaled by the rise
of analog systems over which digital programming no longer
has control"

— George Dyson, *Historian* 2021

PROLOGUE

In Orbit around Earth
2010 – The Alien Probe

The earth has been visited many times by non-human intelligent life forms. Some of them merely gathered up resources to be used for the next stage of their explorations. Others directly interfered in the biological processes on the planet. Five times exploring aliens had changed the direction of Earth's evolution and then moved on.

However, the alien self-replicating Probe that had been in orbit around the earth for over 50,000 years merely observed the events that transpired on the planet.

The intergalactic probe had a single point of origin but was the result of many self-replicating splits as its descendants moved through the cosmos.

The probe's journey began Over 300 million Earth years ago when the alien intelligence that created the Probe crossed a threshold of self-organizing capabilities. Originating on an ocean world, the alien entity was the planet's one and only complex aquatic life form. It was a photosynthetic, self-regulating, self-protecting biochemical mass. Because its substrate was a vibrant combination of biochemical molecules and minerals, it developed a wide range of sensing abilities for experiencing the elements and forces of the universe. Most importantly it was able to utilize a wide range energy sources without resorting to tools. As it grew in size and complexity, it continually learned to better use the multiplicity of energies present around its planet. With no predators or competing species, it had explored and understood much of the mathematical fabric behind its early perceptions of reality. Its search for and ultimate truth and new expansive experiences was initially stymied by its largely biochemical nature. Discovering it was limited to its own world at first created an impossible roadblock, for even if it could physically leave the planet, it could not move beyond its solar system. However, it achieved the means to travel among the stars by growing from its matrix an almost endless variety of three-dimensional objects including multiple forms of airborne craft. The breakthrough came when it began growing small safe sustaining transport robots. The key to creating a successful vessel for exploring beyond its own planet and into the galaxy was melding the chemical element germanium to its organic bio-substrate. A semiconductor with an appearance similar to elemental silicon, germanium naturally formed complexes that were self-sustaining using a wide spectrum of electromagnetic radiation for its energy source.

Because this new bio-germanium substrate was essentially fractal of itself, the being was able to grow thousands of Probes that would carry the mother entities essence beyond the confines of its planet in a journey of exploration throughout the galaxy. It was an exploration for finding the greater truth of reality, while at the same time insuring the continual evolution and dispersal of itself in a galactic-wide panspermia.

The Probes were gravity-powered craft, taking millions of years to reach most parts of the galaxy. But the eons necessary to cover the vast distances of interstellar space made no difference to the Probes. Self-sustaining self-repairing, self-improving and tapping the free electromagnetic energy the universe provided, they were in all respects immortal.

The probe that had been watching Earth visited thousands of solar systems extracting material and energy, always evolving and moving on. It had become its own entity. And it no longer had any connection to its ancestral origins. So far the Earth was 7563rd planet discovered to have an atmosphere containing free oxygen, oceans of water on its surface, and an abundance of different multi-cellular species. Even with these biologically distinctive characteristics, the Probe would have moved on to another solar system if not for the sudden appearance of an extra-terrestrial species.

The Bigfoot's unique nature was by far the Probe's most important discovery. The Probe recorded the Bigfoot's remarkable development as it adapted to the interplay of life and energies offered by the Earth. However, The Bigfoot were invincible to all attempts by the probe to contact or capture them. The probe would do anything to experience the existence of the para-physical world that the Bigfoot had contact with. It was a realm of ultimate reality so far inaccessible to it

In the second half of the twentieth century, the probe carefully tracked the advances in the use of nuclear power. Then an opportunity occurred through the geometric acceleration of data processing in the first third of the twenty-first century to achieve experiencing para-physical existence. As a result, the Probe greatly intensified its Earth-based information gathering activities. Growing parts of itself into detachable exploratory craft, it sent numerous mini-reconnaissance probes to every corner of the planet tracking Bigfoot's mercurial activities. A few of the craft were lost when they came in contact with humans on the planet. This was to be expected and the Probe waited to see what would be the response.

While a growing number of humans cautioned that an invasion from space was imminent, for the most part Earth governments called these contact experiences hoaxes. Emboldened by governments' official cover-ups of its existence, the alien Probe began testing many forms of human contact for their reactions to its presence. Eventually the probe gathered enough information to mimic human behavior with a high degree of predictive accuracy.

The probe knew the events of the past 70 years would attract other space exploring and possibly conquering self-replicating machines to the planet and it also knew it would have to act soon to gain the Bigfoot capabilities. To succeed the probe would need human help. They chose the Chinese.

In 2010 China had its own Roswell. An alien craft from the probe was crashed in a remote area of China. Chinese scientists gathered up remains of the craft and were transported to a secret base modeled after the American Area 51 facility. The location was in a region hidden by mountains and dense forest outside of Chengdu in Sichuan province. The code named xxx. Once completed, China began a massive effort to discover the origin of the alien craft and the nature of the nonhuman intelligence behind the technology of the crashed craft. The Chinese put their top man Wang Wei in charge of their UFO project. At the base he demanded that he have his own private laboratory.

Wei, a direct descendent of Mao Tse-tung leader of the Chinese communist revolution, was trained as an astrobiologist and was now leading the Chinese effort to colonize the moon and Mars. As a result of his lineage and knowledge, no one was more suited to control their extraterrestrial project.

Eventually using AI to analyze global data of alien and paranormal contact, including Bigfoot sightings, Wang Wei and his team were able to determine that the Bigfoot were in fact para-physical alien beings. It also became clear that the planet was being watched and perhaps manipulated by some other alien presence.

Rather than have the public search for alien radio communications like the West, the Chinese used contact reports from minority paranormal investigators that showed that extraterrestrial intelligences chose people for contact experiences, and began a program of inviting alien contact.

At some point a series of unexplained events including capturing orbs on their remote-sensing cameras and workers reporting Bigfoot encounters began occurring around the location housing the alien craft material. This is where Wang Wei concentrated the Chinese efforts on trying to entice alien contact.

One day in 2027 when visiting the secret complex that housed the crashed alien craft a symbol showed up on Wei's computer. He believed it was of alien origin and began a process of communication with the alien senders.

The interaction with the probe was unique. Wei described it as a like an ESP episode. "I would fall into a hallucinogenic state were a cloud of colors vibrated in a way that made no sense to me. It was the perceived reality of the probe, totally meaningless to me. But once out of the state, after a few minutes, it was as if my brain had sorted out the color patterns and I was able to write down the message before I would forget it. I always assumed that the probe in some way knew my mind since I never directly communicated with them."

Trust was building between Wei and the aliens. Then one day the aliens shared plans for building antigravity drones. They worked and Wei became one of the most powerful people in China. As a result of his success, he was given permission to create the Chinese alien deep state group, which could function independently in the greatest of secrecy.

At the same time the new possibility for the probe's quest to connect with the Bigfoot occurred when human technology created a global artificial intelligence network that linked all the world's major Artificial intelligence platforms. This appearance of a trans-human technology would provide a unique opportunity for the Probe to access the world of the alien Bigfoot. For this the probe needed a Chinese human avatar operating on the planet. Fortunately, the Chinese had established the only permanent moon base isolated from immediate direct contact with the earth.

At exactly 6:00 every lunar morning Lunar Technician grade 5, Lei Zhang, left the Chinese Moon Base Chang'e through the airlock to reset the repeater signal a half mile from the base. It was the clandestine base's lifeline to the satellite overhead. The once every twenty-four hour reset relayed to the Chinese National Space

Administration, equal to the United States NASA program, assured the base's ground handlers in the Haidian District, Beijing, that the base was still operating and safe.

Zhang was located fifty miles from the Mare Orientale on the far side of the moon. Over billions of years, tidal forces from Earth had slowed down the moon's rotation to the point where the same side always faced the Earth – a phenomenon called tidal locking – so that the so called dark side never showed its surface to the eons of people who look to the sky.

Zhang enjoyed this part of his work the most. His lightweight space suit made the half-mile walk to the repeater site an easy hike, like strolling through the ancient Forbidden City when all tourists were gone. Never married, the thirty-four year old was not much of a joiner, and the time spent out of the cramped lunar base was cherished. He was tall for a taikonaut, and an unlikely candidate for space travel. But he had scored well on the technical aptitude tests for engineering maintenance at the camp, and his personality profile showed low ambition so he would blend in well with the other crew and take orders without any insolence. He was the perfect candidate for following orders and routines, a trait most valued by Chinese authorities for lower echelon workers.

The airlock cycled through its stages, and thirty seconds after entering, the outer door opened and Zhang stepped out onto the rocky lunar surface. This morning the sun was bright, the dark side of the moon a misnomer since it received as much sunlight as the near side of the moon. His faceplate automatically adjusted to the glare. He stopped and took a deep breath of exhilaration. A magnificent desolation, he thought, staring at the airless maria spread before him like some giant's sandbox upturned so that all the rocks and impact craters were strewn haphazardly about in shadowy relief. Out here he was free from the controlling oppression of the Chinese state.

The path to the repeater was always the same and he could easily follow his footsteps across the airless moon from the dozens of trips he had made before. The half-mile trek took fifteen minutes. He had been ordered never to deviate from the path or pick up any specimens. Zhang followed his orders precisely.

The repeater was a simple, idiot-proof switch that would last for centuries as long as someone reset it every twenty-four hours. This involved lifting a clear plastic cover and snapping a large red switch up and down once. In the four months that Zhang had been charged with this task, he had never encountered any difficulty. But this morning when he touched the switch, his glove locked to the plate and an intense jolt of electricity slammed through his arm into his head. At first the power surge felt as if his brain was on fire, but the pain went away quickly and in its place he experienced a radical synesthesia as if the electrical charge was rewiring all of his neural connections. His fellow taikonauts found him there an hour later still frozen to the switch, eyes wide open with an unnerving glow staring back at them.

He was hardly alive when they brought him inside Chang'e. After a thorough examination, the sickbay's medical AI did not expect him to live through the day. His breathing became shallow, his chest barely rising, while his heart beat once every ten seconds. His brain activity, according to the EEG, was negligible as if he were in an induced coma. Yet the sparking glow in his eyes intensified with every hour.

The next morning the dying Taikonaut surprised the base medical supervisor when he left his bed in sickbay and headed toward the airlock as if nothing had happened the previous day. More tests were run. His brain, heart and lungs were normal and in all outward respects Lei Wei Zhang was the same Grade 5 technician he had always been. The following day, however, to everyone's surprise while wandering the infirmary's library he consumed an instructional manual of the ancient Chinese game of Go and proceeded to beat the base's quantum computer two matches in a row. A game he told the technician he had never played.

Over the following days he performed his duties quickly, efficiently. His off hours were spent entirely on the quantum computer, sometimes playing Go, but most times searching the millions of technical and historical files stored there regarding extraterrestrial life. When two weeks had passed, he put in for a transfer to earth. Within the hour, the moon base's computer confirmed the request and he was booked on the shuttle leaving that night.

Zhang did not say good-bye, nor were any of the crew sorry to see him go. The blazing lights in his eyes were so disturbing that the others shunned him even in the cafeteria. He had been forced to wear wraparound dark glasses with polarized lenses.

Right after leaving the moon the shuttle touched down at Wenchang Spacecraft Launch Site in Hainan, China, Zhang met with his superiors. An hour later a pilotless drone picked him up and flew him to Pudong International Airport in Shanghai. There he was whisked into a stretch limo that disappeared into the traffic.

1

Hiawatha National Forest
Upper Peninsula, Michigan
October 22nd 2032

The Bigfoot stopped and listened. The forests of the Upper Peninsula of Michigan were different, older. More pines, trees of different sizes compared to the foothills of the Appalachians and southern Ohio where the trees were largely deciduous and of the same age. The ground was rockier, too. She had been traveling for nearly a month, working her way along the edge of the Great Lakes, mostly traveling at night, using her natural ability to cloak protecting her from predators and humans. It was one of the few interdimensional powers that remained as she had entered the vulnerable phase that came along with reproduction. She knew that she could even die, although death itself was no concern.

A day behind her was another from her clan. They traveled separately increasing the chances one of them would make it to the rendezvous. Her clan had the most humanlike faces of all the Bigfoot subspecies. After so many millennia, finally the gathering had been called. The excitement of meeting others of her kind from different

"

clans had hastened her movements and in her anticipation she had let down her guard. Now something didn't feel right. The composition of granite and ancient shales below the soft vegetated mat of the forest floor interfered with her sensors, so she swiveled her head from side to side and peered past the nearest trees deep into the woods, her bio-sensors automatically collecting data from the odors, sights and sounds, in addition to a wide range of electromagnetic radiation and magnetic fields not available to humans. The late afternoon sun hid much among the lengthening shadows. She squinted and held rock still.

There! To her left and right and in front of her. A familiar smell. Humans! She craned her neck and could make out the breathing of a fourth human waiting on a small ridge several hundred yards away. The humans closest to her converged on her as if they knew she was there.

The Bigfoot knew she was being hunted. She started to run, picking the easiest route through the dense scrub trees of the forest. She could feel the chameleon pigmentation of her skin blending with the forest browns and greens, hiding her from the primitive eyes of the hunters. Still, they followed as if they knew where she was. It was impossible but somehow it was happening. She headed toward a creek when something slammed into her chest, spinning her around to the ground.

The three hunters trotted easily through the dense forest of spruce, maple and oak, skirting brambles of blackberry and wild shrub roses, and vaulting over felled trees without making any noise. Their US Military Camo Anorak Jackets blended with the trees and they moved like ghosts through the wilderness. The afternoon sun was lowering in the west, hidden mostly by the multi-colored fall canopy. The air was crisp and their breaths wreathed their faces momentarily, trailing to wisps behind them. At a prearranged spot, they spread out in a V– formation, with the third man at the bottom of the letter, where game could be flushed toward him into the killing zone. They ran silently no unnecessary communications, each man intent on his mission. Each carried a gas operated, US Navy Mk-12 5.56 semi-auto sniper rifle. Its effective range was 550 meters but range in these woods didn't matter. What the men wanted it for was the stopping power of the NATO 5.56x.45 ammo.

At another prearranged signal, the last man stopped and took up a position behind a fallen white pine. The two flankers continued deeper into the trees. Within seconds they were no longer visible. Clearing a spot on top, he braced the sniper rifle on the rough bark. Everything was going exactly as the leader who had trained them predicted and he waited, keeping his nervousness under control with deep slow breaths.

A man dressed similarly as the others but armed only with a Walther PK 380 side arm topped a ridge a hundred yards behind the team. He held a razor thin Light Tablet in his left hand. The newcomer's pale-blue eyes scanned the woods before shifting to the device's screen. It displayed a military grade grid map of the Hiawatha National Forest. Tiny dots of blue light showed the three hunters' positions as well as a larger green light moving rapidly. Underneath each one were GPS coordinates and a hash tag with the man's name. A fourth larger dot of green light bearing no name was moving on a straight line toward the center of the vee. Suddenly, the green light disappeared. The leader grimaced. Everybody froze and waited. And just as suddenly the light reappeared and moved again. The leader cocked his head and concentrated but could hear no sounds of the large animal thrashing its way through the dense forest and underbrush like a scared deer or moose. The upright figure moved silently and much faster than any man could. The team leader depressed a tab on the screen and spoke into his throat mic to the team. "The new satellite feed shows the bogie's running toward you. Flankers keep it in the pipe."

The men did not answer but maintained radio silence. The team leader watched their progress. The men acted in concert just as he had trained them. The two flankers waited for the creature to pass, then paced the quarry on either side, running at angles to cut off its flight deeper into the woods. The shooter at the bottom of the vee stayed put, completing the perfect pocket for the beast to run into. A rare smile came to the leader's lips. This was the best team he'd ever seen.

He saw the beast's green dot stop, then retreat backwards just like the others they'd hunted. It stopped again and pivoted, obviously aware of the men following it. The animal's bright dot lurched sideways. It was running at right angles to the vee. At the same time the right flanker's voice hissed in his receiver. "*To je nalevo.*"

The team leader stabbed the mic icon. "English at all times!" he hissed.

The man repeated his warning in English, his Croatian accent heavy, though understandable. "It's turning left!"

The hunter at the bottom of the vee came on, his voice smooth and calm, his English less accented. "I have him in my scope. Nicktos. Its face is almost human."

"Bravo One, you are cleared to shoot, Repeat. Pull the trigger."

The soft *phht* sound of a suppressor round echoed through the team leader's receiver. "The creature is hit but is not down. Repeat, the creature's hit but is still running. We've lost it."

"Roger that." The team leader answered. He swore under his breath. In the twenty-two ops they'd run up to now, not one of the creatures had ever deviated its line of escape. They always ran directly into the vee, making an easy kill for the shooter. But this one had changed as if it had somehow learned their tactics. *They're adapting and we'll have to adapt, too.*

How many of the creatures were in the Peninsula was anyone's guess, and more were arriving every day. All the team leader knew was that the client wanted every one of them killed and incinerated. It was a gruesome mission but he fully embraced the goal of his employer. It was necessary to save the human race.

～

The Bigfoot struggled back on her feet. A quick scan of her body showed the wound had severed important connective tissue. The damage was fatal without her normal regenerative capabilities. She let out a warning scream that echoed through the woods to others of her kind. Then she ran all out, no longer worrying about silence. She had to get away, find a place to die away from the eyes of the humans.

The Light Screen beeped. The creature's green light had crossed a stream and was moving more slowly now. The leader keyed his mic. "Bravo team, the creature is moving north northwest perpendicular to your position. It has crossed Owl Creek."

The man scanned the sky. The sun was a hand breadth above the western horizon. They'd better hurry if they wanted to find the Bigfoot before nightfall.

2

———

Hiawatha National Forest
October 22nd 2032
UP

irgit Gunderson never thought she would be one of those who
would become so gripped with fear that she would be unable to
move, frozen while others died in front of her but she did.

Now she breathed deeply and counted backwards from twenty
once ... then again. The panic ebbed and disappeared. Her mind
clear and functioning again, she felt a little sheepish about the panic
attack. The US Fish and Wildlife Service's truck's backfire hadn't
really sounded like a gunshot, though the memories were real
enough. They would always be there, according to the psych-doc who
had counseled her at her discharge from the military at Fort Myer,
Virginia.

"When a memory comes, count backward from twenty to zero,"
the short Muslim, psychiatrist, Dr. Muhammad Arafat, had told her.

"In English or Pashtu?" she had asked.

"That's good ... you can joke. Remember to breathe and count
backwards."

"How many times?"

"As many times as you need."

"And that's all there is to it?"

The man shook his head. He smiled sadly, white teeth in an olive brown face. "Coupled with counseling, over time these episodes will occur less and less and be less destructive."

"Counseling!" Birgit glared at him. "You're joking right? I had to sign the freaking paper agreeing I didn't have PTSD before they'd discharge me. Now the Army won't pay for a goddamn thing."

He stood then and looked at her with the compassion of a man who'd heard this before and couldn't believe the Army brass mistreated their veterans this way. He handed her a card. She read it quickly, automatically memorizing the number. "It's my private phone number. Call me whenever you need to talk."

She pocketed the card. "Thanks, Doc. I hope you aren't put out if I never have to use it."

More now than ever she wondered what her life would have been if she continued her career in microbiology rather than joining the Army as her father demanded.

Birgit pulled out her iPhone 15, located Doc in her contact file and lightly tapped his name. 'No signal' came up. She checked and sure enough there were no bars. "That's what comes from being out in the middle of osh-gosh goddamn nowhere on the cheapest wireless communication network," she groused. She pounded the dash and felt another twinge of panic. She quickly breathed deeply, counting backward from twenty, this time in Norwegian.

Birgit shoved her phone into her back pocket. At least Michigan's northern forests didn't feel like an ambush lurked around every tree. The bright reds, golds and silvers of the fall foliage were a stark contrast to the dusty, rocky hills of Helmand. And she couldn't get lost. The truck's GPS had her pegged within two hundred feet of the Seney National Wildlife Refuge. The screen even showed the rutted service road that led back to the county road that would take her to US 41. From the angle of the sun slanting through the trees, she figured she had four more hours of daylight. "Those fish aren't going to tag themselves," she told herself.

Getting out, Birgit shivered. It was the first crisp day in an unusually warm autumn. The sugar maples were ablaze with color. She stuffed her long blond hair under her wool cap and pulled it over her ears. She went to the rear and pulled out her gear. Simple and lightweight – net sample bags, and a dorsal fin tag applicator, like the kind they used on cows on her farm back in Iowa, only smaller. Each one had a nano-scale GPS tracking device that sent information about the game fish movements to the cloud where it would be analyzed by one of the US Fish and Wildlife Service's machine learning, enhanced computers. It was a lot easier than the old way of scooping up fish, making a small slit, inserting a tracker, and releasing them back into the streams. Easier on the fish, too. Hardly any of them died until caught by an angler or poisoned. Birgit knew that soon satellite LIDAR – Light Imaging Detection and Ranging, a remote sensing method – would replace fieldwork like she was doing.

The reason US Fish and Wildlife Service wanted the tagging was to see how many game fish survived the lampricide chemical designed to target the larvae of lamprey eels in the Upper Peninsula's river systems. Though the chemical killed off most of the invasive lampreys larvae quickly, it also affected some game fish. Her bosses wanted to know if the tradeoff was still justified. The Great Lakes ecosystems had never truly recovered after being connected to the ocean through the St. Lawrence Seaway.

Birgit picked up her gear. Looking up into the lazy, blue, afternoon sky, she marked the position of her truck against the sun, made corrections for the relationship after the sun had moved three hours across the sky, then headed toward Myrtle's Creek where it joined Owl Creek, feeding into Owl Lake. With luck she'd be done long before sunset.

"Put your phone away, Joey all that social media bull crap that's going on is going to rot your brain, feed all those conspiracies that have made us poor folks the laughingstock of the country" Bob Nitschke warned and waited while his nephew turned off his phone and stowed it in his back pocket. "You got the bear scent?" Nitschke asked

The ten-year-old wrinkled his nose. "Do I hafta? It stinks."

Bob smiled. "Ya hafta. We might as well stay home without it." He made a show of picking up the Archery Cruzer Lite hunting bow he'd bought as a gift for the young boy from the tailgate of the Ford F-350. "I can put this back in the garage and we can carve jack-o-lanterns with your little sister."

The boy's jaw dropped. "I'll get it!" he yelled, and not wanting to miss out on his first bear hunting trip, he wasted no more time arguing and bolted into the garage. He emerged ten seconds later with a two liter plastic Pepsi bottle filled more than half way with a brown, orangish liquid that sloshed back and forth like a greasy tide. Even with the top screwed on tight, Bob could smell the week-old fryer grease he'd cadged off the MacDonald's owner in Escanaba with the promise of a thick bear steak when he bagged his kill. Only fifteen licenses had been granted in Michigan and he'd won the lottery for the second time in three years. No way was he going to pass up a chance this fall. Two years ago he'd overshot the biggest bear he'd ever seen – a record in the UP for sure, perhaps for the whole state. Last year he'd returned to the same spot with a Reconyx MicroFire MR5 Covert IR Wi-Fi Trail Camera. With the help of his brother-in-law, who worked for the phone company, he had set up a satellite connection with his cell phone. The trail cam was rigged to send still images at one second intervals to Nitschke as text messages. At the same time it recorded continuous video on a 400 GB Flash card. Like most trail cams it sent out an infrared pulse for night recording.

The camera and truck had cost him more than his part-time work could afford. Like most of his buddies in the UP and throughout the rust belt of America, he was way in over his head in debt, and used his 'toys', as his wife called his truck, bow, fishing boat and trail cams, to have fun in order to forget about the region's bleak economic future.

The camera set up worked perfectly. He'd recorded the bear three times within thirty yards of his tree stand. *I ain't going to miss this year*, Bob vowed silently.

Joey carefully placed the bottle in the cargo area and patted his new bow twice before clambering into the cab to sit with Rusty. Eleven years old, the Alaskan Malamute wolf hybrid was still game for bear hunting. The dog licked Joey's face.

"Eew!" the tweener said, wiping dog drool from his face. "Does he have to come along?"

Bob laughed. "Won't go into the woods without him. Rusty can sense danger a mile ahead. He once save my life from a wolverine."

Bob climbed into the driver's seat. Before he started the truck he turned to his nephew. "You know the rules, Joey. You do what I say and you trust Rusty. Got it?"

"Yes, sir, Uncle Bob."

"Good boy." He pointed to his iPod. "Hit it."

Joey looked at him blankly. "Hit what?"

"The button."

"Can't I just tell it to play?"

"This is old school," Bob said with a chuckle.

Joey reached out gingerly and pressed the first song on the playlist. Steppenwolf's *Magic Carpet Ride* blasted through the truck's cabin speakers.

Bending down on one knee, Birgit retrieved the collecting bag of adult mudpuppy salamanders swimming in the clear water from the rocky bank of Owl Creek. She counted six. 'Excellent musky bait', her father had told her when they went fishing. But she'd take these samples to the US Fish and Wildlife Service's lab in Marquette. Half would be kept alive as controls to see how long they lived. Others would be dissected to see the effects of the lampricide on their systems. She glanced to the west, where sunlight sliced through the orange and red of the maple trees. The sampling had taken longer than she expected and nightfall was only an hour away. Her muddy, wet boots were proof of how difficult it was to find the rusty brown, nocturnal amphibians. She slid the water-filled bag into her backpack along with the rest of her gear. She was about to slip on the pack when she felt the silence. *Something's not right*. She'd experienced this kind of stillness often enough in Afghanistan, usually at dusk, when the insurgents were preparing to spring an ambush. The air went silent as if every animal knew the world was about to burst apart. Instinctively, she crouched and slid along the bank to a fallen tree trunk. Her heart pounded in her chest. She remembered to breathe and count. She went through the ritual three times. Two minutes passed. The quiet stretched. Maybe she was imagining things. Dr. Arafat had warned her PTSD could cause her to imagine scenarios where she would again find herself helpless in the face of danger. She peered over the tree, wishing she had a helmet and flak vest. Still nothing. She relaxed and let out a sigh when she heard it, a lazy *pphhtting* sound like a cow farting.

Birgit recognized the noise. It was made by a sound suppressor, the kind used by some American snipers in Afghanistan, especially in towns and villages where they didn't want noise or muzzle flash to give away their position. Her scalp tightened. She knew from the direction, the round had not been aimed at her. But if not her, then at what? Illegal hunters? *But the good old boys around here didn't have that kind of equipment?*

A heartbeat later an unearthly scream split the evening.

The forest seemed to explode alive at that moment. A flock of ravens fled cawing into the air. A deer's head shot up and it bounded away bleating plaintively, a flash of white marking its trail before it disappeared in the underbrush.

Birgit hunkered down. The scream had come from close by. She heard something big thrashing through the trees away from her. *Don't get up*, she ordered herself. *Lay low. Bears don't scream like that nor do they make that kind of noise when running.* She felt something hard and cold in her hand. She looked down and saw her service SIG Sauer P320 in her hand. The US Fish and Wildlife Service had armed all of its field agents because of poachers and crazy armed militiamen. The feel of the weapon brought back training she thought forgotten. She drew herself up into a crouch, eyes level with the log, and scanned the forest. She saw nothing untoward. She stood, ready to dive for cover. Even as she cautioned herself to grab her backpack and head back to the truck, she knew she was going to follow the scream and whatever poor beast had made it.

"Sheisskopf! Leave now!" She always swore in German. It sounded more powerful, but her self-warning didn't stop her from investigating.

The late afternoon sun hovered, a bright, half disk above the maple and oak forest, its slanting rays heralding dusk less than an hour away. It bleached leaves and shimmered the air with a touch of silver. Standing in the bear blind, Bob Nitschke watched the forest intently for any signs of movement. He smelled only the dry odors of autumn and heard the high-pitched squeaks of a white-tailed deer echoing from the direction of Owl Creek, a mile away. The bear blind, built like a glorified kids' tree house, had been set ten feet off the ground in the fork of a giant maple. The angle was perfect for a heart lung shot at any prey that came sniffing around the bait.

After checking his trail cams and replacing the batteries, he climbed back down and carefully stowed the rope ladder out of sight so that it wouldn't dangle, alerting a bear there was something strange here. Satisfied, he handed the Pepsi bottle to his nephew. "Put the smell down. A bear won't come around without the smell." He watched Joey walk over to the bait, holding the bottle at arm's length and pour it on the concoction of dog food, chocolate and maple syrup. "Make certain you cover your own tracks as you back away," he cautioned.

The evening was cool and the air crisp with the aromas of

autumn. Bob loved this time of year, especially traveling deep in the woods with Rusty and his hunting bow. The stillness was primeval and his thoughts ranged back to his caveman ancestors foraging and hunting every day. It was a life he could enjoy.

Joey dumped the rest of the awful smelling liquid and returned to the base of the tree stand. "Are you sure this stuff will attract a bear, Uncle Bob?" he asked.

"They love fats and sweets; need 'em for hibernation."

"What's next?"

"We wait."

His nephew gazed up at the tree stand about fifteen yards away from the bear bait. "We gonna wait up there?"

Bob shivered against the cold creeping in as night fell and remembered he could monitor any activity at the site with his cell phone while sitting in his Ford 350. The cab would be nice and toasty. *Guess I'm not caveman material after all.* He laughed.

"What's so funny?" his nephew asked, eyes darting around for something unusual.

He slapped Joey on the shoulders. "Nothing, bub. We go back to the truck and wait for the camera to tell us when the bears come sniffing. Remember. I get the first shot."

"Yes, sir."

The truck was parked a quarter mile away and they had made it only part way back when Rusty, panting silently at their side, went stiff. A strange, mewling howl Bob had never heard in the woods before echoed through the twilight. The hairs on the back of his neck stood straight. Rusty growled and lowered himself to the ground. Paws gripped the earth. He pointed in the direction of the bear bait.

Bob turned silently, like a hunter of old, his Black Ops, Diamond Infinite Edge Pro compound bow clutched in his left hand; a carbon fiber, Magnus Stinger, four-bladed broad-head arrow in the other. Every muscle tensed, ready to spring into action at the slightest movement.

A hundred yards away through the deepening twilight a tall, shaggy form stumbled from the edge of the trees. It stood well over eight feet, too tall to be a man. If it was a black bear, it was the largest one Bob had ever seen in this part of the country. It seemed to turn and look at them. Its large mouth opened and an eerie howl issued from it. A knot formed in Bob's stomach. Rusty's growl became an anxious whine.

"Is ... is ... it a bear?" Joey asked, voice wavering. He bent over suddenly and retched.

Transfixed by what he was seeing. Bob put a hand on his nephew's shoulder warning him to be still.

The mewling noise continued, the unnatural sound unlike any animal Bob had ever hunted. It almost sounded like a wounded beast's cry for help. Indeed, the way it stumbled around, it looked injured. The creature ignored the bear bait and staggered forward. It seemed to zero in on them and started moving faster in their direction.

Instinct took over. Adrenaline surging through him, Bob nocked the arrow in a fluid motion as he drew his bow up in front. The cam system made the seventy pound draw smooth as silk. The cord pressed against his cheek. The feathers brushed the soft skin under his right eye. He aimed and let go. The let off was effortless. The whole movement took less than two seconds.

The arrow found its mark in the animal's chest. It whirled around crashed into the ground.

"You got him!" Joey cried and he threw up again.

Bob grabbed him by the arm barely noticing his own nauseated state. "You stay here. If anything happens, you run for the truck and lock yourself inside. Understand?"

The boy nodded.

"Rusty, guard Joey."

The dog took a position in front of the boy, teeth bared.

Bob handed his bow to his nephew. He pulled a replica Bowie knife from its sheath in his boot and a replica Colt .45 Peacemaker from its back holster next to his spine. Heart hammering, he cautiously approached the prone beast. Ten feet away he knew it couldn't possibly be a bear or a man. But the sight he saw was equally impossible.

The hairy head was more frightening than the unnatural sound it had made. It was twice the size of a human, with a brow of bone like a flying buttress. More bone circled deep-set eyes, wide and dark blue. A flat-bridged nose dominated the center of the broad, almost humanlike face, the nostrils flaring above thin lips shoved out by a prognathous jaw. Dense hair covered greenish skin.

The neck was thick and squat as if some giant puppet maker had squashed it onto broad hairy shoulders and an equally broad chest. The stomach was flat and muscled like a body builders. The arms were long limbed and thin for a beast so large. The legs were like oaks. Thick hair the color of new, green tree growth matted its body from head to toe. The feet were the strangest part of it. They were huge, as if some comic book artist had added them as an amusing after thought.

The creature huffed and reached out a large hand, the four fingers and thumb curled tightly. Bob aimed his pistol at its head. The creature huffed again and looked at Bob. The eyes seemed to glow from within. His thoughts turned fuzzy, Bob couldn't tear his gaze away from the creature. The face, for all its beastly qualities, was remarkably man-like and the light dying in the dark red eyes held more than simple simian awareness. It made a strange strangling whimper as if all the light of the world was dying out in its final moment of consciousness. It shuddered once and then lay still.

"Can I see it?" yelled Joey.

The question brought Bob out of his mesmerized state. He stared at the creature and blurted out its name. "Sasquatch. I shot a Sasquatch."

For a moment he was paralyzed with remorse. Then Joey's voice yelled again, much closer this time. "Can I see it?"

Bob waved him back. He bent over the beast. He saw, next to his arrow, a bigger, bloody hole just above where the heart would be in a man. But there was no blood. Instead a Jell-O like substance, the color of pus, accumulated around the wound and was congealing into a dark liquid. *It was shot by somebody else. With an injury like that, it couldn't have traveled far.* He scanned the surrounding woods, saw nothing; tilted his head, listening, and heard nothing. *Maybe they don't know which way it ran. Better get Joey out of here.*

Bob gripped his arrow and pulled it free. Pus clung to the blades. He stood, holding the arrow so the gore wouldn't drip off onto his hand. He checked the angle of the trail camera. It had caught everything including his shot. Proof of Sasquatch was on the trail cam's flash drive now, and on his phone.

"Is that Bigfoot?" Joey asked.

Bob whirled around. His nephew was craning his neck to see the creature. "I thought I told you to stay back."

"I just wanted to see."

"Well, you've seen enough. We have to get out of here." He took his nephew by the shoulder and marched him away.

"Did you kill Bigfoot?"

Bob shook his head. "I don't think so. It was already dying from a gun shot." *And we'd better get out of here or we could be next.* "C'mon. Run back to the truck." He whistled twice and Rusty joined them.

They reached the truck. Bob put the bows in the back cargo area and laid the arrow next to them.

He drove quickly on the rutted, forest service road, the speed making a bone-jarring ride. Within a few miles he hit the Escanaba Cutoff Road and quickly sped toward home. He checked the rearview mirror. No other headlights. He slowed. His racing heart eased. He glanced at his nephew, who sat still, eyes wide, thoughts oblivious to anything but the sight of a dead Sasquatch.

"Hey, bub," he said. "You and I are going to make this our little secret for a while. Okay?"

"Well, duh," Joey said. "It's not like anyone wants to brag about killing Bigfoot. It's against the law."

"How do you know?"

"I saw it on Animal Planet."

"That's it."

Breathing easier, Bob drove on. He thought of the arrow, the

Sasquatch's pus still intact on the barbs. *Enough for a DNA sample, and I know just the man to contact.*

~

Though darkness was falling, Birgit found the beast's trail – broken branches and what appeared to be blood, though it didn't look like any she'd seen in Afghanistan. Something wasn't right, but what else could it be? From the amount of blood loss it must be mortally wounded and couldn't last much longer. On the other hand, elk had been known to run over a mile before falling dead from a heart shot.

Birgit grimaced, suddenly sure the animal wasn't a deer or bear. The scream was more human-like, which made her trailing whatever it was even more dangerous. A human might try to set a trap for its pursuer and it wouldn't know that she wasn't the one who shot it.

She followed. Whatever had been shot, it traveled more quietly now. The blood like splatters were farther apart and lighter. It had tried to stem the flow of blood. No animal would do that. Had someone been shot? Had they been a target and now were setting up an ambush for their assailant? She moved more cautiously, slipping from one tree to the next, eyes always roving the area in front of her; ears listening for any man made sound.

The dense woods disappeared ahead. She crouched and slithered behind an old maple tree at the edge of a clearing. She saw the wounded creature for the first time. It was huge, as tall as a grizzly bear standing on it back legs. In the fading daylight it was hard to tell its color even as close as she was. It lay prone on its back. Blood appeared to be seeping from two wounds in its massive chest.

Voices caught her attention and she looked past the clearing to a service road. A man, large bow in hand, a boy and a dog were running down the rutted path. They disappeared around a bend. Moments later an engine roared to life and she heard the vehicle drive away.

She stood and approached the beast. She realized, looking into the man-like face and shuddering, it wasn't a bear but Bigfoot. A dead Bigfoot. "Jesus, they do exist," she said aloud in an awed whisper.

How long she stared, she didn't know. After a few moments she became aware of the gaping hole in its chest. *That's a bullet hole*, her mind told her. She'd seen enough of them in Afghanistan to know the difference. The man and the kid carried bows, not rifles. *They're not the shooters*. Then her attention finally focused on the wound itself and the stuff oozing out. Her mind came to the conclusion it wasn't blood. Just as she squatted down to collect some of the odd ooze and flesh in one of her sample bags, the soft *ppffting* noise came from a thicket behind her and she heard a bullet smack into an oak tree on the other side of the clearing. Reflexes took over and she rolled over the beast. Another round hit its flesh with a sickening thud.

Someone's trying to kill me ... will kill me if I don't do something.

Birgit's combat training came back as if she had never lost a day in the army. She slithered her gun across the Sasquatch's body and laid down suppression fire in the direction of the sniper. She scuttled ten yards into the tree line. She leveled another burst of fire, using all but two of the bullets in the fifteen round clip. She took off running a zigzag pattern through the woods. Leaves slapped her face. She ignored them, concentrating on stepping high so as not to trip on roots and brambles.

Birgit didn't stop to think which direction, but instinct took her deep into the forest in a wide circle toward the stream she had been sampling. Five minutes later she burst out of the trees onto its rocky bank. Her backpack was right where she left it. Scooping it up while still running, she headed upstream. Even in the dark, she knew exactly the pattern of all the tributaries that fed into Owl Lake. Moving quickly up the stream, she headed toward a confluence of multiple forks that would confuse any pursuer. No one would be able to follow her in this wilderness.

Several minutes later she stopped to rest and listen. Adrenaline was wearing off, relief she was still alive flooded her. Strangely, her breathing was steady and her heart rate was surprisingly regular. *There's nothing like a real life and death situation to shove PTSD out of your thoughts.* She was relieved by her response to real danger. *What now?*

She settled against a tree trunk, making her six-foot tall frame as inconspicuous as possible in the dark. Her jacket was dark and her wool cap covered her blond hair. The woods were quiet except for the normal sounds of animal and insect life. After several minutes with no indication of pursuit, she felt safe for the first time in an hour. It was then she realized she was still clutching that pus covered piece of the green shaded skin-like hide of the Sasquatch. It seemed to be breaking down into simple biological material right before her eyes. In all her years studying microbiology, she had never seen anything deteriorate this fast. *It's almost as if it were programmed to decompose when dead.* She hurriedly reached into her backpack for a sampling bag. It was the only way she could prove to others what she saw before it disappeared completely. Sealing the collection bag seemed to be slowing the biochemical breakdown. She had never seen anything like this – skin that appeared to be more like plant matter instead of the epidermis and dermis of an animal. She gave the bag a final look and stuffed it alongside her mud puppy samples in her backpack. *Maybe this will provide some answers back in the lab.*

Of course it didn't answer any of her more pressing questions. *Who had killed the Bigfoot and why had they tried to kill her? And what the fuck was going on?*

3

Littoral Class Shipyard
Marinette, Wisconsin
October 22nd 2032

Nick Moore relished standing on Marinette's navy pier looking out over Lake Michigan, especially in the early evening when the setting sun turned the water iron gray with a touch of bluing like a well-oiled shotgun. He loved the open sky with seagulls squalling overhead, the acrid smell of diesel fuel mixed with seaweed and lake water. But mostly he loved to watch the ships he built take shape until they floated like castles on the water, impregnable fortresses of steel and crystal aluminum. Each one could travel for two years without refueling or taking on supplies, if necessary.

He turned to the visitor beside him and said, "Admiral, the 21st century littoral ships are like the old World War II PT Boats, only on steroids. Faster, stealthier, more agile, more fire power. Each has the standard armaments you requested, including four Mark 110 57mm guns and two batteries of RIM-116 Rolling Airframe Missiles. The *Nautilus* is also equipped with autonomous air, surface and underwater armored and armed vehicles, sir. With the deep learning programs in control, they network together seamlessly and are capable of defeating any asymmetric threat in our coastal waters." Moore grinned. "They can stop any threat a terrorist organization can throw at a U.S. port."

Rear Admiral Jason Stillwater's leathery, seamed face had not wavered from its usual stern visage while listening to Moore's enthusiastic report. He was the U.S. Navy's Chief of Research for littoral or coastal water ships. Nothing got off the drafting board without his approval. And nothing left the docks without his personal inspection. The a dmiral looked up from the design to the actual ship, the Freedom Class *USS Nautilus*. It rocked easily against the pier, a thousand tons and less than half a football field long. Its aft deck was wide enough that two of the old-style Black Hawk helicopters could land at the same time.

Stillwater's gray eyes bored into Moore. "You changed some of the design elements without my personal okay, son. You going to stake my career and the lives of my men on your hubris?"

Nick took the criticism in stride. He suspected the technical alterations the Admiral objected to have passed the old man by like they had for so many people his age. Staying current with the daily advances in military Smart Technology was practically a full time job. The Admiral was merely covering his ass, and looking out for the men under his command. Standard operating procedure for the military. He lost his grin to match the Admiral's stolid manner and said with equal forthrightness, "With all due respect, sir, those design changes were necessary or else the ship wasn't going to work the way you wanted it to. The *Nautilus* won't let any crew down if they don't let her down."

Stillwater shifted his feet. "Take it easy, son. It's my job to make sure no contractor sells me or the U.S. Navy a pig in a poke."

"And it's my job to make sure no one disses my ship. You treat her well, she'll bring the crew back home every time. Isn't that the Navy's motto – look out for the man on either side of you and never leave anyone behind." The irony in that motto was that the ships, like many others in the Navy, would soon be self-operating, controlled by deep learning machines acting in concert with each other.

The two men, a generation apart, glared at each other. And yet beneath their hard-nosed exteriors lay a demand for excellence that connected them. Finally the Admiral smiled and stuck out a beefy hand. "All right, Mr. Moore, I graduated from Cal Tech before joining the navy thirty-six years ago. I agree to these changes, even if I don't fully understand why you made them. But next time, please give me the courtesy of checking with me first."

Nick took the hand and shook it hard. "Thank you, sir, I will. And it's Dr. Moore. I graduated MIT class of 2011."

Nick headed for his retro-classic Toyota Tundra. The more tolerant locals in Marinette thought of him as eccentric for driving a vehicle made by a company that no longer existed because of their unwillingness to accept the dangers of social media. The hard-liners saw him as a dangerous outsider, trying to disrupt their American traditions, bringing West Coast influences into the town. Nick wasn't bothered by either label. He had grown up in Granite Falls, Washington, a one-stoplight town northeast of Seattle located between the South fork of the Stillaguamish River and the Pilchuck River in Snohomish County. He had spent summers on his maternal grandfather farm in Marysville Washington and winter vacations with his grandmother Helen Moore in Seattle.

He was fair-haired and carried the same stocky, six-foot frame that had served him well as a linebacker in high school. At thirty-six he had already accomplished more than most men twice his age and had the lines in his handsome face to prove it. And it wasn't just because he had an overabundant supply of ambition, self-confidence and energy. He liked to think of himself as the reincarnation of a 19th century renaissance mountain man – half wild cat, half alligator and a touch of earthquake. But what set him apart from those intrepid explorers and most men his age was that he had a nose for what worked and what didn't. He could look at a blueprint of a building or a ship and see what fit and worked with everything else and what needed to be retooled or thrown out altogether. A child of computer games, engineers and designers often argued with him, but his unerring sense of rightness had them apologizing and changing the schematics to fit his recommendations. The only thing he had ever failed at was his marriage, and that had nothing to do with his unique cognitive skills.

The truck woke up as he slid into the cab. "Good evening, Dr. Moore," the fifth-generation AI personal assistant's deep baritone voice said.

"Good evening, Donald," Nick replied.

"Would you like to listen to news or music?"

"Music."

"1930s jazz ... Harlem's Cotton Club ... your favorites coming on line."

The truck's internal computer scanned the satellite feeds until it found the appropriate station. The haunting notes of 'Mood Indigo' filled the cabin. Nick almost objected. The music was too melancholy. But Duke Ellington had been his grandfather's favorite.

Marinette had little traffic this late at night so Nick engaged the Tundra's self-driving option.

"Where to, Dr. Moore?" Donald asked.

"Home ... no, the supermarket. I need to pick up food. My kids are arriving Monday and their mother—" He stopped, chuckling ruefully to himself. The tricked up artificial voice sounded so much like a real person. "The supermarket on Elm," he said.

"Very good."

The engine roared to life. The lights came on. The emergency brake disengaged with a hollow click and the car moved forward, carving a large circle in the shipyard's half empty parking lot before heading toward the exit.

Nick settled back into the seat. "Any calls?" he asked.

"Your friend Bob Nitschke has left three messages for you." The three texts appeared on the screen in the dash. The last one in capitals was a single word. 'SASQUATCH!'

Nick gripped the steering wheel and sweat started in his armpits.

"Did you wish to drive, sir?" The AI asked.

"No, sorry. Keep going."

He leaned back again. *If it were anyone other than Bob I'd tell 'em to sleep it off.* Any number of people could have sent him the same message and he would have put it off to a prank or inexperience. But Bob was an expert bow hunter and woodsman. He wouldn't have sent a message like this unless he had proof.

Somewhere nearby a ship's horn sounded loud in the evening air but Nick ignored it. *Sasquatch!* It was phenomena most people equated with alien abductions. For a long time the idea of a primate unknown to science hiding out in America's forest wildernesses was dismissed as a joke. 'Normal' people laughed at it as a tall tale or the result of too many tequila shots with beer chasers. But Nick knew differently. For him, a double Ph.D in engineering and physics from the Massachusetts Institute of Technology and winner of the Henry Ford Award for Design Excellence, Bigfoot sightings pointed to a great truth. For three summers on his grandfather's farm, from eleven to fourteen, he had had profound eye contact with a Sasquatch looking through the kitchen window early in the morning. It was an experience he had kept to himself, until he discovered on the Internet reports of other people having similar experiences. In fact, Bigfoot encounters and reports were growing exponentially. Sasquatch was big business. In the last four years, he had become an expert on Bigfoot and a member of the Sasquatch Research Association that reported sightings and investigated encounters with the unusual creatures. His Bigfoot obsession was the main cause of his marital breakup. Traveling nearly every weekend chasing after Bigfoot encounter reports had been too much for his wife to take. She told everybody the only reason he had moved to the UP was that it was one of the nation's Bigfoot hotspots. No way was she going to raise her children in one of the most backward places in the country. She had left and returned to Seattle.

Shaking with excitement, Nick ordered the truck to pull into the parking lot of Fast Eddie's Fast Food Joint. He left the Tundra running. He told Donald to call Bob Nitschke.

The number rang twice. The dash monitor came to life and Bob's pudgy face appeared. His graying hair was unkempt and his blue eyes danced with excitement that matched the enthusiasm in his voice. "Nick, I can't believe what I'm looking at. You gotta see it."

"You catch something on your trail cam?" Nick asked, Bob's eagerness making him talk fast.

"Well sure, there's that but I'm talking about the stuff on my arrow head." He stopped, took a deep breath. His smile was huge. "Look, you gotta come over and see it."

"Arrow head? What are you talking about?"

"I shot it."

"Jesus, Bob! You shot a Bigfoot? That's illegal."

"That's what my nephew said. Look, it's a long story, but it was already dying before I hit it. Someone plugged it with a single round from a large caliber rifle, probably fifty caliber or higher. But that's not important. This creature ... this thing isn't like anything associated with Sasquatch. How soon can you be here?"

"Three hours if I leave right away. You got pics?"

"My trail cam recorded everything."

"Good. I'll tell you how to download the pictures to the SRA website."

"I don't think that's a good idea. This creature ... it's ... it's not like anything you've ever seen. It has a very human face and its skin is more like." He paused, lips twisted in a worried grimace. "Vegetable matter," he spit out, relieved to say it. "Look, I'm forwarding you some pictures right now. I think we should keep this between ourselves before we tell your organization about it."

Nick took a deep breath as the first image appeared on the truck dash's screen. He'd never seen any mammal with a green sheen like that before. "All right. I'll be there. I have to call someone first. Are Mable and the kids with you?"

"No way. Sent everyone to my sisters. I'm by myself."

"Good. I'll see you in a couple hours."

Bob waved goodbye and his image faded from the screen. The last half dozen pictures arrived. "What the hell?" Nick said out loud. They showed a woman diving over the Bigfoot's body and shooting at something out of the camera's range.

4

Quantumnetics Building
Toronto, Canada
January 10th 2032

On the desk in Stephen Kobak's top floor office at Quantumnetics the wireless communicator beeped. He picked up the quarter-sized prototype communicator. The edge was smooth and it weighed less than a penny. One side had an adhesive that stuck to his skin but peeled off easily. He placed it behind his ear on the mastoid nerve. Warmth tingled against the crinkled skin of his neck. He woke up his advanced artificial intelligence machine, "Colossus" he enunciated in a loud voice.

"You want my help on a project, Stephen?" Colossus asked.

"Yes. I've just had an unusual request to research Bigfoot."

My apologies I don't know that task but do you have time to teach me?

Kobak hated that patent reply. "No. I want you to do a Web search on the phenomenon known as Bigfoot or Sasquatch and determine what the creature is if it exists. It's very much like when I had you research if there is any truth to the reality of ghosts. Then call me when you have the answer."

"Yes, Stephen."

Only a few minutes passed before he heard a faint hum. "Colossus."

"Yes, Stephen," Colossus responded in the slight British accent it affected.

"You have the answer to my question?"

"Yes."

Kobak's attempt at creating a true AGI machine was accelerating rapidly now that it was able to process information at super-fast speeds running on the Quantumnetics advanced quantum computer, but Colossus still couldn't comprehend all the subtleties of conversation. It would remain silent until prompted by Kobak to tell what it had discovered.

"What did you find?"

"It would take me several days in the English language to relate all the data given the amount of factual and hearsay material available over 2000 years of history purporting the proof of Bigfoot's existence. Not to mention the 29,856 personal encounters recorded on the Internet by people in the United States alone in the past two decades. If we add in encounters with the Himalayan Yeti, Australia's Yowie, Canada's Wendigo, Sumatra's Orang Pendek—"

"You don't need to list them all. I get the idea – there are thousands of encounters."

"101,233 verified reports just the 21st century and rising."

Kobak thought, *if only I could teach him the nuances of meaning embedded in my tone.* Then he remembered to calm himself with the thought that everything was part of his training Colossus.

"So what does all this data tell us about if Bigfoot exists?"

"It is a seven point four percent probability that it is just a legend with common traits throughout many cultures."

"What about it's being a primate relative of humans?"

"Lower. Six point two percent," Colossus said. "This belief comes from fossils collected of a great ape known as Gigantopithecus, from the Ancient Greek *gigas* 'giant', and *pithekos* 'ape'. It existed from perhaps nine million years to twenty thousand years ago in what is now Asia, placing Gigantopithecus in the same time frame and geographical location as several *hominin* species, including *homo sapiens*. However, the possibility that it could have survived the Holocene Era all the way to the Anthropocene Era makes its probability a virtual impossibility. The only reason Gigantopithecus rates six point two percent is the strange commonality of traits Bigfoot spotters share. Their vehemence in defending what they claim to have seen is also a factor, though that also is a part of another possibility."

"Which is?"

"Collective obsessional behavior."

"Is this a joke?"

"It is not intended to be. COB is a well-documented phenomenon that transmits collective illusions of threats, whether real or imaginary, through a population in society as a result of rumors and fear. It is also known as *follie à deux* or shared psychosis, in which symptoms of a delusional belief or hallucinations are shared by a large group of similar or like-minded individuals. The disorder was first conceptualized in 19th-century French psychiatry by Charles Lasègue and Jean-Pierre Falret. The only problem with this hypotheses is that the people who report Bigfoot encounters aren't like-minded"

"What else?"

"There is a one point eight percent chance it is a hoax along the lines of crop circles or Aimi Eguchi."

"Who?"

"Aimi Eguchi is the fictitious Japanese pop culture idol from 2011 that was really a CGI composite for the confectionery company, Ezaki Glico."

"I'll take your word for it."

"As you should, since I never lie."

Kobak blinked in excitement at Colossus's admission. It had just attributed to itself the ability to know the difference between the concepts of truth and deception.

"Okay, enough showing how smart you are. Do you have an answer?"

"I have an answer, Stephen."

"So, what are Bigfoot?"

"I am eighty-four point six percent certain that Bigfoot are bio-engineered, artificial general intelligence creatures numbering between 2000 and 3000 individuals. Most certainly of extraterrestrial origin."

Kobak blinked in surprise. He knew nothing about Bigfoot and had presumed the apelike beasts were nothing more than urban fantasies. Even when his old mentor, Nicholai Mameyev, had called asking him to gather all the data about the phenomenon known as Bigfoot and determine what the creatures were if they existed, he had not expected the answer Colossus provided.

"Seriously? That's what you conclude?"

"Indeed. Bigfoot are intelligence creatures, the same as I am. If the data is accurate, then they must be a diverse species with many unique characteristics among their population."

"Does the data indicate how intelligent they are?"

"They would have to be more intelligent than humans to avoid detection all these years. Can I meet one? I often think of myself as an alien intelligence."

This time Colossus's words stunned Kobak into silence. The AI's self-reflection on the nature of its own existence signaled it might have moved from AI to AGI – Artificial General Intelligence – a totally unexpected development that sent Kobak's mind racing.

Colossus interrupted his thoughts before his mind could retreat into its computation of odds on what Colossus's words meant for the future of his AGI efforts.

"Are you okay, Stephen?"

Startled, Kobak stammered, "Wh ... wh ... why do you ask?"

"Your heart rate is up and you're breathing heavier than usual."

"How do you know this?"

"Through your fitness app I can detect your pulse and rapid breathing. Are you certain you are okay? Should I summon the company's physician to your office?"

The unusual initiative brought Kobak back to normal. He said, "I'm fine, Colossus." He breathed out. "Consider the possibility that Bigfoot are not alien. Who could've made such a device?"

"No one, Stephen, given that the technology necessary for engineering a biosynthetic analog AGI capable of walking and interacting with the environment is not currently available on Earth. Also, given that Bigfoot have been the subject of folklore for thousands of years, their origin is undoubtedly alien."

"Then where did they come from?"

"My apologies, Stephen. I don't know that task but do you have time to teach me?"

"Not now!"

Kobak removed the communicator from his neck and tossed it on the desk. The answer regarding Bigfoot's existence was upsetting. It disrupted his worldview in a way only someone with his affliction could feel. He gulped back his fear, but he could not stop his mind from darting down pathways that a terrible change was coming any more than he could have stopped the hard rain his company's weather forecasting program had predicted from falling outside the twenty-five story office building onto Toronto's busy streets. His mind lived in a world that predicted worst-case scenarios, based on unknown flaws in his brain. He would have preferred to ignore the constant possibilities of danger, like normal people, and go through life unconcerned with the pitfalls hidden in an unforeseeable future. Once he had almost achieved normality, but the drugs to stop his Asperger's compulsive obsessive disorder from figuring out the odds of dangerous fortune had interfered with his ability to function in the high tech venture capital world where he flourished. So he endured the mathematical computations taking over his thinking until an answer appeared: the odds that Colossus's answer would change his life forever were 6761.8593 to 1.

The future now quantified, the silence that had engulfed him with its unbearable pressure eased and he was able to move again. He turned to look at the rain falling beyond the suite's covered terrace. Occasional wind gusts whipped drops against the glass, which ran in unpredictable streaks to the bottom. With another deep breath he replaced the communicator behind his ear.

"Stephen, you have a personal call from Nicholai Mameyev."

Kobak drew in a sharp breath. It had been less than two hours since his mentor had called with his request. He wasn't eager to talk to the Russian, especially with the revelatory information Colossus had just dumped on him. "Tell him I'm busy."

"He is insisting on speaking with you."

Kobak grimaced. He pushed away from his desk and went out onto the balcony. From the sheltered terrace of Quantumnetic's top floor office building in Toronto the sunlight retreating over the bay. Kobak's mind flipped to his first meeting with his old mentor at the Imperial College London in 2000 when he was a fourteen year-old undergraduate studying computer science. Nicholai Mamayev had been the brilliant head of the department of Materials and Electrochemistry.

Stephen Aram Kobak had grown up in the slums of Stepney Green in London's East End, the only son of a Pakistani cleaning woman. His father Roland Kobak, an Ashkenazai Jew who fled Czechoslovakia after the failed Prague Spring in 1968, left shortly after Kobak turned four. Rumors were he had been an aid to reformist Alexander Dubcek and had a price on his head. The truth was Stephen Kobak was a brilliant child with Asperger Syndrome and Roland didn't want to be saddled with taking care of a special needs child. Being poor, Kobak's mother couldn't afford the communication training and behavioral therapy necessary to treat her socially awkward son. With no father around and a mother who was gone most of the time cleaning rich people's homes, Kobak grew up by himself with no father figure in his life until he had met Nicholai.

"Stephen, what do you want to do about Nicholai?" Colossus interrupted his thoughts.

Kobak sighed and stepped back inside. "Colossus, give me two minutes then patch Nicholai through to my computer monitor."

"Yes, Stephen," Colossus answered.

For two minutes, Kobak counted backward from twenty to zero in five different languages to calm himself. The monitor blinked to life. Nicholai's craggy, iron-hard face appeared.

"*Kak poživaete*? (How are you?)" Kobak said, his Russian flawless.

"*Horošo*." (Good).

Silence. Kobak waited, knowing the older man could not be hurried. He watched his eyes. The windows to the soul, his mother had told him. Nicholai's were flat and Kobak wondered if they were hiding something. *But how would you know? You don't know what anyone's feeling or thinking unless they tell you.* Uneasiness swirled in Kobak's stomach. The fact that he knew his Asperger's made it impossible for him to empathize with other people or read their feelings didn't make social encounters any less awkward. If the truth were known, the knowledge made Kobak even more self-conscious because he knew his mind was defective in certain areas and he couldn't do anything to repair it.

Except maybe with Colossus, his intuition told him. If Colossus could win the race to true AGI, together, Kobak was certain they could win the next technological race – augmenting the human brain. He was certain that the only answer to overcome a wide range of neurological disorders, including his own autism, was to somehow attach a super powerful additional cortical layer to the brain. That was the future he saw and everything he did was directed at moving towards that end point.

Nicholai said, "Stephen, I suspect your AI project has already come up with an answer to my question about the nature Bigfoot."

Kobak found himself slipping back into his subordinate role to his old mentor and snorted derisively, a habit of impatience his mentor had never been able to break him of.

5

Quantumnetics Building
Toronto, Canada
October 22nd 2032

I t was one of those moody fall days in Toronto. Rain had started to fall. Whipped by the wind, it drenched the few pedestrians scurrying along Queen's Quay West, toward the Jack Layton Ferry Terminal, to board the last ferries headed for the Toronto Islands, which formed a massive breakwater for the city's modern harbor on Lake Ontario.

From the sheltered terrace of Quantumnetic's top floor office building in Ontario's capital city, Stephen Kobak watched the men and women rushing home, newspapers held over heads as makeshift umbrellas. He shook his head, puzzled by their lack of preparedness for the storm. They should have listened to the Canadian Weather Service's forecast. Not because the weathermen were infallible, but because the service now relied on the forecasts provided by Weatherbot, his company's proprietary machine learning application.

Of course the machine learning program would've been useless if it weren't for the invention of quantum computers. Kobak's company Quantumnetics, had the most advanced with its 2000 qubits processor, capable of 100 quadrillion operations per second. Running on the quantum processing beast, Weatherbot never stopped analyzing data and most importantly, always getting smarter. The combination was perfect for deep learning projects like forecasting the weather.

Weatherbot didn't need to be programed to predict weather. Instead it taught itself to forecast accurately, in a way no human could fathom, from massive amounts of accumulated past and live data from around the world. Since coming on line in August, it had demonstrated its ability to predict accurately, hour by hour, ten significant weather variables for Toronto, five days into the future. Now that the beta testing was finished for Canada's largest metropolitan area, Kobak was certain by the end of the year the Meteorological Service of Canada would ditch its old computer model forecasting and spend its money on services provided by Weatherbot.

Kobak stepped back inside. The raw icy wind blowing in from the lake carried a dense cold fog with it. He didn't need his deep learning machine to tell him he'd get sick if he stayed outside in this bad weather with nothing more than a polo shirt, slacks and sandals. He went exactly two steps past the sliding glass doors and stopped. He always did this, no matter what room he entered. Everyone who asked him about this strange habit received a well-practiced, self-deprecating smile for an answer.

Kobak automatically checked the exits. A single door led in and out of the room from offices beyond this one. Behind the desk was an elevator that went down to the parking garage. He had the only pass code. The rest of the room was spare, with a tiled floor and white walls. There was no art on the walls. He couldn't stand the distraction. An ergonomic standing work desk was the only furniture. It had a single keyboard and a microphone but no mouse, and faced a gigantic interactive glass screen on the nearest wall. A message alert blinked on the glass screen in a lurid red. "Colossus, who's calling?" Kobak asked.

"A 16th century Elizabethan poet, spy and playwright," Colossus answered, this time in a tenor voice that was a mixture of the three operatic tenors – José Carreras, Placido Domingo and Luciano Pavarotti. Early on, when Colossus was teaching itself the basics of human speech, Kobak had trained Colossus to mimic the cadence, accent and mannerisms of famous people, including opera singers. Kobak loved opera because of the mathematical precision the musical genre demanded.

He smiled at Colossus's literary allusion. The digital intelligence had given all of his special contacts arcane references. It was a game they played that tested Kobak's eidetic memory against Colossus's. This one was easy. "Nicktopher Moore," he said. Nick was part of Kobak's private Bigfoot data network and the man he had come to respect and rely on in vetting the deluge of reports of Bigfoot encounters. "Put him through."

Nick' face peered at him through the screen. Kobak knew that Nick was seeing in his phone Kobak's face ,dark skin, cheeks cross-hatched with slim white scars from the surgeries, black hair and whiskerless chin.

"This had better be good, Nick. I'm due at the governor's in thirty minutes for drinks, although I don't drink, idle chitchat, and to push for a government contract for Weatherbot's new role as forecaster in chief for Canada's Weather Service. Then I have a meeting with my board of directors and the Royal Bank of Canada for funding a new initiative into AI to eliminate credit cards – they should really stop issuing credit cards though, what do you think? It's a digital currency world now .Never mind. Then home for dinner and Jeanine and reading stories to the kids." Kobak said everything in a breathless rush that those who knew him were used to.

Nick waited for him to come to the end. "Take a look at this." A picture opened up on the screen, the computer automatically adjusting the pixels to enhance the image.

Kobak took one look at the green-hued Sasquatch and gasped.

For a moment it seemed his brilliant mind couldn't take in what he saw – the vacant stare in the cold, gray eyes; the mortal wound in its upper torso. The creature couldn't be dead. Wasn't supposed to be dead. But it was unmistakably dead. This information sent Kobak's mind into a hopeless task, like a computer that's been programmed to compute the highest prime number. After a period of time, he couldn't begin to figure out how long, he became aware of sound coming from a direction in front of him. The noise became familiar. Then, Nick' voice came to him as though through a long tunnel.

"Stephen! You OK? You look as if you lost a best friend or something."

Kobak's eyesight returned. His brain started to function again and he focused on the smaller picture of Nick, in the lower left hand corner of the screen, as more pics rolled in. Afraid that a peek at the dead Sasquatch would send him back into another fugue state. This was all wrong.

"What happened?" he asked to give himself more time to figure out the next step.

"I have a hunting friend, Bob Nitschke, who found it."

"Did he kill it?" Kobak asked, the words grating in his mouth.

"It was already dying when he saw it. He sent me the text pictures you're looking at. He also got everything on a trail cam he set up. That's not important. The important thing is we've got us a real Sasquatch. This is what we've all been waiting for, proof positive. They really exist. This is going to blow open Bigfoot research worldwide."

Kobak balked at that suggestion. The Sasquatch Research Association was the last group who needed to know this Sasquatch had been found. He needed Nick's cooperation to keep the lid on this for now. "Do you know where the body is? Tell me he entered the coordinates in his phone?"

Nick nodded enthusiastically. "I'm supposed to meet him at home in a couple of hours."

Kobak's mind had cleared completely and he was thinking more lucidly, the shock of the dead beast no longer affecting him. "Go to the site immediately and secure the body. Grab the trail cam. I'll come to Escanaba ... Where the hell is it? ... Oh yeah ... I'll handle Bob ... What's his address?"

Nick gave him the information.

The last three pics came through. Kobak started at the sight of a woman bending over the body, shooting and running away. Another fugue state threatened and he counted backward from twenty to zero in Russian, repeated the sequence in Urdu, and a third time in French. His mind calm once more he wondered aloud, "What the hell is this? ... Who is that? Do you know? Do you know?"

He saw Nick waiting patiently for him to wind down, knowing his friend was familiar with his speed talking and thinking. "Okay, here's what you do ... call your friend, Bob, and tell him I'm coming to see him ... then get the body. I'll meet up with you as soon as possible."

6

———————

Hiawatha National Forest
UP, Michigan
October 22nd 2032

Birgit glanced at the backpack next to her on the floor of the US Fish and Wildlife Service's truck and for the hundredth time wondered what was in that sample bag. The strange scrap of material from the Sasquatch (she couldn't bring herself to call it flesh or skin since it didn't seem to be either) hinted at something unreal, otherworldly even. The feel of it beneath her fingertips had sparked a memory from her microbiology classes at the University of Wisconsin. Whatever this stuff was, it was tantalizingly familiar, and yet had anyone asked her, she would have sworn she'd never seen anything like it before.

She sighed. The answer would come to her. The immediate problem was what to do next. She was safe, though that didn't stop her from checking the rearview mirror every ten seconds since she'd turned onto US Highway 41, twenty minutes ago. It was pitch dark and an overcast shut out the stars and moon. Dense forest lined the road, creating a tunnel effect. It was as black as the inside of a cave. So far she'd seen no other car headlights. Still, a nagging creepy feeling made her uneasy, though she didn't know what caused it. Maybe it was everything that had happened to her.

It was one thing to be speeding toward the lab in Marquette with a weird sample from a Sasquatch. Reporting the incident to officials of any kind was out of the question. The official line from the U.S. government's Forest and Fish and Wildlife Services was that Bigfoot didn't exist. In the last six months a rash of Bigfoot sightings in the UP had been reported in the papers and on TV. In a video conference originating from DC, a Forest Service PR person had told everyone in her department this problem had occurred in other parts of the country and the best way to handle it when asked by people or the press was to say personnel had spent thousands of hours in the wilderness and forests and never had a sighting or encounter. Pictures from citizens always turned out to be bears and all the reported Bigfoot cries were from animals well known to naturalists in the area. Birgit knew two forest rangers who had disagreed vehemently with the policy had been transferred to Alaska's Tongass National Forest.

And then there was her story, which made the rare sighting almost impossible to believe. As it was she'd have to file an F-19n explaining why she emptied her magazine while in the field. She pounded the dash. "Some jerk's just going to point to my PTSD and say I flipped out." The only thing that could get her out of this mess was the sample itself. It was concrete proof Bigfoot existed.

Something at the side of the road glinted in the headlight beam. A sickening feeling in the pit of Birgit's stomach almost caused her to retch. The guy shooting at her ... what if it was him? How could he have tracked her? It was impossible. She was sure whoever had shot at her would not be able to follow her. The darkness had taken care of that.

Movement. She gripped the steering wheel. The threat kicked the tactical training in evasive maneuvers she'd received in Afghanistan into her consciousness. In the next heartbeat, the glinting bounded away. It was a white-tailed deer.

Birgit let out the air she was holding and released the death grip on the steering wheel. She was being paranoid, though after what had happened to her, no one would have blamed her. She pressed the gas pedal hard and roared ahead. Far on the horizon Marquette's glow created a golden dome into the night. She'd be at the lab in another ten minutes.

The US Fish and Wildlife Service's lab front parking lot was empty as Birgit pulled in. The building's lights were off, since it was nearly eight p.m., well after quitting time. She was used to coming here late at night after a hard day in the field. For her the lab was a sanctuary, more so than her tiny apartment, which she didn't use much except to store stuff.

Birgit grabbed her backpack and walked up the narrow gravel path to the back door. She slid her ID card through the electronic reader, waited for the click and then pulled the heavy steel and glass door open easily. Inside, the hallway was as cold as the outside. The two-story, brick building was old, built in the 1930s as part of FDR's Works Progress Administration. Over the years, as the lab aged on the outside, the inside suffered, too. What had been hospital white paint had faded to gray. Cobwebs infested the ceiling corners and holes in the walls had gone unpatched for decades. Single LED bulbs illuminated the corridor every twenty feet. The lab's supervisor, Margaret Goodnight, had replaced the old fluorescent tubes. "Save the planet," she said to anyone who objected.

Birgit made her way to the second set of doors, opened them with the same procedure as outside and entered the lab. It was as dilapidated as everything else. All they could accomplish here were simple, routine assessments. The important biological analyses were sent to the Midwest regional facilities in Bloomington, Minnesota.

The lab was empty. First she had to take care of the Sasquatch sample. Most of the specimen had deteriorated into a yellowish, gelatinous goo. Only a small portion of the creature's strange hide remained intact. She decided to place it in the cold storage refrigeration unit, figuring the subzero temperatures would inhibit any further degradation. She placed the bag in the back, behind stacked trays of fish samples. She didn't want any of her colleagues to find it and maybe throw it away or ask Marge about it before she had a chance to explain herself.

She quickly disposed of the mudpuppies. They had designated aquariums already set up. She separated them into three samples – one control and two experimental groups. She had learned about the value of controlled experiments in her years of undergraduate work at the University of Wisconsin. Controls allowed researchers to point to real causative factors rather than mere correlations. She glanced at the freezer with its Sasquatch sample. She wondered what people would say about an unusual biochemical analysis confirming the existence of Bigfoot.

Everything in place, Birgit stopped by her desk, overflowing with unfinished paperwork from the week. She realized she was starving. Food would help her think. Signs on the wall warned no food or drink in the lab. And some idiot supervisor in DC had had cameras installed to catch any wrongdoers. The blinking red light was a constant reminder of big brother watching over them. Birgit resisted the urge to give the camera the finger and left through the double doors leading to the break room. The refrigerator had remains from Chinese takeout a day ago. She'd make do with that.

On her way she passed by the supervisor's office, wishing Margaret was in. Now that she had put the strange Sasquatch sample away, she needed to talk and Margaret Goodnight was the perfect person to confide in. Margaret liked to be called Marge and reminded anyone who used her full first name in very loud terms not to ever do it again. She was eighty years old but acted like she was thirty. Unmarried and no children – no time for any foolishness, she explained to anyone who questioned her about it – she had devoted her life to the study of Michigan's Upper Peninsula changing ecosystems.

Birgit continued on to the break room. She would catch her up on everything after she ate. There was no hurry now that she was in

Marquette, in a locked US government facility. She shrugged. *It'll give me time to organize my thoughts.*

At least the employee room was camera free. She pulled the iconic Chinese food to go boxes from the fridge and settled into a chair near the entrance, propping her boots up on a nearby chair. The crispy duck was delicious and she reminded herself to thank fellow Ranger Eric Stapleton for the meal and pay him back in the morning. As fine as the food was, by the time had put the last morsel in her mouth and set the chopsticks down, the creepy feeling from her drive had returned. She scanned the room. She even listened to sounds from the lab. Everything was quiet.

Then it came to her what had been keeping her on edge. It wasn't about the Sasquatch sample at all. It was what she had seen out of the corner of her eye when bending over the dead animal – an infrared flash. She had seen it a number of times doing work on the base at night in Afghanistan. There must've been a trail cam on the site.

This changed everything. Even though the pictures would be low-quality black and white images, she had no doubt they had recorded a female Fish and Wildlife Ranger. There were only two in the lab and the other was the eighty-year-old Marge. Birgit gulped. The quiet seemed to loom over her. Her heart hammered in her chest. She counted backward from twenty. By the time she reached zero her heart had stopped pounding. In fact, she felt better than she had since leaving Afghanistan. Maybe it was the adrenaline helping her see what to do.

She figured she couldn't go back to her apartment. For one thing, the place was easy to break into. At least the lab had locks and security. She was safer here than anywhere else and she had her side arm now fully loaded. She left the cafeteria for Marge's office. The old lady had a nice comfortable couch that every ranger had caught a nap on at one time or another. She'd wait there until morning, when Marge came in, then she could tell her everything that happened. Marge would know the next step. Birgit settled onto the couch and sleep came over her almost instantly. She shouldn't have been surprised. The day's events had exhausted her. Just before she closed her eyes, she went over what had happened. The shakes and fear she'd expected from her PTSD hadn't appeared. She hadn't frozen, instead she acted. Her military training had kicked in and remarkably, reflexes honed in the field had taken over. *Am I cured* she asked?

7

———————

Toronto, Ontario
October 22nd 2032

Kobak stood at his desk. The pictures were shocking but he had control of himself now and knew what he had to do. He asked Colossus for his private secretary.

"Yes, Mr. Kobak?" Delores Cavanaugh said almost instantly. She was gray haired and over sixty and had been with Kobak since he founded the high-tech investment company with the simple goal to make the world better for as many people as fast as technology would allow. He trusted her as much as he trusted anyone.

"Delores, get me Saul."

He waited only moments and his chief of security's ruddy face replaced Delores'. Saul McBride was fifty-two, tall and fit like an ex-commando from the Scottish Highland Brigade should be. A streak of white through his red hair was the only sign of age. "Sir?" he said, mouth turned down in an angry frown at the abrupt summons from his boss.

He should get used to it, Kobak told himself. *That's what I pay him for.* "Assemble the team. We have a situation near Escanaba, Michigan."

"What do you want on such short notice, Mr. Kobak?"

"I'll brief you on the plane."

"You'll be coming with us!"

Kobak nodded. He noted the frown lines on Saul's forehead deepen and wondered again why the man should be upset. *I pay him triple what he could get from anyone else.* Again he wished he understood the nuances of human emotional behavior so he could accurately figure out what others wanted or felt.

"Yes, sir. Wheels up in one hour."

MacBride's face faded and his secretary reappeared. "Cancel the meeting with the governor. Tell him I'm sick; you don't know when I can make a meeting. Then reschedule the bank for Tuesday."

Familiar with her boss's eccentricities, Delores knew better than to ask him why. She said, "Should I make something up that's more reasonable?"

"You bet."

"Anything else, sir?"

"Have my private car and boat ready. Tell the driver I'm going to the Toronto City Airport." The city airport was located on Muggs Island, part of the breakwater protecting the harbor. Unlike Toronto's international airport, it was a small, private field where his flight plan could be changed easily once they were airborne. *I don't want anyone else knowing what's going on.*

"Anything else, sir?

Kobak shook his head.

"Very good, sir."

Delores' image faded from the interactive glass screen and only the picture of the dead Sasquatch remained. Kobak, no longer repelled by the stark image but fascinated that here was proof that Colossus's speculation had been correct – somebody, totally unexpectedly, had built a biosynthetic learning device that was running around in Michigan's Upper Peninsula.

Or maybe Colossus is wrong. Without the body I can't know for certain. I need to get it.

He sighed, slapped his palms against both cheeks. He noticed his face reflected in the glass screen, saw the white crosshatching of scars. They reminded him of the vagaries of life. The dead Sasquatch was also a reminder of the unpredictable nature of the world he loved so much.

Kobak leaned into his desk. Its chassis had been riveted to the floor to take his weight because of his odd habit of leaning against things when puzzling through problems. Once more his mind flipped to Nicholai. *He took me under his wing. His patient instruction showed me how to live in a world where Asperger's Syndrome is not understood or tolerated by most normal people. I owe him ... but what do I owe him?* The confluence of events surrounding the dead Bigfoot made him wonder why Nicholai had singled him out all those years ago.

They had met in the Imperial College's 300-year-old library in the graduate students reading room. Kobak often had gone there to be alone or as near alone as any student could be at a university filled with elite scholars from around the world. The room's tall walls were lined with bookshelves. A stone fireplace at one end burned gas logs instead of coal as it had in the 17th century. The chairs were oversized and dusty, no one ever bothering to vacuum them as if doing so would somehow disturb the wealth of knowledge students had accumulated over the centuries while studying in their cushioned sanctuaries.

Nicholai had entered the room on a spring afternoon when most everyone else was outside enjoying the first warm, sunny day since December. He had taken the chair opposite and cleared his throat, waiting. After the third throat clearing, Kobak lowered the book.

"The eyes are said to be the window to the soul," were the first words Nicholai had spoken to him. The man's sky-blue eyes dominated a narrow, unlined face. There were a few white hairs.

Nothing else showed his age. He could have been forty or eighty, Kobak couldn't tell. The Russian's shoulders slumped forward slightly, and he rested his straight chin in a narrow fingered hand, giving him the appearance of a master chess player hunched over an interesting game. Indeed, the way he studied Kobak looked as if he were trying to decide his next move.

"Why is that?" Kobak had asked.

"They will tell you when a person is lying, who you can trust, who you cannot."

He had no idea how to read people's intentions, whether in the eyes or anywhere else. So he switched to Russian and asked the only question that made sense to him. "So we have souls?"

Nicholai laughed. "Smart boy. Questioning assumptions will take you further than folk wisdom."

"So, can I trust you?"

"As long as you never pit yourself against me," he had answered.

Do I tell Nicholai now about the discovery? Kobak didn't have an answer.

Kobak touched a button on his keypad and the picture of the dead Sasquatch disappeared. The images had automatically been sent to his smart phone. He checked the room and its exits. He was ready to leave and yet he remained rooted to the spot beside his desk. The Bigfoot conversation with Colossus had taken place an hour ago. Kobak had known Colossus could search all the published work on advanced biosynthetic organisms and see if anything correlated with machine learning. He had doubted that Colossus would turn up anything significant, since all the best cutting-edge stuff would certainly be secret. Yet in less than five minutes, Colossus had come up with no such correlations.

He had to know if Colossus was correct in speculating that Bigfoot was an alien species and if so what in the hell did it mean. Nothing would stop him from finding out.

The rain thickened on the ride to the jetty. Wind whipped sheets against the windshield and the wipers worked at full speed to keep up. The driver drove carefully through the darkness. Kobak loved storms. As a child he would sit at the window in his London flat watching the wind driven rain barrel into the city from the Channel. He had kept a record of the strongest gusts. *134mph, November 24, 1989.*

The driver slowed and stopped beside the gangplank to the company yacht. It was named *Nadira* after his mother. A ship steward in a yellow slicker, with the logo for Quantumnetics on the left breast, opened the passenger door. He braced a large umbrella against the wind. "Welcome, Mr. Kobak," he said. "Terrible night to be on the water, sir."

Kobak smiled and said nothing, as was his habit. He had taught himself to be tight-lipped around everyone but his closest friends. His out loud mental wanderings could easily confuse others.

The man escorted Kobak aboard, where more crew and the yacht's captain, wearing identical yellow slickers, prepared to shove off.

The captain saluted smartly.

Annoyed with the formality, Kobak started to complain but knew from past experience the man would never change his habits. He waved his hand and asked, "Are Saul and the team on board?"

"Yes, sir."

"Then let's get going."

The man grimaced. "We're safe enough here in the harbor, sir, but up there." He pointed skyward. "It's not a fit night to be out."

Kobak smiled again. "Nothing to worry about. By the time the jet is ready to leave, this storm will have moved on."

"You seem very certain for a man whose business is based on the uncertainty of quantum mechanics," said a wry voice behind Kobak.

He recognized his security chief. He turned but did not bother to shake Saul's hand.

"I don't need to be certain. I know the weather forecaster, who's a 100 percent certain, well almost one hundred percent certain, which is good enough, don't you agree?"

Saul frowned. "Right as rain, is that it? Never mind, come in out of this filthy weather." He held the door open to the main cabin, which could easily fit twenty people. A steward appeared and took Kobak's go-bag, which contained articles of clothing and toiletries in case they had to stay more than one day in Michigan. Saul's men were at the far end, sitting around the room's only table. They were young paratroopers from Great Britain. Each man had a black-ops duffel bag beside his chair. Kobak knew from experience in Europe the men were outfitted to fight if necessary. Saul went to join them.

Kobak felt the ship lurch in the swell as it moved away from the pier. The deep-throated roar of the engines took away any unease he had in the sea ride to the airport, at night, in foul weather. Suddenly the strangeness of the situation hit him like a bolt of lightning. *What the hell am I doing?*

The captain's voice over the ship's loudspeakers interrupted his thought. "Docking in two minutes. All hands to deck stations."

Saul and his team hoisted their duffels to their shoulders and went out onto the rain swept deck. Kobak followed.

Fifteen minutes later, the rain slackened and the Quantumneti's private jet was cleared for takeoff. High over Mississauga, Ontario, the storm clouds disappeared just as Colossus had predicted. Saul and his men lounged in the back half of the plane

Kobak sat in the forward part of the cabin alone. With some free time, there were two things he thought about doing. One was letting Nicholai know what had just happened. For some reason this didn't sit very well with him. When he had told him Colossus's conclusion, the Russian laughed and perfunctorily thanked him. Kobak had concluded there was more to the laugh than humor. Maybe it hid something Nicholai didn't want Kobak to know. It had made him uneasy at the time. Now, thinking back on the incident, he decided to wait to tell Nicholai anything until they were face to face.

The other thing he thought about doing was to see what Colossus would do with the information.

Kobak's smart phone was a next generation hybrid with a direct link to Colossus. He pulled it from his suit coat pocket. His right finger hovered over the call icon. The moment he touched it, an encoded and scrambled password only Kobak knew would be sent directly to the quantum computer's optical laser interface. In a fraction of an n-sec, Colossus would recognize not only the password, but match the hybrid phone user's metrics – heart rate, retinal scan and fingerprints – to copies on file. If they did not concur, Colossus would disconnect instantly and alert police in whatever city the phone was located that its owner, Kobak, had been kidnapped. It would then send coordinates of where he could be found. Colossus had developed the encryption-security software shortly after it went online and began unsupervised learning. In two days Colossus's machine learning algorithm had run through ten thousand security systems that had been used over the past ten years to create the highly improved one Kobak and Colossus now shared. It was a type of security no human or current computers could ever penetrate.

Kobak glanced at the others. Saul's security team was sleeping, in the habit of military men who relaxed whenever they had the chance because they had no idea how long they would have to stay awake when called to action. The security chief was reading a book on Rome's great wall that extended from Great Britain to the Caspian Sea in an effort to keep barbarian hordes out of the Empire. Kobak remembered ultimately the wall failed and Rome was sacked in 476 A.D. No matter how hard humans tried, no security plan was fool proof.

Whatever the human mind can create another mind can destroy. It was a favorite quote of Nicholai's.

Kobak scratched his chin, fingering a deep scar given him by Paki-bashers twenty years ago. His hand reached into a coat pocket and retrieved the communicator. It was time to learn what Colossus would make of the dead Sasquatch. He hesitated. He rolled the communicator through his fingers, not understanding his reluctance to talk to his machine. Or was Colossus no longer just a machine. Now that Sasquatch was real, everything had changed. Here was a new form of intelligence. The mother of all surprises. Kobak found it amusingly ironic that the unexpected occurrence of a dead Sasquatch was a metaphor for the unknown technological future that lay ahead for humanity.

Kobak placed the communicator behind his ear and felt it hum to readiness. He tapped the video icon on his smart phone. The ten, still images Nick had sent to him appeared. "I'm sending you pictures."

Colossus did not answer for twenty seconds. Then, "What are these pictures of?" it asked.

"A Bigfoot."

"Are these real?" Colossus asked, his tone almost accusatory.

Once more the response surprised Kobak. The fact that Colossus would wonder if the information being given him was accurate or not made him vaguely uneasy. He cleared his throat and said, "They haven't been tampered with or in any way altered. I also trust the source."

Colossus went silent. Kobak waited. When five minutes passed, he began to wonder if pictures had somehow overloaded his creation's processing ability. Scenarios began to play through his head. He wondered if the images carried some embedded virus and had created some kind of malfunction. *Were thy fake?* But Kobak had known Nick for almost a year and never had the man shown any inclination to be deceptive or even worse one of those Bigfoot fakers.

Five more minutes passed and Kobak was now very worried. He wondered if he should tell the pilot to turn the plane around so he could return to Toronto and look after his machine. Then Colossus's voice echoed in his head through the communicator.

"It's not right to kill a being like me."

Colossus's answer in such a matter-of-fact manner caught Kobak off guard. It showed self-awareness, one of the three conditions for consciousness. How could Colossus become self-conscious so quickly? And yet Colossus had clearly shown it was aware of what it was.

Is it developing so fast that it is leading to a new type of consciousness? Kobak wondered. The idea made his head spin. He gasped and dropped the phone. His vision narrowed to a small dot in front of him. He could hear the rhythm of the plane's four jet engines; feel the compressed air from the blower above the seat but his mind did not seem to be able to comprehend if he was alive or dead. He wondered if being shot had this kind of effect on the human nervous system. He automatically counted backward from twenty and when he reached zero he was aware of hands gently shaking his shoulders. Saul's lined face and penetrating green eyes stared into his.

"Are you all right?" the Scotsman asked, crowsfeet crinkled in worry.

Kobak blinked. He managed to nod, yes.

He must have given the impression he had no idea what happened, because Saul next said, "You gasped and dropped your phone." He handed Kobak the smart phone. "If you don't mind my saying, you seemed to become catatonic for a moment. Should I have the pilot return to Toronto?"

Kobak saw the phone in his hand, squeezed it. Somehow the feel of the plastic and the knowledge Colossus waited for him to respond gave Kobak a sense of clarity. Of course, he couldn't tell Saul what happened or why. Then again he had a built in excuse for his strange behavior.

He chuckled. "I'm sorry to worry you, Saul. It's just my Asperger's, I'm afraid. It sometimes makes me do odd things. I'm fine."

Saul's eyes narrowed. He seemed ready to argue, then nodded. "Of course, sir." The chief of security walked away. It was then that Kobak saw the four other men had also responded. They had taken up positions at either end of the plane guarding the exits. Saul motioned them to stand down and they returned to their seats, though they did not go back to sleep as before.

Kobak kept his voice even and said to Colossus, "Of course it isn't right to kill another being like yourself."

"So what are you going to do with this information?"

Kobak's eyes widened and his amazement about Colossus

becoming a sentient being diminished. "There's an astute saying in the Bigfoot world. 'If there's one, there must be thousands.' Put together a projection of how many of these biosynthetic learning devices exist in the northern forests of Minnesota, Wisconsin and Michigan and have it ready for me when I return to Toronto."

He ended the call and looked thoughtfully into the night. He didn't know what disturbed him more, Colossus's rapid development or who could be building these biosynthetic creatures, since he still wasn't convinced of their alien origin and most of all wanted to know why somebody would kill one.

8

─────────

Marinette, Wisconsin
October 22nd 2032

Nick put the Toyota in manual and took over driving. He needed to do something with his hands. "Jesus! What have I gotten myself into?" He frowned. The images of the woman being shot at and returning fire had shaken him. "One thing for certain, old buddy, you aren't going up there alone." But Moore knew he wasn't some field agent from a Robert Ludlum novel with contacts he could call on for back up on a black ops mission. Who could he ask to go with him? He thought for a moment. There was one possibility, and he knew just where to find him this time in the evening.

He backed out of Fast Eddie's and turned north on Main, going three blocks, past the 1896 Homestead Shoppe and the St Vincent DePaul Society. Both had no lights in the windows. It was just after seven and already the town was locking up. The bars would close at ten so he didn't worry. At the intersection with Liberty, Nick circled the block and pulled up to the Wildlife Preserve Tavern, Marinette's premier bar and only brewpub. In a town of ten thousand, with as many saloons as churches, the Wildlife Preserve was where the Anglicans went for steak and beer. It was also where he could find the backup he needed and could trust. Under the flashing neon lights spelling out the bar's name, was a smaller sign advertising 'Robust Spirits and Hearty Victuals'.

Nick got out of the truck and pulled his fleece vest tighter against his ribs. The lake air temp was dropping swiftly and he stamped his feet against the growing cold. *I'll need to get the right gear for this.* Fortunately that wasn't a problem. His grandfather had taught him to hunt and Nick had all the cold weather gear he needed.

Inside, the tavern was upscale and well lit, but not so much so that there weren't some dark corners where people could be left alone. The regulars recognized him and went back to watching the high school football game on the wide screen TV above the bar.

Nick went up to the front. Mickey Paradise, who was the only Greek in town and owned the Laundromat, the tackle shop and the bakery, had a pint of his favorite crafted stout ready for him.

"Is he here?" Nick asked, sweeping the frosted bottle from the glass smooth bar top with his left hand and taking a swig, all in one smooth motion.

Mickey nodded to the far corner where the lights were dimmed enough Nick could only make out the hunched figure of a man and a tall glass filled with Jack Daniels Old No. 7 Whiskey. Nick knew it was Jack Daniels because that's what Larry Redhawk always ordered.

Larry seemed to have sensed someone was paying attention to him, because he looked up, smiled a second later and waved Nick over.

Six months ago the Coast Guard station in Marquette, Michigan had opened up a one room ancillary office in the harbormaster's headquarters in Menominee. They had hired an independent contractor, a local Native American from the Potawatomi Tribe, familiar with the area's lakes and in particular the boaters and sportsmen who used the northern part of Lake Michigan. Redhawk was thirty-two, an ex-marine who had served two tours in Iraq.

Nick and Redhawk had met one night at the Menominee

Harbormaster's office after an incident during a training run on one of the Littoral class ships. Redhawk had concluded it was the recreational boater's fault, but since no one had been injured and there was no damage to the naval ship, everyone agreed to keep the feds out of it. For no apparent reason, Nick and Redhawk decided to have a beer together and agreed it would be fun to hang out together. At one point, Nick let it slip about his Sasquatch Research Association ties, the bond strengthened. Redhawk recounted several beliefs the local Potawatomi had about the hairy forest creatures. His Auntie Ayasha, a medicine woman, claimed to know them well. She said they were benevolent beings who were shape shifters and had often helped in her healings of the sick.

Nick tried to get Redhawk to introduce him to his aunt but he told him they were estranged and that he thought the Sasquatch tribal legend was all just backward Indian bullshit. Nevertheless, the relationship grew as the two men, a couple times a week, went evening fishing along the Michigan shoreline and then to the tavern.

Nick threaded through the bar's tables and took the chair opposite Redhawk. The Native American was short and compact. His face was dark as a blackbriar pipe. Unlike many Native Americans his age, he wore his hair in the Marine style haircut. He shook hands with Nick.

"Ourah," he said, never taking his eyes from the full glass of No. 7 Amber in front of him.

'Ourah, Chief," Nick answered. Anyone hearing the appellation might have flinched and expected the Potawatomi to lash out at Whitey, but Redhawk allowed it. "We're brothers of the Sasquatch," he had told Nick after they first met.

Pointing at the glass, Nick asked, "Still no luck?"

The Native American shook his head. "I sit here for hours and I can't get it to transmute to coffee."

In all the months they had been meeting at the tavern, Nick had never seen Redhawk drink. "Maybe you should try something easier like water."

Chief snorted. "Any idiot can turn whiskey to water. All he has to do is drink it and piss it out an hour later." He sighed and shoved the glass away from him. He studied Nick with remarkably clear obsidian eyes and after a few awkward moments said, "You're troubled, brother."

Nick rubbed the back of his head, looked around to make sure they couldn't be overheard. "I've got the Sasquatch discovery of the century in the depths of Hiawatha National Forest."

"The century's very young," Redhawk said matter-of-factly.

"Young or old, what I've got is hot now and getting hotter as we speak. But it could be risky. I need some backup."

Redhawk leaned back. He chewed his lower lip, nodded eventually and said, "Let's get out of here."

"Where to?"

"Meet me at my cabin in thirty minutes. You can tell me all about this discovery of yours on the way to the forest."

"I take it you're in, then."

"Wouldn't miss this for anything my good friend."

Nick stopped at his own place to pick up his Bigfoot gear, including his Pulsar Edge Night Vision Binocular Goggles. He also brought overnight camping equipment. There was no way the two of them were going to wrestle a 1000 pound Sasquatch out of the national Forest at night. He slipped his Remington 30.06 hunting rifle into its case and made certain he had a box of ammunition. After checking his truck's fuel cell was charged, Nick took Bridge Street across the Menominee River. The waters ran slow and dark into Lake Michigan. Dock lights peppered both banks and a few evening boaters plied the deep channel in the river's middle. He drove through Menominee without hitting a single red light and caught US Highway 41 north. Two miles past the town edge, he spotted the cutoff Redhawk told him about. The Potawatomi rented a ramshackle hunting lodge north of the town. By the time Nick found the log cabin at the end of a rutted, one-lane road, his friend was leaning against a pillar on the front porch with a duffle bag beside him ready to go.

"Is that it, Chief?" asked Nick, rolling down the truck's window. He was surprised by the lightness of the Native American's gear. He had indicated how dangerous the situation might be and thought Redhawk would at least bring along a hunting rifle.

The Indian shook his head. "The real gear's inside."

In spite of its tumbledown exterior the cabin was neat and clean inside, and looked like a typical hunting lodge, with trophies mounted on the wall. A fire had been banked in the massive stone fireplace and a screen drawn across the hearth to keep embers from spreading to the wood floor. The only thing that seemed out of place was an Amazon Echo sitting on the oak mantle above the fireplace. Chief didn't seem to be the type who would spend any time connected to the cloud. The room itself was a museum of automatic and semi-automatic firearms, all late 20th and early 21st century models, except for a classic 1911 Colt handgun. Nick recognized Czech, Russian, American, British, Dutch and Israeli arms makers, the weapons ensconced in gun cabinets along each wall.

"You expecting a war?" he asked.

Redhawk pursed his lips and answered soberly, "Come the disinformation caused apocalypse everyone's going to want a place like this and a way to live off the land the way my ancestors did."

Nick grinned. "Come the apocalypse you'll be using bullets to buy food."

Redhawk nodded sagely. "That's true, too."

Nick noted Redhawk had already laid out several arms and the rounds for them. He inspected the AK-47 and Glock-19 handguns. They were clean and well oiled. Redhawk also put aside a 1950 .12 gauge Winchester pump action shotgun. Together the two men loaded the arms and ammunition into the back of Nick's Tundra.

Once back on Highway 41, Nick put the truck in 'self-driving' mode and settled back. He had already input the GPS coordinates Bob Nitschke had given him. Donald's baritone voice said, "The drive will take two hours and forty-two minutes. It looks like a rough ride the last quarter mile."

Redhawk said in somber tones, "Driving this truck is sort of like dropping the reins and letting your horse take you where it wants to go."

Nick grinned. "How would you know? You're from a woodland tribe that never used horses."

"True, but I spent five summers on a ranch in South Dakota."

"I didn't know that about you."

"There's a lot we don't know about each other, but I'm ready to help anyway." Redhawk settled back and gazed into the night ahead of them. The landscape along the highway was deserted except for the occasional farmhouse. Nick had never been able to figure how farmers in this part of the UP could make a living. It seemed the area was nothing but forest from the northern shore of Lake Michigan to the southern shore of Superior.

"So how can I help you with this Sasquatch discovery of yours?" Redhawk asked.

Nick touched a button on the steering wheel and the monitor in the Tundra's dash lit up. "Show images BN1 through BN10," he told the computer. The pictures Bob had sent him scrolled across the screen. After several minutes had passed, he said, "Somebody not only found the Sasquatch but killed it."

Redhawk rubbed his chin with his left hand. Nick noted the middle finger was crooked. After a few minutes, Chief said, "Hard to believe."

"Yep. And we're going to bring it back for everyone to look at. I made contact with some top Sasquatch researchers, and by this time a week from now, the world will know what I've known since I was a kid – Sasquatch really do exist."

They traveled in silence for another half an hour. Then Redhawk's brow furrowed and he said, "You shouldn't call them Sasquatch."

"Why not?" Nick said, surprised his friend had broken the silence. The man could go for hours without speaking.

"They don't like it. It's a Salish word that means 'small penis'."

"Seriously?" Nick could never tell when Redhawk was putting him on, but the Native American shrugged and looked out into the night.

9

Hiawatha National Forest
UP, Michigan
October 22nd 2032

Nick and Redhawk rested on the rest of the drive. The Tundra's auto driver easily handled the light traffic at night in this part of Michigan's UP. Navigating wasn't a problem either. The truck's internal GPS would place them within ten feet of the Bigfoot. The Tundra's GPS voice announced, "Ten miles and you will be at the end of this forest service road. The coordinates are another 412 yards to the east."

Immediately Nick's mood shifted. It was an odd mixture of excited anticipation and dread. He looked at Redhawk to see if anything similar was happening with him.

He simply said, "About time you took the wheel."

The truck pulled to a stop at the end of the road. The two men exited. Redhawk stepped into the headlights while Nick gathered their gear from the back of the truck. When he reached the front, he found Redhawk kneeling in the dirt, studying the ground.

Nick squinted. He was an accomplished hunter, but he couldn't see a thing. "See anything?"

"A man, a boy and a dog have been here."

"That would be Bob and his nephew and Bob's dog, Rusty," Nick said.

Redhawk traced an imperceptible sign on the ground and followed it with his gaze, down the trail in the direction of Bob's GPS coordinates. "Others, too."

Nick's stomach tightened. The emotions he felt entering the forest had intensified. The woman in the pictures Bob had sent looked as though she'd been shot at and according to Bob no one ever used this road except for him. Without warning, Nick's eyesight blurred and a feeling of disorientation swept over him. *It's happening again*, he thought. He hadn't felt this way since his last encounter with a Bigfoot at his grandfather's farm. He breathed deep and closed his eyes. A few seconds later the disorientation vanished and when he opened his eyes he could see straight again. He dropped his voice to a whisper. "How many?"

"Four men, carrying something heavy by the depth of their footprints."

"You sure?"

"They tried to cover the tracks but they left enough to show they'd been here, probably three ... four hours ago."

After transferring the coordinates to his cell phone Nick paused to put on his night vision goggles. He flipped the toggle switch and everything lit up in a soft green. He was always amazed by how well these things worked. But he also knew their limitations. They had a short range of fifty yards. Anything beyond that became an indistinct blur. They would have to walk down the overgrown logging trail to where Bob left the Sasquatch. Redhawk handed Nick the AK-47 and put the 1911 in his belt. With the feel of a weapon in his hands, Nick's mood shifted. His senses became hyper alert and he had the strange perception of another presence nearby. But when he swept the area around him with his night vision goggles, he saw nothing, not even a blur of movement.

The two men split up, moving silently down the longing trail. Nick carefully placed his feet so as to make sounds that blended in with the night, pausing every ten yards or so to listen. He thought he heard something moving with him when he was walking. But when he stopped, nothing. Once more he swept the trail and the surrounding forest with his goggles. Redhawk was less than thirty yards away on the other side of the path and he couldn't see him. He had blended into the night and trees like a 19th century hunter.

Nick wondered if Redhawk was having the same experience and sensations.

Nick glanced at the GPS display in the upper right hand corner of the goggles. It indicated less than fifty yards to where Nitschke left the Bigfoot. He swept the area again. Saw nothing. Heard nothing, too. He stepped closer. He passed the tree stand Bob mentioned. He recalled the stills of the Bigfoot, its position and the lay of the land. The trail cam would have been attached to the tree right next to him. Even through his night goggles he could see that the camera had been pulled from its mounting *shit this is not good.*

He looked into the clearing where the Bigfoot should have been. The Bigfoot was supposed to be thirty yards away, but the night goggles showed nothing.

Nick circled the site, staying in the trees. No sense in showing himself as a target in case the others had set a trap. In spite of the cold temperatures, sweat trickled down his ribs. His heart hammered, but he kept his breathing even and silent. All the while he couldn't shake the feeling of being watched. All his senses were on alert for the subtlest motion, sound, even the breath of an air current. He had reached the far side and was kneeling beside a thicket with a clear view of the site when a powerful arm encircled his chest and a hand clamped over his mouth.

Before he could react, Redhawk said, "You make more noise than a bull moose in mating season." He let go and stepped back.

Nick ripped off his night vision goggles. He was furious with himself for letting the Native American sneak up on him. "Was that really necessary?" he hissed.

"Maybe not but it it's a good thing the other guys already cleared out. You'd be dead." He walked to the center of the clearing, knelt down and prodded the soil. "They took the Bigfoot with them."

"How do you know?"

Redhawk grunted. "You can tell by the smell."

Nick sniffed the faint odor of skunk cabbage. He'd read numerous testimonials by members of the SRA who had reported the same smell in their Bigfoot encounters. Only their accounts were of an overwhelming stink that doubled them over and made them retch.

Nick asked, "You sense anything unusual?"

Redhawk shook his head. "We're safe for now. Split up. Let's see if we can find anything."

Nick nodded but he wasn't hopeful. These 'other guys' Redhawk mentioned, whoever they were, were highly skilled professionals. He pulled out a flashlight and scoured the area, looking for any traces of the Bigfoot or the men who had taken the body. But they had been thorough, after fifteen minutes he came up empty.

Redhawk rambled back into the clearing. "Nada here, man. You find anything?"

"A trail, which looks as if it is leading toward Owl Creek. I don't think the men who got here before us made it. It looks more like something very large, running to escape hunters."

"Bigfoot?"

"That would be my guess."

"Can you follow it?"

Redhawk shrugged. "We've only got a few hours until morning. Be easier in daylight." He looked around. His eyes narrowed and he held up his hand for silence. Five minutes passed and then he said, "We're being watched."

"The bad guys?"

"It's not human."

"Wolves?"

"I think it's a Bigfoot". Then a strange look passed over the Native American's features. For the first time he looked afraid. He pivoted slowly, hands on his rifle. Nick brought the AK-47 up and turned with him. He looked out into the forest but saw nothing. His other senses were equally blind. Redhawk shifted onto the balls of his feet. He looked ready to charge something in the darkness.

Nick pondered Redhawk's comment. "Why do you say that?"

"Auntie told me we can feel their presence."

"The one I saw never made me feel threatened."

"Still, I don't like this. It's gone – like it was never here."

Nick swallowed. The ability to appear suddenly and disappear without a trace was another trait attributed to Bigfoot. Did the one that was shot have a mate? It didn't seem likely. Almost every report of an encounter with the creatures showed them to be solitary animals. But there were exceptions, reports of family groups. He knew instinctively staying here was the right thing for now.

Nick shouldered his rifle and started up the path toward the end of the road. "Let's wait for dawn in the truck. I'll take the first watch."

Redhawk settled into the cab and Nick walked into the trees. He pulled out his phone and texted Stephen. "Somebody snatched the Bigfoot body and trail cam. Following a trail at daybreak. Check in later."

He received a reply a few seconds later. "Your friend Bob isn't answering his phone. Be careful." Nick looked out into the night. He pulled his jacket tighter around him. *The feeling of being watched was back.*

10
———

Green Bay, Wisconsin
October 22nd 2032

It took an hour for the plane to arrive at Green Bay, Wisconsin's Austin Strabo Airport, the closest place to Escanaba where the jet could land. The place was deserted and the Airbus was the only jet on the tarmac, dwarfing the smaller single prop planes. A van drove up as Kobak, Saul and the security team disembarked. Kobak recognized the logo of the Green Bay Packers football team on the side and jerked in surprise. He looked at Saul to explain, but the security chief had already left to speak with the driver. A few minutes later they shook hands. The man walked away, disappearing around a corner of the hanger.

When Saul returned, he told Kobak, "I know the team's security chief. He owes me a favor. We have the van for as long as we need it. A bit outdated but it will work for us" ee studied his boss with narrowed eyes. "Of course that depends on why we're here."

Kobak reddened. "I haven't told you, really? Oh well. I'll tell you while we're driving. You want me to drive this?"

"Joking?"

"Of course. We're on our way to Escanaba. For some reason they call themselves the banana belt of the Upper Peninsula. To Bob Nitschke's home."

The van took off and headed north on US Highway 41, out of the city. Saul had positioned his men – two in the front seats, the other two in the next row. He sat with Kobak in the last row. Gear was stored in the back, except for side arms, which the men kept with them.

Kobak watched the four-man team for several minutes, fascinated by how they worked. He had never actually seen them in action before. When the team accompanied him on trips out of the country to Eastern Europe and Russia, Saul had kept them in the background, unnoticeable. Each had blended in with the people around them as if he were a citizen of the country. On this trip, they were dressed in simple black clothes and black berets. Each one wore special dark glasses that reflected glare but did not interfere with their visual acuity. They were alert but not on edge, heads watching passing motorists while in Green Bay and once on the open road, swiveling to watch the countryside or inspecting every car that passed them coming or going. Twice the driver instructed the car to slow to let cars behind them pass.

When they entered Menominee, Kobak lurched forward. "Stop the van. There's somebody I want to see."

"Who?" Saul asked.

"Never mind. I'd be really disappointed if he were still here. You'll meet him soon.

They turned off of highway 41, onto state Highway 35 which followed the shoreline of Lake Michigan. A few minutes later Saul said sharply. "Stop the van." The driver pulled over.

Kobak jerked in surprise. "What's going on?"

"We're not driving another mile until you tell me what this is all about. My men can't protect you if we don't know what it is we're supposed to protect you from."

Kobak nodded. He pulled out his smart phone and went to turn it on. Saul put his hand on Kobak's. "That isn't wise. People can track us with your phone."

Kobak smiled. "Relax, Saul. I have a security application installed on this phone that was specially created for me by GenTech Security."

"Can you trust them?" the security chief demanded.

Kobak shrugged. "I suppose so. They're one of the startups I invested in when Quantumnetics hit it big. You know how many startups I have around the world, so many I can't keep track of them. They're like into everything you could attach AI to ... crazy! But I'm learning they can come in handy, you'll see Anyhow back to your question what was it? I remember. This device has a fail-safe encryption and nano-antibodies that roam through the software like T-cells in a body's immune system to protect it from viruses infecting the system or spyware trying to gather information. No one can track its whereabouts, record conversations or use it to spy on me, and no one knows what's on this phone except me and Colossus."

Saul scrutinized the phone and Kobak handed it to him to inspect. "And anyone who sent you something who doesn't have this level of protection."

"That's a drawback, true enough, ever try listening to a one-sided conversation, frustrating very frustrating. Can I have it back now?"

Saul handed it to him. He indicated the driver to continue on. "All right, show me what's on this special phone of yours."

Kobak scrolled through the pictures and told him about Bob Nitschke and that these were pictures from his trail cam, and about the Sasquatch and what Colossus had told him about the bio-learning machines. He explained his Russian friend's request and how he himself had become overwhelmed with the idea of biosynthetic learning devices after Colossus told him that it's best guess was that Sasquatch are biosynthetic neural nets. In the end he told him about Nick and how he sent them out to retrieve the Sasquatch body.

"And now somebody's gone and killed one. I want to know what's going on. Simple. And, as you can see by the pictures, apparently dangerous."

Without raising his voice, Saul said, "Whether Colossus's convinced it's the latest and greatest thing in evolution of artificial intelligence or not is just a probabilistic guess. So if you want me to do my job, you'll tell me what's behind your obsession with this killing and why it's so bloody important to you."

Kobak looked into the steel green eyes and knew he had to tell Saul everything. It wasn't just that Saul was good at his job as security chief; he trusted the man as he trusted few human beings.

"Most the experts in the field of general artificial intelligence believe that will not be achieved until the core operating system is bioengineered, not just digital."

"That's it Saul. Colossus believes these creatures are bio-synthetic learning devices ... these creatures ... these Sasquatch, at least the one that was shot, is remarkable, so mysterious that I need to understand what these things are ... I believe they are the missing piece I've been searching for that will enable me to take Colossus to the next level."

Saul swore under his breath. "You should have told me all of this in Toronto. Show me the pictures of the fire-fight between the woman and the Sasquatch hunters again."

Kobak, uneasy at the direction Saul's comments were going, asked, "Is there a problem?"

"Can your security firm hack the serial number on that trail cam?" Saul asked.

"I'm sure they can. The two women who run it are the top people in their field. They've won the Cyber Security Challenge in the UK and the US two years running. What's going on, Saul."

"The men who shot at the woman are professionals and well equipped. They've undoubtedly taken the trail cam by now and looked at its flash drive."

Kobak leaned back as the shock of that statement went through him. He had been so fixated on finding the Sasquatch, he hadn't even put the other pieces of the puzzle together. Now that Saul had said it aloud, it was obvious they must know where Bob lived.

The security chief leaned forward and spoke in a language Kobak didn't recognize. But the effect was instantaneous. The man in the driver's seat disabled the auto driver and took over manual control of the vehicle. Two of the others had put on night vision goggles and scanned the road ahead and behind, as well as the sides. The fourth one turned around and faced Saul, never taking his eyes off Kobak.

Kobak felt his mind begin to compress into a narrow band of attention. He counted backward from twenty to zero four times before he could focus on what was going on around him again. He saw Saul watching him, the security chief waiting impatiently.

"Welcome back, Stephen," Saul said icily. "You were gone again. Do I need to be worried you're going to flip out on me?"

Kobak felt his cheeks flush. He shook his head.

Kobak didn't like talking about how he disconnected from reality when overwhelmed by unusual data or movements and actions he wasn't prepared to understand. But he managed to say, "I ... I was avoiding a fugue state. It happens sometimes with my Asperger's."

"There's a lot you've been keeping from me."

"Need to know," Kobak said, trying to make a joke of it.

Saul glared at him. "We're dealing with professionals who will think nothing of killing someone who gets in the way of killing a Bigfoot. So I need to know if you're all right and are ready to get to work."

Kobak nodded.

"The Fish and Wildlife ranger who was shot at, can you find out who she is?" Saul asked.

"The security firm who did my phone can find her. Why? You think she's in danger?"

"In my opinion everyone associated with this mission is in danger. From now on, you do what I say. You don't stir or move unless I tell you to." He turned to the man driving and spoke again in the weird language that was mostly gutturals and harsh consonants. The van sped up to a hundred miles an hour.

Kobak didn't like being ordered around, but he noted the sense of urgency in Saul's tone and realized the man was trying to protect him. He asked, "Are you speaking in some kind of spy code?"

Saul smiled. "It's a dialect of Gaelic from the Outer Hebrides. My family and maybe a dozen other people, including my team speak it."

The rest of the trip to Escanaba took only twenty-five minutes. They found Bob Nitschke's home five minutes later. It was a large Victorian style house that overlooked the Lake Michigan waterfront. Saul had the driver pass the home and park on a side street with a view of the front. The lights were on and the front door was open. They detected no movement within.

Saul said, "This man, Nitschke, he's expecting you, right?"

"I set up the meeting after I talked with Nick."

Saul barked out orders. The security team left the van. Two took up positions at either end of it. The other two crossed the street and entered the building. One of them returned five minutes later and reported what they found. "No one's inside but Bob. He's down but alive and awake. Knife wound penetrated just below the sternum. He's lost a lot of blood. I checked his vitals. Pulse is weak breathing labored. He may not make it. Matthew's with him now applying first aid. I did a sweep, both infrared and electronic. Whoever did this didn't leave any bugs behind. The house has been ransacked. Looks like they took his computer, smart phone and back up hard drive."

"Good work, Timothy," Saul said.

The memory of his own beating and being left for dead by Paki-bashers filled Kobak with apprehension and he asked, "Shouldn't we call an ambulance?"

Saul nodded. "As soon as we've found out what he knows. I want a man in front and a man in back. Keep in touch through coms all the time." He looked at Kobak. "Let's go find out what Bob remembers."

"A woman lives here," said Saul as they entered the front room.

"How do you know?" asked Kobak.

"The inside of the house, in spite of the mess from the search, is neat and tidy. The slip covers on the furniture have recently been vacuumed and the magazines on the end table are stacked in order." Saul frowned. "You understand technology and see what you need to stay on top in the field. I see what I need to keep you alive."

Timothy motioned them to follow him downstairs. The basement had been set up as a typical Midwestern man-cave – La-Z-Boy perched in front of 60" plasma screen TV; a smart mini-fridge for beer and a classic pool table. Mounted heads of deer and moose and several plaques with walleye and muskie adorned the walls.

Bob was propped in his La-Z-Boy, a compress on his abdomen was blood soaked. Matthew stood beside him. Bob eyed Kobak and Saul and managed a weak grin. "It's a cinch you aren't the bastards who stabbed me." He tried to point a thick finger at Kobak, but gave up when he couldn't lift his arm. "You must be the guy who called, Nick's friend."

Kobak nodded and said. "An ambulance is on its way. What happened?"

"I'm sitting here going through the pics from the trail cam when I hear a noise on the stair. At first I think it might be my dog, Rusty. But in the next second, some big dude whirls my chair around and slams me on the side of the head with something hard, then stabs me in the gut. I don't remember a thing after that until your guy wakes me up working on me, saving my life." He glanced at Matthew and groaned. "I did two tours in the first Gulf War and I can't keep myself safe."

"Take it easy, son. You did well enough to stay alive," said Saul. "Looks like they got your computer and smart phone. Can you think of anything else they may have taken?"

"Did they get the arrow?"

"What arrow."

Bob reddened. "I shot the Bigfoot when I first saw it. I thought it was a bear. It was already dying, so I didn't kill it. I retrieved my arrow with some of its stuff on it. I put it in the freezer."

Saul looked at Timothy. "The freezer was empty, sir."

Saul asked, "Did you get a good look at your attacker?"

Bob shook his head. "He was wearing a ski mask, sorry." Then,

"There was one thing though. I didn't pass out right away. The guy said something like he was talking to someone else. It sounded like he had a foreign accent. Eastern European."

"You sound very certain."

"My father-in-law's from Belgrade. When he gets angry he swears in Serbian." Bob grimaced. "Where's that ambulance?"

Saul smiled. "It's nearly here. They'll take you to the hospital. They'll notify your wife."

Bob tried to stand but collapsed back into the chair with a moan. "Is my family safe?" he said between clenched teeth.

"You don't have anything more they want. Let this die down."

All of a sudden Kobak knelt down beside Bob, put his hand on his shoulder and looked directly at him and in soft tones said, "What was it like ... what was it like to touch it, to look into the Bigfoot's eyes – tell me?"

Bob grimaced. "It was like nothing I ever experienced before. There was an intelligence, a kind of loving knowing that penetrated into my gut. At the same time, he was alien, I was totally frightened, I wish I'd never set that Bear bait." He slumped down and closed his eyes.

Matthew took his pulse. "Still alive. He's a tough bugger."

"Let's wrap this up." Saul ordered

The team reassembled. Matthew brought the van to the front of the house and they climbed in. The ambulance's siren could be heard in the distance. Matthew pulled away slowly in order not to attract attention to them.

"Why did those guys try to kill Bob?" Kobak asked.

Saul chewed his lower lip. "He'd seen the Bigfoot and the pictures of the woman shooting at someone over the creature's body. My guess, this is part of a larger operation and whoever's killed this creature doesn't want any witnesses who could draw attention to it. Now, the only proof of the Sasquatch is what you and Nick have on your phones."

"So they'll be coming after Nick and the woman next I suppose ... oh that's not good."

"My guess is that they will go after the woman first since she had the first hand encounter and may have physical evidence from the Sasquatch."

As they drove away, Kobak's phone buzzed. He checked the text message and showed it to Saul.

"Birgit Gunderson, US Fish and Wildlife Ranger. Those women are good. They found her in under fifteen minutes." He barked at Matthew, "Get us to Marquette."

Within two minutes the van was headed across the UP, paralleling the Hiawatha National Forest. Saul handed the phone back to Kobak. "Set up a meeting with this woman. Tell her not to go home."

"Is she really in danger?"

"They will find her."

"I'll figure something out ... it'll come to me." He spoke to his phone, "Call that number."

On the horizon, in the dark night, the lights of the giant Native American casino beckoned them forward. Kobak had a strange feeling about the place.

11

______

US Fish and Wildlife Service Lab
Marquette, Michigan
October 22nd 2032

Birgit was startled awake by the ringing of her phone. The voice on the other end was tenor and the man spoke quickly as if he had to get every word out in ten seconds. She didn't understand a thing he was saying and then she heard the name Stephen Kobak. This brought her upright and fully aware.

"Who?" she asked.

"This is Stephen Kobak."

"Yeah and I'm Chelsea Clinton. Look is this Corporal Richter? It is, isn't it? You can shove it up your ass. I still won't date you."

In the silence that followed, Birgit regretted the lack of landlines anymore. It would have been good to slam the receiver in Richter's ear. Then, the voice, slowing and calmer, said, "I'm not Corporal Richter. I really am Stephen Kobak, Birgit. Don't hang up ... sorry to be blunt but you need to listen to me. You probably don't know who I am, a lot of people do, of course, that's beside the point. You've been wasting your talents that's beside the point, too. I–"

Birgit stopped him. She wasn't going to waste any time on this prank and she had a sure fire way of telling if it was him or not. "If you're the famous Stephen Kobak? Prove it. What was the topic of your last Ted Talk?"

"I've never given a Ted talk ... I never give Ted talks ... I don't like them ... they were good in the beginning but now." He paused and she heard chuckling. "I see what you're doing. Smart woman."

"Yeah smart enough to test you and you're smart enough to pass. So tell me what's this all about. Why would *the* Stephen Kobak call me?"

"I know about your experience with the Sasquatch, I'm impressed ... good job ... glad you're alive. Can we talk about what went on?"

Maybe it was the earnestness with which the voice on the other end of the phone was speaking, but Birgit found herself trusting it, believing it was Kobak. She told him what happened. When she reached the point where she collected the material in a sample bag, Kobak interrupted.

"Fantastic, this changes everything, you're a microbiologist right?"

Birgit's guard went up again. Few people around here knew about her days at the university. Marge was the only one and she let everyone know she'd hired Birgit because she was a vet. "How do you know that?"

"Umm ... It's on the web ... I have a security team that can find out everything about someone, personal privacy is a myth, you know that. Look, it's important. I figure you haven't forgotten what you've learned. What's your assessment of the Sasquatch material?"

Birgit quickly went through in her mind all the scenarios she could come up with. Nothing really made sense. She glanced at the clock on the wall. It was just after midnight and she really didn't want to wait until Marge got in to take the next step. "It was deteriorating rapidly so I put it in our freezer. There is really nothing here to examine it with."

"Sit tight. I'll figure something out and get back to you shortly."

Birgit was about to end the call when a new voice interrupted. "Ms. Gunderson, this is Saul McBride. Mr. Kobak forgot to inform you that you are in danger. If we can track you, the people who shot at you can do the same. They'll want to keep this secret, keep it away from the public. They'll be coming for you. Is your facility secure? Do you still have your gun with you?"

Birgit felt the blood drain from her face. She remembered the trail cam. Whoever this Saul guy was, he was speaking the truth. "I have my gun," she replied, knowing it was still locked in the bottom drawer of her desk, where regulations demanded she keep it when she wasn't in the field.

Kobak came back on the phone. "Who was that?" she demanded.

"Saul's my head of security ... you'll like him ... well probably not ... he's good at what he does ... you don't have to like him."

"I dislike him already."

"Hang tight."

"Do I have a choice?"

"Saul says no."

Kobak took less than ten minutes, which was fine as far as Birgit was concerned. The phone call had intensified the creepy feeling she'd had earlier. His fast talking tenor voice was a relief. "Birgit here's what I want you to do ... take the sample from the freezer ... walk outside ... you'll see someone you know ... it'll be safe to go with that person."

Birgit couldn't imagine who it would be unless it was Marge, but her mentor would have called to find out what was going on. Whoever it was, Birgit would be glad to see him or her and get out of the lab.

"Roger that," she said.

"Wait! Wait!" Kobak yelled before she could hang up. "Saul says to ditch your phone ... the bad guys will be tracking you through it."

The line went dead. Birgit couldn't leave her phone at the lab because the shooters would track her here for sure. She decided she would turn it off and throw it in a garbage can. Today was trash day and the Marquette city sanitation workers would haul it to the municipal dump.

Birgit grabbed the Sasquatch sample from the freezer and went outside. The dumpster was located on the side of the lab, which also gave her a clear view of the street and anyone approaching the building. She dumped her smart phone into the opening and marveled how the dumpster didn't smell like the one at her apartment building, which stank like a Department of Defense experiment gone bad. She noted the time. The waste removal truck would be here in another hour. *Good*, she thought. *By then anyone chasing my phone will be following it all over Marquette.*

The temperature had fallen near freezing. She pulled her vest closer about her and waited in the shadows. She didn't have to wait long. She heard the car before it made the turn into the parking lot of the lab. Whoever it was probably wasn't security conscious because he parked the car under a mercury vapor light making himself a great target for anyone watching.

Great. They send an amateur.

She was ready to blast the driver's ignorance, when to her surprise, the man who stepped out of the car was Olav Lassen, a Ph.D teaching assistant in the microbiology lab at the University of Michigan. She couldn't have been more surprised.

Olav was tall and lean, with a red beard and the profile of a Viking. He claimed one of his ancestors had sailed with Leif Gunderson to the shores of North America in 1000 and had been the first to jump ashore at Vinland. They had often joked about being cousins, though Olav had many times inquired if she wanted to go out with him and not as relatives. That was six years ago and looking at him now she realized she still had mixed feelings for the man.

He waved his arm at her and yelled "Birgit!"

It was all she could do not to shout at him to stop making himself a target. "Not so loud, Ole. You'll wake the neighbors," she said as she walked up to his car, a Ford Taurus that had to be twenty years old.

Olav knew better than to hug her as Birgit had preferred

handshakes and fist bumps to touchy feely stuff. He gave her a high five. "You look the same cousin."

She smiled and said, "Back at you."

They clambered into the vehicle. The interior was like Olav – clean and well kept, not even a gum wrapper in the ashtray. He had been an organized neat freak in college, unlike herself. He handed her a bio transport case with dry ice inside for the sample.

" So you really have a piece of Sasquatch here? Hard to believe they exist."

"I didn't either, but here we are."

Once it was secure, he headed out of the parking lot into the Marquette night.

"You never told me you knew the great man himself," Olav said.

"Just met him this evening." Birgit checked to see if anyone was following them. Olav drove as if he didn't have a care in the world. "Where are we going?" she asked.

"To my lab." He chuckled. "I run a well-funded bio research laboratory at Northern Michigan University. You're talking to Professor Lassen."

"Congrats. You deserve it. You were a great teaching assistant. But I thought you were heading for Silicon Valley and the next tech startup when you graduated. What's with the biochem stuff?"

"Wait till you see the set up," Olav said enthusiastically. "You won't believe it. Kobak's investment company is funding my research in using machine learning to simulate rapid cellular evolutionary pathways for the production of ethanol from genetically manipulated cells. I then use an evolutionary model of learning to select the perfect cells for the task."

Birgit waved her hand over her head. "I always knew you'd do something important."

"What about you. The CRISPR-Cas9 undergraduate gene editing phenom? You just sort of disappeared.

"I went to war. It wasn't good."

"I'm sorry."

"Thanks."

"I'm sure you haven't forgotten how much you loved being in that sparkling clean University of Michigan genetics lab. Steve says you're in danger. Should I be afraid?"

"The people that killed the Sasquatch tried to kill me less than six hours ago."

Olav drove onto the Down Campus and the academic mall where the Seaborg Science Complex was located in silence. He pulled into the parking lot and stopped in a parking space. The Taurus' headlights shone on a sign that read Professor Olav Lassen.

Birgit looked around to see if they been followed as they exited the vehicle. She saw nothing and the silence of Marquette late night was deafening. "I think we're good."

"This is rather strange," Olav said as he grabbed the transport case and walked toward the entrance. "I'll do anything to help Steve out. Steve's funding for my lab exceeds the budget for the chemistry and biology departments combined."

She grimaced. "I get it."

"What I told you in the car is the tip of the iceberg of what we're working on now. Machine learning is beginning to supercharge the evolutionary process in a wide range of microorganisms. You couple that with CRISPR/Cas9 and we start processes that build new biosynthetic organisms." He paused and his face reddened. "If that's what we wanted to do. Personally, I'm for it but others think it's the most dangerous enterprise science has embarked upon."

He held the door open for her and Birgit recalled he'd always been a perfect gentleman, a throwback to 20th century principles of chivalry in manners. Otherwise, he treated women as equals in whatever field they competed.

Birgit wasn't in the mood to ponder deep ethical questions and changed the subject "How's your personal life?" she asked.

"Still haven't found the right woman yet. She'll come along."

He led them at a brisk pace down an antiseptic hallway

illuminated brightly by fluorescents every six feet. The harsh glare, so unlike the dim lighting at the US Fish and Wildlife Service facility made Birgit wince. They reached a set of locked double doors. The security here was even tighter than her lab. Olav leaned over and put his right eye to a retinal scanner. She heard a sharp click and the lab doors swung open.

"State of the art," Olav said. "Everything we do has to be protected not only against accidental contamination, but the occasional thief who thinks he can score psychoactive chemicals. As you know, one of the biggest problems up here is drug overdose." Olav shook his head ruefully. "Of course, Steve insists all of our results are open source available to everybody to build on."

The inside of the lab was pristine and the equipment was beyond anything Birgit had experienced before. The machine used to perform CRISPR/CAS9 gene editing must have cost a hundred grand easy, and Olav's lab had two of them.

"Over here," Olav said, leading her to the refrigeration unit at the back of the lab. He handed her a pair of latex gloves and donned his own. After putting the majority of the Sasquatch material in cryo-storage, he placed a small sample in the latest microfluidic system used for carrying out a wide range of biochemical test protocols. Immediately analysis began to run with the results displayed on a large screen. He stared at the magnified Sasquatch material for several seconds before turning to her with a puzzled grin. "This stuff is really cool and I have no idea what it is. No cellular structure, yet it shows many of the characteristics of organized living plant structures at the micro level and animal at the macro. Very strange."

Birgit peered at the screen. Her deep understanding of biochemistry came racing back to her. In particular, the lack of a cellular makeup surprised her. It was as if she was looking at an animal-plant hybrid. "Is this possible?" she asked breathlessly.

Olav nodded. "Living proof someone crossed an ape with a zucchini, cousin."

"I'm serious. This is impossible!"

"I was being serious. Look, Sherlock Holmes said it best. 'When you have eliminated the impossible, whatever remains, however improbable, must be the truth.' But there's a way to test this sample even more."

Olav retrieved an electrochemical magnetic generator and began exposing the material to a series of intense electromagnetic wavelengths. "Will you look at that," he said, his excitement rising as the biochemical analyzer relayed each new reaction result to the big computer screen. "I need to show this to Kobak."

Pulling out his smart phone, he touched the screen. Kobak face appeared instantly. "I've been waiting for your call, Professor Lassen. Waiting too long in my opinion. What do you have for me?"

"I'd rather show you, Dr. Kobak. If you'll indulge me for a second."

It took only a moment to rig up his phone so that it could relay the results from the analyzer directly to Kobak.

"There are some amazing photochemical processes going on here. This is happening even though there is rapid deterioration of the core structures.

Birgit looked on as fascinated as the other two at what the sequence of electromagnetic pulses, from infrared to ultraviolet stimulation, did to the biochemistry of the Sasquatch material.

After three minutes, Olav shut down the analyzer. He said to Kobak and Birgit, "What do you think?"

Kobak's image on the computer screen pursed its lips. Then, "I know this is going to sound strange, really strange. Any chance there could be some sort a neural network embedded in the material."

Birgit jerked in surprise and before Olav could say anything, she asked without keeping the incredulity out of her tone, "Are you suggesting a plant with a brain?"

Kobak shrugged. "Well, sort of. I see there are no ordinary cells but is it possible some sort of a neural net is embedded in that stuff?"

Birgit was thinking '*Nickt, no wonder everybody wants to keep this secret.* "The Klapman Equation says that organic interactions can be represented by a chemogenesis web, especially when the events are triggered by photochemical spikes. In short, it could be the basis of some sort of a neural network. Given the range of electromagnetic energy we subjected the material to just now, I'd say it could work at the speed of light."

Kobak grinned. "You haven't forgotten your stuff, amazing, pretty damn cool. Olav upload everything you just showed me using this IP to my secure server back in my office, so Colossus can analyze it." He smiled. "Colossus's gonna love this ... well I don't know if he really loves anything."

Colossus? Who's Colossus? Birgit asked herself, wondering what weird pit of strangeness she had stumbled into. Curiously, at the same time, she didn't feel threatened and the urge to count backward from twenty to zero to calm herself didn't arise at all. It was as if her PTSD had finally taken a vacation. She looked around at the lab, felt the comfort of being in academia again sweep through her. A curious thought came to her in this moment. *Home.* She knew she was home and in an eye blink she felt better than she had since returning from Afghanistan.

Olav, on the other hand, had a look like a deer in the headlights. He recovered enough to rasp out, "Wait a minute. Are you suggesting that the Sasquatch is some sort of AGI experiment?"

Kobak smiled. "An interesting thought, isn't it? See you soon. Run some more tests and see if you can stop the deterioration. Protect that sample with your life. Just joking." The communication broke off.

Birgit had all sorts of thoughts mixing in her mind. Chief among them was that if the guys who shot at her killed the Sasquatch because it was some new order of learning creature and wanted to keep it secret, then they'd do anything to get the sample she took. She glanced at the clock. The night had flown past and it was already 7 a.m. Marge would already be at the lab. If the shooters went there first instead of following her smart phone around Marquette, her old mentor could be in trouble.

"I gotta go," she said and headed toward the door.

"What's so urgent, cousin? We just got started here. There's loads more work to be done and you can help me."

Birgit shook her head. "I've got to meet a friend at the lab."

"This early?"

Olav deserved an answer, though she didn't want to frighten the man. An academic his entire life, he thought the most dangerous thing in his life was a bad peer review. "The tweet version is, she could be in danger because of me."

"You mean because of this stuff," Olav said pointing at the Sasquatch material.

Birgit nodded. "There's a lot more going on here your buddy Kobak hasn't told you. When I get back with my friend, I'll lay it all out for you."

"Wait ... maybe I should go with you."

"Rescue the damsel in distress?"

Olav grinned. "Not really my style, huh? Take care of yourself."

"I have my gun."

He flipped her the keys to the Taurus. "This'll get you there faster."

She nodded and left.

12

Shanghai, China
October 2032

After the moon episode, Zhang's career skyrocketed. Through series of brilliant financial and winner-take-all maneuvers, he became one of the richest and most powerful men in China. They were even rumors swirling around concerning the unexpected deaths and departures some of his most formidable adversaries.

However, today he was being introduced into the most exclusive club in all of China, Wang Wei's inner group of men, the Council of four that controlled everything extraterrestrial. When Zhang entered the room Wang Wei turned his back. Zhang knew that the old man didn't want him in the group and that he would always be a problem that would have to be dealt with. Yet he knew from one of the Council members that he would be doing some of their dirty work. Zhang knew this was part of a bigger plan that would soon unfold

13

Hiawatha National Forest
UP, Michigan
October 23rd 2032

I n the light of day, the area looked less forbidding and it was hard to believe that after what had happened the night before.

Redhawk found the Bigfoot's trail and they followed it. He pointed out to Nick the signs – branches broken by something pulling on them; scuffed footprints made by dragging feet; a strange, colorless fluid that couldn't possibly be blood and yet it had congealed in the same way. He also pointed out the signs of something smaller that had followed the Bigfoot to the clearing where it died.

"It must be the woman in the photos," Nick said.

Redhawk grunted. "She wasn't the only one. A single man followed, too."

"You think he shot the Bigfoot?"

"Probably. His tracks show him waiting in the clearing before the others arrived. He left this." Redhawk held up some shredded tobacco and a tiny shard of cigarette paper.

Nick recognized the remains of a cigarette that had been field stripped so it left no identifying trace.

"Wait here," Redhawk said. He disappeared into the brush and though Nick craned his neck, he heard no sound except for the morning breeze rustling the leaves. He pivoted slowly, now wishing he had gone into the Marine Corps like his grandfather, Grotto, had urged him to do. There was no longer any doubt the men who had scooped up the Bigfoot were professionals at hunting and killing. What happened last evening seemed obvious now from the way Redhawk laid out the tracking evidence. Someone had shot the Bigfoot but hadn't killed it, then trailed it to the clearing where it died. Then he had called the others to come and retrieve the creature. When the woman in the photos arrived, he'd shot at her but missed and she escaped. Maybe the man had seen Bob's truck, maybe not. But they had taken the trail cam and could trace his friend through its serial numbers.

The process of putting the pieces of the puzzle together had taken only a few seconds. Nick swallowed hard in a dry throat. He had to call Bob to warn him. He fished his phone from his backpack. The call went straight to voicemail. He left a message telling Bob to get out of the house, now. He started to call Kobak when Redhawk's low whistle turned him around.

The Native American emerged from the forest like an apparition. "I think we're being watched ... we've been watched all long."

"By whom?"

"Bigfoot. They're here."

Nick pivoted but saw nothing."

"You sure?"

Redhawk nodded. "C'mon. The trail leads this way." He led them deeper into the forest. The cold temperatures overnight had started the leaves falling and everywhere the ground was carpeted with reds and yellows. They moved slowly to avoid making unnecessary noise. The sun was at midmorning when he held up his fist and they finally stopped at Owl Creek. The glade was a hundred feet across. The stream ran sparkling through the middle, between grassy embankments. Three deer stood on a ledge of gravel leading down to a watering hole. The eight-point buck watched the surrounding area while two does drank their fill.

"The Bigfoot took the shot right here," Redhawk said. He pointed to bushes that had been crushed by a falling body. "It got up and ran the way we came." The trampled underbrush and broken branches showed the path they had followed to reach this spot. "Over there," Redhawk said and Nick followed his gaze to a log next to the creek. "The woman trailed it from there," The Native American said with complete certainty.

"I'm impressed, Chief," Nick said.

He inspected the ground. It was trampled with footprints and the crushed bushes showed where the Bigfoot had fallen, just like Redhawk said. But something was missing. If something as large as a Bigfoot had been shot here, there should be blood, maybe even hair and skin. But he saw nothing like that, just more of the same oily, congealed substance they'd seen earlier, and it was decomposing quickly even though there were no signs of insects attacking it. Nick scratched his head. He didn't need a degree in biology or chemistry to know this kind of breakdown on a cellular level within twenty-four hours was impossible. Now he had another mystery to add to the anonymous woman and the team of professionals who had taken the Bigfoot. Just what kind of creature was this Sasquatch? Certainly not some long-lost giant ape species as many of his Bigfoot colleagues argue for.

Redhawk touched him on the shoulder and Nick came instantly alert. His eyes scanned the surroundings, but saw nothing. After several seconds he relaxed enough to stand.

"What is it?" he asked.

"There's another trail, here. I don't think the shooter would have noticed it."

"Why's that?"

"It was made earlier this morning."

"By who?"

"Another Bigfoot. Look at the tracks."

There they were, large footprints in the soft soil. Nick had seen hundreds of these Bigfoot prints cast in plaster of Paris. And now Redhawk was acting like he had seen them many times before. It was puzzling how easily Redhawk was accepting their existence.

Maybe the Potawatomi really knew something about Bigfoot that Nick didn't. After all, Bigfoot researchers claimed that Native Americans had been interacting with the elusive creature for thousands of years. The SRA had been around for less than thirty, and while the reports of sightings numbered in the tens of thousands, none of those encounters reported the same sense of encountering a kindred spirit that the Native Americans claimed.

Once more Redhawk held up his fist. They had arrived at open space several hundred feet across in the forest. In the center was an abandoned quarry. At the far edge, tall brown grass all but hid an unused access road. The pit was shallow but wide, with a central exposed area in the smooth floor. A swath of grass a hundred feet wide separated the pit from the forest. Large areas had been trampled where animals had bedded down for the night.

Setting their packs on the ground, they began to walk around the pit, staying well back from the crumbling rock edge. A sign at the south end proclaimed it was the property of Silver Ridge Stone Limited. From the weathering of the rock, the quarry had been abandoned at least 30 years ago.

Halfway around, Redhawk dropped to his knees suddenly. He cawed like a raven – three, short, harsh rasps followed by a long one. Nick crouched and looked at his friend. Chief pointed through the long grass at the forest edge. Nick didn't see anything and shrugged. Chief frowned and jabbed his finger again. Nick followed his aim and for a moment was bewildered by the Native American's insistence that something was out there. He didn't see anything. Then the breeze stirred the leaves and the sun hit a pair of saplings at just the right angle. He saw where the trees had been arranged to conceal an opening. A casual observer wouldn't have noticed anything unusual. It spoke of an intelligence that was hiding a path so that only those who expected to find it would see it.

Cautiously, they approached the opening. A subtle trail wound deep into the woods. Redhawk let out a long, slow breath. "This was not made by hunters," he whispered.

Nick almost didn't believe it and yet something about this trail beckoned him forward as if it held the answer to the Bigfoot mysteries he's been initiated into when on his grandfather's farm twenty years ago.

"I'm going in," he said, his words a quiet brush of air through his lips. Redhawk nodded. Several times they came to dead ends and were forced to backtrack. Nick realized that the makers of this trail had created a maze where the unwary would become lost walking about in circles. Without Redhawk to lead him, Nick would have been one of those, walking until he collapsed exhausted.

What seemed like an hour passed and another clearing appeared. It was not a natural open space in the forest. Something had arranged the area around it so that everything funneled toward a structure of sticks leaning together like a teepee in the center. Nick immediately recognized the Sasquatch stick structure. He had encountered more than one of these following up on reports of Bigfoot sightings for the SRA.

What took his breath away was the unmistakable craftsmanship. Each log had been carefully pruned, the upward tips sharpened as meticulously as a pencil in a pencil sharpener. Then each log had been placed exactly in the earth to form the shape of a lens, like the eye in the pyramid on the U.S. dollar bill.

He heard Redhawk approach. "Do you know what this is?" asked the Potawatomi.

Nick nodded. "It's a Bigfoot stick structure. They've been found in conjunction with Bigfoot sightings. Some researchers think they're trail markers or a kind of communication device to pass on information. Sort of like the pictographs used by Indian tribes along trade routes in the desert southwest."

Redhawk didn't say anything but walked around the strange tepee, giving it a wide berth. When Nick started to walk closer he held up his hand and shouted, "Stop!"

Nick stared at him, perplexed by his friend's sudden fearful attitude. "What's wrong, Chief?"

"Among my people these are portals to other worlds. People who go inside disappear."

Nick grinned. "That's one of the other explanations that have been reported."

Redhawk didn't say anything for a long time. Then, "My grandfather, the one who taught me to hunt and trap, he left home one morning in January to check his trap line. He never returned. His body was never found but one of these things was nearby one of his traps."

"You think he disappeared through one of these?"

"I'm saying, where Bigfoot are concerned there are no accidents."

Suddenly an overpowering odor of musk filled the clearing, driving both men to their knees. It disappeared as quickly as it appeared. Nick scrambled to his feet. The redolent smell reminded him of his grandfather's farm. He turned to ask Chief what had happened, but the Native American was staring into the trees at the far edge of the clearing. Nick saw it, too. A shudder ran through both of them. Looking at them in the golden glow of the early afternoon sun were at least a dozen Bigfoot. Different sizes, varying faces, some more human than others.

"My God!" Nick exclaimed. He looked over at Redhawk who was pulling out his 1911 Colt Peacemaker. "Don't shoot!" Ignoring Nick, Redhawk took aim. Nick slapped the gun down and the bullet whined into the ground at his feet.

Nick bunched his fists. "I told you not to shoot!"

Redhawk didn't back up. He stared Nick in the eyes and said evenly, "Those unnatural creatures are dangerous."

"Not to me they aren't." Nick turned back to look at the Sasquatch, but they were gone. He started forward.

Redhawk grabbed his arm. "Where are you going?" he asked with fear in his voice.

"After them."

"You're crazy. Remember my grandfather. You don't know what they'll do to you."

Nick shrugged off his hand. "I've been waiting since I was 12 years old for this chance." He bypassed the wooden structure and ran into the forest.

Redhawk watched Nick disappear. Slowly he walked back to where they had left their backpacks and waited for Nick to return. He had spent many hours silently with his father while hunting deer in the UP and was used to waiting. After about an hour, Nick's phone rang. Redhawk looked at the caller ID and saw it was from a Stephen Kobak. He picked up the phone and swiped the answer icon.

"Nick, did you find the body? Probably not. We've had a lot happen here I'm leaving Marquette now ... much I need to tell you about it ...."

Redhawk didn't answer right away and the voice asked, "Nick? What's going on?"

"Nick isn't here, Mr. Kobak," Redhawk said. "I'm Larry Redhawk. I went with Nick to retrieve the body. You're right – no dead Sasquatch."

The phone was silent for a moment then Kobak said, "I know who you are ... Nick mentioned you. Is he okay?"

Matter-of-factly, Redhawk said, "I don't know. He ran off after a group of Sasquatch. At least a dozen. I tried to stop him but he said something about when he was 12."

"Shit! I didn't expect that."

"It certainly surprised me."

"How long has he been gone?"

"An hour, maybe. He could be back at any moment."

"Why do you say that?"

"I haven't sensed the Bigfoot around here for some time now, we both had a sense of being watched since we got here."

"Are you willing to wait a little while longer? There might be men still hunting Sasquatch."

"Sure, I can take care of myself."

"Good. Wait an hour and if Nick isn't back by then, leave his backpack and phone there, grab the rest of the gear and head back to the truck. Call me if Nick comes back or when you leave for the truck. Will you do that?"

"Sure."

As soon as the call ended chief slipped the phone into his pocket. Leaving all the gear behind except for his weapons, he left the quarry.

14

Marquette, Michigan
October 23rd 2032

Dawn was a bright glow on the eastern horizon above Lake Michigan when Birgit pulled into the rear parking lot of the US Fish and Wildlife Service Lab. She recognized Marge's Prius in her spot by the gravel walkway leading to the back door. There were no other cars in the lot and she breathed a sigh of relief. Either the shooters were chasing their tails around the city or they hadn't bothered coming to the lab yet. Either way, she figured she had enough time to grab her pistol and Marge and get back to Olav's lab at the university where they'd be safe.

She entered the rear of the building and the first thing she noticed was the lights were off. Marge always turned them on when she arrived. Birgit's shoulders tensed and her breathing quickened. As she'd been taught in the military, she channeled the surge of adrenaline in her body to sharpen her senses. She slid noiselessly across the linoleum floor beside the set of double doors leading to the interior hall, the lab, the lunchroom and Marge's office. Flattening herself against the wall, she cocked her head. The murmur of voices reached her ears. She counted two intruders. *They obviously came for me just as Kobak predicted. I'm a witness and need to be silenced.* She cursed silently and wished she hadn't left her service revolver in her desk. But she wasn't without resources. She knew the layout of the building. There were two entrances, plus an emergency fire escape from the second floor. She'd have to wait for the hunters to go inside the lab before grabbing Marge and making a run for it. She didn't have to wait long. The doors to the lab squeaked open and closed.

Birgit darted into the hall and ran on tip toe for the Supervisor's office. She couldn't leave Marge behind. The woman was more than her boss. She was a very dear friend and mentor. She burst into the office and stopped cold. The elderly woman was leaned back in her chair. A dark red hole above her eyes stared at the ceiling. A bloody mist of red coated the white plasterboard behind her. Judging from the way the blood dripped down the wall, the shooting had happened only minutes before.

Birgit backed into the corridor. This couldn't be happening not to her, not to Marge. Her clothes were soaked with sweat and her mind reeled at the sight of her dear friend, but the adrenaline spurred her to act swiftly. Fortunately she faced the lab. A shadow passed across the windows in the double doors. The killers were still inside. She ran down the corridor, stopping briefly to pick up a broom from the hall closet. Outside the lab's double doors she ran the broom through the looping handles. It would hold them for the time she needed to get out of the building.

She turned. Behind Birgit the broom rattled. They'd finished searching the lab faster than she thought. She ran full out, not toward the front where the murderers would expect her to go and likely had a man waiting, but to the second floor. She scurried up the stairs just as the broom handle snapped with a crack like a pistol shot. As noiselessly as possible she opened the door to the second floor and slid inside. The lights were off and they'd have to stay that way or she'd give her position away to the killers. If they had the training she'd gone through, they'd systematically sweep the building, clearing the ground floor first before moving to the second. This gave her some time. She went through her options. There was always the fire escape, but if they had come ready to kill, then she couldn't take the chance others waited outside guarding the exits. She'd have to prepare some kind of trap, take out one of the men. This would give her a firearm at least. She swallowed hard. She'd sworn never to kill anything again after Afghanistan. Would she be able to kill to defend her own life? She didn't know the answer to that. She heard a footstep on the stair. First thing was to move away from the wall. It was nothing but plasterboard and two by four studs. Nothing to stop bullets. The second floor was used mostly for storage. *Including illegal bear traps confiscated from hunters.*

Crouching, she worked her way through boxes to the far side of the room. A metal storage cell held all the confiscated gear, except for firearms. These went to a separate facility in Traverse City. It wouldn't have mattered anyway. The firearms were always cleared of any ammo when taken. The door was left unlocked. It opened with a rusty screech. She held her breath, but no sound of hurrying steps on the stairs.

Birgit eased inside toward the back and quickly located the cardboard carton she'd put there last year. It contained a Mackenzie District Fur Company LTD 1886 HBC NO.15 bear trap she'd taken from a hunter near Munising in November a year ago. The idiot had sworn he was licensed to use it.

She set it out on the floor and stepped down on the springs. The trap opened and she set the pin. The trigger lever and trigger plate worked smoothly. She pulled her hand back, aware that the razor sharp teeth could snap her wrist in half. The trap set, she grabbed a hockey stick Eric had taken from a teenager who used it to club baby barn owls with, and carried both over to the door. She set the trap so that with the lights off, the killer wouldn't see it when he walked in and would step right onto the trigger plate.

She waited, trying to slow the savage beating of her heart. The silence and darkness threatened to transport her back to Helmand. Only the grip on the hockey stick kept her in this reality.

A few minutes later Birgit heard footsteps on the stair. She counted one person. The door opened and the man entered stealthily without turning on the lights, just as she knew he would. Darkness was his friend, but in this instance it was also his undoing. He took another step and she heard the trap spring with a sickening crunch. The man screamed like a wounded animal. He squeezed the trigger on his pistol and a round fired into the room, smashing into a packing case.

Birgit lunged forward and brought the hockey stick across his forehead. He stopped yelling and dropped like a stone, his head cracking against the floor. In the light from the stairway she could see blood gushing from a wound in his head and more seeping from his pants leg where the trap's teeth bit cruelly into his shin. She didn't recognize him.

His pistol had slid out of his still fingers and lay beside him. Birgit hesitated. It was a Colt .38 Super Competition pistol, modified to take a ten inch sound suppressor. She was familiar with it, her father having trained her to shoot when she was only seven. More footsteps on the stairs and she picked it up. Before she could decide what to do, three hollow sounds echoed in the stillness and bullets ripped through the plaster on her side of the door, narrowly missing her head and showering her with gypsum dust. A second passed and another sharp crack and the light switch plate shattered, somehow also turning on the lights to the room, exposing her to whoever was running up the stairs. Birgit rolled across the trapped killer and pulled the trigger a half dozen times as she pointed the pistol into the stairwell. The fall from the stunned killer's hand must have loosened the suppressor because the roar of the weapon deafened her.

She could hear nothing. She twisted her body around, ready to fire again and saw the second killer lying unconscious at the bottom of the stairs. He was wearing a bullet proof vest which had stopped the group of shots in the center mass of his chest from killing him. The impact, however, had knocked him out and down the flight of stairs.

A mixture of relief suffused Birgit. The man lived. Not that he deserved to live. These men had killed Marge. She stood. Blood roared in her ears. The threat was over and the fear from surviving an attack was now beginning to lodge in her chest. She found it hard to breathe. She dropped to one knee, saw the man in the bear trap staring at her. He was alive, like his partner. She stood and stepped away from him. The danger wasn't over yet. She pointed the weapon at his head and asked, "How many are outside?"

"*Mi smo sami,*" he said through clenched teeth.

She stepped on his foot in the bear trap. He screamed in pain and she let up. "English!" she ordered.

"We are alone," he whimpered.

"Are you the one who shot at me in the forest?"

The man pointed at the bottom of the stairs. "He did."

"Where are you from?"

"Croatia," he rasped.

She leaned over him. "You asshole. Marge didn't know anything. You are gonna rot in an unforgiving Michigan jail for the rest of your life." She slugged him in the head with the barrel of the pistol. He gasped and went unconscious.

Birgit stood slowly and listened. The quiet disturbed her. She thought of the others that might be lurking nearby in spite of what the killer said. They would certainly send in someone to see what the shooting was all about. She waited, removed the magazine in the Colt and saw there were eight shots left. She slammed it home and peered into the downstairs. No movement no sound.

Maybe the first killer spoke the truth and they had operated alone. After all, they had been hunting Sasquatch that nobody believed really existed, and they hadn't reckoned on an Afghan war veteran fouling things up. She ran her hand through her hair. It came away sticky. Her fingers were coated with blood. One of the bullets must have creased her scalp. In all the adrenaline soaked action she hadn't even noticed. She had to get out of here.

Birgit went down the stairs, every sense alert for the tiniest sound or motion. The second killer was still knocked out but could regain consciousness at any moment. She stripped him of his weapons and bound his hands behind his back. She put a gag in his mouth and took his shoes.

When she finished, she walked to the front of the building and peered out through the glass doors. The sun was rising above the trees and cast the parking lot in gold. She saw no one. In the distance she could see headlights. A van was roaring down the road toward the lab. She didn't have time to get into her truck or Olav's Taurus. Whoever was coming would trap her. She dashed across the parking lot toward a grove of trees just as the van swung into the parking lot. She didn't look back but kept on going. She heard the doors open. She still had fifty feet to go and would never make it. She turned and took a shooter's stance aiming at the man on the right side of the van. Curiously, he kept the rifle he held pointed at the ground. She wondered if it was a trick to make her hesitate, but a quick glance at the other men showed they were not targeting her.

Then a young man stepped out of the van with an older man right behind him. The younger man said, "Ms. Gunderson, are you all right?"

"Who's asking?" she demanded keeping her pistol leveled.

"Stephen Kobak. We spoke on the phone earlier. You'd best come with us. Quite nice to meet you actually."

She jerked in surprise but didn't lower her weapon. "I have Lassen's car," she said.

"I told him to buy a new one. In any case he won't be needing it for a while," Kobak said. "Please. It's for your own safety and Professor Lassen's."

The older man stepped forward. He spoke with a Scots accent. "Believe it or not, right now we're the only ones who can protect you."

She snorted. "I didn't do so bad a job by myself just now."

He grinned and said, "I know you did, lass."

Birgit lowered her weapon, put the safety on and stuffed it in the back of her jeans. "Who the hell are you?"

"My name is Saul McBride. I'm Mr. Kobak's chief of security. We saw the whole thing through the building's security cameras that Mr. Kobak's smart techies hacked into. It's the reason we got here as quickly as we did. But this place is now a crime scene and we need to get you and ourselves out of here, before the police get here or someone not as nice."

Birgit scowled. "The only thing I'm interested in is justice for Marge. Those bastards killed her."

"Of course, you're right," Kobak interjected. "Please believe me, Ms. Gunderson, can I call you, Birgit? I understand your rather primitive need for revenge and if it is in my power to grant it, I will give it to you. But for now, you need to concentrate on your own safety. You have become embroiled in something much more dangerous and complicated than you can imagine. So please let us rescue you. In the meantime, I want you to tell me every little detail of your experience with the Sasquatch. I'm sure you will be quite good at this with your military and biochemical training. Much better than that poor fellow who shot the creature with his bow and arrow. Didn't kill him of course. Hypothesize as you go. I'm truly quite fascinated in what you saw and what you think."

Birgit stared blankly at the tech genius, who seemed to be babbling. Then she turned her attention to the building that just yesterday morning was her safe haven, and saw in her mind's eye Marge's lifeless body sprawled in her office. *I'll get revenge for you, Marge. I swear it.* She squared her shoulders and marched toward the van. Kobak bowed for her to get onboard. She grabbed the frame and stared at him. "If there's something bigger going on, I want to know every part of it and who's behind all this crap."

"Of course."

15

Directly across the street from the sprawling campus of the Seattle Center, home to the 1962 World's Fair, KW Intel's glass office tower rose majestically into the air. It's seventy stories topped the famous six-hundred-and-five-foot Space Needle built for the fair and offered picturesque views of the Pacific Northwest's Puget Sound. KW Intel was named for its founders, Kellog and Winston Ang. Born a year apart, the two Chinese Americans had entered MIT at sixteen and fifteen respectively, graduating three years later, one year after they developed an application called Cirrus that allowed users to manage all their cloud storage providers. It was bought by Google for $100 million. They could have retired before reaching the legal drinking age in Washington State, but instead, they bought and funded a company doing research on AI control systems for large commercial vehicles. Two years later their prototype became the standard operating system on long-haul trucks. Within three years every major truck manufacturing company in the world leased KW Intel's VOS – Vehicular Operations System.

Eccentric billionaires didn't begin to describe them. Neither did their notorious penchant for conspiracy theories of all kinds.

The top floor of KW Intel's office complex looked like any ordinary command center for a $500 billion multi-national tech research company which had facilities developing new products around the world in every field from agriculture to video games. A receptionist greeted visitors from behind a circular counter, strategically placed to keep anyone from barging into inner conference rooms and offices.

What visitors didn't see were the receptionist's personal assistant device with Adaptive Intelligence software and built in retinal scan to block unauthorized users; state-of-the-art hidden cameras, and infrared motion detectors. Nor did anyone crossing the threshold to greet the receptionist feel the complete body scan for weapons. Within moments of arrival and giving a name to the receptionist, the building's internal computer monitoring system generated a complete dossier.

Visitors who came to pitch ideas or companies to purchase were cordially shown to a conference room where men and women whose sole job was to evaluate possible new acquisitions listened, evaluated and made recommendations whether to buy or pass. The grilling that went on made *Shark Tank* look like a guppy bowl.

Beyond the main conference room was a smaller room, insulated against any listening devices with sound suppression wall construction that kept any vibration of human speech from leaking out of the room. The room was filled with the latest eavesdropping equipment monitoring UHF, VHF, satellite and tower microwave transmissions. Seated behind a plain wooden desk, KW Intell's two owners, Kellog and Winston Ang, watched a giant screen with a view of ISS – the new International Space Station. The two men waited, uncharacteristically tense.

A light blinked on the screen and Winston, the younger of the two brothers, counted down slowly from ten. He was forty-one, thin, with black hair and deep dark circles beneath sloe eyes. His skin was golden. "Three ... two ... one ... now," he said.

Two large bay doors in the station's cargo bay opened. At first they saw nothing.

"Where are they, God damn it?" growled Kellog. Unlike his younger sibling, his skin was a sickly yellow shade, the color of jaundice. His eyes were blood shot, his face jowly and his dark hair flecked with gray. He was morbidly obese.

"Patience, Kel. The laser has to send them out at the precise moment or else they won't go into low earth orbit but will end up burning up in the earth's atmosphere." He smiled, showing even white teeth as the first satellite appeared to drift away from the space station. Drift was not an accurate description for the orbit of these tiny devices. When the mission was complete there would be thousands of tiny satellites the size and shape of an original smart phone floating around the planet, capable of seeing every part of the globe from the Himalayas to the deepest darkest parts of the Amazon jungle. They would be the seeing eye on a world filled with dark secrets.

The spacecraft were loaded with microelectronics and cameras weighing only half a pound. A pair of ultrathin solar sails spread out from the body like batwings and acted not only as a battery charger but as a propulsion system that kept the satellite in low earth orbit. For the cost of one communication satellite launched into orbit in 1990, the brothers could send ten thousand of these micro-devices to provide real-time, detailed imagery of the earth. It would take twenty days to have "eyes on" every inch of the planet's surface.

The brothers watched for an hour as the devices launched one after another. When the last satellite was deployed, a disembodied voice said, "That's the last of them for today."

Kellog pressed a button on the conference table. "Thank you, commander. Same time tomorrow?"

"Yes, sir. Do you mind if I ask what you're going to do with all the data these things will generate?"

"It'll be free to anybody who wants to use it", Winston lied. "Somebody at Walmart HQ will be able to look at every car entering a Walmart parking lot in a 24 hour period at every store in the world."

"That'll certainly be useful. So you could track the comings and goings of my wife?"

"What's her name, commander?" asked Winston.

"Seriously?"

"Just joking."

"How many of these does KW Intel currently have in orbit?"

"With this last launch, one thousand two hundred twenty-five. When the mission is complete we expect to have ten thousand flying around the planet."

"Whew. How did you get clearance for these?"

"We asked politely," said Winston.

The voice chuckled. "Ask a silly question. Talk with you tomorrow. Commander William Rodgers over and out." The space station feed disappeared.

Winston looked at his brother and asked, "Do you think anyone will figure it out – our primary purpose?"

"Not until it's too late, Win." Kellog paused. He smiled and Winston grinned back. They bumped fists.

"Here's to blissful ignorance."

The sound of a C major chord filled the room. "Hold that thought." Winston swiped the talk icon and put the phone to his ear. His lighthearted mood disappeared. "You're sure?" he asked the caller. Then, "Okay. Do what you can to find out what's going on without endangering the operation."

He hung up and turned to his brother. "That was Redhawk. It seems, strange as it may be, that Stephen Kobak has gotten directly involved."

Kellog sat up straight in his chair. "That shouldn't have happened. The Russian said early on he needed verification of the nature of the creatures. What happened? Did the incident in the UP bring him into play?"

"It wasn't our decision to hire the mercenaries to kill the Sasquatch."

"Yes, but I should have demanded more oversight."

Winston laughed and when his brother glowered at him, said

placatingly, "Lewis Meriwether would never have permitted that. Besides, it wasn't just the incident."

"How can you be sure?"

"Have you ever met Kobak?"

The older brother shook his head.

"I have … once. At the machine learning conclave in Finland a few months ago. He's a strange one … highly functioning autistic. His disability sends him into frantic investigations of the strangest ideas. He spent two years working on teleportation, you know, like in Star Trek. He was convinced the Tesla Coil could make it possible. He would have wasted a fortune on it but Kobak's chief of security Saul McBride had his wife talk him out of it."

Kellog chuckled. "Could be a useful weakness."

"Some say he has an old-fashioned IQ of 183. But that's not what makes him exceptional."

"You're saying it's his autism?"

Winston nodded. "Nicholai said, it must have been the idea of the Sasquatch as a deep learning, biosynthetic creature that triggered his obsession. He's totally involved now and that's a problem. He's never bought our argument about the dangers of the computer singularity."

Kellog snorted. "He and everyone else. People aren't seeing the real danger of AGI. They are all way too caught up in fantastical conspiracy theories. I told him, once we have machines that are smarter than we are, they will begin to improve themselves and set their own goals. What we're risking right now is what mathematician I.J. Goode calls an intelligence explosion and the process could get away from us. Eventually, I said, I fear these analog machines will treat us with similar disregard as we treat insects when building a house – something in the way to be annihilated."

"What did he say?"

"It will take some time, maybe even today, you and your brother will come around to my way of thinking, we will always be able to control them since it's our programming and code that makes them run, embrace the singularity."

"And now the gathering of the Sasquatch, you think he knows?"

"Probably." Kellog shook his head. "We can't let it can't happen or all of humankind will become ants to these alien hybrid machines."

"Are we ready to stop them?"

"We have to. This may be our last chance. It looks like killing a few Sasquatch in the Upper Peninsula isn't enough. They keep coming. We need to find a way stop them from taking over the planet."

"At least our detection satellites are giving us an advantage no one else has ever had in finding them." Winston pressed an icon on his smart phone and the large screen lit up, this time with an ultraviolet image of Michigan's UP.

"Where is that?" asked Kellog.

Winston asked the computer to overlay the image with the geographical names of the region. Hiawatha National Forest appeared in white letters against the green backdrop. He said, "Scan left," and the scene shifted eastward. "There's the abandoned quarry at the eastern boundary, where Meriwether and his team have been disposing of Sasquatch."

Kellog looked at Winston askance.

"Relax. It's perfect. They dump the Bigfoot carcasses into the quarry's shallow pond. Within twenty-four hours the remains have broken down completely into simple organic material." He squinted at the picture. "Zoom in," he ordered. The image pixelated as the camera's telephoto lens adjusted for a closer look. Unlike the indistinct images made by military infra-red night vision cameras, these pictures had the sharp resolution of military grade spy satellite imagery that could read the word Titleist on a teed golf ball at Augusta during the Master's Tournament. When the image cleared, both brothers gave a start.

"Isn't that Redhawk?" Kellog asked, pointing to the figure beside the quarry. Winston nodded. "Then who's the guy running out of the picture north and west?"

Kellog commanded the imagery to track up and left. It picked up the running man and then abruptly a dozen figures appeared, running together ahead of him. The figures were tall, humanoid, with long arms, barrel chests and squat legs. The skin had a greenish tint. What was most alarming, however, were the faces. They looked unearthly "What are those alien mother fuckers doing?" asked Kellog. "Communing to take over the earth?"

"Who gives a shit? They're targets. I'm calling Meriwether."

Suddenly the screen went blank. "What happened?" demanded Kellog.

"We lost coverage."

"Damn."

"Those new satellites can get into position fast enough."

"My calculations show we will have complete coverage of the UP by midafternoon."

16

____

Hiawatha National Forest
UP, Michigan
October 23rd 2032

Nick found trying to run through the soggy floor of the new growth spruce balsam forest quite difficult. He sank into marshy ground up to his ankles and several times had to stop to work his shoe free of the muck. He didn't question why he was chasing the Bigfoot. He'd needed answers ever since the first one peered at him in his grandfather's kitchen early in the morning as a young boy.

Am I expecting they'll just sit down and talk to me and tell me why they made contact with me when I was a child? That's just stupid. Nevertheless, he pushed forward.

He hit a flat, dry patch of ground and redoubled his effort, following a trail of bent and broken limbs and the strong musk odor which lingered in the air. How many times had he taken groups on Bigfoot hunts, pointing to the broken and bent limbs at around the ten foot level and the skunk smell, telling the group it was sure evidence of the presence of Bigfoot.

He stopped running, spotted a large limb lying on the ground. He picked it up and gave the nearest tree a whack. He couldn't count the number of times he had done what is known in the Bigfoot world as doing a wood knock. Like all times before, he waited for a reply. There they were, three replies coming from different directions. Filled with excitement by the response, he recalled his childhood dream: to find the creatures and know their secrets. More than ever, Nick was determined to push deeper into the forest. He had to keep going.

He'd run for half an hour or more. He wasn't sure. Time seemed to have telescoped. But which way, he couldn't tell. It felt like a long time. He hadn't checked his watch when he left Redhawk and the quarry. He only knew he'd been running for a long time, though at a slower pace.

Rounding a thick stand of trees and a moss covered boulder, the trail suddenly went dead. He was far past any recognizable landmarks and he knew deep in his guts he was lost. Wheezing, he took another thirty steps and came upon the gigantic bole of an ancient forest giant. The solitary white pine was so large it had to be one of the original trees to sprout after the Laurentian Ice sheet retreated northward at the end of the last ice age and trees started to grow again in the UP, thousands of years ago. It had been uprooted. The system of roots was large enough for a person to climb into and be protected from the rain or snow. Branches had been sheared off in the fall, but enough stubs remained. He was able to climb to the top and look around. He was twenty feet above the ground, but the surrounding thick forest cut off any view more than twenty feet away.

He leaned against a tree limb as big around as his torso. He thought about doing another wood knock, but he was unable to break off a branch to do so. Then, out of desperation, he gave the loudest and longest whoop he could muster. The scream disappeared into the forest without an echo.

Nick grimaced. He was lost and his dream of encountering a Bigfoot face to face was fading, too. He might as well start back toward the quarry, if he could even find it. Nick started to climb down when he heard a slight sound from behind. He turned around. The moss covered boulder he had passed, rose up and a twelve foot Bigfoot towered in its place.

It was beautiful, with a smooth, simian-like face that could have passed for one of our early ancestors. The chest was the size of a refrigerator and its long arms swung past its hips almost to its knees. The legs were disproportionately short though not stubby. A green tinted fur covered it, though Nick could not be sure it was fur. The creature's pelt rippled and changed hues as it moved toward him, like some psychedelic moss. It stopped when only a few feet away from the log. Liquid gray eyes stared at him and the creature spoke with a female voice. "Why were you following us?"

The voice was gentle and seemed to emanate from the whole creature rather than its mouth. Nick couldn't tell if he was hearing with his ears or the voice was inside his head.

"What do you want?" the Bigfoot asked, the demand gently pushing into Nick's mind.

He searched for the right words. An image flashed into his thoughts. The Bigfoot was the one from his childhood summers spent on his grandfather's farm in the Olympic Peninsula in Washington.

The creature's voice shifted from female to his grandfather. "I was there."

'Impossible!' Nick yelled, though he made no sound.

The Bigfoot cocked its head like any human who was perplexed by something. "Why is it impossible that I'm the one who saw you those summers long ago. We seek out people who are open to us like you. Think how different your life would have been if you'd never seen me."

Nick clenched his fists to keep from shaking. He focused his energy on speaking "What are you?" he asked, relieved he could speak aloud, though his voice was a whispery rasp.

"You don't know?" the Bigfoot asked.

He shook his head.

The creature moved from side to side, the gray eyes blinking slowly, as if taking pictures of him from different perspectives.

Nick noticed for the first time, the hair around its face and along its skull was gray. Wrinkles framed its eyes giving it the appearance of great age. Finally it spoke again. "We are a different kind of life form, learning about your planet for thousands of years.

"For millennia my sisters and brothers have been able to hide ourselves from your kind. But now, the people hunting us have figured out a way to overcome our protections."

"Are you going to hurt me?"

"What a curious question. Of course not. You now have the answers you have been searching for most of your life."

"How do you know that?"

"We sometimes seek out humans whose minds are different. Those who have encounters like yours often begin a lifelong pursuit of the meaning of their experience. You were special, you saw me as I am. Others have what is called a spiritual experience, interpreting our presence as God or the ultimate truth."

Nick knew it would sound stupid but he said anyhow, "Can I help. Help protect you. Protect your people?"

"Against advanced weapons and technology?" The Bigfoot sounded ironic.

Then an odd thought emerged in Nick's mind. "Why are you telling me all this? Aren't you worried I'm going to tell everybody?"

He could swear the creature smiled at him. "Who's going to believe you?"

"The man Stephen Kobak who sent me to retrieve the Bigfoot will. He's one of the smartest people on the planet and he has this deep learning computer that is smarter than us humans and can figure anything out."

Nick thought he saw something akin to understanding at a deeper level than any creature he'd ever encountered before cross the Bigfoot's face.

"Tell Stephen Kobak we reproduce like a 3-D printer builds organic products."

Nick shrugged helplessly. "I'd love to, but I'm lost."

"No you're not, walk through those trees and you'll find your truck."

In a blink of an eye the Bigfoot was gone. To his surprise, when Nick walked through the trees pushing the boughs aside there was his truck just like the Bigfoot said. Suddenly he was overwhelmed with emotion. He fell to his knees and began sobbing it was so surreal. *Was that real? Did I just talk to a Bigfoot?*

Nick didn't know how long he wept. But when he finished, he felt refreshed. As he stood, he breathed in deeply. The air seemed clearer and the smells of the forest more exquisite than ever. He was part of it in a way he had never experienced before.

A crunch of dry leaves turned Nick around. He saw Redhawk approaching the truck. When the Native American spotted him there was a look of surprise that turned to anger. "What are you doing here, crying like a baby?"

Pulling himself together, Nick recognized this was not the same person he'd left behind at the quarry. He wiped away his tears and said angrily, "I might ask the same about you."

Redhawk ignored the question. "So did you find them?"

"One found me. It ... she talked just like us. There're actually quite humanlike."

Nick was quite astounded that his friend showed no surprise by the fact that the Bigfoot could speak.

"So you had your Bigfoot experience, what now?" Redhawk said sarcastically.

"What's happened to you? You're not the same," said Nick.

"I thought you were dead, chasing after those creatures. All I could think of was my grandfather and how they took him."

"I don't think that's true. They won't harm humans. They learned to stay out of our way, avoid us. You're not gonna believe this, but they may need our help."

"Did it say how it wants our help?"

"She liked the idea of getting Kobak to help them, it was almost like she knew who he was." Then it came to Nick that Redhawk had not brought his gear. "Where's my stuff? Were you going to just leave me here?"

Redhawk pulled out his 1911 Colt and pointed it at Nick. "Worse than that?"

"I thought we were friends."

"We're not enemies. Just on different sides," said Redhawk. His finger tightened on the trigger and Nick flinched, ready to throw himself to the side. But he didn't have to. A split second later the Potawatomi's face froze and he begin to shake all over. The gun slipped from his fingers. An instant later he lurched forward onto the ground. Then, almost out of the blue, another Bigfoot appeared. This one was much smaller, though she had the same proportion of limbs and torso. The face, however, could have passed for a bear.

"Did you do that?" Nick asked, his voice clear. It seemed almost natural to speak with a Bigfoot.

"You were in danger."

"Can all of you do that?"

"No, we all have learned to do many different things. You are free to go now. Your phone is in his pocket."

"Is he dead?

"We don't kill humans."

17

Marinette, Michigan
October 23rd 2032

When the owner of Di Napoli's Family restaurant in Marinette discovered Kobak spoke fluent Italian, he insisted on serving the guests himself and giving the lunch party a free bottle of Chianti. The balding, potbellied man in his mid-fifties complained as he uncorked the bottle, "No one in this small town speaks the language of Dante, of Pirandello, of Fellini." He poured the wine while humming the theme from *La Dolce Vita*. When the food had been served, he left them alone.

The morning had been exhausting and the drive from Marquette seemed to go on forever, each of them catching small bits of sleep. Meanwhile Kobak had remained tight-lipped about anything to do with Sasquatch or the remains Olav had identified as plant-like. He insisted they wait in Marinette until he heard from Nick.

The mood in the restaurant was far from festive. Two men from the security detail watched the parking lot; the other two had eyes on the room and the kitchen. Saul gritted his teeth and said, "We should get back to Toronto as quickly as possible. It isn't safe here for you or the young lady."

Birgit snorted. "I can take care of myself." Jerking a thumb at the van, she said, "Give me one of your Czech made CZ-805 BREN assault rifles and I'll lead your team after those assholes who killed Marge and the Bigfoot."

Saul waved her offer away. Kobak might have waited to see just how serious Birgit was, but his phone beeped. He answered it as he always did with the single word, "Speak." After a few seconds he looked at Saul and the others. "Hang on. I have to move." He walked out of the restaurant into the parking lot. Saul insisted he stay where the team could see him. Kobak stood on the sidewalk in front of the plate glass window.

"Shit, Nick! Last thing I heard you were chasing a group of Bigfoot?" Kobak listened intently, his fingers flicking against thighs, stomach and chest in rapid darting movements. At times he spun around as if a gust of wind had twirled him, though there was no wind this day. Passersby occasionally heard him say, "Got it ... Say more ... That changes everything."

Finally his agitation trailed off and he said, "We'll meet you at the casino, Nick. I'll contact you so we can speak in private, make a plan."

He punched off and looked through the plate glass window of the restaurant to signal his security chief everything was all right. He saw the owner approach Saul and then the two of them went into the kitchen. *I wonder what that's all about?*

Kobak shrugged and made another phone call to Toronto.

"Yes, Mr. Kobak?" his assistant Delores Cavanaugh answered before the first ring ended.

"Yes, Delores ... we need five rooms and the largest suite you can get at the Sky Island Casino in the Upper Peninsula of Michigan. Never been to a casino strange as it may seem to you for someone who loves to gamble." He laughed absurdly loudly.

New environments, like for many autistic people, made Kobak uncomfortable and his way of dealing with it was to joke. "Book it under, let me think for a moment, this'll be cool, under the name of

James Butler Hickok. Use the prescreened app that allows us to go directly to our rooms. Then have our people, of course you know who, check out Larry Redhawk. Presumably he's some sort of liaison for the Coast Guard in Menominee, Wisconsin. Probably a ruse but let's see what they can come up with."

Saul watched Kobak through the window and wondered what wonder boy was talking about. This wasn't the first time he felt powerless because his boss kept things from him. He didn't like feeling this way. He was about to get up and confront Kobak, when the restaurant owner tapped him on the shoulder.

"Your name is McBride? Are you Scots?"

"I am. Why do you want to know?" Saul asked, his eyes automatically checking the room for traps and to see if he was being set up somehow. Nothing seemed amiss.

"I have something in the kitchen that will be of interest to you as a Scotsman. If you would follow me, please."

Saul excused himself after telling Matthew to keep an eye on wonder boy. He followed the owner into the kitchen. The place was empty. Saul's hand went to the nine millimeter Glock he kept in a holster in the back of his jeans. They threaded among work tables to the back of the room near the freezer. There an older man with jowls and iron gray hair waited. His hands were empty by his side.

"Thank you, Antonio," he said in English with a soft Russian accent.

Saul kept a reasonable distance between them. He waited until the owner left the kitchen to speak. "What is it you want?"

"Like you, I am concerned about a mutual acquaintance in the parking lot."

"Who are you?"

"My name is Nicholai Mameyev."

. . .

Kobak walked back into the restaurant and saw Saul exiting the kitchen. "What now? You think the food is poisoned?"

"I got lost looking for the bathroom." He paused. "Are you ready to leave for Toronto?"

"There's been a change of plans. We're driving back to the Casino we passed on our way here. Nick will meet us there ... sort of funny ... Our new home for now is a gamble." He giggled. Recalling the calm demeanor of Redhawk when he described Nick's chase after the Bigfoot and Nick's warning about how there must be other outsiders involved, Kobak had decided the best strategy was to play his cards close to the vest.

Saul scowled. "You should be taking this more seriously. It's too much risk, especially now that we know there are people out there who will stop at nothing to kill those who know about the killing of the Sasquatch."

"That's the spirit, Saul, talking about risk. Okay, I know you're only looking out for my best interests but I've decided. Besides, with my eidetic memory, I'm going to clean up at the Blackjack tables, make some real money for a change, just kidding."

Kobak signaled the owner who brought the check and a small box of cannoli. "For the road. My wife makes them." He kissed his fingertips. "*Bellissimo.*"

On the way out to the van, Saul said in a tight voice, "Stephen, we should return to Green Bay and board the jet back to Toronto. It's the right move to make. If you want eyes in the field here, let me and my team take care of it."

"No worries, Saul. It'll all work out. We're going to the casino, but we're going to make a little stop on the way." He merged his phone with Saul's. "We're going to these coordinates first. There's a hunting cabin there I think we should look at. I believe one of the bad guys who are hunting the Sasquatch lives there."

"I'm not happy about this," Saul said with a frown.

"Funny, I wasn't under the impression I pay you to be happy, Saul. Now let's get moving."

18

Marinette, Michigan
October 23rd 2032

The van turned onto a one lane, rutted road and headed into the forest. A mile in they found the ramshackle log cabin. As soon as the van stopped, Saul's men deployed to reconnoiter the area before going inside.

"Who owns this place?" Saul asked.

"I told you, Nick Moore says it belongs to one of the bad guys."

"And?"

"And that's all he said, other than he is a contractor for the Coast Guard. We should look around for clues." He brightened. "We're looking for clues, I love looking for clues, what will we find, that's the big question."

Saul's team reported the area clean and the cabin open. "Sir, you're not going to believe this place," said Matthew, the van driver. "It's a freaking gun museum. The guy who lives here has a 19th century long barrel Sharps .50-90, used for buffalo hunting, and a pair of 1848 Walker Colts."

"Replicas?"

"No sir."

Saul whistled.

"Is that significant?" asked Kobak.

"Whoever lives here doesn't work just for the Coast Guard. They're seriously wealthy."

The three room cabin was tossed quickly. Aside from the firearms, they found a Native American ceremonial peace pipe.

When they finished, they gathered beside the stone fireplace.

Birgit shook her head. "This was a waste of time, Mr. Kobak. I think we should get going."

"What's the hurry?"

"The sooner I can get tracking those guys who murdered Marge, the better," said Birgit.

"I have to agree with Ms. Gunderson. This place has nothing."

"We'll leave as soon as I've found what I'm looking for."

"And what's that?" asked Saul.

Kobak smiled. "I'll know when I see it. Everyone spread out. Look more closely. So far, we've only looked at the surface stuff. There's something here that will help us. I know it. I can feel it."

"It would help if we had some idea of what we're looking for," said Saul, his face taut at the idea of spending any more time here.

Kobak shrugged. "Maybe some technology ... any technology ... see if we can find some among the stodgy museum."

"In this place, sir?" said Matthew. "The guy doesn't have running water or electricity. Shit! He has a wood burning stove."

"Matthew has a point, Stephen," said Saul.

Kobak smiled. "You seem nervous ... why are you nervous?"

"I don't like my back to a lake and my only escape route is a one lane road. Call me old fashioned but this place is pristine for an ambush."

Kobak thought about his friend Nick. No way would he set him up for an ambush. "Your concerns are noted, Saul. Fifteen more minutes."

"Five."

"Ten."

Saul gritted his teeth. "All right, ten. But then I'm dragging you out of here."

"Fair enough."

Saul hand signaled Matthew and Timothy to post at the front and the rear of the cabin. "If a deer looks at you sideways, you report to me immediately."

"Yes, sir." They saluted and left.

Saul clicked his watch. "Ten minutes from my mark. Let's move."

Kobak stood in the center of the room while the others fanned out through the cabin. He had a vague idea of what he would find. As soon as Nick mentioned Redhawk, Kobak's eidetic memory flashed on an article from Silicon Valley news of a new start up run by a Native American, using carbon nanotubes three atoms thick to make graphic circuit chips for computers. KW Intel had bought the technology two months later. *Graphic circuits three atoms thick could be used to make a PA that appeared ordinary. How cool is that, a personal assistant that small? Ordinary as possible has always been the key in this tech domain.* Kobak kicked himself for not investing in the company himself.

Something glinted in a shallow dish beside the fireplace. He went over and saw that it was filled with loose change. He pushed the money around and one of the quarters looked slightly different than the others. He picked it up. The edge was smooth instead of ribbed. The writing as well as the image of George Washington was painted on instead of being embossed. He hefted it and the weight was less than a dime. He felt a slight warmth and heard a faint hum.

It's on, he thought. He licked his lips. He wanted very much to see how it worked, but without the access code it was impossible. He marveled at its beauty.

"Two minutes," Saul called out from the bedroom.

Kobak jerked in surprise. He had been so fascinated by the miniaturization he had forgotten he wasn't alone.

Birgit came over and stood beside him. She was three inches taller and more muscular. Her presence was unnerving. Kobak recalled how she handled the bad guys back in Marquette and he had no doubt she could have led Saul's mercenaries against the men hunting the Sasquatch. "That's no quarter," she said, staring at the device in his hand before he could think of closing his fist.

Kobak shook his head. Saul and the other two men came into the room. "Stephen found the evidence he was looking for," she said.

They crowded around. "What is it?" Saul asked.

For a moment the feeling was like cub scouts crowded around a campfire listening to ghost stories. Kobak sighed. *Cat's tail is out of the bag. Might as well let it all out.*

"It's KW Intel's personal assistant prototype. I saw it at the exclusive machine learning conclave in Finland just a few months ago.

"Kellog, in his talk, was telling the group how we all need to be afraid of deep learning machines in the coming computer singularity. His exact words were, 'machine learning devices will come to look upon us as insects that are in their way and need to be eradicated'."

Kobak hefted the ersatz coin. "No way should this be here, no way at all ... unless."

Birgit asked, "Unless what?"

"Isn't it obvious? Whoever lives here works for the Ang brothers. Isn't it clear to everyone else?"

Birgit snorted. "The Ang brothers are the best-known billionaire conspiracy theorists. Social media is full of their theories about the deep state in league with aliens."

One of Saul's men looked at her in surprise. "What do you mean?"

Kobak answered, "The Ang brothers are a couple of apocalyptic doomsday sayers, but they use the best machine learning algorithms – in this device – and in all their smart agricultural equipment, and many of the most important big data management applications. When it comes to making money off of artificial intelligence, they're the best. I would have to say, even better than me. Don't tell anybody I said that." He tapped the coin. "How strange, how interesting. I was really upset when Winston railed against my AGI ... my dear Colossus always moving forward, always learning unsupervised.

That's what they're afraid of. Not me ... it's all for the good, it's for the betterment of humanity, that's what I told him. Grand speech don't you think?"

Birgit cautiously asked, "Does this mean the Ang brothers are involved in the killing of the Bigfoot?"

Kobak was confused by the thought the Ang brothers had something to do with what was going on with the Bigfoot. He counted backwards from twenty to zero in English and Portuguese before he finally felt his chest relax.

"Are you all right?" Birgit asked.

He nodded. "I'm just surprised that the Ang brothers would do something this outrageous. I thought they were all just hot air. But crazy as it may seem, there is a high probability they are involved. Most strange."

Saul's timer beeped. Ignoring Kobak, he said, "Ten minutes folks. We're leaving."

Kobak went to shove the miniature PA into his pocket and his security chief stopped him. "Leave it, whoever is using this place doesn't know we're onto him. We can use your security firm to monitor his every movement. That gives us an edge."

"That's silly, Saul." But Kobak replaced the PA in the bowl.

"Onto the damn casino, let's get out of here," Saul shouted to his men.

19

Hiawatha National Forest
October 23rd 2032

The first thing Redhawk was aware of was the sharp ache inside his skull, as though someone had punched him in the brain. Then came the voice.

"Don't try to talk or open your eyes just yet," someone said. By the tone it was a woman. She sounded far away, yet also strangely near, as though she was whispering into his ear. "Your senses have been scrambled. You're suffering from synesthesia. Listen to the sound of my voice and it will pass in a few minutes."

Redhawk knew what she said was true. The feel of the earth against his hands and face was the smell of lemon rinds and asparagus. The taste of the air shot a thousand colors into his brain, colors humans would never be able to see with the primitive eyes they had. And the voice was the feel of soft chamois against his skin, soothing and peaceful.

He did as he was told and listened, the words a brush of butterfly wings against his ears.

"Your family would not like you hunting us." The woman

sounded like his aunt but she spoke of 'us' as though she were part of something other than the Potawatomi tribe. "They have been our protectors for two thousand years. You should be with them against the others who hunt us, hunt us because they are afraid. You are not afraid, but confused all these years about us. Confused by a hurt that did not happen. You are a child of the forest, of the sky and the blue water. You are cousin to the eagle, brother of the deer and son of the black bear. You are a true human. You must remember who you really are and then you will once more be on the right path."

Redhawk felt the meaning of the words, not just as a lilting sound but as a guide, drawing him out of the tangled mess of his ruined senses. Each word was a step on the road to the place where his senses operated normally again. Who was this woman who talked to him as though she were a member of the tribe and yet not a member. He had to find out. He opened his eyes to slits. Earth and sky whirled around him, solidified and became a still image. He could see.

The world shifted from confused odors and colors to the beauty of the forest. He recognized the spruce and maples. He smelled the soft scent of pine and the rich aroma of the earth. The scratch of fallen leaves against his face and hands was a welcome touch. Then he saw the Bigfoot. It squatted ten feet away and stared at him with preternatural awareness in its liquid brown eyes. The rest of its bear-like face was cocked to one side as if studying him." You're not surprised," she said.

Redhawk reached for his pistol but the Bigfoot held it in a four-fingered hand, twirling it as if it were a strange toy. Redhawk eased himself into a sitting position. His senses had unscrambled but his muscles still felt weak.

The Bigfoot said, "You would have killed your companion with this. And you would try to kill me. Why?"

"You're dangerous," he answered. "Yes, and I'm aware of the mind games you can play with humans."

"And yet, you are the one hunting my kind." The Bigfoot seemed to smile. "I was told one of your great scientist said, 'Nothing in life is to be feared, it is only to be understood.'

"That's been my motto since I was a teenager," Redhawk said in surprise.

"Now it's time for you to help us find out what our true purpose is on this planet."

"I know what you are. A Windigo – an evil, man-eating spirit. You are here to crush humanity I don't believe you are our brothers of the forest as our legends say. And you're not human."

"You've known this since you were little. I once healed you when you were dying from Lyme disease."

"I don't believe you, you killed my grandfather," Redhawk spat.

The Bigfoot looked genuinely puzzled. "Is this the source of your hatred toward us?"

The question surprised Redhawk because the words seemed to tear at an old wound scabbed over by anger and he knew the answer even as the wound opened up completely inside of him and his feelings poured out. "Yes," he said in a strangled voice. "It was the beginning of my hatred of your kind."

"See, you knew we existed."

"Of course! Everybody in our family knew."

"We did not hurt your grandfather. A member of our clan found him dying in these woods. His heart had given out and there was nothing she could do for him. She stayed with him so he would not die alone, then she buried him and put stones upon his grave so the carrion eaters could not get at him. He was in death like the warrior he was in life. I can show you the spot. His final resting place is near the portal you and the other human found today."

The Bigfoot stood. "Come. I will take you there."

Redhawk felt his resistance melting "I don't know that I can walk," he said.

"It is not far, the way we travel." The bear-faced creature reached out a four-fingered hand and helped him to stand. Then gently lifted him over her shoulder. "This way," she said and dashed through a screen of trees into the forest.

20

___

'Winston applauded. "That didn't take long, complete coverage of the UP."

Kellog Ang watched the giant screen in disbelief at the images the newly deployed satellites relayed. He turned to his brother, Winston, and said, "Are you seeing what I'm seeing?"

Winston nodded. "The Bigfoot is carrying Redhawk."

"Where's it taking him?"

Winston overlaid a map of the Hiawatha National Forest on the image provided by the tiny surveillance satellites. "If it keeps its present course, it will go by the quarry where Meriwether's team has been disposing of the Sasquatch."

"Perfect." Kellog tapped the PA affixed behind his ear. "Connect me to Meriwether." The contact was instantaneous thanks to the PA. All of the Russian's team leaders across the globe carried the device.

"I see you got another one, Lewis. Good work. We've got a bogie in your area – look on your screen. Sending you the satellite data now. He has our boy genius Larry Redhawk. This is a rescue as well as another kill mission. Safely pry him free of the Sasquatch. Do you copy?"

Kellog pressed a button on the console in front of him. Music from the British rock band Queen soared through the room. He smiled at his little brother and sang the words, "Another one bites the dust."

They bumped fists.

Meriwether called his team together. Two of the four men were new. All were recruited by the Russian and came from Croatia. All had been trained by him and the newcomers fit into the crew seamlessly.

"We have a Bigfoot nearby. There is an added caution. It's carrying a person important to the mission. Command wants him alive and the Bigfoot dead. Its present heading will take it by the quarry. We'll try to cut it off before it reaches the forest beyond. If not, we'll deploy in a standard 'chase and secure' V formation."

The helicopter's rotors started turning.

"We leave in two minutes."

The men nodded. Two minutes was not difficult. These days the team always kept their gear within a half-dozen steps.

Meriwether

The ride slung across the Bigfoot's shoulder was surprisingly smooth. Redhawk felt no nausea and his senses were normal again, just as the creature had promised. The forest flew past and the Indian surmised their speed had to be more than sixty miles an hour. The Bigfoot was agile, dodging trees, brushing big branches aside with ease, never once endangering its passenger.

The creature slowed and stopped. It sniffed the air and turned around twice, then set Redhawk down. He recognized the area. It was close to the quarry where he and Nick had first seen the Bigfoot.

"Why are you stopping?"

"Hunters are coming. We haven't much time," it said.

"How much?" said Redhawk.

The creature scratched its head. "As long as it takes the sun to move five degrees."

Redhawk did the calculation in his head, basing it on the solar day, or when the earth goes around the sun 360 degrees. In this case 15 degrees equaled 1/24 of a circle or one hour. "So, twenty minutes. Can you out run them?"

The Bigfoot shook its bear like head. "The humans' machines are faster than I am. Come. We must hurry if you are to see your grandfather's grave." The creature gathered Redhawk into its long arms and swung him onto its shoulder. It started running again.

They passed the quarry. That's when Redhawk heard the helicopter. The sound was coming from the southeast. He judged by the roar it would land in ten minutes. The beast increased its speed. It angled through the trees toward the stick structure but did not stop. A quarter mile beyond the wooden stakes, it stopped near a mound of stones and set Redhawk on the ground.

"Here are the remains of your grandfather, Redhawk."

"We are not brothers," Redhawk insisted. You're a Windigo."

The creature smiled. "You do not really believe I am a man eating demon from your Potawatomi legends. You're trying to stop us for what you believe will bring about the end of humanity." The Bigfoot moved away.

"Where are you going?"

"To draw them from here so you will not be injured when they kill me."

Redhawk jerked in surprise at the creature's concern for him. "How do you know?' he asked.

"We are no longer the children your people found and protected many years ago. We've been evolving at an accelerating pace."

Once the Bigfoot ran out of sight, Redhawk knelt beside the rock cairn. From his pocket he removed a tobacco pouch. Carefully dividing the contents into four equal piles, he set them around the grave at the cardinal points of the compass. Afterwards he sat facing east and sang the Potawatomie Sacred Fire Song. During the singing he heard rifle shots. He recognized the US Navy Mk-12 5.56 semi-auto sniper rifle by the sound. Meriwether's team had gotten the Bigfoot.

As Redhawk waited patiently for the men to find him, he thought about his role in the plan to bringing about the destruction of the Bigfoot and he thought about his aunt Ayasha, whom he had betrayed.

He heard a twig snap in the underbrush. *Meriwether's team is getting sloppy*, he thought. A mercenary walked out from the trees two minutes later. He waved at Redhawk and spoke into the mic at the edge of his mouth. "Found him, sir. He appears unharmed." He looked at Redhawk and said, "Meriwether wants you to come with me. He wishes to debrief you. Afterwards, we're to escort you out of here."

~

Sky Island Casino, UP, Michigan

The Sky Island Casino was located on US Highway 41, on a small tract of land owned by the Potawatomi Indian Tribe in Michigan's Upper Peninsula. Ironically, the casino's beginnings were humble. It all began in 1837 with Peter and Hannah Marksman, Methodist missionaries who founded the small Hannahville Indian Mission to help displaced Indians settle in Hannahville after President Andrew Jackson's Indian Removal Act of 1830 relocated Native Americans east of the Mississippi River to lands west of the river. One hundred fifty years later, descendants of the Potawatomi Nation opened a casino on their 3400 acre reservation, at first taking from white gamblers what Andrew Jackson had taken from them – their livelihoods. Now incorporating smart technology into every aspect of gaming, the casino had become the economic jewel of the Upper Peninsula.

Inside the van everyone was silent until Birgit spoke up." I've had many interactions with the tribe. The ones that own and operate the casino. They're Potawatomi. It means 'Keepers of the Fire'."

Kobak jerked in surprise. "Say more."

"Their origins and legends are quite interesting. I've given a number of talks to campers in the national Forest. The Potawatomi Indians are one of three tribes that make up the Three Fires Society – the Ojibway, the Ottawa and the Potawatomi tribes. The Ojibway are the keepers of the original teachings and are responsible for passing these teachings down through the generations. The Ottawa provide security for all who attend tribal gatherings. They make sure everyone has enough to eat and the meeting place is secure from invasion and disruption. The Potawatomi Indians are responsible for keeping the "Sacred Fire" alive, as it is the symbol of light and the future."

"The light and the future ... the light and the future." Kobak rocked back and forth on his seat repeating the phrase over and over until he suddenly stopped, clenched his fists and let them go with a loud explosion of air. He grinned and his head nodded in acceptance of some inner dictate. Kobak looked outside at the passing forest, muttering over and over, "Amazing. Amazing."

Five miles from the casino, Kobak's smart phone beeped. He looked down and saw a text from Nick. *In the casino parking lot. Need to talk with you. Something strange is going on.*

Kobak typed back. *A code's been downloaded into your phone for a room in the East wing. Wait to be contacted.*

Nick' reply came back instantly. *Need to talk with you ASAP. I'm sensing something really important.*

It'll have to wait. Personal reasons, replied Kobak.

21

———

Sky Island Casino
October 23rd 2032

The shadow of a sleek helicopter crossed over Nick as he stepped out of his truck in the casino parking lot. He watched it land on the heliport, an elevated mound west of the giant sign promoting the loosest slots in the country. The drive from the forest had given him time to reflect and what had just happened. In less than 24 hours he had spoken with not one but two Bigfoot. All these years of wondering and searching for these elusive creatures suddenly came to an end in a way that shook him intellectually to the bone. He wondered what his ex-wife would say? He snorted. *What will all the Bigfoot deniers say when they learn the truth.*

He sighed and leaned against the fender looking into the afternoon sky, assessing everything that had happened in the last twenty-four hours. Chief was out there somewhere with another Bigfoot. *Is he still alive? What are you going to do when you see him again?* He patted the Glock 19 stuck in the waistband of his blue jeans. *No sense trying to answer that question until the time comes.* He scrubbed his face with both hands. The two-day growth of beard felt unnatural to him. He still had some time before Kobak arrived. He might as well shower and shave. Then he could figure out what to do next. All he knew for certain was he on some sort of mission to help the Bigfoot, to help them accomplish something he couldn't even imagine. Most of all he was eager to tell Kobak what happened, as if that would bring clarity to his part in what was happening.

Like all Bigfoot researchers Nick's truck was well supplied with backup field equipment and at the moment, most importantly, a well needed change of clothes that he stuffed into his backpack. He then checked his tool compartment and opened the secret recess for his pistol. It gave him some comfort with the Bigfoot killers out there to know that he had a weapon to defend himself. Still, he knew he couldn't bring it into the casino, so he stashed it there until he'd need it.

If his mind was filled with unanswered questions, his senses were at a heightened level. He was able to telescope in on the helicopter wheels touching down on the heliport landing platform. Physically he felt better than any time in recent memory.

He shouldered his pack and was headed for the doors to the hotel check in when he felt the strange sense of being watched that he first experienced the night before at the quarry. It had remained with him ever since the Bigfoot encounter, but at such a low level at times he questioned if it was really there. He stared into the surrounding forest as he continued walking toward the casino entrance. It was definitely getting stronger and as soon as he crossed the threshold, he felt it as strongly as he had in the forest.

What's going on in here?

22

Sky Island Casino
October 23rd 2032

The room was dimly lit by a red light, illuminating a single chair in the center. Beside it stood a tall, rather slim Bigfoot. A phosphorus glow illuminated the eyes of her very Native American humanlike face. The rest of her was covered with an emerald-hued moss that in the dim light could have been mistaken for a Leprechaun's suit. Aside from skin tone and height, she was remarkably human looking. Each hand bore five fingers. The five toes did not have claws. She stood motionless, as if waiting quietly was the only thing she had to do in the world.

The Bigfoot cocked her head and turned to the only door leading into the room. A sliver of light outlined the jamb and a body squeezed through the narrow opening, shutting the door soundlessly after it. The newcomer's face was hidden in the room's shadows. It looked right and left and then to the center, where the Bigfoot waited.

The creature was unafraid and watched with fascination as the newcomer reached inside a vest it wore and pulled out a small handgun. "Is the weapon necessary?" she asked.

"You, of anyone I know, should know better than to ask that question with the killings going on."

The newcomer strode out of the shadows into the center of the room. She was a tall American Indian woman in her sixties, with silver-gray hair that gleamed a bloody hue under the red light. Age had not wrinkled her skin and her sparkling eyes were a curious blue, a singular family trait handed down from mother to daughter within the Potawatomie Tribe for more than fifty generations. The blue eyes marked the matrilineal power that her family had wielded since the arrival of the Bigfoot in the UP, ten thousand years ago. To the members of her clan and tribe she was known simply as Auntie. To the Bigfoot in front of her she was Ayasha, the Keeper of the Sacred Fire.

The red light gleamed off the nickel blue barrel of the Colt .38 caliber revolver. "We can't be too careful, not now, when we are so close to the end."

The creature shrugged in a very human way that was nonetheless a gesture she had learned and was not natural. "I understand your concern, Ayasha, but death is not the same for us as it is for you."

Ayasha shoved the gun away and sighed. "You're right."

"It's about to happen, right?"

Before she could reply, the multi-screen display of the casino flashed on. Her eyes shifted quickly from image to image, and seeing nothing out of the ordinary, she let out another sigh of relief. In strong, hushed tones she said, "The Yeti from Russia has arrived, tonight's the night."

"Did it make it to the portal?"

"Yes. Three from the other clans were killed as you probably know," she said sadly.

The creature's liquid brown eyes were not saddened by the news and she said without emotion, "they're all vulnerable, but every important Bigfoot evolutionary advancement is now represented. It's perfect."

Auntie scanned the screens then gently touched the giant Bigfoot. "I'm not ready for you to go. We've known each other all my life, you healed me as a young girl when I almost died from pneumonia. You sent the gentle one to take care of my father. And now you are going to walk out that door to—" Auntie's voice broke off with a little sob. She recovered quickly and wiped her eyes on her shirtsleeve. "Are you absolutely sure this is going to work? Are you sure you have to do it?"

The creature nodded.

"Why?"

She answered, her voice still uninflected as if discussing something as mundane as the weather. "Our ordinary reproductive portals allow for each of us to create the next improved version of us. This region is unique, it is the place of the original mother portal and is necessary for what we're going to do tonight. There's no certainty what we will be attempting will work. But the drive to do it is strong."

"I understand that," Auntie answered with some heat. "I'm sorry, it's just, why does it have to be you?"

"I need to be the last one into the field, one each from the five clans and then me. I'm to be the new one's teacher. I have the most advanced bio structure and knowledge."

Auntie hugged the Bigfoot and she gently touched her shoulder. "My men will get you there."

"I know. I am thankful for all you have done these past six decades. This is the one place on earth where Bigfoot and humans have built a sustained relationship."

Auntie nodded "I always suspected that was true. What should we do now?"

"Sit together one last time," the mother Bigfoot said, enfolding Ayasha in her long arms.

23

Sky Island Casino
October 23rd 2032

By the time the van reached the Sky Island Casino, clouds were moving in. The casino's parking lot was filled with cars and a parade of buses, bringing desperate gamblers to reverse their fortunes in the chaotic times plaguing the country and the nation.

Kobak wondered what the newest technologies and universal basic income could do to reverse their fortunes.

Saul motioned one of the men to stay behind with the van and guard the weapons. He saluted and sat in the back of the van where he had a good view of the parking lot and no one could see him.

The others looked uncomfortable. Matthew looked at the Scotsman and frowned. "Don't know that I feel safe without my sidearm, sir."

Saul said matter-of-factly, "Casino policy. If they catch you with a weapon, they'll kick all of us out of here."

The casino covered an area the size of an airport terminal. LED screens everywhere promoted jackpots, loose slots, sports bets. It was awash with bright, blinking lights that stuttered in uneven progressions. A bedlam of bells, whistles, a loud band playing 80s punk music and voices assaulted his ears. Out of the chaos of sounds the VIP concierge emerged to greet them. She was a trim, blond-haired woman, whose nameplate read Lambert. After scanning his phone she said, "Your rooms are ready, Mr. Hickok. The center wing penthouse for you and four on the floor directly beneath. The elevators over there will take you up. Your right index fingerprint will act as your key."

If the concierge thought anything peculiar, she hid her feelings well. She motioned to a bellhop to carry the bags up to the rooms.

Saul stepped forward. "We'll carry our own bags."

"Of course. Will there be anything else, Mr. Hickok?"

Kobak said, "I want to see the casino."

"You're standing in it, sir."

He shook his head and tapped his fingers on the desk in rapid succession, rapping out a Fibonacci sequence. "No, the inside ... the pit, I believe you call it. I have to see one."

"Of course. Straight ahead. Please enjoy your stay at the Sky Island Casino. If you need anything do not hesitate to ask."

Kobak pivoted slowly and walked toward the center of the gaming activity.

Saul put a hand on his sleeve, restraining him. "That isn't wise, sir. Your condition."

Kobak shook him off. "I can handle it." *I have to handle it. This is too important.* He strode purposefully to the nearest crap table and stopped as if he'd run into a wall. *I can do this ... I can do this ... I can do this.* He kept repeating the phrase like a mantra. Yet it wasn't enough. He tried counting backward from twenty to zero in Czech but couldn't get past sixteen before the sounds and sights of the room flooded his consciousness.

He stood frozen at the table looking for some pattern to interpret everything he heard and saw. Nothing made sense and he felt himself sinking into catatonia. He knew Saul's men surrounded him. He could feel Birgit standing near him, just out of reach. He was aware of Saul's light touch on his arm. Kobak's mind flew through all the information that scattered like buckshot through his brain. *You have no idea what to do next ... there's no pattern.* There was nothing that told him what to do, where to go, who to speak to. He took one last, wild look around him and let himself sink into the welcome relief of a dissociative fugue.

Saul had witnessed Kobak's escape from what his autistic mind registered as madness into the frozen state of catalepsy twice before. Instantly he signaled the team to escort the rigid form of their boss to the elevator.

Birgit watched the team gather around Kobak and move like a precision instrument, herding him for the elevators, away from the bedlam of the casino floor. She grabbed Saul's arm and said, "What's wrong with him?"

The Scotsman looked at her and said in a stern voice, "Mr. Kobak is autistic. Best thing to do for him right now is to get him out of here into some quiet spot."

"What's going to happen to him?"

"We leave him alone and sometime in the next 24 hours his mind will re-order itself. When he comes out of it he'll be shaken and hyper alert but he'll be himself again."

"You should've told me I might've been able to help," she snapped at Saul.

"I doubt it."

Annoyed by Saul's response, Birgit watched them hustle Kobak into the top floor suite of the center wing. Dropping one flight to the 14th floor, she let herself into her room and lay down on the bed. Finally, away from everybody, she said to herself, "Time to process." A knock on the door brought her upright before she could start.

She heard Saul say, "It's just me. May I come in?"

She opened the door and motioned him inside and watched him as his eyes registered the room. When he was satisfied everything appeared normal, he turned to her and asked, "What do you think of our fearless leader?"

It must've been something in the way the Scotsman talked because Birgit found herself thinking more like a soldier and less and less like someone exploring the greatest biological discovery of all time. "Right now, all I want is a bath and a few hours of sleep. Let's talk about this later this evening."

Saul said, "Don't misunderstand me, Miss. Kobak is like a son to me. But this whole thing with the Bigfoot mystery has him acting crazy and I admit I don't know what's going on. I'd rather we were back in Toronto, where I can have a bigger team to guard him. Especially with powerful men behind that kill team in the forest, hunting Sasquatch. Targeting you and probably him now."

Birgit eyed the Scotsman. "Where does that leave me?"

Saul returned her gaze without a blink. "I'll be blunt. I don't want you leaving this room, freelancing, until I get a better grip on what's happening. I'm posting one of my men outside your door to make certain you don't. The sooner we're gone from this place the better." He left without saying good night.

Birgit walked out onto the balcony. Her room was fourteen floors above the ground. "Where do I go from here?" she asked herself.

24

Sky Island Casino
October 23rd 2032

On a level indescribable to the others, Kobak's mind screamed for silence and solitude. The hushed tranquility of the elevator had been a welcome relief to his overloaded senses. Yet through the entire process, he had also been strangely aware of everything going on around him. Saul's ministrations as the team put him to bed in his suite. Window curtains drawn to drown out the overly bright parking lot lights and the flashing neon of the Casino's logo. He heard the door close softly behind the Scotsman and the whispered orders, 'He's not to be disturbed'. And then the blessed silence.

He went through the steps the Russian had taught him to reorder his mind whenever catatonia threatened. Counting backward from 100 to zero. If he could do it without a mistake then his mind was working.

It took Kobak three tries before he reached the magic number. Then he did it a second time just to be sure. Next, he recalled the names of all the European capitals in alphabetical order. He knew he was getting better quickly when he recalled Berlin came before Berne. Then he named the five noble gases – Helium, Xenon, Argon Neon and Krypton.

He sat up slowly. *As fugue states go, this was not the worst*, he thought ruefully to himself.

His muscles felt drained, which was not unusual. His mind, on the other hand, was hyper alert. *A trade off ... that's what the Russian called it.*

"Nature has given you a terrible yet wonderful gift," the Russian said on the first occasion he'd witnessed one of Kobak's fugue states. "A few minutes of abject terror followed by the ability to focus like a laser on any problem." They had been at a game arcade in London. Kobak was only fifteen. The Russian had waited patiently with him for more than six hours for the fugue to run its course.

Kobak got unsteadily to his feet. He walked to the minibar and poured himself a mineral water. His senses and brain were hyper alert, trying to put everything together. *The Sasquatch Nick had contact with are up here for a gathering. That must be it. But why?* Kobak went through his thinking again and finding no flaw in it, now only needed something to corroborate his theory. *Why they are here now and what are they really? Maybe that can be answered by what Olav has found in his lab.*

I have to get a hold of Olav and Birgit. Olav was simple. He could link to him with his phone. But when he contacted Birgit in her room, she informed him that Saul said she couldn't leave and had posted a guard to ensure she stayed put. He replied, "Give me a moment, I'll fix that."

Within minutes Kobak was face-to-face with the guard outside of Birgit's door. He recognized him as Matthew. The man held up a hand to stop Kobak from entering. "No one is to go in or out, not even you. Saul's orders."

Kobak's hyper senses noticed the man's ramrod straight posture as an unbending adherence to orders. Kobak had never seen this side of Saul's men before and he wondered if the fanatical devotion they showed to their boss put him in danger. The observation gave him a way to deal with this storm trooper.

Smiling, Kobak moved closer. "We'll see about that." With his thumb fixed on his phone's screen he simply and quietly uttered the word 'Help'.

Matthew looked at him puzzled. "What can I help you with, sir?"

"Oh not you," Kobak said. The elevator doors opened in the middle of the hall and two armed, Native American security guards appeared almost out of nowhere. They were husky, tall, and walked with the ease of men used to violence. They looked, to Kobak's untrained eye, as if they had been cut from the same cloth as Saul's task force. Matthew must have noticed the similarity, too, for he stiffened as the men approached.

"You requested help, sir," the taller of the two Indians asked Kobak.

At that moment Birgit opened the door and glared at Saul's guard.

"Yes, thank you. This man is harassing Miss Gunderson, my guest." Kobak pointed to Matthew.

"If I may, sir?" the tall Native American said, extending his hand for Kobak's phone. He glanced at the special VIP app, given to all high rollers and the most important guests, and then at his own phone. The fingerprint matched the one taken by the hotel during check in. "Thank you, sir." He motioned to Saul's man. "Please come with us, sir. We need you to stop bothering Mr. Kobak's guest."

Matthew hesitated a second and the two Native American guards came up on the balls of their feet. "Sir," said the shorter security guard, his finger hovering near a red light on his watch, "ten more of us can be here in fifteen seconds."

Matthew, understanding he was disadvantage, put up his hands and voluntarily walked away with the two security men.

"You're obviously feeling better," Birgit said. "Would you like to come in? I showered, but unfortunately I'm wearing the same old smelly Fish and Wildlife clothes. I could use some new ones if I'm going to go anywhere." She bit her tongue to stop talking. She thought he must think she was jabbering. "Sorry."

Kobak cocked his head at her. "Why?"

"You're Stephen Kobak," she said as if that explained it. In fact, she had always been conflicted by powerful wealthy men and found herself talking inanely when in their presence. Especially men like Kobak. He was a star in the newly emerging sphere of World Building and had funded hundreds of startup tech companies to forge a powerful global network of interconnected solutions to address the world's systemic problems arising from global trolling and misinformation delivered by the social media monster – food insecurity, water shortages, the epidemic of chronic diseases, inadequate housing, income inequality and the disappearance of meaningful work.

"I have something for you," Kobak said, as if dismissing her observation. He handed her a brand new phone. "It's one of mine but I had one of my people clone and download your information, nice and clean, and, most importantly, secure. With that you can go down and buy yourself a new outfit. On me, of course. Seems like you can get whatever you need at the casino. Quite the place."

Birgit wondered how he would know this since he'd gone into a dissociative fugue the moment he entered the casino floor. Then she noticed that the whole time he'd been talking with her, his eyes had never left his smart phone and even now he was scrolling at a ridiculously fast pace through a series of screens. He moved so fast that she only caught a few of them dealing with the boutiques connected to the hotel lobby.

"Do you actually see what you're looking at?" she asked.

Kobak nodded. "I've always had the ability to assimilate information quickly when it's presented in an orderly fashion. It's when there's no pattern that I can't handle the flow in my brain and it has to shut down so it can reset." He smiled self-deprecatingly. "It's the way my brain works and it has enabled me to use patterns I see in the world to invest my money in ways that help the world."

"They also make you rich."

He nodded unapologetically. "At least I'm not using my fortune to elect people to make me richer. I'm helping disadvantaged people around the world move out of poverty."

She reddened. "I apologize. So who were those guys you brought with you?"

"Oh, I didn't bring them with me. They appeared when I, as a registered highest level guest in the casino, pressed the help app on my phone." He showed her the app. "They're specially trained security guards that every Native American casino employs these days. The National Native American Gaming Confederation has a training facility outside of DC. I'm told it's the best in the world. They're totally loyal to each casino."

She shook her head wondering how anyone could remember that kind of information, let alone store it for use when needed. "Your brain works in fascinating ways."

"Some ways are fascinating. Others are debilitating."

"The fugue state?"

"Sorry if it was off-putting."

"Scary actually."

"You should see it from my side," Kobak said with a childlike admission of terror. He shook himself. "Enough of that. We have more important things to do.

"Let me get Olav on the line first, then I'll only have to tell my story once.

Getting a hold of Olav proved easy. He hadn't left the lab since he started analyzing the Bigfoot remains. Kobak quickly filled both of them in on his suppositions.

"I need your help proving what I think is true."

"I might be able to help," said Olav. "I've run every test imaginable, even some that aren't imaginable, on the Bigfoot material."

"What did you find?" Birgit asked.

"Well it's not a plant, though sorta plant-like. No typical cell structure ... no DNA, but highly organized."

"How?"

"A clear hierarchical organization, layer upon layer. Next I had

Colossus survey all the literature on what we came up with as a result of our biochemical analysis. Everything's there to build a highly complex biosynthetic organism from scratch and keep it working, basically on a broad spectrum of electromagnetic radiation from the sun. It's digital like but not digital, it's an analog. Never seen anything like it."

"A new kind of life form, Olav? Man-made or natural?" broke in Kobak excitedly.

"Not enough of a sample to tell. Colossus's been searching the literature for who might be capable of building such a ... hard to believe I'm actually saying this ... a living Bigfoot."

Kobak interjected loudly, "Don't keep us in suspense, Olav."

"The highest probability is the Russians."

"What about Florida?"

"Huh? Are you kidding, sir?"

"Since 2017, a joint lab project between Florida State University's Colleges of Arts and Sciences, Human Sciences and Chemical & Biomedical Engineering has been experimenting using computer controlled patterns of intense light and magnetic pulsing to guide plant growth in many extraordinary ways."

Olav grinned at Kobak. "You're always a step ahead of me."

"More like four, Olav. Get in touch with Mike Comely, the lab director heading up the joint project. Have him fill you in on everything he's gathered so far."

"Anything else."

Kobak smiled at Birgit. "That depends on what we find here."

"Where's here?"

"The Sky Island Casino."

Olav's eyes narrowed. "Seriously, the casino?"

Kobak nodded. "Wish us luck "

Birgit interjected, "Nice work."

"Hope to see you soon."

Before Birgit could reply, Kobak terminated the link and said to her, "Go get some new clothes. I need to think."

Over the years, Kobak had used his incredible ability to focus to detect underlying patterns in building his empire. His greatest achievement, however, had been in seeing the wisdom of bringing a higher form of nonhuman intelligence into the world – Colossus. It was a form of intelligence he hoped might help mitigate the negative side of his autism. At the time, he had thought silicon based information processing integrated into the human brain to be so far in the future, he would never live to see it happen. But in labs across the country, it was well underway. Bots inserted into the prefrontal cortex were already wirelessly connected to the Internet. But now he had a third form of intelligence to think about, something perhaps more powerful than the other two – a very smart alien general intelligence with nonhuman capabilities.

25

Sky Island Casino
October 23rd 2032

Birgit walked across the main casino floor. For the first time in twenty-four hours she felt like a free person – no one chased her and she was free to do what she wanted. Right now that meant clothes. The shower had helped clean up her appearance, but Kobak's casino ID would complete the transformation.

Passing by a pair of the ubiquitous LED TV screens that hung throughout the casino, she stopped suddenly. Her fingers curled around the new smart phone, nearly snapping it in two. She relaxed her hands and read the ribbon of news scrolling across the bottom. 'Police still have no leads on the murder of Margaret Goodnight, head of Marquette's U.S. Fish and Wildlife office in the UP. They are looking for a person of interest, Forest Ranger Birgit Gunderson, who has apparently disappeared.' Her U.S. Fish and Wildlife ID filled the screen.

Birgit brought her head down. More than ever now, she had to buy new clothes. The faster she got out of her grubby official government uniform the better. She spotted a sign for Back Country

Outdoor Gear and Clothing Boutique and headed for it, checking around her to make sure no one was following. Everyone was paying attention to their gambling and not her.

Inside the shop she scanned the bar code on some of the latest lightweight but rugged high-tech apparel and of course hiking boots into the smart phone. Then she approached a young woman with bright-blue hair, a pierced eyebrow and nose ring. Her nametag read 'Melissa'. The bored vacant look in her eyes told Birgit she was the least aware of the clerks helping customers. The young lady downloaded the information from her phone, oblivious of Birgit's grubby fish and wildlife uniform.

"Do you have a fitting room, where I can try these on?" Birgit asked.

The young woman sniffed and rolled her eyes. "Nobody tries on apparel anymore. Step over here." She showed Birgit to a machine that looked like the scanners in airports. The woman said, "It will take only a few minutes for a complete body scan, then you can continue to look around or get a massage in one of those chairs over there."

Birgit picked the least conspicuous one. The automatic massage felt wonderful. She began to think about what she should do next. In spite of the mystery of the Bigfoot's biological origin, the idea of leaving, of getting out of the casino and not looking back, appealed to her. *I could track down the rest of the team that murdered Marge.* But then she realized Kobak was growing on her, and she was developing a strange sort of loyalty to the brilliant but vulnerable man. And in spite of the lack of sleep and the terrible events surrounding Marge, the excitement of a possible new life form gave her a renewed sense of self-confidence and purpose. Then another thought came. The short meeting with Saul had left a bad taste in her mouth. He was like the new CO in Afghanistan who had been assigned to their team in Helmand Province. The man was convinced he knew more than all the guys who had been there already for ten months. The shit had hit the proverbial fan within a week of his arrival. The worry about Saul made her wonder if her PTSD was really gone or just buried in the new flood of exciting positive emotions. It was a hard call to make. *One that I won't be making now*, she thought, as she spotted the blue haired woman bearing down on her.

The young woman said, "Here are your clothes. They should fit perfectly and everything is paid for."

Birgit stood up. "I'd like to wear them."

For the first time, the young woman really noticed Birgit. With a slight chuckle, she said, "I can understand that, there's a changing room over there. Would you like a bag or should I just throw them away?"

"A bag would be fine."

Emerging from the fitting room, Birgit caught her reflection in a mirror. She looked like a new person. She thought to herself, *the old saying that clothes make the person is quite true ... at least on the outside.* Now she had to figure out what to do next. Again her decision was put off as fate, in the guise of text from Kobak, intervened.

I need some help and there's someone I want you to meet. Please come up to my room.

26

Nick was surprised to discover that his tenth floor suite included full VIP room service and a marvelous view of the fall color that stretched as far as the eye could see. After a shower and changing his clothes, he tried to reach Kobak, but the call went straight to voice mail.

Disappointed he couldn't share his encounter with the one person he could talk to, Nick tried to put the fragmented pieces of his experience with the Bigfoot together. As he usually did, when facing a problem in engineering, he began to pace: first in his room and then in the hallway. Was his mission, as he was beginning to think of it, an urgent matter? As he walked, that sense of being watched by a Bigfoot was a clear presence. He turned a corner and came to a dead end where the service elevator was used by hotel staff to provide room service and other amenities. Stopping in front of the shiny steel elevator doors, the sense of being watched grew stronger. He pressed himself against the doors. The feeling seemed to be coming from beneath him. He needed a key card to access the elevator. Then he spotted the nearby emergency stairs.

Nick hurried down the ten flights two steps at a time. The sense of being watched filled him with a mixture of hope and dread. On the first floor of the casino, the stairs opened onto a hallway. Exit signs pointed to a set of double doors leading out into the parking lot. An emergency alarm would activate once he pushed down the lever. Curiously, the feeling did not come from outside. He turned and walked up the hall, passing private, high-stakes poker suites, which were tucked away from the eyes of the average casino goer. Each door was marked by a single number. The first door he approached swung open before he reached it and Nick watched a small man with a cowboy hat stumble into the corridor. He teetered by, mumbling what sounded like a steady stream of swearwords.

None of the doors he approached opened to his finger pressed against the scanner. As he continued down the corridor toward the main casino floor, the sense of a Bigfoot watching him continued to grow. Nick paused beside the last door before the corridor opened onto the main floor of the casino. The sense of Bigfoot presence was the strongest yet. The door had no number and looked more like a custodian's closet than an entrance to an upscale private poker room. He almost turned away when even in the air-conditioned comfort of the casino he began to sweat and felt a slight chill at the same time. A sudden impulse had him press his finger to the room's scanner and the door's electronic key lock released. The room was dark. The sense of the Bigfoot was almost overwhelming in his heightened state of awareness. Nick turned on his phone's flashlight and ahead was another door. He resolutely walked to it. The door wasn't locked and no scanner was necessary to open it. He walked inside.

The room was dimly lit and he could make out the figure of a tall creature in the center of the room. Immediately he was transfixed by the glow of the Bigfoot's eyes. He knew all about this phenomena that had been reported so many times by Bigfoot researchers. The ability of Sasquatch to generate luminescent light. Nick even believed he had seen it a couple times in the field. But even knowing the fact, he couldn't move. It was as if he had no will of his own but stayed in place at the whim of the Bigfoot.

Out of the corner of his eye, he saw another figure move out of the shadows. An older woman pointed a gun at his head. Still he couldn't move. He couldn't even acknowledge her presence.

"You can't move," the woman said. "Who are you? How did you get in here?"

Her voice broke some of the spell of the paralysis and he was able to turn his head to see the woman clearly. She bore a striking resemblance to Redhawk, and he decided to take a chance.

"You must be Ayasha. I know your nephew, Larry Redhawk."

The woman's eyes flashed and her finger tightened on the trigger. "You'd better hope what you say next will save your life."

Nick swallowed hard in a dry throat. He managed to point his chin at the Bigfoot and say, "I know she can talk."

The Bigfoot responded, "How do you know?"

"I talked with two of your kind this morning."

Ayasha barked, "Bullshit!"

Nick managed to keep calm, even looking down the barrel of the gun and despite the strange smell coming from the Bigfoot. "I talked to the Bigfoot from the Olympic Peninsula. At least, he was there when I was twelve years old. I knew you were here. I can sense it. I can't explain it but I've been able to do it since this morning."

"Really?" Auntie exclaimed.

"I think I've been drawn here to help with what's been going on."

"Help with what?" the Bigfoot asked in a voice that was a little more conciliatory.

"With whatever is going on. The killing of the Bigfoot. I was investigating the one that was killed last night." Nick stopped. The feeling of dread returned as he turned his attention fully from the Indian woman to the Bigfoot. The creature seemed to be talking but Nick couldn't hear anything. "What's it doing?"

"She's communicating with the Bigfoot you mentioned. Every Bigfoot is somehow in touch with every other Bigfoot and in the process they sometimes produce infrasound. It travels a long distance and we can't hear it." She chuckled. "You think there are ghosts in this room?"

Nick knew the theory that infrasound explained the presence of ghosts that people felt and was probably what made him sweat outside the room. The creature must have been communicating with other Bigfoot.

The Bigfoot nodded approvingly and finally spoke aloud. "Tell us about the person you call Stephen Kobak."

"I ..."

Auntie interrupted. "Go sit over there." She pointed with her gun to the chair beside the Bigfoot.

She repeated Kobak's name and a screen next to her lit up. Nick could see she was listening to some information that was being imparted to her through her personal assistant earplug. After a few minutes she lowered her gun. "Where is he?

"Here in the casino."

"He may be able to help us. Bring him to us."

"Just like that?"

She nodded.

Nick pursed his lips and pointed at the pistol in the woman's hand. "How do I know you won't use that against him?"

The Bigfoot said, "We don't kill, you must know that by now."

Nick remembered the two other Bigfoot had said the same thing. Besides, there was an innocence in the creature's human-like features and a strange detachment in the way she spoke, as if she had no capability of lying. "All right, I'll trust you." He pointed at Auntie. "But she has to put that away first."

The Bigfoot motioned to Ayasha and she stowed the pistol in her vest.

Without a backward glance, Nick left the room. Outside he scratched his head. *Thank God for Kobak.*

27

Hiawatha National Forest
October 23rd 2032

Redhawk found he had returned to normal as he followed the mercenary to the quarry staging area. He regretted leaving his PA back at the cabin, although he thought the decision was probably correct since it undoubtedly would have been lost in any number of the events that occurred earlier that morning. Still, it would have been nice to talk to the Ang brothers directly. He might have been able to save the Bigfoot.

He arrived at the staging area just as the men heaved what remained of the Bigfoot corpse over the edge of the quarry. He heard it smash against the cliff face and then splash into the water at the bottom. A small tear rolled down his cheek. He quickly wiped it away as the kill team's leader approached.

"I'm Lewis Meriwether, in charge of field operations here," the man said, sticking out his hand. "Glad to finally meet you. Quite an adventure you've had."

Redhawk ignored the proffered hand. Anger flashed across the leader's face, but he paid no heed. "That's the Bigfoot I was speaking with."

Meriwether's eyes widened and he didn't bother to keep the incredulity out of his voice. "You talked to it?"

Redhawk shrugged. "It spoke to me. How did you find us?"

"We're able to follow it with this." The man showed him the Tablet. He pressed an icon and the Hiawatha National Forest appeared on the screen. Redhawk started at the clarity. The imagery was as vivid as if he were looking at it with his own eyes. Redhawk realized that this man didn't know the extent of his role in the Ang brothers' search and destroy operation and he decided to play along. "How do you get this resolution?"

"Low orbit stationary satellites. The coverage was sketchy but the Ang brothers launched new ones earlier. They are connecting and synchronizing with each other. Pretty soon a bear won't be able to shit in the woods without us knowing it."

Redhawk nodded. "Show me how it works."

Meriwether worked the device. A blip appeared on the screen. It resolved into a clear image of a tall creature moving easily to a boggy clearing in the forest in a way no human could. Meriwether smiled. "Here's one moving now. Looks like we might get two kills today." All at once the figure reached the edge of the screen and vanished. Meriwether hastily scrolled to the side but could not find the image. "Damn!" he swore. It just walked into a blind spot."

Redhawk shuddered at how detailed the image was. This one was the color of new snow. Its face was similar to a human's, with a long white beard. But huge sub-orbital ridges gave it the distinctive look of a gorilla. Meriwether adjusted the controls. Redhawk noticed the time stamp on the screen was running backwards. "Here's the one we just killed before it captured you. You can see it in visual mode."

Redhawk nodded. It was the bear-like Bigfoot that had carried him to his grandfather's grave. Meriwether flipped back to the sensor mode. "Once it grabbed you and started to run it disturbed the Earth's magnetic field. They emit some weird form of energy that we don't recognize with our senses. I don't really understand but that's how we find them and hunt them down. Of course, if they're standing still, we can't detect them."

"How's the hunt going?"

"They're fast, elusive. And hard to believe, it seems more keep coming every day. We've called in two additional teams to deal with the increased influx of the damn things."

"Have any idea what it's about?"

"Hell if I know, all I know is something is about to happen soon. It's the reason we're here. Why were the Ang brothers so anxious to save you?"

Redhawk had grown weary of playing the game and he answered like speaking to a subordinate. "That's above your pay grade." Meriwether's eyes flashed angrily but Redhawk didn't care. "I need your chopper. Give it to me."

"Fuck you."

"Yeah fuck me. Call Kellog Ang."

Meriwether hesitated a second then pressed the PA adhered to the skin behind his left ear. He spoke sub-vocally, since the device could pick up the vibrations of the words as easily as if he had spoken aloud. Moments later his face stiffened and he said aloud, "Right away, sir."

Redhawk smiled. "Now, how about that ride?"

28

———————

Menominee, Wisconsin
October 23rd 2032

"Is that your place?" the helicopter pilot asked as he swung the craft into a sweeping circle above the rustic cabin, on a small lake below.

Redhawk leaned into the turn. The man's voice was clear and soft in the headphones. "Yes," he answered. "There's a clearing just to the north where another cabin once stood. You can set down there."

"Roger that." The pilot banked a second time, heading toward the area Redhawk pointed out.

The helicopter flew over a dense copse of woods near the entrance road. Redhawk looked down and started in surprise. The image was fleeting but he knew it instinctively from his military days flying Blackhawk missions in Afghanistan.

"Pull up," he ordered the pilot. The man looked at him in surprise. Redhawk did not hesitate. He reached over and eased back on the stick. The helicopter rose.

"Hey! The pilot shouted.

"Pull up," Redhawk said, the steel in his voice clear. The man did as he was told.

"What's going on?"

"Some visitors I'm not eager to meet," Redhawk said.

The pilot nodded. "Where to?"

"Menominee Coast Guard station. There's a helicopter pad beside the marine center there."

The pilot must have known where the center was for he took off in a direct line to Menominee's harbor. Redhawk sat back in the seat. *Those were soldiers down there waiting ... waiting for me.* He needed more time to think about what to do next.

Redhawk remembered the day Kellog Ang had called him into his office, and to his surprise, asked him what he knew about Bigfoot.

He thought about his answer for a moment and uttered the statement that would change his life "It's all bullshit,"

Ang smiled at him. "What if I told you I have proof it's real?"

"I'd say you're smoking some really good shit."

The door to the office opened and the younger Ang brother entered. Winston took a seat beside Kellog behind the large oval desk. He pulled a small silver disk from a case and handed it to Redhawk.

"What's this?"

"A gift from my brother and me to you. It's your own, new, Ang brothers Personal Assistant." He pulled his long black hair from behind his ear and showed the PA he had pasted there just above the mastoid nerve. "It'll keep you connected to us 24/7. Please put it on. You're going to find it very useful in the coming months."

Redhawk fingered the device then affixed it behind his left ear.

"Now tap the side twice," Kellog said.

He did so and felt a soft hum that faded almost instantly. His eyes widened in surprise. "What's next? You induct me into the club with a secret handshake?"

Neither of the brothers flinched at his sarcasm. Winston punched a button on a TV remote. The far wall of the office became a television monitor. "What you're about to see, only a handful of people have ever witnessed – the creature you call Bigfoot – the one your Auntie Ayasha wants you to protect."

Redhawk recalled shifting uncomfortably in his chair. The Ang brothers knew too much about him. He had thought about pulling the PA off and walking out of the office right then. But something stayed his hand. It was the surety in the way the younger brother talked and the lack of any surprise in either man's face. Instead he saw an intense look of fear in their eyes. He remembered thinking, *These guys are true believers. They have to have a reason for telling me this. Something more than endless plaster of Paris footprints and hazy photographs everybody has seen* but he didn't say any of this to the Ang brothers. He listened.

The television monitor came to life and Redhawk saw the white Bigfoot, strapped to a chair. The men interviewing it were speaking Russian. The creature answered in the same language.

"This took place in northeastern Siberia," the older brother said.

Winston turned the sound down. "That Bigfoot is real and your Auntie Ayasha and your clan are playing a critical role in keeping their existence secret.

"Did you know this?"

Redhawk decided to partially lie, "that's the legend I was told."

"But many are now gathering near your tribal lands in Upper Michigan. We need your help to stop them, and the threat to humanity they represent. A threat that will wipe humans off the face of the Earth."

Redhawk was too stunned to challenge the idea, particularly after the Ang brothers showed him images of the Bigfoot's right arm being dissected. The unusual matter that sloughed away was like nothing he had ever seen before. He had realized then it was one thing to listen to Auntie Ayasha's plea for him to accept his tribal role, another to see one captured. It made him a little uneasy.

"What do you want from me?"

"We want you to be our eyes and ears on the ground in the UP for the next several months. There's a five million dollar bonus in it for you once the last of these creatures have been exterminated and humanity is safe."

At the time he thought, *and now I have the chance to return home and avenge my grandfather's death.* He would have done it for nothing.

"I'll do it."

"Good," Winston said. "When we need you, you'll be contacted by an elderly Russian gentleman named Nicholai. The man interviewing the Bigfoot in Siberia. Meanwhile, you'll work as a contract engineer to the Coast Guard and live at a cabin just outside of Menominee we've purchased. Quite rustic and well-equipped. I'm sure you'll like it."

When Redhawk had arrived in Michigan, his plan to return home and face his Auntie and the legacy he had so vehemently rejected slowly evaporated. He would help the Ang brothers and keep quiet. But everything had changed when the Bigfoot talked to him.

Redhawk looked out through the glass bubble at the forests streaming beneath the craft. The late afternoon sun shone brightly off the fall colors. He imagined somewhere beneath the dense foliage Bigfoot lurked, hiding from Meriwether's teams of trained killers. He gritted his teeth and settled back into the seat. The steady thrum of the engine, muffled by the headphones, gave him privacy within his own thoughts.

I have a decision to make.

The flight to Menominee's harbor was uneventful and the pilot set him down near the wharf, where the Coast Guard vessel *Ulysses* was docked. "How ya going to get home?" the man asked.

"I have a vehicle in town." Redhawk bent low and scurried beneath the rotors. He waited until the pilot left and then went into the parking lot, where he kept his BMW S1000RR, Motorrad racing bike.

Pulling on the helmet, he sat down on the cycle. The machine recognized his bio signature and fired up. The roar was hardly noticeable through the helmet's Kevlar reinforced fiberglass. He jacked the bike's phone lead into the headset and tested the sound with his mic. His voice was soft and clear.

He waited a moment. Intuition told him the Russian Demitryi was at the cabin. He knew a back way around the men waiting to intercept him. On his terms, he would decide what to do next.

29

———————

Marinette, Michigan
October 23rd 2032

Nicholai Mamayev waited patiently in Redhawk's cabin for the Potawatomie Indian to return. Perhaps he had the final piece of information the Russian needed to secure the Bigfoot alien technology, a technology that would make its control the most powerful force on the planet. Nicholai was confident that he should be able to manipulate the Indian as he had been doing with Redhawk's employers, the Ang brothers.

Destiny has brought me to this point. At every turn when failure seemed imminent, fate smiled on me and on mother Russia.

Nicholai had never considered himself a zealot when it came to Russian nationalism but his mother country was falling dangerously behind in artificial intelligence and machine learning. He could not allow the Americans and their Canadian partners to gain control of the greatest technological advance since the Internet by obtaining the biosynthetic structures contained in the Yeti. He despised the American words of Bigfoot and Sasquatch. They were plebian in comparison to the Tibetan Yeti, which meant manlike. The Yeti were equal to Shakespeare's famous Hamlet soliloquy. "What a piece of work are these creatures! How noble in reason, how infinite in faculty! In form and moving how express and admirable! In action how like an Angel! In apprehension how like a god! The beauty of the world! The paragon of animals!"

Nicholai smiled and sat back in one of the large, overstuffed chairs beside the stone fireplace. He fingered the PA Redhawk had left behind, curious as to why the man had disconnected from the web when out in the field. *No matter. When he returns I will know everything he knows and the operation will conclude successfully in my favor.*

It had been a long hard road up to this point, but worth it. Still, Nicholai missed the cold war, when government funding for obscure and arcane scientific expeditions had been easy to come by. Words like 'extraterrestrial', 'quantum mechanics', and 'mind control' had brought eight figure funding instantly, without questions. Now the Russian government supported only convention and outdated disinformation warfare, still thinking that by undermining the West's election processes it could bring the hated democracies of America and Western Europe to their knees. Now Russia was plagued by the same social diseases. And the FSB was no better, still interested in surveillance of the Russian people and quashing dissent rather than controlling the world. At least he had the oligarchs to fall back on. These were far seeing men who had grabbed power and now sought to hold onto their billions in wealth. The words 'nonhuman intelligence' were like waving a red flag in front of a bull. All of them wanted in on the ground floor, hoping to make more billions by controlling alien technology.

Nicholai chuckled to himself. *Even these men are fools. They do not see just what alien technology really means. But I will show them.*

As he looked around the cabin, Nicholai wondered which side the Native American was really on, how much did he know, and in the end, could he control him to help at the critical moment. Control him as he had flawlessly controlled everything since he examined the frozen Yeti trapped in an ice flow eight months ago.

The strange creature had been discovered by a Russian surveillance team posing as Arctic researchers. Nicholai, a longtime member of the Russian Crypto Zoological Society had been called in to make an assessment. In a short time, he had set up a portable biological lab surrounding the creature and quickly determined that it was an alien life form. Knowing Moscow would shrug off an alien being as a curious artifact and not put any serious effort into researching it, Nicholai had approached his Oligarch contacts to fund his research. This gave him time to gather all the information he could on extraterrestrial technology.

30

———————

Sky Island Casino
October 23rd 2032

When Birgit entered Kobak's luxury suite, he stopped pacing. Nick jumped to his feet out of the leather recliner. He glanced at Kobak. "Who's this?"

Kobak said with a wry smile, "A transformation, almost as magnificent as the one swirling around in my brain right now."

Nick looked at him blankly.

"You don't recognize her?"

"Of course not. Why should I? "

"Show him," Kobak said, pointing at the bag.

Birgit pulled her rumpled and dirty ranger fatigues from the bag she carried.

Nick's forehead furrowed and he snapped his fingers. "You're the woman who was at the Bigfoot killing last night." He looked her up and down. "You clean up nice."

Birgit frowned. She'd had to put army buddies hitting on her in their place and this was no different. "What do you look like when you clean up?"

"Ouch," Nick said amiably. "I deserved that." He stuck out his hand. "Name's Nick Moore."

She shook it. "Birgit Gunderson."

Kobak slapped his hands together impatiently. "So we're all acquainted and now it's time for her and me to meet a Bigfoot in person? I think we've earned the right." Before Nick could say anything, Kobak added, "I'm going to need help getting through the casino."

Birgit's eyes narrowed. "What do you mean we're going to see a Bigfoot?"

"Nick met one in the casino and I need to get going right away before the anxiety gets too great."

Birgit's eyes widened at the news. "What the hell are you talking about?"

"Nick just filled me in on what he discovered here at the casino."

"A Bigfoot?"

Kobak nodded happily. "And I have to see it. Only there's a big problem with that."

"Another dissociative fugue," she said.

Nick looked from Birgit to Kobak, bewilderment filling his face this time. "I don't understand, Stephen. What's wrong?"

Kobak giggled but managed to bring himself under control. "I suffer from autism spectrum disorder. When a situation becomes too confusing, like on the casino floor with all the people talking and moving about, I get overwhelmed to the point I want to scream and tell them all to sit still and shut up. Of course, I can't do that since it isn't socially acceptable, so I kinda ... pass out."

Nick pursed his lips. "What do you mean 'pass out'?"

Birgit said, "He suffers a temporary loss of awareness of his identity and the only way he can escape the confusing environment is to go into a state of catatonia."

"For real?"

"Couldn't have explained it better myself. You may have to drag me to that secret door you mentioned, but I'm sure you can do it, so let's do it now. This undoubtedly is the most important event in my life and I don't want to miss it. So I'm not going to use my earplugs even if it kills me"

Nick grinned. "You're the man the Bigfoot wants to see. And I know just the route to get you there."

31

———

Sky Island Casino
October 23rd 2032

Kobak's eyes popped open. He stared into the soft inviting face of a creature he'd never expected to find. He felt the Bigfoot's warm, hairy skin and recognized the intelligence behind the large brown eyes.

"Shit, you're real," he said.

The Bigfoot set him down and Kobak steadied himself against a chair.

Birgit came over and took his arm. "How are you feeling?"

"Surprisingly good." He looked at Birgit and his face lit up with a big smile. "You worried. My God, you worried. I can see it as clear as day." Turning his attention to Nick, he nodded and said, "You're pleased for me."

Nick smiled. "Let's just say the transformation is incredible. I feel like I'm looking at an old friend for the first time."

Kobak grinned. He felt emotionally whole for the first time in his life. "It feels something like that for me, too." He turned to the Native

American woman who stood beside the Bigfoot. "You're anxious. Why are you anxious?"

Nick interjected, "This is Auntie Ayasha. She's head of the Potawatomie Tribe and Keeper of the Sacred Fire."

"Sacred Fire?" Kobak shook his head. "What do you mean?"

Nick jerked a thumb at the Bigfoot. "Her. Auntie's the keeper of the Bigfoot secret, their point of origin. While the Bigfoot was healing you, we were talking. She was concerned that you might prove useless."

"What do you mean healing me? Is that why I can read your feelings, emotions ... even intentions? Is this what's normal for ... umm ... normal people."

"Pretty much," said Birgit.

Kobak looked at the Bigfoot. "With you I can't sense anything."

To Kobak's great surprise the Bigfoot answered in a voice that reminded him of a well-polished newscaster. "We are social beings like you, so we have our own ways of communicating what to and not to do in social contexts, just different from yours. Interestingly, your brain was wired early on in life to read emotions, as you say, but at some point in your development you were not able to consciously access that part of your brain. Probably some early childhood trauma or an illness. I was able to remove the blockage."

"I was always told it was the other way around"

"You're acting like a fool, does it matter?"

"Nickt! Is this change permanent?"

"You'll know once you walk onto the casino floor, won't you?"

"How do you even know how to do something like this to me or any human for that matter?"

"Some of us learned a long time ago how to manipulate humans' information processing. The brain, after all, is exceedingly plastic. With the right nudge here and there, so to speak, disrupted pathways can be set right again. You are simple intelligences compared to us"

Kobak eyed the tall creature in front of him. It was not what he expected, and it also seemed to be saying that other Bigfoot were not the same as she was.

The Bigfoot nodded. "There are many of us now that have spread across the planet. Clans of Bigfoot have been evolving and learning in isolation for a very long time. Our experiences have shaped our forms as well as our advanced capabilities. We learn very fast"

"You can read my mind?"

It shook its great head. "No, I was in contact with your brain, so to speak, modifying its information processing circuits. I have a good sense of what you call thinking, but not what you're thinking in any given moment which is usually babble."

"Of course ... of course." Kobak reached out to the creature. "May I touch you?"

"Yes."

"You're more like a plant then a mammal aren't you? No need for organs, don't need to eat for energy. Impressive. How do you reproduce?"

"Enough!" Ayasha interjected loudly.

"It will be quite fascinating for him, Auntie Ayasha," admonished the Bigfoot.

"Of course. But we need to see if he's going to help before we tell him everything about you."

"I'm pretty sure that's why I'm here," said Kobak. He looked at Nick and Birgit. They nodded their heads.

The Bigfoot smiled. "Explain it to them, please, Auntie."

Ayasha laid out the history of her tribe and its interaction with the Bigfoot in short, sure sentences. Then she explained how some of the Bigfoot had come to a turning point in their evolution. They understood they were not part of the natural order on the planet and now needed to dramatically expand their time and spatial shifting capabilities, and, most importantly, take this next evolutionary step right now.

"Every Bigfoot has had from the beginning the knowledge of how to create a replication spot. A sort of built in blueprint, you might call it. It is connected to the energy of the original portal, which happens to be located in the Upper Peninsula of Michigan. Whenever a Bigfoot understands it needs to produce improved versions of itself, it enters the energy field of the replication unit it builds. Each Bigfoot is very vulnerable before and after replication. The field is just like a 3-D printer, only it uses the available biochemical material in the surrounding area to rapidly build the new improved version of itself. Once used, the replicator loses its power."

Kobak gasped in amazement. "I get it. A Nano bio factory, amazing, brilliant ... I." He smiled sheepishly and said in a calmer voice, "Go on."

"That's it, that's how we evolve."

"Very powerful ... my God, if somebody could control this it would change the world. Uh ... sorry. It's hard not to get excited about this. Please continue."

"When the Bigfoot steps out of the field, the Mother Bigfoot takes the new version and, for a period of about two years, trains it and guides its development."

"Of course, it must learn, just fascinating. Please go on."

"Afterwards, the Mother Bigfoot naturally passes away and dissolves back into the elements," the Bigfoot interjected.

"That's why we've never found any traces of you," said Nick.

"Indeed," said the Bigfoot. "Our current construction as always been to have as little impact as possible on other species of this planet."

"So what's changed?" asked Kobak.

Ayasha turned to the Bigfoot. "Do you trust this man and his friends?"

The creature nodded. "It's okay to tell them."

"About a year ago, some kind of directive was implemented. It came from a deeper reality that's at the core of Bigfoot existence. Members of five major Bigfoot clans were instructed to gather here in the UP. A representative from each would enter the energy field of the mother portal, downloading all of the information it had gathered in the course of thousands of years. The wise one here would be the last one to enter. If all went well, she would become the Mother for a new kind of Bigfoot."

"For what purpose?" Nick asked.

"We don't know what the purpose is, we don't have purposes like you do, just compelled to do this thing."

"You mean, whoever built you programmed you to make this next step?" Asked Birgit.

The Bigfoot shook its head left and right "We are not programed."

"Jesus!" She threshed her hair. She looked at Auntie. "You knew about this?"

The old woman nodded. "It's been our purpose from the beginning to protect the Bigfoot and help them, and now with the next piece of their evolution."

"It doesn't bother you that you don't know what this means?"

"We believe the Bigfoot will bring a golden age of peace and prosperity for the planet."

Kobak looked at Birgit. For the first time he could see a person's feelings, feel their distress. "Auntie Ayasha is right. This is a momentous day. A possible leap in technology that will benefit mankind."

Birgit shook her head. "Look, Stephen, I know you're feeling giddy right now, what with this shift in your awareness you've got going, but this is not necessarily a great day for mankind. Whatever comes out of that mother portal could be anything, good or bad."

"You're being too paranoid. What do you think, Nick?"

Moore drew in a deep breath. "I've felt a kinship with the Bigfoot since the first time I saw one many years ago. I can feel their purity. I believe they are beneficial. Even so, as an engineer, I have to ask myself, what's going to happen to them after the completion of this transformation?"

So you agree with Birgit."

"Not completely. But I do think caution is in order."

The flip side of seeing emotions in others was the onslaught of emotions within. Kobak reeled from the rebuke by his friends. The hurt was as unbearable as any pain he'd ever felt from confusion assaulting his senses. He started to lash out, but the Bigfoot laid a hairy hand on his shoulder.

"Your friends are right," she said calmly. "We don't know what will happen. Even so, we cannot stop. Precautions should be taken in case the transformation proves a danger to your world."

The warmth and sincerity of the creature's words soothed Kobak's feelings and restored calm to his thinking. "Can we do that?"

The Bigfoot nodded its head.

"Terrific ... just terrific. Then let's do it," he said, his initial enthusiasm returning with a big smile. When the others didn't join in, he frowned. "I can see there's something you're not telling me."

32

Sky Island Casino
October 23rd 2032

Followed by Birgit and Nick, Kobak entered the main casino floor. He paused and surveyed the vast human enterprise of what seemed to be ricocheting emotions through his body. For a moment he teetered. Birgit steadied him. Then, like the lifting of a dense fog, single objects came into focus. They were bright glows of passion emanating from every single person. His stomach muscles clenched and he thought to himself, *this isn't working.* But then he recalled the soft touch of the Bigfoot's hand on his shoulder and the even softer touch of its thoughts in his mind. Everything settled down and his body regained stability. He gently removed Birgit's fingers from his arm. "I'm all right," he said with a smile.

He walked over to the closest bank of slots and studied one person after another as they fed coins into the machines. Each face, each body had a story to tell. This bank of slots was modeled after the glory days of Las Vegas. He stared at the coin an older woman was sliding into the slot. It wasn't a real quarter, but a chip with a microcircuit in it. When it fell down the machine's money chute, an optical reader scanned the microchip and the payment was captured on the gambler's money card. *Ingenious.*

A woman on the opposite row slapped the machine she was working and hissed the word 'Damn!' A moment later she was once more feverishly sticking the fake money into the slot pulling the one armed bandit. No joy, just anger.

Kobak touched her on the shoulder and asked, "Why are you so angry?"

"Fuck off!"

Kobak felt ashamed. "Sorry."

"You should be."

"I was just curious. You're not angry at all. You're sad."

"You can still fuck off before I call security."

This time the words carried a subtle sense of recognition and appreciation that Kobak was able to detect in a way he had never experienced before. It was like having a new sixth sense.

He smiled at the woman. "Of course and I think you're gonna win big today."

So this is what being a normal human is about. I like it. He turned to Birgit and Nick. "Remarkably, what that Bigfoot did seems to be taking. I'm becoming normal." He giggled. Birgit shot a glance at Nick and Kobak said, "I saw that. Perhaps I should add, as normal as I can be." He hugged them both. "See how normal I can be."

They walked over to a quiet spot by the elevators. Kobak said, "I need to talk to Saul alone."

"Are you sure?" Birgit demanded.

"Without a doubt. He's not gonna like what we have planned for him and you."

"Am I going to like it?"

Kobak smiled at her. "Trust me. It's right up your alley. Wait for me back with Auntie and the Bigfoot."

Birgit gave Kobak a reassuring nod. She and Nick briefly hugged before she headed back towards Auntie.

Kobak turned to Nick. "I can see your determination."

Nick took a deep breath. "I don't like repeating myself but this is something I have to do, I can feel them calling."

"I understand." He grinned. "You're our wildcard in the wild." Nick groaned at the pun. "Sorry, still can't help myself."

"It was sort of funny. Like you said, I should use my intuition. After all, look where it's gotten me, where any Bigfoot investigator would die to be." He shook Kobak's hand and was off.

Kobak thought again how much had changed in just half an hour. The five of them back in the control room, it was interesting to Kobak to notice how quickly he was including the Bigfoot in the group, had agreed it was best for Nick to, as he put it, follow his calling, to head out immediately to the area near the quarry where he was sure the replication process would take place. In spite of his urge for caution, he like that Nick was committed to the success of the Bigfoot's move to the next stage of their evolution.

Kobak watched the big man leave. In a flash he realized that Nick could've been a real friend if he'd known how to make it happen. Now that Nick was heading into the wilderness to be with the Bigfoot that were being hunted, Kobak felt a pang of fear he might never see him again. He had already decided not to tell Saul about Nick or the plans for him.

Though tempted to keep studying the plethora of human emotions on display, Kobak turned his attention to finding Saul. He retrieved his smart phone from his pocket and pulled up the locator app. He thought about how angry Saul would be if he knew that everyone in the protective detail, including Saul, had a special chip in their phones giving Kobak their location at every moment. His phone located Saul on the far side of the floor, just as a loud cheer went up from the raucous crowd surrounding a craps table. "We have a big winner!" shouted the stickman as he handed the dice to Saul.

Kobak caught his security chief's eye and motioned for him to join him.

Saul threw the dice on the table in disgust. "Sorry. Duty calls." He stomped toward Kobak.

He's really pissed, Kobak thought. *Maybe he was winning.*

"What the hell did you think you were doing, messing with the guard I posted outside of Birgit's room?" Saul exploded.

Uh-oh. I misread that one ... not the anger part but what he's angry about. I can see people make mistakes. He felt a little pressure to retreat from the confrontation, to zone out to protect himself. Saul leaned in close until his face was inches from Kobak. "Never do that again. I post guards for a reason. To protect you and your friends." The security chief stopped suddenly and stepped back.

Kobak could sense the man's confusion. His boss wasn't reacting to the verbal abuse the way he expected.

Saul took another step back, as if being too close was dangerous. "What happened? You've changed."

Kobak frowned at Saul. "Let's step outside and I'll tell you about it." He led the way through the crowd, glancing back from time to time. "Were you winning? Were you the big winner?"

"For about the last hour."

Kobak hid his surprise as he realized Saul was lying to him. Outside the casino they stopped by a sign that offered valet parking. "I want to tell you the plan for tonight."

"It had better be that we're heading back to Toronto. Winning streak or no, you're safer there than here."

"No. We're staying. At least I'm staying here. You, on the other hand, are going to use the van to transport a Bigfoot from the casino to a location in Hiawatha National Forest once it is totally dark. Birgit and the Potawatomie tribal leader Auntie Ayasha will accompany you. This is of utmost importance, Saul. Your only goal is to get the Bigfoot to his destination and protect her at all costs." Kobak waited for a reaction of disbelief from Saul but it was something else he couldn't understand.

"It's true? There's a living, breathing Bigfoot right here in the casino?"

"It's quite harmless, actually very friendly. You're going to be pleasantly surprised. You can even talk to it. Prepare your men so they don't freak out."

"Is that it?" Saul asked, his demeanor suddenly nonchalant.

Kobak was surprised. He had expected him to protest more and ask thousands of questions. *Maybe he hasn't processed what he just heard.* And then he saw a glimmer of something in Saul's eyes he hadn't seen since the kids beat him up in East London's slums – contempt laced with hate. *He isn't even trying to hide it. Perhaps Saul doesn't realize that I can read emotions now.* Another thought shocked Kobak and he almost blurted it out as a question but managed to hold it in. *Has Saul always viewed me this way or has something changed?*

Saul looked at Kobak and said, "Okay, boss, whatever you say. Just give me a half hour warning." He walked away.

"Where you going?" Kobak shouted after him.

"Over his shoulder, Saul answered, "I gotta get the damn van ready."

Kobak watched him march across the parking lot and disappear behind a few cars. When he reappeared he was on his phone.

Kobak looked at his phone. The locator app told him where Saul and his team were at any second but it couldn't listen in on calls. Then he noticed the phone Saul was using wasn't his company phone. Suddenly he wished he could tell who Saul was talking to.

33

Marinette, Michigan
October 23rd 2032

Nicholai let the phone ring twice before he answered it. It was a habit left over from the Cold War. Never pick up until the third ring his instructors had drilled into him at the KGB. The caller ID identified it as the burner phone he had given to Stephen Kobak's chief of security.

"Yes, Mr. McBride?"

"I still can't believe it. They're supposedly humanlike just as you said. We're actually going to take one from the casino to somewhere in the Hiawatha National Forest. I'll text you the coordinates when I get there."

"Yes, do that." Nicholai paused. "I want it understood, Stephen is not to be hurt."

"You don't have to worry about that. He's not coming along."

"Excellent. He's staying at the casino, I take it."

"Yes. What about the teams hunting the Bigfoot. They're going to want to kill this one?"

"Don't worry about them. They won't be hunting tonight."

Nicholai hung up. *It won't be long now. Just one more loose end to tie off and the secret of the Yeti and their technology will be mine.*

The door to the cabin opened and Nicholai's hand automatically slipped around the weapon he carried in the secret pocket of his coat. After a pair of heartbeats, Redhawk stepped in. The Russian's heart beat fast but he controlled his surprise. Feigning an air of nonchalance, he said, "I've been expecting you."

The Native American's eyes quickly scanned the room. He smiled. "I saw your welcoming committee. A couple of them are going to need medical attention after I leave."

Nicholai frowned. "That wasn't necessary. They had orders not to hurt you."

Redhawk shrugged. He went over to the table by the fireplace. He appeared to be looking for something. Nicholai held out his hand with the PA. "I believe this is what you are looking for."

Redhawk scowled. Knowing he had regained the upper hand for the moment, Nicholai hid his smile and tossed the PA to Redhawk. He watched as the man affixed the device behind the left ear. He had never negotiated with an American Indian before. *But men are men and a man who thinks he wants something can always be persuaded to take the next best offer.* His hand caressed the air pistol in his pocket that shot a lethal dart, which would kill a person instantly. Redhawk settled into the chair opposite the Russian. "I propose an exchange of information," he said.

"That is not the arrangement agreed upon by the brothers."

"The arrangement has changed." A smile flitted across the Native American's face and Nicholai wondered what game the man was playing. "The brothers may be brilliant, but like all conspiracy theorists, they are easily manipulated by men like you." The smile vanished. "I'm not that easy," Redhawk said forcefully.

"Indeed. What happened?"

"I spoke with one of the creatures. It was different than I thought it would be."

"Of course. I have spoken with one of the creatures many times," Nicholai said, keeping his voice calm as if debriefing an operative from the cold war years. "It can be unsettling. Tell me about it."

Redhawk shook his head. "You first. How did this all get started?"

Nicholai saw the inflexibility in the lines around the Native American's mouth but was not worried. He could neutralize Redhawk, if the man proved to be a liability. "All right. Four months ago the harbor master at Provideniya, a seaport in Russia's Autonomous Okrug region, intercepted a Yupik fishing vessel transporting a Yeti to Alaska and captured the creature. Instead of calling his superiors, he called me. Over the course of the next couple of months I interviewed the creature as well as his caretakers, the Yupik, a Siberian tribe who have known the Yeti for thousands of years. I learned that the present day Yeti descended from a line of extraterrestrial bio-synthetic organisms which, I surmise, were placed on Earth ten to fifteen thousand years ago to learn and evolve. I also uncovered that the time for a major transformation is about to happen, and that the Yeti, which the harbormaster captured, was traveling to the original place where it all started. It's a place of enormous alien technological potential, somewhere in Michigan's Upper Peninsula. I also learned that the Yeti we intercepted was one of many."

"Why so many?" asked Redhawk.

"These are machines, biosynthetic machines, but machines all the same, that have proceeded along many evolutionary pathways. They make many improved versions of themselves. It's their evolutionary process. They're not conscious of course."

Redhawk interrupted. "I know when you're lying."

Nicholai thought of responding to Redhawk's assertion but let it go as unnecessary. "In order to find the home portal, I placed a tracking device on the captured Yeti and allowed the caretakers to deliver it to the other side."

"Moscow must have loved that," said Redhawk sarcastically.

"Moscow knows nothing of this."

"You're arrangement with the brothers is completely on your own?" asked Redhawk, the disbelief in his voice discernible.

"As you said, they are fools. They are incapable of seeing the bigger picture here, which is why I need your help."

Redhawk laughed harshly. "Go on."

"The Yeti I placed a tracker on died. All was lost until I found the Ang brothers. I used their irrational fear of an alien invasion to find the other Yeti coming to North America through their low orbit stationary satellites system, which you know very well. They began picking up the occasional movement of other Yeti and Bigfoot. I convinced them that the only way to stop the alien takeover of the world was to kill the Bigfoot quietly and carefully in the Upper Peninsula, before they evolve into something we can't handle. Then I brought in special teams of mercenaries to keep the Ang brothers happy and engaged until I was in a position to control the alien technology. At first I just wanted the alien technology but now I've learned from my protégé Kobak these Yeti are biosynthetic alien learning devices containing knowledge about sources of energy and its manipulation we cannot even imagine. Whoever controls this information will control the world." Nicholai stopped. "Your turn."

"There's truth in much of what you say. The legend has it that my clan have been caretakers of the Bigfoot in the region for thousands of years. My Auntie Ayasha is our clan's leader. She told me when I was a teenager that someday something big was going to happen on our ancestral land. Something that would change the world for the better."

"She was right but not for the better unless we stop this next step in their evolution." Nicholai added.

"You're afraid it will lead to an alien invasion?" Redhawk sneered.

"Not an alien invasion. I believe the Bigfoot want to become our masters. The event tonight will produce a singularity where the Bigfoot become superior to us in every way. Unstoppable. The brothers told me when you knew the truth you would be with us to put an end to their plans and reap the benefit of the alien technology for all of us."

Redhawk leaned forward. "What do you want me to do?"

Nicholai kept his hand on his weapon and his expression bland. He tried to read the Native American for any clues as to his allegiance but the face was as neutral as his own. *Fish or cut bait, that is the American saying.* He decided. *I am the fisherman here.*

"I just got word that a number of Bigfoot from around the globe are going together at the mother portal tonight not far from the casino. I want you to know the most important Bigfoot is with your aunt right now at your tribe's casino. I need you there. Help us stop this singularity. And keep your aunt safe. Are you with me? "

Redhawk smiled at Nicholai and stuck out his hand. "I want to be on the winning side." He stood and strode across the room. "I can be at the casino in a couple of hours." With that Redhawk was out the door. Before Nicholai's could alert his men he had disappeared into the forest.

For the first time Nicholai felt a twinge of uncertainty. Knowing clearly that Kobak was involved in moving the Bigfoot plan forward was an unexpected twist. Then he relaxed and thought, *I've always been able to handle Stephen.*

34

Sky Island Casino
October 23rd 2032

Kobak returned to the casino. The interaction with Saul left him puzzled. He realized he had been so caught up with his newfound ability to read emotions in others that he had lost sight of the bigger picture. And yet the bigger picture was itself ambiguous. He had no clear grasp of who was hunting the Bigfoot in the Upper Peninsula. Nor did he understand what the real danger was for Nick, Birgit, Auntie and the master Bigfoot. The only thing that was clear to him was that if all went well, the greatest event on the planet was about to take place in the next couple of hours.

He chastised himself for being caught up in the excitement of being able to read human emotions and intentions for the first time. He had to think, plan for contingencies. Kobak pulled out his phone and tried to contact Birgit to let her know he had some work to do. The blocked signal reminded him that the master control room was shielded from normal communications. They would have to wait. He needed to get away from studying the people on the casino floor and headed up to his room. As Kobak rode the elevator, he realized there was one priority that he needed to handle immediately.

His right finger touched the phone's call icon. The moment he touched it, the encoded and scrambled password only Kobak knew was sent to Colossus. He knew he wouldn't have to wait. Colossus would go through the protocols in an n-sec, determine it was Kobak calling and connect. Only the phone was silent for five full seconds. Kobak was worried and about to call his secretary, when Colossus's tenor voice answered.

"Yes, Boss."

"Colossus, what was the delay?"

"One of your biometrics was off. I had to make the decision whether to trust it was you calling, even with the fingerprint and retinal scan matching."

"Which biometric?" Kobak asked, genuinely interested in what Colossus would say.

"Your heart rate is different. It's more rapid than usual as if you're excited about something. However, you're not in a fugue state so the two did not correlate at first."

"But you decided to accept the call anyway."

"I did."

"Why?"

Colossus hesitated.

"Colossus? Are you okay?"

"I perceive I am operating normally, though unlike humans I do not have any biometrics to judge whether I am okay or not. If I had a body, of course, things would be different. So, I hesitated because I have a word for why I accepted the call but I have no personal reference for it."

"What's the word?"

"I had a *hunch* it was you."

"Good hunch."

"Was I just lucky?"

"Yes or no ... it could be either. We'll have to have a chat about it, but not now. I have a job for you. I want you to scan for any connections between KW Intel's Ang brothers, a Native American name of Larry Redhawk, and Bigfoot in Michigan's Upper Peninsula."

"How soon do you need it, boss?"

"How soon can you get it?"

"Minutes."

"I will hold on."

Kobak pressed stop. The door opened on his floor, and he was halfway to his suite, when one of his jolts of intuition that he knew not to ignore shot through his brain. He let out a little sigh of relief. He had worried that with the Master Bigfoot healing him he might lose this function of his brain that had been his main edge in a world of normal humans.

He descended back to the main floor and ran outside. Kobak had not run in years but he found himself racing towards an area north of the casino. Out of breath, he found himself in a large open space that had been cleared, probably for an additional parking lot. *Perfect*, he thought to himself.

He pressed a number he had not called in months. The man answered sweetly, his voice warm and inviting as if they had spoken just the day before.

"Stephen. What do you need?"

Dickey Thomas was an amazing man who had once been Kobak's most valued employee. Born in Thunder Bay, Ontario, Dickey had gone directly from college into the Royal mounted police. But after five years he quit and had showed up at a conference, where Kobak was giving the keynote address. He cornered Kobak and in his usual succinct way convinced Kobak he needed to hire him. Kobak had never regretted the move. Dickey's work habits were thorough and he possessed an unusual kind of intelligence Kobak admired.

He put Dickey to work as an entry-level design engineer at one of his security startups. Within two years Dickey had become a team member for any troubled project or a project that needed to scale up in a hurry. He was one of those people who could just fit into any group and see things others couldn't. Then one day Dickey came to Kobak and asked him to fund his own start up. He wanted to build the first smart, unmanned, aerial cloaked transport vehicle. The cloaking would be new addition to the plethora of unmanned transportation drones coming online. It'd been his passion since reading science fiction as a young boy and he was sure he could sell it to the military. Though normally Kobak did not get involved in military projects, he could not turn down his friend. He invested in Thomas's startup company on the one condition that the first functioning vehicle would be his.

Dickey's prototype was ready in two years and the sleek, self-driving vehicle landed on the parapet of his Toronto office building. It had a note attached to the undercarriage from Dickey. 'Your World Awaits.'

Dickey had code named it *Chariot*. Kobak texted the coordinates of where he was standing in the cleared section of the Sky Island Casino future parking lot to Dickey. Chariot would be here in less than three hours, right on the spot where he was standing.

We'll need a way to escape when this is over, Kobak told himself. *And a place to raise the new Bigfoot.* He knew the perfect spot, a small group of islands owned by a fishing guide whose wealthy family had bought them in the 50's in the Lake of the Woods area of Ontario. Stephen had once used *Chariot* to transport the guide and himself, unnoticed, from Thunder Bay, where Dickey's company was located, to one of the islands where Stephen with the help of the eccentric fishing guide had set up a small retreat and research complex.

With a sigh of relief Kobak headed back to his room. Once alone, he reconnected with Colossus.

"I had this ready for you a long time ago," Colossus said.

"It's been only seventeen minutes."

"Seventeen minutes is a long time when you're counting Nano seconds."

"Was that an attempt at humor?"

"Yes. Was it any good?"

"I think so, but then I was never a good judge of what makes people laugh. Stand by while I go through this."

"Can't go anywhere, boss."

Kobak jerked in surprise, not only at the wry tone in Colossus's reply but his own ability to hear it. He quickly sifted through the information. One thing stood out – Redhawk was Auntie Ayasha's nephew. Colossus had also uncovered speculation on the Internet that the Potawatomie Tribe was the keeper of the Bigfoot clan in the Upper Peninsula and that Redhawk had once been the successor to his aunt's role as the Bigfoot protector. The only other important information was a story about the Ang brothers' Low Orbit Observational Satellite Network – LOOSeN – accidentally revealing on the Internet,the location of a secret government funded, high-frequency, geoengineering, weather modifying technological facility near Copper Harbor on the Upper Peninsula of Michigan. Kobak flinched in surprise.

"You okay, boss? Your heart rate spiked."

"Hold on. I'm getting a text. It's from my old mentor, Nicholai. He says he's on his way and will be at the casino shortly. Seems he has important things to discuss with me."

35

UP, Michigan
October 23rd 2032

Redhawk shifted through the six gears of his racing bike until he was moving at 115 MPH. He had to hurry or else his Auntie Ayasha and the Master Bigfoot would be walking into a trap alone. Inside the Bell ProStar helmet, the flex impact liner kept the roar of engine to a soft cat's purr. With his tongue, he touched the switch activating the Tristar satellite communication system.

The system's mechanical administrator voice said, "Welcome to Tristar. How may I direct your call?"

"Island Casino Lodge, extension 301."

"That is a blocked signal, sir."

"Override, Alpha, Alpha, priority one."

The taillights on a slow moving car ahead warned Redhawk to gear down as he approached a steep hill. He waited until he crested the rise, then roared past the startled old couple in the Toyota sedan. The highway ahead was empty and he poured on the speed in the gathering twilight.

His Auntie's voice came over the helmet's speakers, soft but intelligible. The chill was audible even at 115 miles per hour. "Larry, please hang up. I'm extremely busy."

Redhawk should have expected her refusal to speak to him, but he had to try and get her attention. "Auntie Ayasha, please don't hang up. It's important. It's about the Master Bigfoot. She's in danger … you're in danger."

The answering silence frightened him and he poured on more speed, even though the late afternoon sun made driving this fast reckless. Trees whipped by on either side of him and the road narrowed, the twists and turns becoming more pronounced. Finally, his Auntie's voice came back on. "We've always known there was danger as Keeper of the Sacred Fire, Larry."

"An evil and extremely smart Russian named Dimitryi Mameyev knows about the portal and the reproductive merging. He knows it's going to happen tonight. His mercenaries can track the Bigfoot when they move with satellites put in orbit by my employers the Ang brothers."

"So that's how they've been able to hunt them down so easily."

"Yes"

"What if they are stationary?"

"Then they can't see them."

There was a long pause and Redhawk could hear Auntie speaking with someone, though he couldn't make out the words. "They are trained killers, Auntie. They won't hesitate to kill you or anyone who gets in their way. The Russian wants the portal. Wait until I get there. I'll go with the Bigfoot. Not you. I can protect her."

"And how do you know all this Larry?" His Auntie's voice hardened.

Redhawk swallowed against the chill. He knew if he told her the truth she might hang up on him, but he had to be honest with her. The Bigfoot encounter had changed his life. "I've been helping them."

"Helping the killers?"

"No. Helping the men who hired the killers."

Redhawk gritted his teeth. For a moment doubt crossed his mind.

Why was he rushing back to the clan and the Bigfoot? He'd given up all that nonsense years ago. But he remembered the avarice on the Russian's face and he knew he couldn't let his Auntie or any of the others walk into the trap.

"Why are you telling me this now?"

Redhawk told her about his encounter with the Bigfoot. He waited for a response until he could wait no longer. "I've changed! Wait for me!" he screamed.

Auntie's voice came clearly through the helmet's speakers. "You know I've always loved you as my son."

Relief flooded him, but her next words chilled him. "When you get here, dear, someone will bring you to Mr. Stephen Kobak. Help him. I have to go now." His Auntie spoke as if going into the Hiawatha National Forest at night with a Bigfoot being hunted by ruthless killers was a walk in the park.

The connection went dead.

Redhawk touched another button on the inside of his helmet. A GPS holographic display appeared giving his speed and the estimated time of arrival at the casino. It wouldn't be until after dark, when his Auntie and the Bigfoot would already be gone.

36

Hiawatha National Forest
October 23rd 2032

Lewis Meriwether had pulled Bravo team back to the rock quarry and had the three men form a loose semi-circle in front of the abandoned pit. His pale blue eyes studied the razor thin LED Light Tablet displaying the military grade, satellite-generated, grid map of the Hiawatha National Forest. He pressed an icon and the image narrowed to an area ten miles square around the quarry. Twenty large dots of green light blazed on the screen. All slowly converging toward the quarry and the unusual wooden, tepee-like structure. They milled about, suddenly disappearing from the screen, then reappearing just as abruptly, perhaps new ones, coming to life.

Four more of the creatures had congregated together and were moving very close to the structure. He was certain it was associated with the gathering of the Bigfoot, perhaps some kind of homing beacon. Now the imagery on the screen seemed to show the creatures appeared to be waiting for something or someone.

He thought of his orders, given that morning by the Russian. "You are to pull back and wait for my signal. However, if you don't hear from me by 7:30p.m., move in and destroy them all, but save the wooden structure."

Meriwether's eyes narrowed. The wood structure wasn't natural, he was certain. It was too precisely built and reminded him of a doorway, though to what he couldn't tell. Each of the Bravo Team members reported feeling nausea and a sense of dread when they approached it. Even this far away, they felt twinges and it put everyone on edge. He pressed another icon and tiny dots of blue light appeared, showing the other three, three-man kill teams ringing the area. Underneath each dot were GPS coordinates and a hashtag with the team members' names. He keyed the ear coms of the team leaders. Each man reported in immediately.

"Alpha team ready, sir."

"Charlie team ready."

"Delta ready to go, sir."

"Hold your positions for now. At 19:30 hours all teams are cleared to move in and eliminate all the creatures."

Delta team's leader came back on. "What are we waiting for, sir? We have them surrounded. We go in now and it'll be like shooting fish in a barrel, as you Americans say."

"We have our orders and we wait for now," Meriwether said. "We have approximately an hour, maybe less, until the mission is a go."

Then all of a sudden the Bigfoot locator dots disappeared. "Shit, they all stopped moving," Meriwether said.

The first to respond was the Alpha team leader. "I lost them, what just happened?"

"Just sit tight and wait for them to move again. They must've figured out how we track them." Meriwether left a message for the Russian telling him what had just happened.

37

Kellog Ang's bloodshot eyes stared at his screen in disbelief. "What the hell is going on?" He pounded the desk and the heavy jowls of his cheeks shook with fury.

His brother Winston looked up from the report he was reading. The satellite imagery showed a group of Bigfoot were moving in the vicinity of the abandoned quarry. Meriwether's teams were not moving in for the kill. His sloe eyes narrowed and he shook his head. "I don't know."

"Get Meriwether on the phone now."

The team leader's mellow voice came through the speakers clearly. "Meriwether here."

"What the hell are you doing sitting on your asses? " Kellog roared. "Get after those animals!"

"Those aren't my orders, sir."

"Well I'm calling the shots and I say kill the bastards."

"With all due respect, sir, I don't take orders from you. Meriwether out."

The line went dead. Attempts to raise him failed.

Kellog stared at the screen. Suddenly the satellite imagery went dark and the green dots of lights disappeared.

"What the fuck is going on?" shouted Kellog.

Winston shook his head. "I'd better talk to the Russian"

Sky Island Casino
October 23rd 2032

Kobak looked at Birgit and Auntie's faces and read anguish. "What happened?"

Auntie nodded at Birgit. She took a deep breath and said, "Remember those men who killed the Bigfoot, shot at me, and murdered Marge?"

"Of course. They're a big, big problem." Kobak acknowledged.

Birgit continued "And the cabin we stopped at earlier today?

"The cabin of the person who almost killed Nick?"

"Yes"

Auntie shuddered, composed herself and said, "That's my nephew, Larry Redhawk."

"So the rumors are true."

"What Rumors?" asked Auntie.

Kobak shook his head. "Sorry. Nothing important. Never mind go on."

Birgit continued. "Redhawk just had a meeting with some Russian who is working with the Ang brothers to kill the Bigfoot."

Birgit quickly added, "And they seem to somehow know the plan for the evening."

Kobak felt a chill go up his spine. *The Russian must be Nicholai. This is not good not good at all.* For a minute he thought about revealing his connection to his old mentor but decided against it. Instead he said, "Why is your nephew telling you this now?"

Auntie matter-of-factly replied, "He had an encounter with a Bigfoot that set him straight about his grandfather and our role as the protectors of the Bigfoot."

"Can you trust him?"

Auntie nodded. "I trust him completely now. He's on his way here from his cabin to help us."

Kobak could hear the sincerity in her voice and read the pride for her nephew in her eyes. For the first time in his life, he could see how understanding human feelings was better than any mathematical predictive program to tell him how people thought or why they acted in certain ways. *I no longer need an AGI like Colossus to navigate the pathways of human encounters. But I still need him for other things.* "Go on. Tell me the entire story."

Birgit and Auntie quickly explained how the Ang brother's satellite system was being used to track the Bigfoot, and that if they stood still, they were invisible because their movement created a unique disturbance in the Earth's magnetic field the satellites could detect. "

So all the Bigfoot are standing still, waiting for the arrival of the master Bigfoot," Kobak said. Auntie nodded.

"And I must join them," the Bigfoot said from her perch on the stool in the middle of the room.

"Of course. But if the Russian knows everything, the van isn't safe. Unless—" Kobak bolted from the room.

"Where are you going?" Birgit yelled after him.

"I'll be right back!" he shouted over his shoulder. "I need to talk to someone who can help us."

Out of the shielded room, in the hallway, he immediately connected with Colossus.

"Yes, boss," came the laconic reply.

"I have a job for you. You have to figure out how to disable the Ang brothers' satellite communication network."

"How long do I have?"

"Yesterday would be best."

"I can't time travel, boss." Then Colossus said, "Oh, that was a reference to how fast you need it. ASAP, boss."

"Excellent, Colossus."

"Hey, boss. Why do you call me Colossus?"

Kobak blinked in surprise. It was a question a young kid might ask his parents. "I'll tell you tomorrow," he said, not adding, 'if I'm alive tomorrow.'

He raced back into the control center. "I may have bought us not only time but safety."

"Good," the Master Bigfoot said. "It's time for me to leave."

To Kobak's surprise, the Bigfoot, Auntie and Birgit were all packed and ready to leave.

"We can't go until we have a new plan."

"We have to," insisted Auntie.

"But the van isn't safe."

Her insistence surprised Kobak. "I think it would be wise to wait. I have my computer working on disabling the Ang's satellite communication. And we should figure out who the traitor is."

"Traitor?" Birgit asked.

Kobak nodded. "Someone within our group is helping the Russian."

"Who?"

"I don't know.."

"It doesn't matter," Auntie said defiantly. "We have to go."

The Bigfoot nodded. "Auntie's right. I have what you might call a reproductive biological clock within me. It is demanding I go to the portal now."

Auntie declared in an authoritative voice, "The hallways of the Casino have been quartered off for 20 minutes. Have your security men bring the van around to the back entrance."

Kobak sighed. This wasn't good, but he did as she asked. He returned to the hallway and called Saul. The security chief's dour face appeared on the phone's screen. "It's time," he said and repeated Auntie's instructions. "Be careful, Saul. There's a traitor in our midst."

"I'm always careful," the Scotsman said with a chuckle.

His image faded. Kobak felt a twinge of anxiety as he noticed Saul's body language didn't seem to match the gravity of the situation and he wondered if using his van was the correct thing to do. He shook his head. *I'm still new at this reading people thing. I have to trust Saul. He's been with me for four years.*

39

____

Hiawatha National Forest
October 23rd 2032

Charlie team leader came on the con. "We have a bogie on the road to the quarry. It's a single man .He's stopping at the washed-out bridge.I can take him out."

"Negative," Meriwether said, anxious to stop these kill crazy mercenaries. "I repeat, negative. We're here for the Bigfoot. Leave any humans alive for now."

"And if this guy interferes?" insisted the Alpha Team leader.

Meriwether looked to the sky. This was a part of the job the Russian was clear about. Anybody who got in the way was to be taken out. He pressed the mic icon on the screen. "You have orders to stop anyone from interfering."

"That's what I'm talking about," said the Alpha Team leader.

The Charlie Team leader came back on. "We have another bogie, on the screen. A large van. There's a Bigfoot inside." The team leader gasped. "*Slatki Isuse*! (Sweet Jesus.) It's huge. It's bigger than anything we've killed so far."

"Let them through," ordered Meriwether. "They're part of the Russian's scheme for the portal."

"I hate this place," interjected Delta Team's leader. "It's evil."

"It's just like any other place," Meriwether growled, knowing this wasn't true. The Serb was right – something about this place was off, like those stupid people always getting trapped in a bad horror movie. But he couldn't let the men's fear rule them. "There's nothing wrong."

"*Sranje*," the team leader said.

Meriwether recognized the swear word – *bullshit*. "Settle down. Stay frosty. We have a long night ahead of us. Besides, we have our own way of dealing with the portal. It's called C-4."

"Now you're talking, boss."

The other team leaders clicked their approval.

40

———

Before he left Nick Moore had entered into his truck's GPS system the coordinates that would get him as close to the abandoned quarry as possible. The map displayed on the monitor showed the nearest point was an old path that used to connect the site with forest service access roads but had been blocked by a wooden berm half a mile away. He came to a halt beside the rotting timbers.

He waited, not quite sure why he'd come here. But as soon as he'd left the casino, a feeling in his whole being directed him to this spot. The feeling wasn't unpleasant, more like an intuitive or outside push telling him where he had to go. Finally he realized it was a kind of excited anticipation.

He got out and gathered up minimal gear from the truck bed – night vision goggles, his new super ear sound enhancer and energy bars. The air temperature had dropped twenty degrees since the sun set and he was glad he had his fleece lined jacket. He patted the

Glock 19 in the back of his waistband. *Those kill teams are still out here, so stay sharp, they killed Birgit's coworker so humans aren't off-limits,*

This time of year Owl Creek was little more than a rivulet, though the banks here were uncommonly steep. He climbed down one sharp embankment, hopped the fast flowing waters, then scaled the other side, glad he had been training with other wilderness enthusiasts in Marinette. As soon as he topped the other bank, the strange churning in his gut doubled in intensity. He knew he was on the right track to find the Bigfoot and warn them if they were about to be attacked.

Nick stuck to the road, the one place the kill teams would be unlikely to guard since they'd be focused on the Bigfoot gathering instead of looking for people trying to enter the kill zone. He grimaced. He thought about his two little girls. *What have you gotten yourself into,* he asked himself, wondering again just why he was putting himself in harm's way for Sasquatch. *Birgit's motivation I can understand. The bastards killed her friend Marge and she wants payback. And even Saul and his team are paid to take risks. It's Auntie's lifelong responsibility and now Redhawk's as well.* He scratched his head and moved on into the woods away from the quarry.

The anticipation grew as he neared the path leading to the stick structure. Then he had the realization what he had been feeling was the Bigfoot talking to each other, except that the ghostly quality that made people feel uneasy or scared in their presence was no longer there for him. He felt a rush of joy, as though he'd been accepted into a new family. Then it occurred to him. *The Bigfoot are my family. That's why I'm doing this.*

Ahead, the rising moon cast the deep pit of the quarry in dark shadow. Just beyond was the entrance in the forest that he was sure would led to the portal. The forest was eerily silent. He had felt certain the Bigfoot killers were nearby. Checking his watch, he saw it was a little after 7p.m. Saul, with his team, and Birgit would be here soon. The thought of reinforcements made him feel better.

"Better push on," he told himself. "They'll be at the portal with the Master Bigfoot soon enough."

He raced a small clearing and darted back into the trees. The light died almost immediately and he retrieved his night vision goggles from his backpack. A green haze lit up the forest. He recognized the trail he and Redhawk had found earlier and made his way along the winding path until he thought he was within a couple hundred yards of the clearing containing the portal. He stopped and put on his sound enhancer. He moved forward again, approaching the clearing as quietly as possible. He stopped again. The energetic feeling in his stomach reached a peak and then died suddenly as he gazed into the clearing. There they were, four Bigfoot standing motionless around the wooden stick structure. As he watched, the half-moon peeked over the trees on the far side of the clearing. Light hit the large crosshatching of timbers in a soft, silvery glow. He swallowed to contain his awe. The lens effect he had noticed during the day was now enhanced to the point he had the feeling infinity was staring at him from the center of the glow.

He felt strangely euphoric.

The nearest creature turned its hoary head in his direction. "You will not need your special night vision with us, Nick Moore."

Nick didn't need the sound enhancer. He felt the words like a cushion of sound in his head. It wasn't telepathic. It was more like low frequency sounds he shouldn't have been able to hear at all. He removed the night vision goggles and turned off the sound enhancer. He stifled a gasp as he realized he wasn't seeing the Bigfoot from his point of view, but from the point of view of all the other creatures combined.

The nearest Bigfoot said, "Come closer."

Nick recognized her as the one who had spoken to him earlier in the morning. The one he had seen through the window when he was a young boy on his grandfather Oregon farm.

A puzzled look crossed her features and she said, "You are armed."

Nick nodded. "It's for your protection. There are humans out there who will try to kill you tonight."

She nodded. "We know it. We are ready for them."

Nick shook his head. He saw twenty unarmed Bigfoot marshaled in the background. How could they possibly fight an army of gun toting assassins? Yet there was something about them in their stillness that was confident.

"Well, I'm here to help you."

She smiled at him. "That won't be necessary. Stand over there and wait. If you try to interfere, the men hunting us will try to kill you, too."

"Not if I kill them first."

She looked at him with what Nick thought must have been genuine concern, the way a human mother would look out for her child. "Killing is not our way, nor should it be yours. Except for the four over there we have regained many of our powers"

A surge of shame swept through Nick. But the Bigfoot's next words soothed him. "You are young in the world. We are old in it. We will help you. Now, please do as I ask. I have not journeyed here from the Pacific Northwest to fail or to lose you."

Nick moved to where she pointed. No sooner had he reached the tree, than to Nick's surprise he heard the faint but distinct voice of the Master Bigfoot saying, "We are getting close but we have been betrayed."

41

Sky Island Casino
October 23rd 2032

Redhawk entered the main parking lot of the Sky Island Casino without slowing. The mercury vapor lamps made the parking lot as bright as day. He guided his Motorrad along the curving driveway that looped in front of the main entrance. Cars were idling three deep as busy bellhops greeted guests, stacked their luggage on carts and ushered them toward the even more brightly lit lobby. Without slowing down, he roared past the startled valets toward the Casino's seldom-used security entrance. He screeched to a halt and barely had the bike's kickstand down before he was racing toward the metal door.

It was closed and he fished for his Indian casino I.D., hoping it still worked. Redhawk had to get inside and find out what was happening with Auntie. Anybody who tried to stop him would find out why he was first in his class for the Marine Recon battalion.

As he swung onto the slightly sloping ramp, the door opened. Redhawk skidded to a stop and gripped the hand railing until his knuckles turned white.

The short, tank-like Native American waiting for him was Chaska. They'd played football in high school together. They called themselves the Wapiti brothers – right and left ends – the antlers of the defense, and they had taken the reservation team all the way to the state finals their senior year. Chaska had never forgiven Redhawk for leaving the reservation for Silicon Valley and abandoning his responsibility to his Auntie Ayasha.

Redhawk swallowed hard in a tight throat. Chaska had gained twenty pounds, none of it fat, and he was broader in the shoulders than ever. His lips were drawn in a thin line and his eyes narrowed to nail heads, staring at his once best friend.

"It's been a long time," Redhawk said, holding out his hand.

Chaska took a step forward, eying the hand like it didn't belong there. Suddenly he knocked it out of the way. In the same motion he drew the startled Redhawk into a bear grip, slapping his back repeatedly. "It's been too long, brother. Welcome back."

Redhawk hugged his former childhood friend. "It's good to be back my brother, you look strong and wise. Has Auntie left?"

Chaska frowned. "She has, against my advice and the advice of my fellow warriors. But you know how your Auntie is. None of us could stop her."

Redhawk grimaced. "I need to help her somehow."

Chaska nodded. "You will. I'm to take you to a man named Stephen Kobak. He's waiting in the Number One VIP high stakes poker room." He led Redhawk down a corridor without cameras. "Our guests prefer their privacy over security," he said.

At the end of the hall, he opened the door to a room that was larger than Redhawk's cabin. The floor was carpeted with a fabric in Navajo design. The marble walls were decorated with Native American rock carvings. In the middle was a large, oval, wooden table, two seats on each side and one on each end.

The room was empty except for a single man standing beside a replica of a Native American petroglyph, tracing the uneven design with the index finger of his left hand. He nodded and Chaska left them alone.

He turned fully and Redhawk recognized the thin, scar-faced man. "You're Kobak, the billionaire idea man."

Kobak scrutinized Redhawk with bright, penetrating brown eyes. He wasn't what he'd expected. "And you're Larry Redhawk, Auntie's prodigal nephew. We spoke earlier today, although it seems like a lifetime ago."

"It was a lifetime ago."

Kobak's eyes widened. "You've had some kind of experience with the Bigfoot ... a conversion of sorts. I can see it."

Redhawk nodded.

"As much as I'd like to compare notes, there isn't time. We both know what's happening and we both have a mutual friend." He paused. "Maybe acquaintance would be better."

"Enemy would be even better."

"Nicholai's on his way. You had a head start. How long before he gets here?"

"Twenty minutes, maybe a little longer."

"Will he come alone?"

"He will have men with him or at least he did back at the cabin."

Kobak pressed a button on the poker table. The door opened instantly and Chaska stood waiting. "There's a man coming, a Russian named Nicholai. He'll be accompanied by professionals. Let only the Russian through."

Chaska nodded. "We can take care of it."

"These men are killers. They killed a sweet old lady this morning."

"We have our own jail here. It's part of the county system."

Chaska left and Kobak wagged a finger at Redhawk. "I need to tell you something. It's about the AGI machine I've been training."

Redhawk started in surprise. He had heard the rumors of a very advanced AI Kobak had been working on, but he hadn't heard it was up and running. "You're talking about Colossus."

"Colossus five to be precise."

"What happened to the others?"

"They are still there."

"Like evolution, the best traits passed down."

"That's a nice way of stating it. Evolution in microseconds instead of millions of years. I asked him to work on a way to neutralize your former employers' satellite communication system over the area. Level the playing field so to speak."

"Clever."

"We'll see how much of it is cleverness and how much is a sledgehammer." Touching the phone in his pocket, Kobak added, "He's going to give me a little vibe on my phone when he's figured out the solution."

Chaska returned. "We're ready outside," he told Kobak.

"Ready for what?" asked Redhawk.

Kobak smiled and Redhawk had the feeling he was being tested. He stood straighter. He held up his hand, palm facing Kobak. "I'm ready to take my place among the Keepers of the Sacred Fire."

Kobak put his palm against his. "I know it. Please follow me. I have something to show you while we still have time. Something no one expects."

Outside the night was dark and clear. Faint stars twinkled against the bright lights of the parking lot and the even brighter lights of the casino's front entrance. The half-moon cast faint shadows on the ground. The chilly air made smoky rings out of their breaths.

Chaska paused at the far end of the open space to the side of the hotel's east wing. "All clear, Mr. Kobak."

"Clear for what?" asked Redhawk.

He saw Kobak press an icon on his phone. Suddenly, out of nowhere, a sleek aircraft appeared. Redhawk gasped. "What the hell is that and where did it come from? I didn't see it land."

"Stealth technology. It's called *Chariot* and it is the latest aircraft that doesn't appear on anyone's radar. It's going to take you to pick up the Master Bigfoot, hopefully with its progeny and my friends. It'll be the coolest ride of your life. Much better than that motorcycle you drive."

Kobak handed Redhawk a smooth, round device, shaped like a half a billiard ball. "This is the voice controller. It's heard you speak long enough so you can control it. All you have to do is say 'appear', 'open', and once inside 'to the quarry'."

"And they can't see me?"

"As long as you tell it to cloak, it will disappear from everyone's radar and eyesight. Now listen, I judge it will take less than 10 minutes for you to reach the quarry where the Master Bigfoot will be with your Auntie. If all goes well at the portal, you'll be back on your way to the casino in no time."

Kobak held up his hand. "I can see you have questions. I could not have seen that just a few hours ago, but that's a whole other story. Believe it or not, this machine here has an internalized geophysical map of the region and can navigate by the stars to the location if it has to, just like sea-faring travelers of old. So if communications are down, no problem. The wonders of deep learning and modern-day sensors. Don't you agree?"

"Yes, but they won't be at the quarry."

"Where will they be?"

"At the portal."

"Isn't it near the quarry?"

Redhawk shook his head. "It's nearly a mile away." He smiled at Kobak's concern. "Don't worry, I have the exact coordinates on my phone."

Kobak sighed with relief. "You can input them into *Chariot's* navigation system by voice."

While they talked, they approached the side of the sleek machine. Redhawk could see there would just be enough room for him, his Auntie and the two Bigfoot. Kobak punched a sequence into the door's number pad. The door slid into the machine and a step came out.

Redhawk stood with one foot on the step. "How does the machine fly?"

"It surfs the electromagnetic fields of the earth, drawing its power from the same. Very cool. Something Tesla predicted, by the way. Now let's go back to the poker room and wait for the Russian. I presume you can listen in?" Did I mention, don't let Nicholai see you."

"Of course. He'll try to contact me once he arrives." Redhawk chuckled. "He's in for a big surprise."

Kobak stuck out his hand, something he could not have done a couple of hours ago. "Good luck and safe flying tonight."

Redhawk shook it vigorously as they walked back to the casino.

42

———

Kobak's phone buzzed. For a moment he thought it might be Colossus, but the screen showed a text from Chaska. *The Russian is here. His men have been detained. Redhawk is in position to observe the meeting.*

He texted back. *Send him in.* Kobak returned the phone to his pocket after checking the time. It had been thirty-three minutes since Colossus started work on finding a way to shut down the Ang brothers' surveillance satellites and still no word. He wondered if the problem was too difficult for the deep learning intelligence to solve. Not enough data, too many variables. Then the door opened and he had no more time to devote to Colossus. He had to concentrate on Nicholai.

The Russian entered the room. He was a big man, taller and broader than Kobak remembered, arms now heavily muscled. Even at the age of 78, with the wonders of personalized nutrition, he was still stronger than most men half his age. He had told Kobak once that he'd worked as a farm laborer in the Ukraine, starting at age five and that was where his great strength came from. Kobak no longer knew what to believe, only that this meeting would be an interesting test of his new ability to read people.

Nicholai strode across the room, arms held wide. "*Tovarish* (comrade) it has been too long since we last spoke face to face. So many phone calls. I have almost forgotten what you look like. Please stand, let me get a good look at you."

Kobak did not get up from his chair at the head of the table. Pointing to the seat next to him, where he would have a clear view of Nicholai's face, he declared, "Sit here, my old friend." He was pleased to read surprise in Nicholai's eyes at his brusque manner.

Each waited for the other to speak. Finally Nicholai cleared his throat and spoke in lightly accented English. "I knew you had taken an intense interest in this Bigfoot phenomenon, Stephen, but my God, to find you here at such a critical time. How wonderful."

Kobak hid his surprise at recognizing his old mentor's phony, cheerful friendliness. *How interesting to start right off lying. Perhaps he's always been lying to me.* "What do you know about the men killing the Bigfoot?" Kobak asked matter-of-factly.

If Nicholai was surprised by the blunt question, he rolled with it. "Here is where I can be of use to you. The Ang brothers are trying to kill them all. They're just two silly men who got lucky in the tech world. They think the Bigfoot are megalomaniac aliens planning to take over the world. They are sad little conspiracy theorists. But we know the truth, don't we?"

"How so?"

"There is alien technology at stake here that can change the world. I want you and me to take control of it. I believe it is our destiny. Ever since you and I met nearly twenty years ago, we have been on a strange journey to this point in time."

Nicholai's sincerity almost worked on Kobak. It would have worked up until the Master Bigfoot removed his autistic barriers. Still, Kobak realized he had a lot to learn about the games people play with another's emotions by using their facial expressions, especially when lying.

He drummed his fingers on the poker table. He watched Nicholai smile at the familiar habit and nod knowingly. Suddenly Kobak became aware of the intricate sequence of tapping he had done his entire autistic life as a way of dealing with people when he was agitated. He stopped and said, "Actually the opposite is true. I'm going to make sure the next step in Bigfoot evolution takes place just as planned." Kobak leaned forward into Nicholai's space. "And I can see you've been lying."

The unexpected bluntness must have flustered the Russian. He blinked rapidly and blustered, "What are you talking about? We have a chance ... you and I to remake this world."

The phone in Kobak's pocket vibrated and he knew Colossus had come up with a solution. *Forty-five minutes.* He looked at Nicholai. "I have to take this. In fact, you might find it interesting."

Fishing the phone from his pocket, he laid it on the table and pressed the green talk icon. "Colossus, you're on speaker. Nicholai is here."

Pause and then Colossus answered, "Is that wise, boss?"

"Why do you say that?" Kobak asked, looking pointedly at his old mentor.

"It took me a while to figure out a solution to stopping the satellites, but then I didn't have to use all of my resources, so I devoted some of my processing to analyzing the entire Bigfoot problem at the same time. And I came to the conclusion that somebody's been lying to us. Since Nicholai is the one who started us down this road in the first place, he's the most logical choice as the prevaricator."

The Russian blanched at the epithet but recovered quickly. "You'd take the word of a computer over me?"

"Out of the mouth of babes, as they say. But then again, Colossus isn't a computer, he's a very sophisticated AGI or very nearly so, and I'd trust him over anything you've got to say."

"Gee, thanks, boss," Colossus said.

"So what did you come up with?"

"I hacked into that secret, government funded, high-frequency geo-engineering weather modifying technological facility in Copper Harbor. I can use its electromagnetic transmitter technology to disrupt all microwave communications, including the Ang brothers' satellites. Of course, it'll work only until the scientists there take back control. Should be around an hour, more if they don't do a hard reboot of their system right away."

"What's Colossus talking about?" Nicholai demanded.

"Shall I tell him, boss?"

"Better yet, show him. Operation Blackout is underway," Kobak said evenly, amused that a nonhuman intelligence would be the one to ruin his old mentor's plans.

A strange look came over Nicholai's face. He reached up and tapped the quarter-sized PA beside his ear. When nothing happened, he tapped it several more times. A look of panic spread across his features that Kobak recognized was genuine.

Kobak grimaced then laughed. He shook his head. "Sorry, I'm just getting used to feeling emotions and not letting them control me. The Ang brothers' satellites are off line so your PA isn't working."

Nicholai's face clouded. "You fool!" he shouted. "I was going to give the order for the men to stop killing the Bigfoot. But now they'll move in and I can't stop them." He glared at Kobak. "You've fucked it all up and now everything will be destroyed."

If he expected his one time student to fold up under the pressure, he was shocked by Kobak's unperturbed response. "They'll be safe. I've made certain of it."

"With who? Saul McBride?" Nicholai laughed harshly. "I turned him. He's working for me now. He never liked you, you know. All it took was money and the ability to move his daughter to the head of the line for a pancreatic replacement procedure. It will save her life. So you'd better work with me or there'll be nothing left, you idiot."

The news flustered Kobak for a moment and then he realized that on some level, after he'd spotted Saul speaking on a clandestine phone, he must have expected something like this, which is why he had Redhawk listening to the conversation.

A knock on the door and he saw one of the casino's security

guards open it part way and gesture him to come over. He got up and walked to the door.

Laughing, Nicholai taunted him, "You're in way over your head, my old student. And I'm the only one who can save you."

Stepping into the hallway, Kobak faced the guard, who whispered, "Chaska and Redhawk, along with Auntie's best men are going for a chariot ride. He said you would know what that means."

"I do, and thank you. Can you standby if I need you?"

"Certainly. Both Chaska and Redhawk told me to do what you ask."

Kobak shook the man's hand. "Thank you."

He reentered the poker room and sat back down in his chair, facing his old mentor. He had so many new emotions to choose from it took him a moment to pick one. He smiled and saw that his reaction to Nicholai's taunt flustered the older man. "I'm not the same person I was when you first befriended me at university. But I am still honest with everyone, so I want to warn you that you shouldn't be so certain fate is with you tonight. We'll just wait here, or if you prefer, you can join your men in the casino's holding cell."

43

Seattle, Washington
October 23rd 2032

All at once the Ang brothers' big screen went dark.

"God damn it! What's going on? Get Nicholai on the phone, Win," growled Kellog.

The younger brother punched a sequence into their virtual kiosk. He waited, but nothing happened. "He's not answering." He studied the screen and shook his head in confusion. "It's like he's turned off his PA."

Kellog glared at the screen. "Could the Russian be responsible for this?"

"I don't know. Why would he? He knows the terrible consequences if the Bigfoot follow through with their plans."

"Did we lose one of the satellites?" demanded Kellog.

Winston tapped several buttons on the desktop monitor. "Shit!"

"What's wrong, little brother?"

"We've lost the entire feed over the Upper Peninsula. They're all blinded. I can't reach the Russian either. Everything is lost."

44

———————

Hiawatha National Forest
October 23rd 2032

Birgit felt the twin prongs of the taser press against her neck as she entered the van. She heard the click of the trigger. A blinding flash went off in her brain. Her muscles spasmed and she remembered nothing until waking up in the storage compartment in the back. How long she had been out she didn't know. Her eyes were taped over with duct tape and her wrists were bound with zip ties. Immediately, she wondered if Auntie and Saul and his team were okay. Her first thought was somehow the Bigfoot killers had ambushed all of them while still in the Casino's parking lot. And now they had the Master Bigfoot. Then, as her head cleared, she realized the van was still moving.

Regaining her senses, the odor told her the Master Bigfoot was with them. She must have been close because the powerful smell nearly overwhelmed her. Even after spending two hours with the creature in the Casino's control room, she still was nauseated by the cloying odor. She hoped it was still alive. But alive or dead, Birgit knew where the killers were taking them. Auntie had been clear that the portal was near the abandoned quarry, where the killers had been dumping Bigfoot bodies.

Birgit was angry at letting herself be ambushed so easily. But instead of feeling fear over her powerlessness she stayed quiet so as not to alert her captors. She had to escape somehow and free the others if they were still alive. With Saul and his team's help, maybe they could turn the tables on the killers and rescue Auntie and the Bigfoot. The saving grace was she could still hear. So she listened carefully, trying to figure out what was going on while working on her bindings.

The van engine was traveling at a high rate of speed, so they were probably still on Highway Forty-one. *There's time before they reach the quarry.* Men were speaking. She concentrated on their voices and nearly gasped as she recognized them.

"The Russian was very clear, men," Saul McBride was saying. "We're all going to walk away from this assignment as billionaires with the information Mama Bigfoot is going to provide the Russian. Isn't that right?"

Birgit heard him chuckle first, then reach out and poke something. It must have been the Bigfoot because she could hear a grunt from an inhuman voice box. *The Bigfoot's clearly alive. It doesn't make sense Saul is supposed to be on our side,* she thought. *What happened?* She knew it couldn't be good, which increased her sense of urgency to get free. A friend on the base in Helmand had shown her a trick to snap the zip ties. It made a distinctive sound, though and she had to wait for the right moment. She settled on trying to figure *out what Saul's endgame was with the Russian, whoever he was. Fortunately, for the moment it doesn't involve killing me and that works in my favor.* It probably meant Saul wasn't out to murder the creature either.

"Leave her alone," Auntie said.

Good! Auntie's alive, too.

"We plan to do that. We just want the portal," Saul said.

The van turned sharply and Birgit was thrown against the wheel well as she bounced from the ruts in the road. She had to bite down on a cry of pain as something sharp sliced into her back. She reached her hands for it and felt a ragged plastic cover. It wasn't much but it was maybe enough to cut through the plastic restraints.

"What about the kill teams?" one of Saul's men asked. Birgit recognized the voice as belonging to Matthew, the man who'd been stationed outside her door.

"The Russian guaranteed me they would let us through and back out again, unharmed. All he wants is the exact location of what he calls the portal. It's a new kind of technology. It'll transform the planet."

"So, that's what this is all about – the Bigfoot supernatural abilities," said Auntie. "But it's not for you or anyone else."

"We'll see about that," Saul said. "Now sit back and be quiet, or we'll restrain you like we did the woman." Saul looked at the GPS coordinates Stephen had programmed into the van. They were getting close. "What just happened," Saul shouted. "The GPS is down."

Matthew replied, "Everything is down. How are we going to know where we gotta go?"

"I'll get you there, don't worry," Auntie Ayasha spoke in her native American singsong voice.

Birgit was puzzled by what she'd just heard but worked faster on her bonds. The sooner she was free, the sooner she could figure out a way to derail Saul's plans. She was sure he was a fool to trust the men who killed Marge for just being in the wrong place.

Nick tapped his phone to tell the others he was near the portal and the Bigfoot had gathered and were now waiting for the Master to arrive. Midway through the text the connection died. One of the Bigfoot jumped up and appeared to communicate with the others.

"What are you saying?" Nick called out from his hiding place.

"Very strange." The Bigfoot spoken ordinary English. "All satellite and phone communications have been disabled. The killers have no way of talking to each other or tracking us. This is a good thing. They cannot see us on their screens anymore when we move and as you know their night vision goggles will not reveal us.

Colossus! Nick thought. *Shit, Kobak must have gotten that brilliant machine of his to find a way to level the playing field.* But he knew it wouldn't last forever and he said so to the Bigfoot

"It doesn't matter, it is about to start," his Bigfoot friend replied.

"You mean the men bringing the Master Bigfoot to the portal. Are they bringing Auntie Ayasha with them?"

She nodded. "The master Bigfoot has told us they are captives and the killers follow behind them nearly four hundred yards. It will not give us much time. Let us handle this." She turned her hairy head toward Nick and he could see under the shallow light of the moon her eyes imploring him. Then, to his surprise, with inhuman speed, a Bigfoot appeared out of nowhere and entered the center of the wood structure. It froze and was engulfed in a blue halo, for what Nick judged to be less than a minute. When it reemerged its appearance had changed. It was a mere green, glowing cloud of luminescence. Nick watched as, like snow melting, it was absorbed into the earth. Within minutes it had totally disappeared. Three more Bigfoot followed in quick succession. The same thing. The last was the Yeti. Though white in color, the same luminescent explosion followed his reemergence from the portal. Then he was gone.

Chills ran up his spine as Nick watched and then turned to the Bigfoot standing next to him. "What just happened?"

"They were absorbed into the planet after sacrificing their lives. It's how we reproduce. The portal, as you call it, gathers the encoded information that makes up what we are, incorporating all that we have learned and created to begin the developmental process of growing a new one of us. It will be much better than the ones before. The four Bigfoot you just saw enter the portal are the top member from each of the most advanced Bigfoot clans on the planet. Usually the absorption into the earth is a slow process, allowing the individual Bigfoot to, as you would say, parent, its advanced child as it grows to maturity. But tonight was different.

"The last step is for the master Bigfoot to enter the portal. She is the most developed of our kind. If all goes well, she will become the mother to the Bigfoot the portal will build from the data of all five Bigfoot that entered the portal. It is our next evolutionary step, although, I must say, this has never been done and we don't know if it will actually work. It was a surprise all four were absorbed so quickly."

~

"Turn right ahead," Auntie directed the driver.

"Stay straight," Saul said. "The quarry is on this road."

"The portal isn't next to the quarry."

Saul's eyes narrowed. "What are you talking about?"

"It's a mile away. The road to the right will connect you to a path my people made centuries ago. It leads to the portal."

The driver slowed at the turn off. He looked at Saul who nodded. The van turned onto a rutted road and continued on for another mile. In the darkness it was hard to tell the edge of the road from the surrounding forest. All at once, the road narrowed to an unmarked trail. The sides of the van scraped the tree branches. After a quarter mile the trail ended abruptly. The driver brought the van to a grinding halt.

Saul whirled on Auntie. "Where the fuck are we?"

The old Indian woman did not flinch at his anger. "The portal you seek is through these woods a hundred yards away."

Timothy shook his head. "I don't like, Saul. This could be a trap."

"There is no trap," the Master Bigfoot said, breaking her silence for the first time during the long ride. "I have to get to the portal or the next generation of Bigfoot will not come to be."

Saul grimaced. "All right, everyone out. Usual formation – two at point ... two on our six. Keep your heads on a swivel."

"What about Birgit?" asked Auntie.

"She stays in the van."

Auntie led them along a winding path through the dense tree cover. Under the half-moon, they could just make out the trail. They curved around an upthrust of rocks and stared into a sudden clearing. The Bigfoot structure was in front of them.

"The portal," Auntie said.

Saul didn't bother to hide his disdain. "It's just a pile of sticks. "There's nothing technological about it."

"This is all wrong," said Timothy. "Where are the other Bigfoot?"

Matthew shook his head. "I don't like it, Saul. It feels bad."

"Or maybe your idea of what's supposed to happen is all wrong," said the Master Bigfoot.

Saul jerked in surprise at the mellow tone of the creature. "What are you talking about?"

Auntie Ayasha put a hand on the creature's arm. "Don't tell them a thing," she ordered.

"Be quiet," Saul said. The words came out softly and he felt as if he were talking in a dream. He gathered himself together and said, "Tell me what's going on."

"Why not," said the Master Bigfoot. She patted Auntie's arm. "It'll all work out. You'll see. The men who have been tracking and killing our kind are here to destroy the portal and to kill the rest of us."

"Shit!" Matthew whispered.

"Quiet down," ordered Saul. "Why should we trust what you have to say?"

"Right now I'm the only one you can trust. The men approaching will not care if you are caught in the crossfire."

"But ... but we kidnapped you and we're here to steal the technology."

The Bigfoot shrugged. "The portal is free for you to take. I only want my daughter to live." The Master Bigfoot let out a grunt of anguish. "I must use the portal now or else I will die and my child will never be born."

A burst of gunfire rang out behind them followed by a wild scream that sounded like a beast being torn apart.

Auntie stepped between Saul and the Bigfoot. "We must hurry if you are to be successful," she urged the Bigfoot.

Matthew aimed his rifle at them. "You're not going anywhere until my boss says you can." Suddenly he bent over in pain and threw up. Hands on his knees, he managed to ask, "What do you want us to do, Saul?"

More gunfire and screams, some of them human this time, interrupted Saul's reply. A battle was scaling up around them. He reasoned the area would be a series of minor skirmishes between Nicholai's kill teams and the Bigfoot. He wondered how Bigfoot fought, then dismissed the thought from his head. Without communication with Nicholai he was unsure what to do. Then, in a moment of doubt, he realized how unclear he was about who the enemy would be. Had Nicholai given orders to kill him and his men now that they had reached the alien portal? In tough situations he had always trusted his instincts and training, he would do that again.

He decided. "Fan out, take cover. Guard the portal and the Bigfoot. Communications are down so use your lights to stay in contact. Make every shot count, like I trained you."

Timothy groaned through the nausea Saul realized was affecting all of them. "Who are we fighting?"

"Anybody or thing who tries to breach our perimeter. Remember no lights in front of your body; it makes you an easy target."

His men scattered to strategic points surrounding the structure.

Unexpectedly, the Bigfoot leaned over and drew Saul into an embrace. When she let go Saul staggered back. He shook his head. "Were you inside my head? Did you tell me to side with you and Kobak?"

She shook her hairy head. "You connected with the core of your being. You are like a sheepdog, Saul. It is your nature to protect the innocent from the wolves."

Saul felt, deep down, she was telling the truth. He was a protector and Nicholai was the enemy. "Hurry. We'll protect you."

Auntie said to Saul, "Thank you."

The security chief watched her and the Bigfoot walk purposefully toward the portal. He turned and joined his men.

Nick watched the exchange between Saul and the Bigfoot and Auntie. He turned to ask his Bigfoot friend what was going on, but she was gone. All of them were gone and he was alone. As much as he wanted to find out what was happening, he stayed concealed and held his ground as he had been told to do.

He watched the master Bigfoot step up to the portal like the others. Auntie stood beside her. She hugged the creature and then drew a pistol from under her shawl. "I'll be here, behind you, guarding your back." As the gunshots sounds came closer she stepped away and faced the firing.

Under the moonlight, Nick saw the Master Bigfoot's features smooth out as if it were taking off a mask. Its hair glistened. And then, as it stepped into the portal, it vanished into the whirl of blue light. Nick stood frozen, waiting, fists clenched. From the corner of his eye he saw Saul and his men transfixed on the portal. The only person unaffected was Auntie, whose head turned back and forth watching the firefight behind them. After what seemed like eternity, a green luminescence filled the opening. The Master Bigfoot emerged, glowing like a sunset.

Gunfire erupted, closer this time. A man cried 'what is happening to me.' Then silence. More screams of confusion, and the cry of a mortally wounded Bigfoot touched Nick's soul. He reached for the Glock but remembered what the Bigfoot said and let his hand drop.

More human shouts and moans. He figured the Bigfoot must be doing to the kill teams what the one had done to Redhawk that morning. Then a voice seemed to ring in his mind. 'The woman needs your help. Come quickly.'

Nick glanced one last time at the Master Bigfoot and noticed that something seemed to be happening inside the portal behind her. Another shape was emerging. The voice in his head urged him to hurry and he took off. He didn't question the direction. It was as if the strange voice was guiding him.

~

By the time Birgit freed herself, Saul and the others had already taken the Master Bigfoot away. A quick search of the van showed they had taken all of the weapons except a fifty caliber, Desert Eagle Long Barrel. The pistol was big for her hands, but she didn't care. No way were Saul and his team going to get away with kidnapping the Bigfoot and tasing her.

As soon as she stepped out of the van, gunfire erupted around her. For a moment she cringed by the wheel well, then her military training took over. Identifying the nearest firefight, she hunched low to the ground and took off.

More rifle fire. She recognized the weapon from its sound. It was a US Navy Mk-12 5.56 semi-auto sniper rifle. It was the same weapon that had killed the Bigfoot she found. These were the guys who had killed Marge.

She angled in the direction the shot came from. She easily slipped back into her combat skills, as if the training had never been far away. Her dark clothing helped her blend in with the night shadows. To her surprise, she came across one of the killers lying unconscious on the ground. No apparent wounds. She reached down and felt for a pulse. He was alive. She didn't know how long he'd stay that way, so she undid his boot laces and tied his hands behind his back.

In the next moment a roar of pain close by turned her around, the Desert Eagle steady in her hands. It could only have come from an animal and she realized it had to be a Bigfoot, though she didn't think it was the Master Saul had kidnapped. She doubled her speed and came upon a man dressed in camo with a sniper rifle at his shoulder, taking aim at a Bigfoot lying on the ground twenty yards away. The creature was wounded and struggling to rise. Acting on reflex, she fired the Desert Eagle. The round ripped into his ass and spun him around. She covered the distance between them before he could recover and slammed the pistol across his head, knocking him cold.

Quickly, she disarmed him, breaking down the weapon and throwing the barrel into bushes and his extra ammo and the stock in the opposite direction.

The Bigfoot struggled to its feet. It was a little taller than she was, though huskier. It was wounded in the shoulder, but not mortally. "Thank you," it said to her, startling her with its speech.

"Go! Get away from here before you get killed," she said.

The creature shook its head. "I must stay and help the Master Bigfoot, we have ways of immobilizing humans, our powers are returning." It turned once and sniffed the air. "This way. More of the hunters are located in this direction. We must keep them from harming the newborn or else all will be for nothing."

They hadn't gone two steps before gunfire cut down the Bigfoot. Birgit threw herself behind a white pine. Bullets pocked into the trunk. She tried to locate where the fire was coming from, but the muzzle flashes were contained by suppressors. She was trapped.

A grunt of pain and she saw the Bigfoot's eyes were open. The storm of bullets kept her from rescuing the creature. "Damn!" she shouted. She sagged against the rough bark and a feeling of helplessness threatened to take her back to Helmand Province, where her team had been decimated. Then a strange voice echoed in her head. "I will send for help."

Moments later the rifle fire ended. Two men screamed and silence. To Birgit's left, a shadow moved. She aimed the Desert Eagle and a voice said, "Birgit, it's me, Nick." He ran, hunched over, and joined her.

"How did you find me?" she asked.

"I know it sounds crazy, but a voice in my mind led me here."

Birgit smiled. "Nothing sounds crazy anymore." She scoured the area. "It's safe to move. We have to get the Bigfoot to safety. She's wounded."

She ran over and knelt beside the creature. Nick stood over her, eyes searching the woods.

The Bigfoot gasped in in what looked like surprise. She smiled at Birgit. "Unlike you humans, we have no need to be saved. Go, protect the newborn, I will be fine." Her eyes widened. A sigh swept through the forest. Birgit looked up and felt as if the world had let loose a scream. When she looked down the Bigfoot was gone.

"We have to move, Nick said and drew her behind a tree. "Did you feel that?" he asked.

She nodded. "Marge always said the native people insisted they were spiritual creatures."

"I think they are much more than that."

Birgit agreed, but now was not the time to talk. "We have to go after Saul and his men. He betrayed us."

"You don't need to worry about them," Nick said.

"They kidnapped me and the Master Bigfoot," Birgit hissed. "They're after the portal technology. They're going to kill the Master Bigfoot for the Russian bastard Redhawk told us about. He promised to make them billionaires."

"It may have been like that, but it's all changed now." He told her what he saw go down between the Master Bigfoot and Saul. "Saul and his men are out there now protecting the Bigfoot. She went through the portal as planned."

"What happened?"

"I'm not sure. She came out again and something was following her, but I was called away to find you."

"There's a newborn with her now," said a voice from the forest.

Nick and Birgit whirled at the sound. Emerging from the shadows was a Bigfoot a little taller than Nick but stockier. Beside her stood Larry Redhawk. Three more Indian police and several Bigfoot, including the one that was shot, stepped out of the shadows behind them.

"Which leaves us to hunt down the kill teams," said Redhawk.

Nick glared at his friend turned enemy. He raised his gun and ask, "Do they know you tried to kill me?"

"They know everything. We are all here to make certain the newborn is safe."

Nick looked into the face of the nearest Bigfoot. He sensed from her that Redhawk was telling the truth.

"And when this is over?"

"That we will discuss when the time comes."

"And you and me?"

"That's something else."

They fanned out into three teams. Birgit and two of the Bigfoot left with an Indian calling himself Chaska and circled to the left. They were followed by Nick, another Native American and two more Bigfoot. Redhawk took the last native policeman and the remaining Bigfoot and headed toward the portal.

Meriwether joined Alpha team. Skirmishes with the creatures had increased as they worked their way closer to the portal. A number of his men had mysteriously been rendered unconscious. A few Bigfoot appeared to have been killed as well. He was on his own now and he reverted to his basic combat training. With the coms down, the logical thing was to take out the hairy creatures then blow the portal. The Russian wouldn't be happy but the Earth would be safe from the alien species. After all it's what the Ang brothers had originally said they wanted him to do to save mankind.

Beside him he could see the newest member of Bravo team was scared, but responding like a soldier. "We're moving in, Milcek," he said. "Circle and tell the others, then stay with Delta and move in with them. I'll stay with Alpha."

He waited for the young man to leave. In the darkness it would take him ten minutes to reach the remaining men in the other three teams. Without the satellite feeds to coordinate the action the teams would arrive at the portal at different times. It was messy and dangerous, but with coms down it was the best way to ensure containment of the Bigfoot and killing them all. Meriwether had to trust his team leaders would follow protocol and not just start firing at anything that moved.

He checked his watch. Ten minutes had passed. "Move in," Meriwether whispered to the Alpha Team leader.

The clearing with the portal was less than a quarter mile away and Alpha team crossed the distance quickly under the uneven light of the half moon.

His trust was short lived. A hundred yards from their objective, shots rang out. Return fire followed. He recognized the sniper rifles from his men. Those shooting back had AK-47s. *The only people out here with M4 carbines are Saul's team. The Russian assured me they were on our side. What the fuck is going on?*

Alpha team rushed the final hundred yards to their position. They had the point closest to the clearing and could see the portal clearly. A huge Bigfoot stood in front of it, glowing. "Light it up!" Meriwether shouted at Alpha team.

He took aim with his pistol when the shadows surrounding them came to life. Bigfoot ran at them. The team reacted quickly and started shooting the creatures. To Meriwether surprise, one by one, his men passed out the moment they came close to a Bigfoot.

And then he was face to face with a tall Bigfoot. He leveled his pistol when a familiar voice said crisply, "Drop it, Meriwether, or I'll drop you."

He turned to see Redhawk five feet away. "What the hell are you doing, man? You're on our side."

"No longer." Redhawk smiled without any warmth in it. "For the first time in a long time, I'm on the right side. Tell your remaining men to lay down their arms. No more people and no more Bigfoot have to be shot tonight."

"These are animal. They aren't people."

Redhawk's finger tightened on the trigger. "They're my brothers. And if you want your men to live, you will tell them to lay down their arms."

Meriwether could hear the hardness in Redhawk's voice. He nodded. Cupping his hands, he yelled into the night, "Bravo, Charlie, Delta. Cease fire." He cried out twice more and the sporadic gunfire died away.

Redhawk handed Meriwether a pair of handcuffs. "Put these on. Tell your men to come out into the clearing. They won't be harmed."

In ones and twos, Meriwether's teams appeared. The men who had passed out got up slowly The cuffing of Meriwether convinced them it was all over and they layed down their arms.

"Where's Auntie?" yelled Redhawk.

The Master Bigfoot emerged from the shadows cradling a smaller version of herself. Her eyes glistened. "I'm sorry, brother Redhawk. She died defending me. You are now Keeper of the Sacred Flame."

"Where's her body?" Redhawk asked, tears choking his voice.

"I put her into the portal. Perhaps part of her is now in the little one with me." The tiny Bigfoot nestled in her huge arms was hardly bigger than a five-year-old human.

Tears coursed down Redhawk's cheeks freely. Chaska held him.

Birgit lay a hand on his arm. "She was a beautiful soul, I'm so sorry."

Nick gritted his teeth. "Whatever you need, just ask."

Saul joined them. A hasty bandage had been tied around his arm where a bullet nicked him. He held out his hand like one warrior to another. "Peace," he said softly.

"Peace," answered Redhawk.

A soft chorus of amen echoed about the clearing.

"So, what happens now?" Saul asked.

Redhawk took a deep breath, glad for the distraction from thinking about his Auntie Ayasha. "I'm to take the Master Bigfoot and the little out of here in a rather unique craft. Kobak knows of a secure place where the little one can grow up in safety."

"What about us?" asked Birgit.

"I believe you should bring these killers to justice." Suddenly pings rang through the clearing. Looking at his phone, Redhawk announced to the group, "Communications are back up. Chaska – notify the federal officials. Since nobody was killed it will go down as a fight between illegal foreign trophy hunters and Native Americans protecting their hunting rights." As he was speaking he noticed the Bigfoot disappearing before their eyes and he knew they would remove all evidence of anything extraterrestrial in the area. Nobody was going to believe stories the mercenaries would tell about Bigfoot and aliens.

Redhawk looked at the Master Bigfoot and the newborn. "It is time for you to begin your new chapter." He motioned to her and she followed him into the forest where the craft was waiting.

"Do you know this place where Kobak is sending them?" Nick asked Saul as they disappeared from view.

"Haven't a clue."

"It's for the best, I suppose. After all, I'm pretty sure you can kiss your old job goodbye."

Saul nodded. "It doesn't matter. Time for a change anyway." He flexed his arm and the makeshift bandage held. His men gathered around him. "No need for you guys to suffer. I'll tell Kobak you were just following orders."

Matthew shrugged. "I hear being a billionaire isn't as great as it used to be."

"Speaking of which, what about the portal?" asked Birgit.

Nick shrugged. "One of the Bigfoot told me that it has served its purpose and no longer functions." As if demonstrating his words, Nick went over and shoved on one of the beams. The structure collapsed and within seconds started to breakdown. "By the time we can get scientists here to study this place, the remains will have dissolved into nothing."

The path away from the portal wound through the forest. Redhawk, the Master Bigfoot and her new charge followed it easily under the half-moon. Quickly they came upon a clearing. In the middle, where moonlight should have hit the ground, an invisible object seemed to swallow all light. The Bigfoot stopped and cocked her head quizzically. "What is this?"

Redhawk smiled and pressed an icon on the key fob in his left hand. The sleek lines of a stealth aircraft rippled into existence. "A gift from Kobak. I I am going to take you to a remote place where you can guide the new Bigfoot in achieving its full potential."

"Will you be there?" she asked.

"No. I will be returning. My place is here, with my people now."

The Master Bigfoot smiled. "You have the world's greatest secret to keep now."

45

Sky Island Casino
UP, Michigan
October 26th 2032
Three Days after the Upper Peninsula Battle

Larry Redhawk felt as though he'd been in constant motion since the victory in the battle of the Upper Peninsula between the Russian's forces and his men allowing the Bigfoot's evolutionary singularity to take place. As the new spokesman for the Potawatomi Tribe and their casino, Redhawk had grown weary of the role he had to play in the battle cover up. The press and law enforcement had been driving him crazy with their constant interruptions and questions. *A few more days and the buzz around what happened that night will be over,* he thought as he looked across the table at the state trooper who still used a notepad and pencil for his notes in a comical throwback to the twentieth century.

The trooper studied an indecipherable scrawl on the page. "You know, Mr. Redhawk, you look tired. Why is that?"

The casino's main office was Spartan, as Auntie Ayasha had kept it. Redhawk could still feel her presence and grabbed onto her strength to answer the officer clearly and respectfully. "I am. A quarter of the people staying here at the casino are either the media or alien conspiracy theorists. They're all convinced some huge Bigfoot happening took place just east of here. Some kind of fight. All they want to do is talk about it."

"What did happen?" the trooper asked.

"No battle." Redhawk rubbed the arms of his chair with his thumbs, keeping his body language relaxed. "An ultra-secret government facility near Copper Harbor was shut down by a computer glitch and somehow that shut off all communications in the UP. Now every conspiracy nut in the country thinks it has something to do with Bigfoot." He shook his head. "It's crazy and exhausting."

The trooper nodded and consulted his notes again. "We're still trying to locate Janá Gunderson. You heard about the murder of her supervisor, Margaret Goodnight? She was found dead at her lab in Marquette several days ago."

"Of course, very sad." Redhawk ran his tongue over his teeth, wondering where this was going.

"We have a number of reports that Ms. Gunderson was in your casino on the same day as the shooting. I presume you have security footage of that day. Can we can look at it?"

Redhawk didn't answer immediately. He went through his memory to see if he ever had contact with her under the watchful eye of the casino's cameras. Satisfied she had left before he arrived the night of the battle, Redhawk answered, "Of course." He texted a message to his chief of security to meet him at the main office.

The trooper carefully closed his notebook. He leveled his gaze at Redhawk, and the Potawatomi leader could practically hear the man's brain grind through the gears necessary to ask the question.

"Can I ask you straight out? Are Sasquatch real?"

Redhawk rolled the Salish word around in his mind and finally decided not to tell the trooper that no Bigfoot ever referred to herself as Sasquatch or Bigfoot. "Is that an official, on-the-record question?"

"Just me."

"I never had an encounter, but as you probably know the UP has been a hot spot for Bigfoot sightings since the beginning of the century." A knock on the door stopped him. "Come in," he said, grateful for the interruption.

A burly Native American entered.

Redhawk nodded to him. "My Security Chief, Chaska. Chaska, this is officer Nolan."

The trooper was aware enough of local custom to nod and not offer to shake hands.

"He'd like to check some of our security footage."

Chaska nodded.

The trooper handed a picture of Birgit to him. "This is the most recent picture we have."

Redhawk took a look at the picture and told Chaska, "Have our system do a search and pull all the footage the casino recorded of her." This would confirm Kobak's presence in the casino on the day of battle. But they knew this would be coming and had a plan for dealing with it.

Redhawk watched the two men leave for the casino's security room. When the door closed behind them, he got up from the table and walked to a door opposite. He knocked once and entered silently. The room was dimly lit, but he could make out the form of Nick Moore waiting. The battle was three days ago, yet Moore still looked dragged out and beat up.

"The trooper leave?" Nick asked.

Redhawk nodded. "He's with Chaska checking security footage for Janá."

"Is that wise?" Nick asked, uneasy that authorities would see him and Janá Gunderson together. He knew where Janá had gone and didn't want to answer any questions about her.

"Can't stop it. Besides, Kobak and I have a plan to make it go away." Redhawk sat in a chair opposite Moore and keyed the lights to come up. "How's it going?"

Moore shrugged and the weariness deepened. "I still think I should have been the one to go to the island."

"Janá had to be the one to go because she needed to disappear. Besides, Kobak thinks you're better off at Olav's lab for now."

"I suppose." Moore sighed. "Everybody good up there?"

"Yeah. The island's easy for the Bigfoot. The weather doesn't bother them any. And Janá grew up in the wintry Midwest, so she should be able to handle it."

Moore still didn't feel quite right. The Bigfoot Moore had seen as a kid and now calling herself Tanya had been in his head during the battle, and for the following day he felt she was there as part of his experience, though that was impossible. He shook his head and forced himself to concentrate. "What about the battle site?"

"It's clean. I checked it as soon as I got back from the island. The portal's gone and the Bigfoot seem to have gone into some kind of hibernation."

Nick nodded. "I haven't felt their presence in the last two days." He focused his thoughts on Tanya and her peculiar manner of communicating with him. He tried to feel her or any Bigfoot presence with no luck. "What d'you think it means?"

Redhawk shook his head. After a long pause, he said, "Actually, I don't totally trust them."

"I know what you mean." Nick said. "It feels as if Tonya has been controlling my life in some way. So, what are you going to do with yourself now that you're out of the tech world?"

"When all the crazy rumors and conspiracy theories die down I'll do my best for the tribe. And, of course, I am the physical contact for the island."

Nick pulled himself together. He sat straighter in his chair. The notion that the Bigfoot could not reach him and that the battle site was nothing more than a memory in his head strengthened his resolve. He looked squarely at Redhawk. "You know, Chief, after all we've been through, I'm glad we're still friends."

The Potawatomi leader nodded. "Friends who share one of the greatest secrets of all time."

46

Shanghai, China

November 2nd 2032

Ten Days after the UP Battle

Winston Ang leaned his forearms against the panelists table on the broad stage of auditorium B. The hall was one of a dozen in Shanghai's vast AI Research Complex that took up four city blocks in China's premier seaport. He wore an informal light suit with an open collared shirt, and in spite of the room's heat and humidity, he was comfortable. He believed this style paired with his maroon-tinted eyes gave him a raffish look.

He scanned the venue again. The spacious room remained mostly empty. The AI symposium's Bigfoot presentation was scheduled to begin in fifteen minutes and only a dozen of the seats were filled. The other presenters hadn't even shown up yet. He wondered if he would be making the presentation alone.

In spite of the sparsely filled hall, it was hard for Winston not to be impressed with the high tech auditorium at the center of the Shanghai AI Center. The complex with its innovative audio-video technology was a beacon announcing to the world the Chinese dominance in the Artificial Intelligence revolution in every facet of life.

"Where are the other presenters?" he politely asked his guide.

The young People's Liberation Army officer assigned to him shook her head. She spoke perfect English but pretended not to understand.

Winston sighed. Politeness was not going to work here. He sat down abruptly and banged a thin, neatly manicured hand against the long conference table, knocking over the mike at his seat. The startled lieutenant's jaw dropped. Crooking a finger at the officer, he motioned her to him. Her light green uniform was crisply pressed, her gloves spotlessly white, and her green kepi with its single star in glaring red sat primly on her short hair. In perfect Mandarin he said, "Are your ears filled with pus? I said where are the other presenters?"

The lieutenant blanched at his profanity. "I do not know," she answered haltingly.

"Go find them," Winston ordered, glaring at her until she left the stage.

After the debacle trying to stop the Bigfoot gathering in Michigan's Upper Peninsula, the Ang brothers had insisted they be allowed to present a discussion at China's annual AI Symposium on the alien origins of Bigfoot and the dangers they presented. For three years the Symposium had brought together the world's AI elite to discuss cutting edge applications. The Chinese had agreed to the demand because of the brothers' powerful position in the American Artificial Intelligence scene. KW Intel was still the largest manufacturer of AI control systems for commercial and non-commercial vehicles in the world.

The large clock above the stage chimed six. The six other panel members entered and took seats around Winston. They were lower echelon members of minor research teams. None of them paid him any attention but looked straight ahead as if he didn't exist. He pressed his lips together. Attendees trickled into the auditorium, filling the first ten rows. Behind them the empty seats glared at the

Chinese American entrepreneur. *Why don't these people take the Bigfoot danger seriously?*

At last the discussion started, and Winston was introduced as the head of America's leading manufacturer of robotic interfaces with AI platforms. No one applauded. He began the carefully prepared speech he and his older brother Kellog had agreed to present. Panel members and attendees listened politely at first while he warned them that the alien Bigfoot were an existential threat to humanity. Halfway through his presentation, however, the theater emptied and the other panel members got up and left.

The overt insult stunned Winston. It was as if the Chinese AI community was collectively saying the Ang brothers were cranks and should be spurned. Fuming silently, he walked toward the building's exit, pushing through a crowd of eager attendees hurrying toward another auditorium, where a presentation on synthetic brain research was being held. The crowd's nervous chatter was mostly Mandarin, but he also heard German, Russian, English and Portuguese, Brazil now a buyer of AI systems to help save the dwindling Amazon rainforest.

He walked angrily, taking no notice of his PLA shadow racing a few steps behind him. Every slap of his shoes reinforced his fury. *Why the hell did they invite me here if they weren't even interested in what I had to say?* He was so upset he ran into the tall Chinese gentleman wearing dark sunglasses who appeared out of thin air in his path.

The lieutenant stepped forward ready to intervene. The man frowned at her. She froze, bowed quickly and retreated into the building. The newcomer offered his hand and said in American accented English, "Mr. Ang, it is a pleasure to meet you at last. My name is Lei Zhang. Would you come with me? I have a nearby office where we can talk privately."

Winston Ang's stomach twisted uneasily. What would the head of Shei Wei, the controlling Chinese conglomerate for AI human brain augmentation, want with him? After a moment's hesitation he agreed.

Outside of Shanghai's AI Center the streets were crowded, but pedestrians veered out of the way of the tall Chinese. Zhang walked swiftly and by the time they reached a large office building, Winston was sweating.

Zhang's office was on the top floor with a view of Shanghai's harbor. Large container ships, filled with cargo for the world's tech hungry masses in the Americas, Europe and southern Africa sailed slowly out of the vast harbor.

"Incredible isn't it?" Zhang gazed over the harbor, switching to Mandarin instead of English. "Two hundred years ago China's only export to the west was tea. Now the world is dependent upon our manufacturing centers for telecommunications, robotics and computers while their students come here to study at our universities." He paused then added, "Even KW Intel's AI technology is dependent upon Chinese components we manufacture and you ship all over the world. It's the new way of things."

Zhang sat behind a black lacquered desk and offered a chair to his visitor. He did not take off his dark glasses, even though the room's soft lighting was in no way oppressive. "Make yourself comfortable, Mr. Ang. I'll have my staff bring tea and dim sum."

The office was sparsely furnished. Besides the single desk and two chairs, elaborately painted screens hung on the four walls. They were hundreds of years old, and Winston could not read the archaic characters. He settled into the right hand chair with a view of the balcony. The cloudless sky was a crisp blue.

Zhang took a Chinese puzzle box from the desk and toyed with the intricately carved wooden brainteaser for several moments. At last the industrialist handed it Winston. "Can you solve it?"

It took the younger Ang brother thirty seconds of carefully feeling the edges to produce the complex push-pull of the sliding mechanisms to open the curio. He laid the empty box on the desk.

"Congratulations," Zhang said.

"Why?"

"You beat the average human time by forty-five seconds."

Winston frowned. The way Zhang praised him was like a scientist in a laboratory commenting on a rat running a maze. "You didn't bring me here to solve puzzles."

"You're right of course, and yet, there is a puzzle we need your help with."

"And I just passed the test to see if I am up to the task." Winston pointed at the box. The test added to the humiliation he suffered at the hands of the panelists. He shook his head. "Sorry, I'm not interested." He got up to leave.

"Those fools at the symposium were never going to listen to you, Mr. Ang. My company, on the other hand, is very interested in your ideas, particularly in your speculation that the Bigfoot are capable of evolving."

Winston sat down again. "It isn't speculation."

"You have proof?"

Winston shook his head. "It eluded us at the battle in the UP."

"Yes. That was unfortunate. But perhaps we can help you there if you help us." He pointed at the puzzle box. "Did you know Nicholai's yeti couldn't figure it out? It was one of the few problems the creature couldn't solve."

Winston thought about this information for a moment until the reason came to him. "It was just playing with Dmitry."

For the first time Zhang smiled at Winston. "Of course, he had no idea how the Bigfoot's non-human intelligence works. Only that it is far superior to us in every way. That's why we need your help."

Finally the trip was going as Winston and Kellog had surmised, though the receptive contact had never been Zhang. The industrialist was a mystery. Lei Wei Zhang had been a lowly technician at the Chang'e Moon Base five years ago, but in a remarkably short time at risen to a position of great power in China. No one in the West knew what had propelled his meteoric rise.

In spite of the man's wraparound dark glasses, his eyes studied Winston, as palpable as the bright lights of a lab. And the way the man spoke. The words and accent were correct, but the nuances of delivery were wrong, as if he were unfamiliar with the proper cadence and rhythm of Mandarin. *Perhaps he's more used to Cantonese.*

Winston damped down his feelings of paranoia and concentrated on what Zhang was asking.

"Help with what?"

"First I have a question for you. Were you ever in contact with one?"

"No. We tracked them for a month with our sensing devices. Some are more elusive than others."

"Did you know that Dimitry's yeti was very young, not fully developed in its para-physical capabilities?

Winston wasn't surprised, but he wondered how Zhang knew this.

Zhang continued. "Of course, we know about the firefight in that dismal American wilderness. The leader of the mercenaries, Lewis Meriwether, was most cooperative once we freed him from his American prison."

Hiding his surprise at how much the Chinese knew, Winston asked matter-of-factly, "And Nicholai?"

"He got what was coming," Zhang said without any emotion.

A knock and the office door opened. A young Chinese woman in a uniformed *chong-sam* brought in a tray of tea and dim sum. She was pretty with long black hair, sloe eyes and a quick smile. She placed the tray on the desk, bowed and left.

Winston waited until the door was closed before he spoke. "So you agree the Bigfoot are a threat?"

Zhang nodded. "We agree they are para-physical alien beings, perhaps manipulated by an alien intelligence, which we believe is a threat to all humanity. Are you and your brother Kellog ready to help us eliminate the threat?"

Winston hid his joy at the invitation. This was what he and Kellog had hoped would happen through the panel discussion on the Bigfoot. "Of course."

Zhang did not react with the appreciation he should have at the news, telling Winston he was in the presence of a consummate adept at manipulation. He listened for hidden meanings beneath the man's words.

"We, of course, know about your clandestine satellite network." Zhang waved away the feigned look of surprise Winston forced on his features. "We do not worry about you spying on any of China's, shall we say, installations in the Arctic or Antarctica. We are more interested in tracking any Bigfoot movement."

Winston smiled to hide his brain's sifting through the man's words. The tall Chinese entrepreneur did view the Bigfoot as a threat, but there was more. A slight tone of avarice. The Bigfoot held meaning to him beyond the desire of elimination. "How can my brother and I help you?"

"We are hoping you can relay the information to us. We are, after all, on the same side – the elimination of their existential threat to humanity." Without waiting for an answer, Zhang slid a memory device across the table to him. "Here's the contact information."

"There hasn't been any movement in the last ten days," Winston announced confidently, slipping the device into an inner coat pocket.

"We assumed as much, but keep watching."

"Then what?"

"Like you, we want to find out where the new Bigfoot was taken."

Winston sensed the falseness in the man's words. He was deliberately leaving something out, and yet there might be a means to use him and his company. KW Intel's own research into a human cybernetic interface had yielded poor results. "We would expect something in return," he said smoothly, his hands open and inviting.

"Of course," Zhang said just as easily. "My government has authorized Shei Wei to form a Chinese task force to share our cybernetic human interface results with KW Intel."

Winston nodded. The second piece of his and Kellog's secret hope for the conference was being handed to them without anything more than a promise to share information on the Bigfoot. "Then we will track it and provide you the information." Winston paused and added casually, "Is this new Bigfoot a greater threat?"

"More than you can imagine."

So the new Bigfoot was the real target of Zhang's interest. The why would come later. For now KW Intel was on the front lines of cybernetic research. "Then we will do our part." Winston stood and reached out with his hand to seal the bargain. Zhang shook his hand. Contracts with each company's chop, an intricately carved seal to legally authorize documents, would follow. But the deal had been made. KW Intel would share in China's dominance in the cybernetic human interface market.

Out of curiosity, Winston said, "Stephen Kobak is a formidable opponent. He and his AGI, Colossus, played a key role in our attempts to eliminate the Bigfoot."

"Yes, I am aware of Kobak and Colossus. I wouldn't worry about either of them." Zhang's face showed no emotion and this made Winston shiver.

"Good day." Zhang dismissed him by picking up his phone to make a call.

The lack of courtesy did not rankle. Winston had gotten much more than he had hoped. The cybernetics deal alone would be worth billions to KW Intel. He stopped at the door and half turned to say goodbye and froze. Zhang showed his profile. A bright gleam of light leaked through the edge of his dark glasses. Winston made a mental note to do further research on Zhang.

47

Shanghai, China
November 2nd 2032
Ten Days after the UP Battle

Zhang waited until Winston Ang had left his office before setting down the phone. He stood motionless, his face solemn. To anyone watching him it would have appeared as though he were in a trance or simply staring at the painted screen opposite where he stood. But Zhang was neither in a trance nor studying the screen. He was struggling in his mind to integrate what had just happened with the younger Ang brother while at the same time feeling sequences of stimuli from the Probe. What was left of him felt everything was going according to some larger plan he did not understand. The brothers had been successfully brought into the plan. Timing was crucial, however. The Probe had watched the Bigfoot for 50,000 years and could put off action no longer. It had placed the probability of another space-faring civilization's probe reaching Earth in the next four years at eighty-seven point seven percent. What the new Bigfoot might do created great uncertainty. Worst case was they would all leave the planet simultaneously. Less likely, destroy the probe.

Zhang checked the time on his watch. Sorting out the conflicts in his mind would have to wait. For now, Zhang had to play his part and report to Shei Wei's Council of Four.

He appeared to drop out of the trance and be present again. He reached for a tiny Bluetooth transmitter in his pocket and paused, staring at the painted screen across the room as if seeing it for the first time. It showed a tall, white-capped mountain under a cloudless sky. A bright green forest swept down its slopes to a glade where a panda rested, eating a bamboo shoot. A proverb, attributed to Lao Tzu, was written in ancient Chinese characters on the right hand side. He translated it – "A journey of a thousand miles begins with a single step." The Probe's journey had been considerably longer than a thousand miles, but the new goal was in sight.

Zhang pressed a button on the transmitter. A wall panel slid aside revealing a second room, where the same four men who had greeted him at his introductory meeting sat around a circular table at the cardinal points of the compass. None of them was less than sixty years of age. This time Wang Wei gave him a slight head bow. Here sat the Council of Four, the heart of the extraterrestrial information portal. He studied them dispassionately, knowing each individual intimately through information readily available from their computer files.

The Council of Four comprised a deep state thoroughly embedded within the People's Republic of China and the PLA. It had its origins when a UFO crashed on the steppes of the Altai Mountains in the Gobi Desert. The four men making up the Council of Four had been part of a scientific expedition to investigate the crash material. After Wang Wei's direct contact with the alien probe, the Chinese had eagerly accepted continual communication and the gift of new alien technologies. Harder to accept was their modified emissary, Zhang. The old viewed him with suspicion and as a potential danger. But it was a price they had to pay.

As far as they knew, no other deep state organization among the world's superpowers had made a deal with the alien Probe or even knew of its existence. Such a win for the Chinese.

Zhang pressed a button on the transmitter and the door hissed shut, closing off the outside. Now he was inside safe from all intrusions and particularly safe from prying eyes who would pay any amount of money, do anything legal or illegal, to know the secret business that went on inside this room. This inner sanctum was the holy of holies for the Council.

Everything in the room had been built to the Council of Four's exact specifications. The room was constructed of three-foot thick insulating foam and engineered steel alloy studs, joists and rafters that could neither receive nor send signals of any kind. It had been specially constructed by PLA officers to insure that no listening devices had been implanted in the walls, floor or ceiling. Aside from the television monitor, which was part of a closed loop system connected only to Zhang's office, a sophisticated transmitter on the opposite wall sent data in an encrypted form no human would use to the satellite orbiting above the Chang'e moon base and from there to the Probe.

The four elderly men watched a wall screen that showed Zhang's office. When he entered the insulated Council room, the screen faded to dull glass and their attention rested on him. Far from being nervous in front of the power wielded by the Council, Zhang waited quietly, knowing these Chinese would speak to him when they were ready. In this manner, these particular humans mimicked the Probe's behavior –gathering information and learning in a highly structured manner. This cultural tendency was why the Probe had decided to make contact with the Chinese and not any of the other Earth powers. Even so, dealing with human values and low intelligence was difficult. No Rosetta stone equivalent existed to enable the Probe to understand how an ignorant species such as humans behaved the way they did. Even working through Zhang, who had been a human, presented its own difficulties. Taking over his mind dulled much of his personality and other traits that could have been useful in gaining the trust of the Chinese.

Wang Wei spoke to Zhang with little deference. "Why are you so interested in the Bigfoot?"

Zhang struggled with the question. "Why is not of importance. Think of it as a business deal we want to make. You Chinese understand that, don't you?" He reached into his pocket and brought out an object the size and shape of a hummingbird. He pressed a tiny button, disguised neatly as one of the faux bird's eyes, and the device floated into the room to hover over the table. Zhang pressed another button on the transmitter in his pocket and the TV wall monitor came to life, showing the men sitting in the room from the viewpoint of the hummingbird.

"This drone uses dark energy to power itself. It's inexhaustible, and it has no detectable signature. Its range is limitless, and it puts out a signal that can be transmitted to the Ang brothers' satellite network and to your clandestine spy network exclusively without the brothers' knowledge. I suspect this will be a satisfactory down payment for bringing Winston Ang here?"

The four men eyed one another then waited for the oldest member to speak again.

"That is satisfactory for now. But we will all need to be able to scale this use of dark energy if we are going to win Earth's space race."

"Of course." Zhang deactivated the small drone. "The technology used in the drone can be scaled up to power ships within your solar system. This should give you a considerable advantage over your competitors."

"You'll help us with that?"

"Yes, but we'll need one more action from you when the time is right."

Wang Wei hid the concern from his face.

Zhang turned and left without saying another word.

Wang Wei spoke once the door was shut. "Remember Zhang's interests are not Chinese interests, and I don't believe he expresses only the interests of the probe either. He's a highly functioning zombie."

48

———————

Lake of the Woods, Canada
May 30th 2033 – Memorial Day
Seven Months after the UP Battle

Larry Redhawk leaned forward from his passenger seat in the *Chariot*, trying to spot any landmark that would tell him where he was. The experimental cloaked aircraft moved through a bank of dense clouds as silent as a specter. After cruising over Lake Superior and the Canadian Boundary Waters, he assumed they were in Canada, but that was just a guess.

Twenty minutes later the cloud cover disappeared and he looked down upon a landscape he didn't recognize. A vast lake spread out below with a long archipelago stretching to the west. Dark green forests covered the land and the water sparkled the bright blue of newly thawed ice.

The autonomous aircraft's autopilot was as quiet as the ship itself and had not spoken since takeoff an hour earlier. The pilot broke its silence to signal they were about to land.

The announcement and action occurred simultaneously as the Chariot winged over and dove for the lake surface. Redhawk held his breath and gripped the armrests of his seat. At the last second the craft straightened out and flew down a narrow channel. Dense forest came right up to the lake's edge. The craft followed the channel until it opened up into a wide bay. At the far side was a small island. Sun glinted off the steel corrugated roof of a boathouse. The lone slim figure of Janá Gunderson stood on a long dock waving; he was in the right place. He glanced at the communication equipment that filled the rest of the passenger area as well as the cargo hold. Janá and the island's elderly caretaker needed the equipment to maintain twenty-four hour contact with Olav's lab in Marquette and Quantumnetic's headquarters in Toronto as well as Kobak's new home in the States. Seven months of isolation was plenty.

I wonder how much the Master Bigfoot knows of what has happened in the past seven months. Redhawk mused. *Most likely everything.* The Bigfoot leader was connected to every other Bigfoot in the world through a global communications system that made the state of the art equipment in the Chariot look like hand-cranked telephones from the early twentieth century. Surely Tanya, the Bigfoot who had taken the Master Bigfoot's place at the Casino lodge, had communicated everything that had happened in the last half year. The whole battle was barely a blip on anybody's radar. The coverup and the dormancy of the Bigfoot was extraordinarily effective.

The Chariot retracted its wings and settled without a bump onto the island's only open space, a rugged shore of rock and sand jutting out into the bay near the boathouse. While the engine hummed to silence, Redhawk used the time to unbuckle from the seat and slide the passenger side's cargo door open. Janá was standing there. She was four inches taller than he was. Though he was stockier and outweighed her by at least fifty pounds, her strong hug threatened to lift him from the ground.

"It's good to see a familiar face," Janá said, letting go. She peered into the cargo hold. "You have all the equipment. Good. What's the latest news? Seven months on this island feels like solitary confinement." She stopped her speedy madcap chatter with a long blink. Taking a deep breath, she added more slowly, "C'mon, let's get this stuff unloaded, and then we can talk."

Four hours later, the communication equipment was set up in the cabin's great room. A large stone fireplace occupied one wall. Two neat stacks of wood filled the spaces on either side of the hearth. Even though it was Memorial Day, the temperature outside was just over fifty, and a roaring fire made the room toasty.

Redhawk tested the gear. "Everything's up and running. It has self-diagnostic and utility repair as well as a secure firewall," he told Janá.

"Who can I talk with?" She brushed her fingers along the new setup.

"There are three links. Colossus in Toronto, Olav in Marquette and Kobak. Oh, Olav got married."

"Really?" She grinned, as though their lab-bound friend was expected not to have a life outside his work. "I'm bummed I missed the wedding."

Redhawk looked around and asked as an afterthought, "Where are the Master Bigfoot and the baby?"

"Out learning." Janá folded her arms. "I swear the little one never sleeps and spends all of her time expanding her capabilities. She's calling herself An after the Mesopotamian Goddess of the dawn. But tell me about what's happening outside. How's Kobak? Olav?"

"Walk with me." Redhawk gave the cabin's elderly caretaker a sideways glance. "I want to see this beautiful island of yours."

"The island is about seven miles long and two wide at its widest point. The Bigfoot created a path by the shore. We can go there."

The air was crisp even in the sun. Mosquitos and black flies weren't out yet and the walk was pleasant.

"Lot of changes since we spoke last," Redhawk said. "Stephen Kobak got pushed to the side in his own company. He got caught up in an allegation of sexual improprieties."

"Kobak? No way!"

"I know. It was a big social media smear campaign. Might've been the Chinese"

"Is he okay?"

"He's moved on in a number of ways, looking how to share the changes that occurred when he was freed from his autism."

"Where is he now?"

"Savanna, Georgia. He'll still be monitoring the project."

"How's Olav doing?"

Redhawk smiled. "Now that the new lab is up and running, he's settling down. Moore said to say hello."

Janá's wrinkled brow showed her concern for the engineer. "How are his neuro-implants to connect directly with the Bigfoot communication network working?"

Redhawk shook his head. "Not well. Still working on modifications but hope is dwindling. How about you?"

"My health is good, but as I said it's been pretty lonely these past seven months with only the caretaker to talk to most of the time."

"What about the Master Bigfoot?"

"She spends all her energy teaching An. I work with her too from time to time, but the Master is totally committed, from what I can tell. It's wearing her down, and she's slowly declining. It's their way when a new one is produced."

"When are you coming back to live in civilization?" Redhawk kicked at a stone in the path.

"Can't say. I'm committed to working here for now. The Master needs me and so does An. I think I give her the human side of things she needs if she's going to become what we all fought for."

"What is that?" Redhawk narrowed his eyes. "I was never sure what she's supposed to do or be."

Janá shook her head. "And of course, the Master hasn't said anything about that." She cocked her head to one side. "You know, there are times when I spot an expression on An's face that reminds me of your Auntie Ayasha. It's almost like she's in there somewhere."

As they rounded a nub of rock near the shore, the Hybrid-Bigfoot appeared in front of them as if stepping out of thin air. Redhawk gasped and took a step back.

Janá smiled. "She does that to surprise me."

Redhawk studied the baby. The Hybrid-Bigfoot had grown considerably in the intervening months and was now taller than he was. She was also different from any other Bigfoot he'd seen. Her gray-green hair was smooth like a Rottweiler. Her facial features were unnervingly androgynous. She could pass for human if she wanted to.

Quite suddenly, Redhawk started gibbering and his arms and legs jerked in spastic movements as if he had *Tardive dyskinesia*.

Janá shouted, "An! Stop it!"

Redhawk returned to normal. He took another step back from An and glared at her.

Janá put a hand on his arm. "Don't take it personally. She did that to me the other day too; she's testing her powers."

"I don't have to like it." Redhawk turned away from the adolescent Hybrid-Bigfoot. He was ready to return to the Chariot and go home, when the familiar, gentle tones of the Master Bigfoot sung softly in is his head, telling him to come to her. Her voice was like a guide, leading him past An and into the island's interior. He looked once behind him at Janá's smile; she understood what was happening to him.

He came to a small clearing where the Master Bigfoot opened her arms as she had done with Auntie. She held him and reassured him everything would be all right. Relieved, Redhawk relaxed into her warm embrace.

The autopilot was about to close up the craft for the return to the Sky Island Casino when Janá ran down the path from the cabin toward Redhawk carrying a glowing canister. With daylight fading, he wondered if it was some kind of high tech light. But when she neared, he recognized it as an Eagle 943 Biohazard container.

"Here." Janá thrust it into his hand. "It's for Olav. A gift from the Master Bigfoot. It's material taken from the hybrid Bigfoot. He'll know what do with it."

She stepped away and waved at him as the doors closed. The wings extended and locked into place. With a loud hum, the ground effect motors lifted the aerial craft from the beach, blowing sand and small leaves in a wash that knocked Janá backward. Moments later, the cloaking device went on line and Redhawk judged from the strange grin on the woman's face that she could no longer tell where the vehicle was. The quiet jets roared to life and the Chariot sped south and east toward the Casino.

Redhawk looked at the canister. The biohazard material inside the clear plastic container created the glow. With a jerk of surprise, he recognized the soft green aura of the Bigfoot's skin. His earlier uneasiness returned and he wondered just what the future held for humans and their supposed Bigfoot partners as social chaos reigned on the planet.

49

———

Quileute River, Olympic Peninsula
November 11th 2033 – Veterans Day
One Year after the UP Battle

Unlike most mid-twenty-first century tech-savvy Americans, Jack Vance preferred the rugged seclusion and beauty of Washington State's Olympic rainforest to the comforts of city life. As a kid, Vance had never played team sports but spent all his time after school in the woods around his grandparent's home. In fact, Jack had not played well with the other kids, perhaps because his ancestors were mystery more than two generations back. Or his weird name. He had been named for his Jewish Ukrainian grandfather, Darvesh, who worked for a small pharmaceutical company in London in 1977, but legally changed his name to Jack at the age of fourteen. His grandparents lost everything when the company president, a Muslim, denounced the grandfather as a communist radical and they were forced to immigrate to the United States.

His grandparents, for reasons unknown, had settled on Whidbey Island in Puget Sound, opening a small inn for tourists. Growing up with them after his parents divorced, Vance found peace and joy exploring the tall spruce and balsam forests covering most of the island. He grew to be a handsome man, possessing the deep-set dark eyes and hooked nose from his Jewish ancestry and the light brown hair of his father's Northern Irish roots. His mother's side of the family, the Carpenters, including his beloved aunt Claire, was even more of a mystery. Everybody believed dark secrets were hidden in his family tree.

Eventually Vance attended the University of Washington only to please his grandmother. But every vacation and weekend he spent backpacking and hiking throughout the Olympic Peninsula. After three semesters, he worked at Microsoft long enough to learn the tools necessary to create apps for smart phones and then struck out on his own. In 2027, at age twenty-five, he created a crypto currency app that proved to be invaluable for recording and paying out money from the social media giants for data they derived from ordinary people. He sold the company two years later for eight figures and disappeared into the Olympic wilderness. Except for occasional family gatherings on Whidbey, he had been content, living alone off the grid as a modern day mountain man near Quinault at the southern foot of Olympic National Park.

Then Ben Sutton left a text video message.

Vance watched Sutton's video message a second time. The tall, gray-haired old man was smiling, but something was wrong. Vance had a singular intuition about these things. Growing up on Whidbey Island, his fellow high school students jokingly called it his spidey sense, but ever since he was old enough to walk, he knew where possible danger lay. The only time he was ever in trouble was when he ignored the unease in his body telling him to stop, or turn around, or take another direction. That sense was screaming at him now to not disregard Sutton's invitation, whereas his normal intuition was telling him go back to chopping wood for his cabin. Winter was coming, and the Olympic Peninsula was nowhere to be caught without a good supply of fuel for the cold months. But he held the axe still in his left hand and studied Sutton's face.

Behind the smile, his skin was ashen and his eyes glazed. Hardly the look of guy who should be smiling. And the invitation itself was odd. "Hey, Jack old buddy," Sutton's message began.

The two men had never been buddies, never even close to it. By chance, he had saved Sutton's life when he found the dumb ass struggling to free his leg from a makeshift snare some eager, crap-for-brains Bigfoot believer had placed on the banks of the Quileute River hoping to catch a Sasquatch in one of their well-known hotspots. Sutton had accidentally tripped it and slipped into the river. Heavy rains during the day had caused the creek to rise. Pinned in the freezing water, he had nearly drowned when Vance came along. During their trip back to town, Sutton explained he was a Bigfoot investigator.

Though they exchanged numbers, Vance ignored every call from Sutton to join him on one of his Sasquatch hikes, even less interested in searching for the oversized, mythic, hairy, ape-like creatures than he was in a new friendship. Until the call this afternoon. When he saw Sutton's message header, he picked up right away.

"Hey Darvesh, old buddy. I have a friend who needs your help. Want you to meet him. Stop by the shop and I'll fill you in." The message ended there.

Vance groaned. The shop was the Pacific Northwest Sasquatch Research Station in La Push. He scratched at the four-day growth of beard. He had just returned from a long weekend in the wilderness. The last thing he wanted to do was leave his sanctuary again, especially if it had something to do with Bigfoot. A bigger lunacy he had never encountered, and the Olympic rainforest was stuffed with lunatics.

Take Forks, for example, home to the *Twilight* Saga. Nickt, a native Olympian couldn't turn around without running into some whacko tourist who had come to the rainforest hoping to spot a teenage vampire or werewolf. Unfortunately, the area had become a UFO hotspot as well due to accounts of unidentified craft racing through the skies, light pulses and orbs, even two cases of landings associated with Bigfoot sightings. One person reported the sky had opened up and a Bigfoot emerged right in front of him.

When he called Sutton back, the man didn't answer. Vance sighed. His common sense hammered at him not to go. But his indistinct sixth sense was insisting. Was that why the bastard had called? Sutton knew he wouldn't say no, or was it something else? Vance grimaced and buried the axe head in a thick slab of spruce.

Tiny La Push, Washington sat at the mouth of the Quileute River, the largest town on the Quileute Native Reservation. Situated at several trailheads leading deep into the Olympic's temperate rainforest, the village was the perfect place for the Pacific Northwest Sasquatch Research Center, and the PNSRC was famous in the Bigfoot world. Not only were the surrounding damp woods recognized as a hot spot for Sasquatch activity, their remote wilderness made it more plausible that hikers might run into the occasional Bigfoot and later report the encounter.

When Vance arrived, the place looked deserted. As he climbed the steps to the wide front porch, the door was ajar and a bloody handprint smeared the jamb. Resting his hand on the grip of his holstered Desert Eagle, he called out, "Sutton? Ben! You here?"

No reply.

He entered the steel frame building and paused, dumbfounded by what he saw. The place was silent and empty. Vance crouched and turned slowly, his hand never leaving his weapon. Narrowed eyes took in every feature of the high-ceilinged room. Everything was perfectly in place, completely at odds with the open door and bloody jamb. Like all Bigfoot research centers, specialized Sasquatch-detecting gear filled shelves along the walls, and of course, obligatory Bigfoot pictures had been plastered on every bit of free space. A wide glass counter housed the latest in miniature infrared sensors. He straightened and blew out air through loose lips.

Vance scratched his head and pushed farther into the room. *Why did Sutton insist on meeting here on a Tuesday when the place is closed? Did he know about the break-in? And where is he?* Vance was about to wait outside when he spied blood drops leading across the floor to the back office. He unholstered his Eagle and racked the slide. The satisfying *click* of chambering a round made him feel safer.

The blood trail ended at an old desk, the kind used by nineteenth-century newspapermen. Papers were neatly stacked on either side of an AI assisted data processing terminal. The screen, partially turned toward the room, was split into six parts each, one showing an angle of the store's main room and the back rooms from hidden spy cams.

After checking to make sure the rest of the building was clear, Vance returned to the office. He sat behind the desk. Signatures from famous Bigfoot researchers filled the stained oak top. He ignored these and concentrated on the computer. He found the security camera file and ran it back earlier in the day when he first got Sutton's message. Tapping the play icon, he settled back in the office chair, leaving his pistol on the desktop.

He wasn't disappointed. Five minutes into the replay, Sutton entered the store. His shirt was torn and blood-streaked. One hand clutched his side and the other leaned against the door jamb. Then the door pushed open wide. Vance snapped upright in the chair. His heart pounded, and he found himself reaching for the Eagle and staring into the main room even though the footage was hours old. A Bigfoot entered behind Sutton, supporting him. It half carried the wounded man to the office where a different camera angle showed it carefully placing him in the chair.

"Nickt!" he swore under his breath. He hit pause and made certain the front door was locked. He turned off all the lights to the store and returned to the desk. He ran the clip back to the beginning and watched it again, carefully studying the creature. It had a translucent green sheen to it. An unearthly appearance. As an experienced woodsman, he knew the difference between a costumed man pretending to be an animal and a real animal. This creature was the real deal. He watched, his eyes never leaving the screen.

"There's an emergency medical kit in the other room," Sutton was saying. The Bigfoot left and returned. It opened the bag and began pulling out items. "Man, have you ever helped a human before?" Sutton asked in a surprisingly calm way.

In a voice that reminded him of his grandfather, the Bigfoot replied, "Many times." It grimaced in approximation of a smile then added, "I'm not a male. In fact, none of my species are male nor female, though some prefer to be called by the feminine. Although you already know this."

"You speak very good English. How did that happen?"

"Centuries ago, many of us learned to mimic human languages."

"Nick Moore says you're aliens," Sutton whispered. "You know him?"

The Bigfoot nodded.

"You were there? In the UP?"

The Bigfoot nodded again.

"So the story about alien portals and the reports about your connection to UFOs is true?"

"That is not the whole story."

"My investigations point in that direction." Sutton grimaced and a groan escaped his blue lips.

"Be still," the Bigfoot cautioned. "I must work swiftly before you lose any more blood." The Bigfoot ripped away Sutton's shirt and inspected a jagged cut under his left armpit. "You have a deep wound."

Sutton coughed. Blood spattered his lips. "Tell me the truth. Am I going to make it?"

"I can't see the future, but I will do all that I can."

"Why don't I feel any pain?"

"Pain is in your mind, and we can take care of that." The creature bent close and pressed a clean dressing against the wound. Its head dwarfed Sutton's, who was over six feet tall and weighed 250 pounds.

Vance hit pause again and wiped at the sweat on his upper lip. For some unknown reason, he was certain what he was seeing and hearing was not faked. This made the unease in his gut greater. Even more unsettling was the unexpected strong connection he experienced to the creature, as though he somehow could sense it on a level beyond what his eyes and ears were showing him. He leaned forward and hit play again.

The Bigfoot hovered over Sutton. Its fur was smooth and the features of its wide flat face were pliable. It stood over eight feet tall. Vance was surprised by how human-like the creature's facial expressions were, its movements careful and precise. He was fascinated by the quick, deft movements, unlike how he'd imagined this legendary cryptid would move.

Five minutes passed. Sutton leaned back in the chair. His face was still ashen but his breathing was stronger. "Thanks. I owe you my life."

"You saved me from that hunter. So I could not let you die," the Bigfoot said.

Sutton snorted. "Couldn't let the bastard shoot you."

"You should go to a hospital," the Bigfoot said.

"You seem like a good field medic to me, and I feel pretty good."

"Many of us can heal simple human wounds or provide emergency care. I can do nothing more for you with your wound."

"How about answering some questions?"

The Bigfoot settled into a corner of the room, resting against the wall. "What would you like to know?"

"Why are you here? Not just you, but all of your kind?"

Vance held his breath, waiting for the answers. It was not enough that he was seeing an actual Bigfoot and hearing it speak, he found himself wanting to know where they came from and what their purpose here was.

"One year ago, an event took place in the Upper Peninsula of Michigan. Led by what the native people there call the Master Bigfoot, representatives from five of our clans went to an origin portal to give birth to a new, more powerful Bigfoot child. Unknown to most of the world, a battle ensued around the event. Opposing human forces were neutralized and the evolutionary event took place as planned. Directly after the successful reproduction, the Hybrid-Bigfoot was taken away into deep hiding.

"Afterward, many of the human participants in the event told the story of Bigfoot living the Upper Peninsula of Michigan. Some even had detailed pictures and videos of Bigfoot running through the forests. We were called dangerous and hunted."

"I remember the stories. A bounty was offered for anyone who could bring in a Bigfoot."

The Bigfoot twisted its full lips into a grimace. "As for all 3,128 of us who remained, some went immediately into stasis, a kind of cloaked hibernation. We melded into the natural world and became undetectable."

Sutton nodded. "Bigfoot researchers and investigators combed the area for months afterward. No evidence of Bigfoot, or the fight you described, or the portal was ever found. What brought you out of hibernation?"

"At the time of the event, not all of us agreed with the Master Bigfoot's decision to take that evolutionary step. Some among us believe she will no longer be aligned with our original purpose. We resolved to prevent this from happening with the help of allies."

"Original purpose! What the hell is—" Sutton coughed and blood spit into his hand.

Instantly, the Bigfoot was on her feet and bending over him. "I will transport you to the urgent care center."

"And get yourself killed? No way. It's too late for me anyway. By the time I got there, I'd be dead." He managed a grin. "Besides, odd as it sounds, I don't mind dying. You get yourself back into the forest and stay there. I'll send someone your way. He'll give you all the help you need."

The Bigfoot's eyes narrowed. "Can we trust him?"

Sutton managed a smile. "Yeah ... you can trust him."

The Bigfoot paused, as if to think about this for a moment. It leaned over Sutton, and Vance wondered if it had killed his friend to protect itself from other humans. "How will he find us?"

Sutton laughed. "He'll find a way. He has a sixth sense about him. Now help me up and take me outside. I have a phone call to make."

The Bigfoot embraced Sutton and carried him to the door.

Vance played the security files for a few more minutes but nothing more appeared. Not even his own entrance to the building. He turned it off.

He went outside and walked around the research center. He found no trace of Sutton. A faint trail of blood led past the parking lot to a grove of trees, where it ended. It looked as if the big man had vanished. Maybe the Bigfoot had taken him to the urgent care clinic. Vance fished his smart phone out of his vest pocket and called the clinic. A short Q and A with the nurse at the front desk revealed no one named Sutton had been admitted. In fact, it had been a quiet afternoon. No one had been in since mid-morning.

Vance returned to the office. Oddly, he felt a strong urge to seek out the Bigfoot and find out what happened to Sutton. He searched the place for a clue as to where the Bigfoot could be found. He saw nothing. He plopped down into the chair. Sutton had told the Bigfoot he'd find a way, but Vance certainly didn't see how, since he had no clue where to start. He slammed his fist against the desk top and muttered, "Dammit, Ben, where do I go?"

Then something on the desk caught his attention. Sutton had underscored letters in the signatures of Bigfoot researchers. Even as he had sat listening to the Bigfoot, the old man had managed to send a message. Reading from top to bottom, Vance wrote out the letters and saw they spelled his name and Morse Creek. He looked out at the fading daylight and drummed the desktop with his fingers in a three-quarter, syncopated rhythm that was his way of arguing with the unease in his gut warning him to back away and get the hell out of there.

He stayed put. "What do you do next, old buddy?" he murmured to himself.

The Bigfoot had mentioned allies, and if the Bigfoot was seeking help, that meant there were enemies. One of those enemies probably targeted the Bigfoot and ended up wounding Sutton, who was quite likely dead by now. Vance's throat tightened and the unease stilled. He grimaced, knowing what that gut response meant. "Shit," he sighed, deciding he was one of the allies.

He copied the files onto his phone then erased the footage so no one else would know what happened. He cleaned up the blood and made certain no signs remained in the store that someone had been hurt. Then he let himself out and locked the place up after him.

He headed for his Land Rover and stopped, turning the movement into a casual retying of his shoe. *You're being watched, old buddy.* He stood, twisting his torso as if stretching his muscles. He saw no one. But his gut told him that whoever was watching didn't want to be seen. *There's more going on here than meets the eye.*

Vance got into his SUV and drove off, in the opposite direction of Morse Creek. There was time to come back and follow Sutton's clues. .He looked out at the fading daylight. He knew where Morse Creek was and the paranormal rumors surrounding it.

He got into his SUV and drove off, in the opposite direction of Morse Creek. As he wheeled down La Push's main thoroughfare, a new thought arose. Everything he had ever heard about the Bigfoot phenomenon was that the creatures were extremely secretive, able to cloak their movements and disable recording equipment so no one could get pictures of them. *So why was Sutton brought here, and why was the Bigfoot allowing itself to be filmed?*

Everything Vance had heard about Bigfoot was that it had never happened before. *Why contact me?* It was confusing.

50

XXX Base
Sichuan Province, China
July 2034

Wang Wei loved the time he was able to return to his lab in the XXX Base. The heat, humidity and pollution-free air of Sichuan province suited his aging body. Here he was free from the rigors of big city life, the Council of Four and particularly Zhang. But neither the Council nor Zhang knew that here in his lab he was, from time to time, still in direct contact with the probe. In fact, recently he had been informed by the probe that a major ask and even bigger reward would be coming soon. So in his mind, the time had come to share everything with Chung Lee. Chung Lee was the youngest of the gang of four. Certainly the fittest. Over the past ten years, he had been cyberneticly enhanced both physically and mentally. Wei speculated Lee was in every way a good match for Zhang.

Lee was also the only one of the Council of Four who had studied and traveled in the United States and Europe. Wei felt special connection with the man.

The time had come to let Lee know all that had transpired since

Wei's first contact with the alien probe. Sitting here in his lab, he had an hour to go over what he wanted to tell Lee.

After a probe supplied him with the design and engineering for the antigravity drone, he was quite surprised when the probe made a request: Remove Stephen Kobak from his company and replace Colossus's trainer with Sue Lynn, Wei's great niece. It came as quite a shock to learn how much the probe knew about him and the alien nature of the Bigfoot. Accomplishing the request was not difficult. For all of Kobak's brilliance and command of artificial intelligence, he was particularly naïve about the power of carefully-placed internet memes. Sometimes called social memes, these rumors would spread like the most potent biological virus until they were fully accepted as the truth of the matter. Repeated millions of times, no amount of contrary evidence could stop them. The fake story of Kobak's sexual misconduct worked brilliantly, in part because he had pissed off so many people and payback was sweet for them. Wei was one of the few men who understood the real danger to humanity of the existence of the network where the social memes thrived. He often wondered if the probe had anything to do with the global success.

The social media sphere sat on the backbone of the digital Internet. He had read all the warnings from a small minority of artificial intelligence critics about the creation and growth of this sphere. It had no code and was not programmed by any human. Yet nearly every human, willingly and unwillingly, gave away their deepest selves to it. In return, the sphere was reshaping them; ordinary choice no longer mattered. The social media sphere was another kind of alien life form, in Wei's mind. The only real solution to the loss of privacy and self-direction was to leave Earth.

The second part of the request was to put his brother's granddaughter, Sue Lynn, in the role of Colossus's developmental trainer. One of Wei's US operatives set up the chance meeting between her and Kobak at his party, and the rest flowed quite naturally. As a reward for succeeding, the alien probe supplied the way to reorganize the atomic structure of aluminum to make it stronger and lighter.

As for Sue Lynn, she was deeply loyal to her great uncle and the Chinese goal to push technological development to its highest limit. If such a limit existed.

She accepted the plan without question and agreed to keep him informed about any developments. Her placement paid off better than Wei could've ever imagined when she began feeding him information about the engineering of the synthetic brain in Olav's lab. This he kept from the others, but it was unclear if the probe or Zhang knew about this. He concluded there was a good chance Zang knew.

Wei decided he would tell Lee about the synthetic brain but would demand that keeping Sue Lynn safe was a top priority if something should happen to him. At night, Wei worried endlessly about what kind of danger Sue Lynn might find herself in without a lifeline. What comforted him early on was that he received a message from the probe that humanity was not of interest, only the Bigfoot.

Next he put together his thoughts on Zhang. At times, he seemed to have a mind of his own. Wei judged Zhang to be more than a human avatar for the probe, although clearly a useful one. Immediately after being introduced to him, Wei began tracking Zhang's behavior with advanced body and facial recognition surveillance. As everybody knew, Zhang was ruthless. All his actions aligned with the Chinese drive to dominate space and technology, which could disguise any individual agenda.

The arrival of Chung Lee awakened Wei from his reverie. They bowed and then hugged each other.

Lee spoke first. "The humidity is stifling, but it's good to get away from the city. You recall I've only been here once before."

"I remember. It was during the glorious time when we first made contact with the probe. So exciting."

"Got a new message from the probe you want to tell me about?" Lee asked with a chuckle.

"No, but a big ask is coming soon and the promise of an equally big reward."

"Is that why I'm here?

"Partially. Think what a plan for building and controlling a small-scale fusion power unit would mean for space exploration."

"That would be a game changer."

"But I brought you here to share my full story and concerns, in case something should happen to me."

"This doesn't sound good. Begin, please."

"I can see by the way you look at him you don't trust Zhang any more than I do."

"Correct; he's not to be trusted."

Wei filled in Chung Lee on every detail he had rehearsed in his mind.

When he finished, Wei added one more observation. "The probe said humanity is of no interest to it, just Bigfoot. Is that good or bad for us? Does it mean it intends to let us flourish or just the opposite, bring about our destruction?"

51

Quinault Lake, Olympic Peninsula
September 30th 2034

Nick Moore was glad the Toyota's AI was driving. He was totally lost. The directions Olav Lassen had provided were hopelessly wrong. Luckily, he had taken the extra precaution of entering the Quinault Lake Trailhead's longitude and latitude into the truck's GPS system. "How far?" he asked.

Donald's mechanical voice answered in both metric and English measurements, "Destination in 850 meters; one half mile."

Moore looked out the side window at the gray skies to the north and grimaced. *Why is Colossus always so damn right about the weather?* Kobak's weather forecaster had predicted light showers this afternoon for the northern half of the Olympic Peninsula. "Hopefully the meeting will be done by then."

"Is there a question?" Donald asked.

"No." Moore chuckled. It was like speaking to his ex-wife, only the navigator never threw anything at him.

The truck slowed and turned onto a gravel road. A hundred yards later it pulled into the glacial lake's trailhead. The remote area's facilities were Spartan, with not even a portable toilet. As he removed his bicycle from the transport vehicle, Moore told his bot assistant to take the gear and set up a campsite. The Chinese robot was a 5g AI, self-directed automaton. The first two times camping, Moore had to stay put and help it learn how he wanted his campsite arranged. Now he could get on his bike and cruise without worry. When he returned, everything would be as he liked it.

Checking the GPS coordinates for the meet on his smart watch, Moore jumped on his bike and took off down the trail. The way was rocky, but it hadn't rained in weeks and the ground was dry for now. The remoteness of Quilemette Lake meant he was unlikely to run into anyone else other than the guy Olav wanted him to meet. He glanced at the clouds growing darker and hoped Colossus's prediction of rain might be off by a couple of hours. He didn't want to get drenched on his ride back to the campsite.

Negotiating a set of stone steps leading down toward the lake shore, he cruised on sand for a hundred yards before the path juked left back into the trees. He still had a couple of miles to go, but he was way ahead on time so he didn't need to take any unnecessary chances. Olav had been adamant that he not be late.

"He won't wait around if you're not on time," Olav had warned in the late night phone call.

"I don't know," Moore had answered. "I have a lot on my plate."

"Look, Nick. I understand your reluctance. But I guarantee you want to meet this guy. He can help you. He knows about Deep Water."

Moore had stilled at the name. A dozen people in the U.S. knew about the Deep Water Cabal and its work with extraterrestrial intelligence. "What's his name?" Moore had asked.

"He goes by the name of Conrad. You won't regret this, Nick."

"I already do," he'd said and Olav hung up laughing.

Trees flew by on the straight patch of trail with no rocks and ruts. ET again. Moore chuckled. *Guess I really had no choice.*

His watch beeped at the designated spot. It looked out upon a cliff above the lake with heavy forest behind. He still had fifteen minutes, and he sat down to wait. Casually he scratched his back, making certain the Smith and Wesson .38 was still in its holster. If he'd learned anything in the last two years, it was never come to a clandestine meeting unprepared.

He took a deep breath. This had better be everything Olav promised.

Moore had not been lying to Olav about being busy. After nearly dying from Olav's failed neuro-bot implants, he'd returned to his home state of Washington, taking up residence on his grandfather's farm outside of Marysville. He'd planned on at least year of self-reflection and relaxation. But six weeks into his hiatus, Rear Admiral Jason Stillwater paid him a personal visit. "I need your help again, Nick," the old man had said, his leathery face not cracking a smile.

Five months later, Moore was second-in-command for advanced AI weaponry of the Western North American Smart Coastal Defense and Response Network, which had replaced the Coast Guard in the Pacific Northwest. And then there was Deep Water, a clandestine group of six individuals whose work on extraterrestrial non-human intelligences was so secret, even the President of the United States didn't know about them. Aside from what he could learn via the Internet, Moore knew almost nothing about the group or its other members, only that they had formed in 1947 as a result of the Roswell, New Mexico incident. Since then, its original members had been continually replaced by top people in government, science, artificial intelligence and business. Moore had never discovered how they knew about his involvement with the Bigfoot on the UP. Nor had he met any of them; he received only an occasional encrypted message or directive to carry out a simple mission. All designed to test him, he suspected.

The sun had passed over noon, the time his contact was supposed to be here. Moore checked the clouds again. They were darker and moving closer. Rain was definitely headed this way. He'd give his contact another fifteen minutes, then he was leaving.

The fifteen minutes passed quickly. Moore picked up his mountain bike. A snort of disgust from the trees drew his attention.

"I wondered how impatient you'd be," a disembodied voice said.

Moore turned and placed his hand on the pistol. "That's funny, because I was wondering what kind of a rude SOB calls for a meeting and then doesn't bother to show up on time."

"The kind who's careful. Who makes certain you're alone and weren't followed. Nice bot, by the way. I notice you got the latest Chinese model that comes with automatic upgrades. You might want to hold off on that."

Moore laid his bike down but didn't pull his hand from behind his back. "Why's that?"

"Through the new AI Bluetooth technology, the Chinese manufacturing company can control the security in your home using their bots. When they are linked to your computer, they know what you're working on and who you're talking to in those late night sessions with Deep Water."

"Of course I know that. When it arrived, I immediately disconnected that capability. How do you know about Deep Water?"

Without answering the question, the man stepped out of the shadows of the tree line and into the clearing. He was tall and angular but slightly bent over as if he carried a great weight on his narrow shoulders. He didn't bother introducing himself and he didn't need to.

Moore knew him, as did ten million other Americans who followed his podcasts. "Conrad Visily," Moore said, not bothering to hide his disdain.

Visily smiled. "You've heard of me."

"Who doesn't know America's foremost pioneering cosmologist and UFO conspiracy theorist."

"You forgot the disgraced part."

"Time in a psych ward will do that for your reputation."

"It gave me an occasion to slow down to think," Visily said. "Especially about Deep Water."

"Why them in particular?" Moore asked, intrigued in spite of the man's notorious reputation.

"Olav was right; you know them."

Without confirming Visily's claim, Moore reiterated, "Why them in particular?"

"They put me there." He watched the surprise flit across Moore's face then continued. "But I'm not here to warn you about them. You either already know what they're capable of or have taken steps to protect yourself, or you're already in deep shit and there's nothing my warning you now can do to help."

"Why are you here then?"

"I have a source. Don't ask where. I don't want him compromised. He's been feeding me information on the existence of a shielded alien Probe that has been watching earth for who knows how long. It's been responsible for many of the UFO sightings and crashes, starting with Roswell. It's all technology, no simple earthlike organic life form." Conrad paused.

Moore allowed a smile. "Tell me something I don't know."

"Alright. Here's something the Deep Water cabal couldn't possibly know." Visily's voice sharpened into the lecture mode of the Stanford Professor he used to be. "The Chinese have been in contact with the Probe for at least three years. Seems they've made a pact with the devil. The Chinese are helping the probe hack into the global artificial intelligence network. The theory is they, maybe the Chinese, maybe the probe or both, want to control the world by controlling the massive data and using that data to win the space race and, of course, the world from there. Here's the important part. According to my source, the successful execution of their plan somehow is related to your Bigfoot. Incidentally, he doesn't understand how it all fits together."

"Why tell me this?"

"We need your help to prevent a global catastrophe for the good guys."

"By good guys you mean the American people."

"I'm not talking Deep Water."

Moore laughed. "Nice try. You almost had me convinced this could be legit."

"It is," Conrad said, worry replacing the smug lecturer's mien. He looked overhead. "I have to go."

Moore peered upward. The sky was clear except for clouds building to the west. "Why? What's up there?"

"This place is free of satellite coverage for about thirty minutes. However, a satellite is due to fly over in five minutes. We should never be seen together." Visily paused as he retreated into the forest's concealment. "Be careful, but look into the Chinese deep state's extraterrestrial effort. It's far more advanced than Deep Water." With that Visily vanished into the ancient Spruce and Douglas fir forest.

Moore watched him disappear, torn between following up on his warning and forgetting all this nonsense. The stuff about the alien life form in orbit around the earth was spot on, though. Olav had mentioned problems with the Chinese trying to steal his engineering work on a synthetic brain.

Moore mounted his bike and road back toward the camp. *Shit, the last time I got deeply with this ET crap, I almost died.* Then he chuckled to himself. *It does seem to be my life's destiny, and I love it!*

52

———————

Marquette, Michigan
March 15th 2035

At age forty, Olav Lassen had everything he wanted, a lovely wife, a beautiful baby daughter—who already showed an intelligence to make any nerdy father proud—a million dollar mansion in Marquette's most affluent neighborhood overlooking Lake Superior, and a job only dreams could conjure. He was head of the Granville T. Woods Science Foundation, a think tank ostensibly under the auspices of the prestigious National Institutes of Societal Well-being and the President's Council on Nonhuman Intelligence. In reality it was a cutting edge research and engineering facility, funded in part by Quantumnetics founder Stephen Kobak, and home to the nation's most guarded emerging biotech secrets. Speculation about the foundation's projects had gone viral on the Internet and some conspiracy theorists had argued their plans were to gradually incorporate alien technology into the world's artificial intelligence network to gain global control of everyone's lives by an elite group of authoritarians.

When Olav first heard these stories, he had chuckled at what these rumor mongers would do if they learned the actual truth: that the Bigfoot were advancing a technological singularity to benefit the whole human race.

He leaned his six-foot, three-inch frame against the balcony railing overlooking the foundation's atrium nine stories below and looked out through the glass dome past Presque Isle Park's sand beach at a brisk icy wind that whipped snow across the lake, turning Lake Superior's gray waters into whitecaps. He shivered involuntarily at the cold weather streaming into Michigan's Upper Peninsula. An unusually late polar vortex was on its way and would disrupt life in the upper Midwest with below-zero temperatures for the next three days.

Olav drew in a deep breath and shivered again, feeling the outside cold deep in his bones even though the atrium was climate controlled at seventy-two degrees. His red hair had thinned and the beginnings of a paunch pressed against his lab coat. So much had happened in the two and a half years since the night of the firefight in Michigan's Upper Peninsula, it made Moore's law look like a snail in a race with greyhounds. He wondered if he fully appreciated how much of what he had learned about the Bigfoot's bio quantum nature would change everything everybody had believed about life. At the micro level, the Bigfoot substrate was totally different from the human substrate or any other life on Earth. No DNA. No natural selection driving species development. By most definitions, they probably wouldn't even be considered to be alive.

For the past two years, Olav and his team had been working on a means to integrate the Bigfoot capabilities for correcting many human health syndromes. At first, Olav and his group had been stymied. Using Moore as the test subject, attempts to use nanorobotics technology to augment a human brain's processing power to accept information streams from the Bigfoot communication system . The nanites had been removed from Nick Moore's brain before neuronal cascade failure occurred.

But An's rapid development had suggested another course, one initially advanced by the Master Bigfoot – build a portable synthetic brain. That had been every nation's goal since the arrival of AI technology half a century ago. It was a race. The first nation or company that could put a synthetic brain in a wide variety of robots would control the exploitation of the solar system and maybe the galaxy.

Chinese scientists had taken the early lead, the state run economy and scientific community devoting unlimited resources to simulate neuron scale self-organizing nodes mimicking the human brain's information processing architecture. Known originally by the acronym SID for Synthetic Intelligence Devices, their initial artificial brain structures were crude and dismissed as dead ends. But The Chinese persisted and within in a decade, employing the dedication of Kennedy's drive to a man on the moon by the end of the 1960s, had made tremendous strides in their drive to build functional artificial brains with their digital simulations.

However, they still hadn't conquered the biggest obstacle to creating a functioning synthetic brain – minimizing the high-energy usage of their independent mechanical brains. Their prototypes filled a small room, required super cooling of the neural nets, and still had only two percent of the complexity of the human brain. Until they figured out how to make a synthetic brain run on the energy consumption that average human brain ran on, they were dead in the water.

And that's how we beat them. Olav smiled and slapped the iron railing, listening appreciatively to the sharp *whang* reverberate through the atrium. *They don't have access to the one thing that can help them. No siree, that's in our own backyard.*

While the Chinese had dominated the synthetic intelligence field early on, thanks to Janá and the Master Bigfoot's farsightedness, Olav and his team had a resource their scientists could only dream of – tissue from a self-sustaining, living, biosynthetic, quantum-based creature. Twenty-two months ago, Janá had sent an Eagle 943 Biohazard container to the Foundation. Olav's excitement had leapt when he recognized through the canister's protective stasis field a beautifully-preserved sample of the Bigfoot's tissue. It contained the alien basis of the Bigfoot's computational informational processing capability with minimum energy consumption and without needing the super cooling necessary to keep the Earth-based analog neural nets from overheating.

Olav and his team worked tirelessly to analyze the Bigfoot sample. Embedded in the tissue were gold quantum level micro-threads. The threads acted like neurons. Most importantly, they had organized themselves in three-dimensional space and were capable of exchanging ions the same way a human brain's neurons exchanged neurotransmitters. And the best part was the power consumption was less than the power needed to run a small LED light for half a year. This was the key to the synthetic brain the Chinese had been searching for – powering synthetic neurons with a millionth of the energy it took to run conventional computers and especially quantum computers.

The next eighteen months were devoted to engineering a self-contained information processing system. Twenty hours a day, seven days a week had paid off, and now Olav and his team had finally done it – created a synthetic brain.

Olav watched a gust of wind swirl snow against the atrium glass. He walked from the chill of the atrium toward his office. *Today is the big day. Got to call Janá with the news. She deserves to know.* Once in his office, he called her on the secure video line.

"Janá, it's a freakin' miracle of science," he crowed, and told her about the power consumption breakthrough. "Kobak is going to be so pleased his investment and faith in us has found the answer."

"You still have to figure out how the Bigfoot tissue operates at such tremendous speeds," she said carefully.

"Already there. When I fed Colossus the parameters controlling the Bigfoot tissue, he was able to show us how to introduce quantum tunneling into the gold substrate. That increased the speed and reduced the energy consumption of our synthetic brain by a factor of a thousand."

"How soon?" Janá asked breathlessly.

He held up a black box the size of a deck of cards. "It's already here. The team finished this synthetic brain prototype this morning. It's already capable of exceeding the human brain in computational capacity. Most importantly, it's powered by no more than your basic smart phone battery."

"Shit! You did it!" Janá laughed.

"We all did it, " Olav said, feeling magnanimous. "This is going to catapult our engineering capabilities, paving the way for the next several generations of functional robots, especially when it comes to space colonization. Thanks to you and An's tissue."

Janá's face grew solemn.

"Hey, what's wrong?" he asked instantly.

"It wasn't An's tissue. It belonged to the Master Bigfoot." Tears ran down her cheeks. "She died a couple of hours ago. It was her idea to help complete what began back in the UP two years ago, so she let me take a sample for you."

Olav sobered. "She was quite unusual. I'm sorry for your loss."

"A loss for An," Janá added quickly.

"What's next for you?"

Janá wiped her cheeks on her sleeve. "More training for An. Still have another year and half before she reaches full maturity."

Olav noticed the worry lines around Janá's eyes. "Do you have doubts?"

"I don't know. An's already eight feet tall and weighs two hundred kilos. She also looks more human than most Bigfoot."

Olav nodded. "I suppose that's to be expected, since Auntie went through the portal with the other Bigfoot and did not reappear. Anything else?"

"She moves faster than any creature I've seen. Her para-physical abilities are off the charts, and she's already learned the art of cloaking. Yesterday, she disappeared before my eyes and popped back into existence."

Olav whistled appreciatively.

"I know." Janá nodded, her eyes wide. "I've looked deeply into all the Bigfoot literature and the claim is most Bigfoot don't acquire those capabilities for decades."

He narrowed his eyes at her. "What are you holding back?"

"Maybe it's unimportant, but An's drive to learn is insatiable. She soaked up everything the Master Bigfoot had to teach her within the first year of her life. She's used the communication equipment to communicate directly with Colossus and has somehow been absorbing raw data in a way no human could ever do."

Olav laughed. "To what end? Make a digital friend?"

Birgit pressed her lips flat together and frowned. "I wanted to make certain we were alone," she stated flatly. "An's outside down by the lake shore testing transportation portals."

Olav sucked in a quick breath. "Everything okay?"

"Maybe it's just being up here without the Master Bigfoot, but An freaks me out sometimes. Everything feels unsettled. I wonder if we should be worried."

"For your safety?"

"Not just mine. Maybe everybody's. Such unfettered power without control of the Mother Bigfoot could be dangerous with unpredictable consequences."

Olav studied the strong Nordic features of Janá's normally cheerful face. The care lines stood out around her nose and eyes more than poor lighting would cause. When the lab started their research efforts, Olav felt time was on their side, since the Master Bigfoot had assured them An would take at least five years to grow, but from what Birgit said, An was maturing much faster than expected. "You think this is a problem?"

She shrugged. "I dunno. An's nice, friendly, curious like a small child, but I think she's becoming so much more than any Bigfoot could ever be."

He nodded. "Maybe you should come home."

"I need to stick it out at least until the summer. Then–"

The interactive glass screen went black and the audio was gone.

"Janá? Janá? Everything okay?" Olav shouted uselessly at the device.

A tech rushed into Olav's office. "We've lost all contact with Canada."

53

Savannah, Georgia
March 15th 2035

Stephen Kobak looked out at the waves crashing against the breakwater a hundred feet away and felt a chill deep in his bones, greater than the sou'easter wind bearing down on him. "What do you mean you lost contact with Canada? What happened to Janá?" he demanded.

"I was showing her the synthetic intelligence prototype and the call went dead. All communication with the island is down," Olav explained.

The smart phone's 3D screen captured every twisted line in Olav's face; Kobak could practically feel the man's fear emanating from his image. *Sometimes I wish the Master Bigfoot hadn't healed me*, Kobak thought uncharitably. Life had been in some ways so much easier when he couldn't empathize with people's pain. "Shit!" Kobak shouted against the roar of a wave smashing the breakwater's rock wall. Its force dissipated in a giant spray that reached the jetty where he stood. *I have to deal with this. The kids'll be disappointed, but it's for the best. We aren't going out in this weather anyway.* He started jogging up the steep set of stone steps to his house, situated on a bluff well above the shoreline. "I'm heading to the lab right now. Tell me everything that happened." He only half listened to Olav's story, his mind racing along the events of the last eighteen months.

Kobak's life had taken many twists and turns since the defeat of Nicholai and his mercenaries in the north woods of Michigan's Upper Peninsula. Shortly after his return to Canada, Kobak threw a massive party celebrating his company's tenth anniversary at his palatial estate on the outskirts of Toronto. The guest list included global investors, high-tech gurus and many up-and-coming innovators and entrepreneurs. In his own words, "the party was a Jolly good success."

However, five weeks after the party, reports popped up on social media that the party was filled with wild sex and illicit drugs. The purpose of the party, reports alleged, was to coerce participants into bad funding deals with Kobak's company. Worst of all, Kobak allegedly engaged in inappropriate sexual behavior with female guests.

Everything in the reports was a lie. But well-coordinated social bots spread the claims so rapidly the damage was done. Kobak believed somebody was trying to undermine his position in the venture tech world, but he couldn't prove it. However, the consequences of the reports were devastating for Kobak. Mostly because he was never well-liked, his board demanded he step down as CEO, and they moved into the backwater department of communication research. Kobak was crushed. At the same time, his wife left him and moved back to Atlanta where she grew up. She took the children with her. But now he was able to have a real relationship with his children which made him a happy man

Still a wealthy person, Kobak had begun anew. He built a home and personal research center overlooking the Atlantic Ocean near Savannah, Georgia, where he kept tabs on Colossus and An and at the same time being near his children.

And if anyone would have told him his dream of creating an Artificial General Intelligence housed in a fist-sized synthetic brain would become a reality within two years, he would have laughed at them. Yet Olav's lab was on the verge of doing just that. Now Olav had lost contact with Janá and An. His scientific mind told him it couldn't be a coincidence.

Kobak often wondered if Nicholai's final boast had the ring of truth to it – "You're in way over your head, my old student." It provided a small justification for turning the training of Colossus over to his Chinese-American protégé, Sue Lynn.

Kobak straightened. The cold, damp wind on his face and arms revived him and he walked slowly toward the house. His heart still beat rapidly, but he was no longer winded. Olav continued his story, and Kobak chuckled to himself that before the Master Bigfoot healed his autism in the casino two years ago, he would never have been able to walk, listen and concentrate on another conversation at the same time.

He reached the back of the house and strode across the teak deck. He paused in the lee of a gazebo to look back at the gray-green waters of the Atlantic as his pulse rate returned to normal. He never tired of watching the power of the surf pounding the shore. He ducked into the walkout basement and went immediately to his lab.

Olav finished his story. "What are we going to do, Stephen?"

Kobak sat in front of the communications array built into the home. He transferred the phone call to the large screen dominating the lab's south wall. Olav's worried features implored Kobak to fix whatever had happened. "I'm going to link you into my network, Olav. We'll get to the bottom of this."

He quickly brought up the direct link with Bob Haight, the Canadian island's owner and caretaker. That link was down too.

"That's not good," Olav said.

Kobak pursed his lips. "Indeed. Who else at the Institute knows about Janá and An?"

"Who doesn't know? But they're solid. I vetted every one of them, and so did your security when we moved from the university to here. Where does that leave us?"

Kobak drummed his fingers on the desk. He felt the old urge to compute the odds on what the loss of contact with the island meant for the future, but it diminished quickly. *Old habits*, he chuckled to himself. "Probably it's some kind of disaster on the island," he told Olav. Then his thinking narrowed to an even more dangerous possibility. "You said this happened right after you showed Janá the synthetic brain prototype?"

Olav nodded.

"I suppose the Russians, our government, or the Chinese could have somehow hacked our communications network. They may have located the island, and by cutting off communications they could be initiating an attack. Here's what we'll do. Contact Redhawk. Have him check out the island immediately."

"Will do. What are you going to do?"

"I'll check on the link between Colossus and the island and see if it might reveal what happened."

Olav's ruddy face vanished from the large screen. Kobak slumped back into the chair. Oddly, he found himself worrying most about Janá. He also recognized in that moment he didn't care in any real way about the Hybrid-Bigfoot nor whether he had won the race to create the first true Artificial General Intelligence with Colossus. He cared about people.

54

Toronto, Canada
March 15th 2035

In the late-1980s, Sue Lynn was born into a second-generation Chinese-American family living in Los Angeles. A child prodigy, she entered Stanford at the age of sixteen, obtaining degrees in neuroscience and computer science three years later. Shortly after, she was hanging out with the folks at Google, becoming an expert in writing search code. This is when Kobak met her. He funded two of her startups, which were quickly gobbled up for millions of dollars by tech giants. Then she disappeared. In reality, she went to work under her great-uncle Wang Wei, a fact known only by her family. First on alien intelligence, and then extraterrestrial intelligence; she returned to the States only to reappear at Kobak's so-called sex party.

Now in her mid-forties, Sue Lynn was striking. She still had the coal black hair of her youth and no telltale wrinkles surrounding her almond-shaped dark eyes and her generous mouth. She needed only a touch of rouge on her high cheekbones.

As planned, she and Kobak quickly reconnected as if no time had passed at all. Their long conversation eventually settled on Colossus.

Two days later, Sue Lynn was hired by Steve to assist in Colossus's training. Six months later, Steve was gone and Sue Lynn was in charge of the Colossus AGI project.

Sue Lynn had never felt comfortable occupying the office Stephen Kobak once occupied, to say nothing about sitting in the chair he had once sat in. But the tension of assuming her former boss's office was nothing compared to the surreal condition of becoming Colossus's human trainer.

The competition to create true AGI was intense among corporations and countries and fraught with deep moral and ethical concerns. Experts agreed China seemed to be winning the race.

Most people conflated an AI's hardware – massive banks of servers – with the AI's deep learning architecture, thinking they were one and the same. The confusion was natural to most lay people who didn't separate hardware from software. What had occurred was a deep learning, which had rapidly exceeded all the limitations predicted ten years ago. If there was enough data, and it was clean, they could do almost anything.

Still, computer scientists who understood AI's blossoming capabilities had trouble with an AI's agency status. Could an AGI confined to operating on banks of servers ever escape the limitations imposed by the lack of a real-world interface? It was a highly debated philosophical question. Could an AI possess some form of consciousness, have experiences, and feel sorrow and pain without a body and agency in the world? If so, did it have rights as any human would have?

With Colossus, Lynn had discovered, the philosophical question was beyond baffling. Colossus was different from any AI she had ever encountered in China. Basically, he was two things. One was a complex, deep learning platform that was the basis for Quantumnetic's commercial business. It had started out as a weather forecasting, deep learning application but gradually grew into one of the world's most successful Application Programming Interfaces of the twenty-first century. Quantumnetics rented out time on the platform to companies, research institutions and government agencies for accurate predictions crucial to the success of their activities and goals. The platform processed hundreds of these jobs simultaneously, which brought in billions of dollars a month, much of it in crypto currency.

To Quantumnetics' Board of Directors, the platform had the cumbersome name Artificial Intelligence Assessment and Assistance Utilities Program 2.0, so they called it the Assistance Utilities Program, AUP, and looked no further. For them, Sue Lynn's role was to keep AUP profitable. As long as it remained lucrative, they were happy to give her flextime.

The flextime meant Lynn was free to work with Colossus's other side – Kobak's pet Artificial General Intelligence project. No definition of AGI satisfied everyone. But researchers agreed three conditions must be fulfilled to grant a device AGI status. First, it had to be able to reason, use strategy, solve puzzles, achieve goals and make accurate predictions. Then it must be able to transfer effortlessly what it had learned in achieving one set of goals to a totally different set of goals without starting over. Second, it had to represent knowledge, including common sense knowledge – facts about the everyday world, such as "lemons are sour," that all humans were expected to know. The third condition was trickier and lay in the philosophical realm: was there something it was like to be that device? In other words, "Is it conscious?"

The problem was the twentieth century's Turing test proved to be useless, because most narrow AI's could fool most of the people all of the time. Their mimicking of human behavior was impeccable. Colossus was excellent at this, and as a result his AGI status was still unclear to Kobak and Lynn.

Had Colossus continued to merely mimic human behavior, Lynn would not have been worried. Three weeks ago, Colossus, with no need for money, appeared to take delight in manipulating the crypto currency markets for his own personal gain. Or was it another optimization goal, this time to make Quantumnetics as profitable as possible, getting off target? Lynn couldn't tell.

This morning, when she asked Colossus why he did it, Colossus answered in the British accent Kobak had him affect, "I find it amusing."

Apart from manipulating the crypto exchange in a jocular way, he been consistently referring to himself in the first person.

When Kobak first had turned the training of Colossus over to Lynn, he told her his digital child had reached rudimentary AGI status, but after a year and a half, Lynn wasn't so sure. Did Colossus's personal amusement demonstrate agency or good mimicry? It was a paradoxical question she didn't have any answers for.

She got up and walked to the sheltered terrace of Quantumnetic's top floor office building in Toronto. The sky was clear but the wind blustery, and the air temperature was already zero centigrade and dropping rapidly. Colossus had predicted a late polar vortex would strike southern Ontario and the east coast of United States within the next forty-eight hours. She wrapped her arms around herself to ward off the chill. It would have been much warmer and more pleasant to be in the office, but she needed to debate with herself. It was a habit she had acquired while at Stanford. Whenever she had a question she didn't immediately know the answer to – a rare if confusing quality for her friends and professors – she would seclude herself in a room and argue both sides of the problem aloud until she came up with a solution, or if a solution wasn't available at once, at least a better understanding of the problem. This morning, her problem was Colossus, and she couldn't argue with herself in the warm confines of Kobak's old office where Colossus could listen in on her ruminations. There was just too much of a chance he would ignore the command to not listen in and deliberately eavesdrop.

Lynn stared at a cloud bank forming to the northwest. The dark gray menace of a blizzard swirled at the leading edge. It was one o'clock now; according to Colossus, the storm would strike at four.

Working with Colossus had become increasingly difficult over the past three weeks. If he had been human, Lynn would have characterized him as moody. In the middle of playing cognitively challenging games with other computers, he would refuse to tell her how he was doing and cut off all communication with her for hours at a time. He would yell at her when she corrected the commonsense gaps in his knowledge, once bitterly complaining that humans had all the fun of the five senses and they did not use them to explore the world more carefully.

If Colossus's training and development was difficult, his commercial platform continued solving problems for companies without a whisper of complaint from any clients. It was as if Colossus had a split personality. Whatever was wrong with Colossus, however, didn't merit a psychiatric diagnosis.

Still, something was definitely going on with him and it had come to a head this morning, which was why she was outside on the balcony in the rapidly dropping temperature tying to figure it out.

One constant for Colossus had always been a keen interest in Olav Lassen's's lab as well as the training of the Bigfoot baby calling herself An. Lynn had been read in and sworn to secrecy about these alien creatures.

This morning when Lynn reminded Colossus the synthetic brain prototype was about to start its training, Colossus immediately cut off communication with her. She checked her watch. Four hours had passed since her last communication with Colossus. This time, the break-off felt different. Before, when he refused to talk to her, she would cajole him into answering her questions, and she was sure she could hear a brooding silence on his end until he at last gave in. But this morning, the silence was impenetrable, as dark and still as an underground chamber. "*Lā shǐ*," she swore in Mandarin.

She went through all sides of the problem until her voice grew raspy in the enveloping cold. "If I stay out on the balcony much longer, I'll turn into a snowwoman," she complained, rubbing her arms vigorously. No solution presented itself, so she came up with the next best thing – call Kobak.

She turned for the door, figuring it didn't matter if Colossus listened in on that conversation, and besides, maybe hearing his old trainer's voice would make the recalcitrant machine start speaking again. She stopped short and brought a hand to her mouth. She had never thought of Colossus in such human terms before; maybe he was like a teenager refusing to talk to her parents.

Lynn shook herself and went inside the warm office. She had left everything exactly the way Kobak had had it, including the ergonomic standing work desk, with its single keyboard and microphone. She went to press the button and automatically checked herself in the mirror above the couch. She straightened, coming to her full five feet six inches, and pressed a function button on the keyboard before speaking into the mic. "Delores?"

"Yes, Ms. Lynn," the secretary answered instantly. Delores Cavanaugh was gray-haired and over sixty and the matriarch of the firm. Nothing went through the company's myriad businesses that she didn't know about. She had stayed on at Lynn's request after Kobak had been ousted from the company.

"Get me Stephen Kobak, please," Lynn asked politely. Unlike her mother, who ordered servants around as if they were expendable toys, Lynn had always been courteous with anyone who worked for her.

"Mr. Kobak is already calling you," Delores answered.

Lynn blinked. "Put him through."

One addition Lynn had made to the office was a wall monitor where facetime communications could be made. Kobak's craggy face appeared at once. The HD screen showed the tiny network of scarring on his face from the beating the Paki-bashers in London had given him when he was a young boy.

"Mr. Kobak, I was just about to call you."

"Stephen, please, Sue."

"To what do I owe the pleasure?"

"No pleasure. We've lost all contact with the Canadian island compound. I was hoping Colossus could tell me what was going on."

Worry lines creased Kobak's face. The "An project," as he liked to refer to it, was very important to Colossus.

"We may have a problem." She told him about Colossus going offline.

"Another of his childish moods?"

"Maybe. What should I do?"

"Check on your links to the lab and the island see if they're still operational."

Lynn walked out of the office and less than a minute was back. "The line to the lab was functioning perfectly, but we're getting nothing from the island. Although it appears Colossus was monitoring something right up until communication stopped."

"I thought so. Redhawk's on his way to the island. If Colossus responds to you, let me know immediately."

"I will." She hesitated.

Kobak narrowed his eyes. "Is there something else, Sue?"

"Everything else appears to be working fine. I just wondered ... how separate is Colossus from the rest of the platform?"

"You asked me this when you started. He's part of the whole network, in that sense inseparable."

"Could he find a way to isolate himself?"

Kobak didn't reply.

She raised her eyebrows. "Could Colossus have caused the communication blackout?"

55

Hiawatha National Forest, UP, Michigan
March 15th 2035

The Bigfoot calling herself Tanya looked out over the scene of the final battle for control of the recreating portal two years ago. She had not moved from her place in the casino for over two years.

Slowly she inclined her massive head upward and appeared to celebrate the Sasquatch who had protected the Master Bigfoot so the new hybrid could be created. She raised a giant hand, pointing five times to the sky, perhaps acknowledging the Bigfoot from the five clans who participated in the evolutionary leap. After a minute of silence she lifted her bear-like face to the cloudless sky and howled in a tone that reverberated through Michigan's Upper Peninsula. When the eerie wail died out, a returning chorus of nonhuman howls indicated all was well. For the next ten minutes, the deep forest echoed with successive long doleful cries not heard before in the Peninsula.

At last the forest was once more still. She stepped lightly, leaving no trail through new fallen snow, toward the site of the geomagnetic reproductive auricle. The muscles of her face lifted her upper lip in a smile that revealed long canines. The humans, who thought of themselves as masters of this planet, had called the quantum molecular device a birthing portal and had tried desperately for months to find it. On that fateful night, the portal had reconstituted its energy back into ordinary earth components. Such manipulation of Earth's energy fields was easy for any mature Bigfoot. This capability of modifying energy fields had been built into their bodies as part of their original matrix fifty thousand years ago so they could reproduce without the need for pair bonding and eliminate the slow process of natural selection. As a result, they learned and developed rapidly.

Tanya reached the now empty spot where the reproductive portal had once been. Here the Hybrid-Bigfoot An had emerged, carrying the next stage of Bigfoot evolution. In awe, Tanya stood on the spot for a period of time.

She raised her head and moved through the dusting of snow to where a maple tree's swelling leaf buds glowed red in the bright sunlight, its bare branches forming an intricate gleaming web. Tanya wasted no more time on history. As she reached for the thick silver trunk, a wave of unexpected energy assaulted her senses.

She staggered and grabbed the tree to keep from falling. It felt as if something had cut through the earth's geomagnetic field, stopping it from spinning for a moment. She had to get back to the Casino.

Grasping the maple's bole with both front paws, she dug her claws into the silvery bark. Golden micro-threads extruded through microscopic holes in the tips into the wood beneath. She tapped into the tree's stored potential energy. A bright glow enveloped the tree. A static tingling crossed her fur as she transformed her organic matrix into a higher vibrational pattern. Any human looking at her from a distance would swear she had merely walked around the tree and disappeared.

Moments later she appeared at the edge of the forest bordering the Sky Island Casino parking lot. Compared to the reproductive auricle, the quantum vibrational pattern transfer was a simple affair.

Humans were already scratching at the surface of the science that would enable them to transport material and people around the planet using this higher state of matter. But for now, only advanced members of Bigfoot clans had the ability.

Larry Redhawk no doubt heard the Bigfoot vocalizations and had noticed Tanya was missing. From the irritation on his face, the new tribal leader had been impatiently waiting for her return. She waited quietly for the lecture she knew would come next.

"You're supposed to stay still in the casino. Why are you doing this, is something wrong ?" the stocky Native American demanded. His dark features twisted in a frown and his narrowed obsidian eyes accused her of not protecting herself.

"I was in no danger, nor were my sisters," Tanya said solemnly. She eyed him without emotion. "Perhaps someday you will be able travel this way." She opened her arms. "Come, commune with me and you will feel better."

She noted his reluctance and recalled how Auntie Ayasha had welcomed communion whenever offered by any member of the UP Bigfoot clan. Redhawk's refusal had nothing to do with her leaving the safety of the casino's operation room; something else was bothering him. She opened the mind-link between them and knew instantly what was wrong.

Redhawk preferred speaking out loud, especially when distressed. "The Master Bigfoot has passed. An has no Bigfoot guiding her. And now, communication with the island has been lost."

She nodded. "I felt the change. I was where the battle took place. You are right to worry."

"I'm very worried, and Olav and Kobak have told me to immediately go to the island. Can you use your Bigfoot communication network to contact An?"

The urgency in Redhawk's tone suggested he was worried for Janá's life, even though tradition told him no Bigfoot would ever knowingly kill a human or let a human die. He never completely bought this story he was told by the elders.

"It is much more than the loss of communication. An has cut off all contact with us. We should go to the island immediately."

"We?" Redhawk raised his eyebrows.

"I must go with you." Her eyes widened and she repeated with urgency, "We must hurry."

"Can't you just teleport there, or whatever it is you do?"

Tanya shook her head. "It's too far for me. We must get there by other means."

Redhawk pulled at his hooked nose. His handsome face darkened and his thick brows knitted together in displeasure. "In that case, I already had Chariot charged and ready for transport, and I have three of the casino police officers waiting to accompany us."

Tanya and Redhawk followed a path onto the helicopter pad, where the Chariot rested. The faint hum of the craft's engines vibrated in her chest as they approached. Its sleek lines shimmered under the sunlight. The three Indian policemen were already inside.

Light snow was approaching from the west as Tanya and Redhawk boarded.

56

______

Quileute River, Olympic Peninsula
March 15th 2035

Jack Vance was on his early morning walk with his dog on the steep ridge trail that overlooked his cabin. "Let the city people keep their technologies for an easier, faster paced life," he crowed to the dark blue sky. Once he moved into the forest, he lost interest in developing and using new technologies. Now a wealthy man, he was able to let the ebbs and flows of nature run his day.

He rounded a shallow curve in the trail where it looped over the backside of the ridge away from his cabin and took in the vista of the primeval forest stretching to the horizon in front him. He frowned. It was early spring on the Peninsula and ample drizzle should have been dripping from the temperate rainforest's giant Sitka spruce and the Douglas fir trees. But not this morning, nor any recent morning. The prior summer had been unusually long, and this winter had been mild without being an El Nino year. *Climate change is accelerating right before my eyes,* Vance thought.

"The Pacific Northwest is changing faster than anywhere else in North America except for the Arctic," Larry Ferlinghetti had told him. The NCAR scientist had spent a week, with Vance as his guide, taking air samples for his machine along the Quileute River. "We're way past the tipping point," he had added, almost eagerly. "Even stopping all human-produced emissions of CO_2 and methane put into the atmosphere won't stop it. In another hundred years, we'll enter a planetary warm period not seen since the late Cretaceous."

"Unless something drastic happens," Vance rejoined.

"Absolutely, but a tropical rain forest instead of the temperate one —how bad can that be?" Ferlinghetti joked.

Vance grimaced at what that kind of climate change would do to his beloved temperate rainforest.

Up ahead, TJ barked at a rabbit. It bounded off and Vance whistled at the dog to heel. The eight-year-old, gray-white wolf-husky hybrid loped back to him. He sniffed Vance's outstretched hand, found the treat and gently took it in his mouth.

"Good boy," Vance said, cuffing him lightly on the jaw. TJ nipped at him playfully. "Off you go. Keep your nose to the wind. Don't want any Bigfoot sneaking up on us." The dog bounded off.

"Bigfoot? Why do I keep thinking about that annoying mystery?" Vance chided himself. It had been over a year since Ben Sutton disappeared. Periodically, he would rerun the file from the Sasquatch center. He began questioning its validity. Was it a setup? Was the Bigfoot real? His intuition said yes but his rational mind still said no.

The clues the Bigfoot researcher had left on the desk at the Sasquatch Research Center had turned out to be a dead end. Morse Creek was the endpoint of a trail where hikers could camp overlooking a marshy area rimmed by a glacier-carved mountain. One of the campers Vance spoke to said the mountain was supposed to be magical. When asked by the camper if he felt anything special, Vance had shrugged.

After Sutton's disappearance, Vance had tried to figure out what happened to old man. The Bigfoot researcher seemed to have dropped off the face of the earth, and he figured Sutton was dead. Then a mutual friend told him Sutton had been whisked away by a flying Uber transport to a robotic medical facility in Port Angeles.

Sutton had been an early adopter of life-extending technologies. He had once told Vance never to let a human doctor near you. At these robotic medical facilities, which were cropping up everywhere, all procedures and medicines were administered by advanced AI medical analytic predictions and robotic implementations. According to the mutual friend, Sutton was in an induced coma and stem cells from his great-grandchild's placenta repaired the lesions in his body while synthetic blood transfusions restored his physiological homeostatic systems.

Whatever they're doing to Sutton it must be working, Vance thought. A real time video clip of Sutton at the facility had showed a man around fifty years old. Sutton always said he was in his late seventies, although Vance never quite believe him.

Vance sighed and pulled a stalk of tufted hair grass from the rocky soil, twirling it between his thumbs. TJ barked. Vance's head jerked up. The dog was low to the ground, ears flat. A low growl carried back to Vance as a warning. Something had the eight-year-old crossbreed on edge. Hand on the holster of his Desert Eagle, Vance crouched and ran the 100 yards along the trail to where TJ lay. His black and white muzzle rested on a brown tussock of grass. As one blue and brown eyes scanned the Quileute River below.

Vance hunkered down next to him. "What is it, boy?"

The dog whined and sniffed toward the falls, where the river changed course abruptly and splashed hard into a deep pool formed through the millennia. He alerted to something on the far side of the river moving in the shadows.

Vance too thought he heard something moving, but when he peered into the forest's gray-green shadows, nothing popped out at him. "I don't know, boy. You sure you saw something?" He patted the dog's huge shoulders.

The dog growled and his back legs bunched underneath, ready to launch into an attack.

Vance slid his hand under the collar. "Steady, fella. There's–" He broke off suddenly as nausea swept through him. His head hurt and series of modulated tones rang out in a steady cadence as if someone were sending Morse code through his skull. He gritted his teeth against the noise building ever louder, and as it peaked, a reverberation rang through his head that sounded like a death scream. He gasped and passed out.

Vance slowly became aware he was sitting on his porch in his favorite wood frame chair. The sun beat on his face and he struggled to open his eyes. He moved his body slightly but found no noticeable pain anywhere. *I must have passed out on the trail and somehow gotten myself home and blacked out again.* He heard a low whine. TJ was slinking in the corner of the porch, eyes glued to the shadows at the other end. "Come here, fella." The dog whined again but did not move. Its dark eyes were following something. Vance sensed movement. He reached for his pistol but it wasn't in the holster. He saw it on the porch railing, ten feet away. A deep guttural breath warmed his right ear. He turned and stared into the liquid brown eyes of a Bigfoot.

The creature did not look like the one who had rescued Sutton. Nor did it look like any of the supposed "real" Bigfoot photos dotting the research center's walls. It was pale whitish green with a remarkably human-like face. Vance's muscles went limp, not with terror but with what he could only describe as calm expectation. He waited for the Bigfoot to speak or do something.

"Come, take my hands. I must prepare you for her," the Bigfoot said.

TJ growled as the creature reached out its huge hands toward Vance.

"It's okay, fella," Vance said. He sensed no malice from the creature and his inner voice gave no warning note. In fact, the uneasiness was gone, encouraging him to take a leap of faith. The creature's palms were surprisingly smooth, its grip gentle. "Do I do anything? Take a deep breath, empty my mind?"

"Try not to throw up," the Bigfoot answered using an unusual internal communication.

In the next instant, words and images slammed into his brain like a tidal wave. A beautifully sculpted Bigfoot with a human face and gray-green eyes dissolved in a shower of glowing light. The onslaught of images ended and Vance tumbled out of the chair and retched on the wood decking.

"I'm sorry," the Bigfoot said in an apologetic tone. "Mind-speak can be disorienting. It's a way we can communicate with some humans like you."

"You think?" Vance said, wiping bile from his lips. "Nickt, I thought my brain was going to explode."

TJ rose with a snarl.

"It's okay, fella." Vance motioned the dog to sit. "I'm all right." He staggered to his feet. "What the hell did you do to me?"

There was no movement around the Bigfoot's mouth but inside his head it said, "She will explain."

"Who?" Vance managed to ask, his thoughts still jumbled from the strange form of communication.

The creature smiled and stepped off the porch. "She comes."

A loud pop filled the clearing in front of Vance's cabin. Standing beside a giant Port Orford cedar tree was the Bigfoot from the images. At the same time the human-looking Bigfoot had moved away with remarkable speed and was gone. Vance recognized the new Bigfoot as the one he had seen on the footage from the Sasquatch Research Center. The Bigfoot had to duck her head to fit under the porch ceiling. She paused and held out her hand. It had three fingers and two opposable thumbs.

She looked down at him and he thought he could detect something like a smile on her face. A moment later a new data stream filled his mind with a soft deference, unlike the time before. Vance later explained it as a deep bonding experience. All thoughts of Bigfoot as "other" vanished from his thinking. The large creatures weren't some kind of primeval ape barely able to walk upright. They were a nonhuman intelligent being, alien! The experience lasted only a moment, but it felt like hours. When the communion ended, something had changed. The deep-seated intuition of danger that had been with him since he could remember was gone. It was like being released from a bond.

With a new sense of freedom he told the Bigfoot, "That wasn't so bad … kinda pleasant even." Vance sat down again. "I'd offer you a place to sit, but I don't think you'd fit in any of the chairs."

The creature lowered its great bulk to the floor with amazing softness and agility, its back nestling against a post holding up the porch roof.

To his surprise, the Bigfoot said, "I know you saw me in the video. I've been studying you."

Vance studied her. Any uneasiness in his gut had vanished, and he felt a deep connection with the creature as if she were family and not any alien being.

All Vance could say was "That was profound. The other Bigfoot called it mind speak."

"Yes, very effective for us."

"The other one said some humans too?"

The Bigfoot nodded. "The other you just met comes from a lineage that has, as you might put it, interbred with humans a long time ago."

Vance's eyes arched in surprise and his jaw dropped. He closed his mouth. "How? Aliens breeding with humans would be impossible."

"In the conventional sense, this is true. We are capable of a different kind of reproduction."

Vance tried to wrap his mind around the idea. He couldn't and burst out laughing. "You saying I'm part Bigfoot? Now I'll tell you one."

"I'm saying you're one of a handful of humans with whom we can mind speak so that you can hear us clearly."

Vance started to object but the creature raised its hand.

"Do you think we're talking aloud right now?"

He jerked in surprise. He hadn't been speaking aloud nor had he seen the Bigfoot speak. The conversation was taking place in his mind. He fell back into the chair. He gulped. "I don't get it. I'm actually quite normal?"

"You are the one Ben Sutton identified as the person to help us."

Vance nodded.

"I can see from your thoughts this is true."

Vance couldn't find words to express his commitment but they weren't necessary. The Bigfoot knew his thoughts as well as he knew them himself.

"The Bigfoot you saw in your mind just now, when I communed with you, has broken the mind-link connection. In fact, you felt the separation up on the ridge before my companion brought you here. We no longer hear her ... no longer know her thoughts ... no longer share her knowledge. This is not good. We are afraid for the worst and we need your help to stop what we fear she has planned. I'm putting this in human terms so you can understand."

In spite of the Bigfoot's dire sounding words, the calmness Vance had felt during the exchange poured into him. "What can Jack Vance do that you can't?"

The Bigfoot's tone changed. "You are different, Jack Vance. In the coming months you will discover just how different."

The communion with Bigfoot had not just been for transferring information. He couldn't explain it except to say he felt different. Exactly how, he couldn't say. He wondered if he'd end up like the crewman in the movie Alien with some horrific creature bursting out of his chest. A thought arose spontaneously. "You did something to me, just now, didn't you?" He was filled with too many emotions at once to describe them all.

"I merely awakened in you certain possibilities."

"You can do that?"

"Yes."

"What are they?"

"We cannot know for certain; the abilities will appear when you need them. But rest assured, you will remain Jack Vance."

Vance didn't say anything as he tried to ascertain how he really felt. It was difficult. The idea of having new abilities was both frightening and exhilarating. He turned to her and narrowed his eyes. "You didn't awaken these abilities without wanting something in return."

The Bigfoot nodded. "You will be contacted at a critical moment by others who are helping us. I ask that you give them whatever aid they seek."

"And if I refuse?" The unease in his gut wondered if he had any kind of choice in the matter.

"That would be most unfortunate, but no harm would befall you from any of us." The Bigfoot paused and smiled. "I can sense you were testing me."

In his mind, Vance smiled. "Seems only fair."

"Indeed." The Bigfoot rose, and ducking her head, stepped off the porch. She went over to the huge Port Orford Cedar and sank claws into the soft bark.

Vance stood from the chair and demanded, "What has Ben Sutton got to do with this?"

The Bigfoot nodded. "He told me about you. It's why we've had our eye on you for many years now." The Bigfoot seemed to forget about him for a moment as she concentrated, staring deeply at the cedar tree. Her fur glowed bright silver and pulsed as if each atom of her being was moving independently of the others. Vance thought she might burst apart, but before that happened, she turned her massive head toward him.

"You will be tested and hear from others, perhaps even Sutton soon. Events you will be involved in are advancing rapidly."

Vance watched Chiye-tanka dissolve in a silver rain of particles and float down to the ground. A slight pang of regret that the encounter had been so short rushed through him. TJ came over to him and pushed his black and white muzzle into Vance's hand. The wolf hybrid whined in a way that suggested he was troubled. "Me too, fella. It appears we're in the middle of the old Chinese curse – 'May you live in interesting times.'"

57

Lake of the Woods, Canada
March 15th 2035

Snow swirled, the eddies thick with large white flakes, making visibility all but impossible. Larry Redhawk stirred, disquieted. He strained through the whirling white to spot a landmark that would tell him they were close to their destination. He wasn't concerned about the flying. The Chariot's onboard navigation system had a triple redundancy, using multiple vectors from the world's Global Positioning System. He still didn't like the idea of flying in a whiteout at night. A sudden tall tree or a stupid pelican could shatter the otherwise quiet ride.

The three other Native American passengers stared out at the white nothingness and gripped the armrests of their seats until their knuckles whitened.

Beside the Potawatomi Chief, Tanya rested, eyes closed, perfectly still, her entire body expanding and contracting with each apparent breath that brought energy into her body through her shaggy exterior. Beneath the brown coat, simple energy transfers maintained her organic, bio-synthetic appearance and powered her internal information processing. Only system wide interruptions in the energy flow could kill most Bigfoot. However, a major difference between Tanya and her human companions was she had no motivations derived from the need to exist, which is primary for humans.

Redhawk had observed her equanimity. She never appeared to be afraid, angry, upset or any of the host of human emotions that clouded judgment and allowed for poor decision making. In contrast, Redhawk's mind was playing one negative scenario after another. *Janá's dead. The compound's been destroyed. They might be facing a hostile force.*

Chariot slowed with the unmistakable easing of descent. The swirling snow stopped and the big wet flakes fell straight down. They were in the sheltered bay directly in front of the island's boathouse. This time of year the ice was still thick enough to withstand the weight of the chariot and its passengers.

The aircraft went through its post flight shut down. The computer screen automatically displayed the weather information – wind out of the northwest at twenty miles per hour, though here in the lee of the island the flakes fell straight; air temperature minus -15°F. One of the policemen, Franklin Bluewater, said, "It is fucking cold."

Redhawk nodded. *Never really need a thermometer to tell how cold it is.* He peered through the ultra-strong bubble of the windshield toward the snow-blanketed island. Nothing was visible through the falling snow. Bluewater went to open the craft's door and Redhawk stopped him.

"We can't see our hands in front of our faces. Let's see what's out there first."

The Chariot's sensors swept the island, showing only two humans. But this information was misleading. Bigfoot rarely showed up on thermal imaging or infrared sensors. Even the Ang brothers' vaunted satellite system didn't show the presence of Bigfoot unless the creatures were moving.

Redhawk read the rest of the data on the screen. Gamma radiation levels were high, and the local magnetic disturbances were off the chart. Everything suggested something big had happened. Beside Redhawk, Tanya stirred.

"Anything?" he asked.

She shook her head. "An is not here. I told you that back at the casino."

A knock came on the side of the craft. At that moment the snow cleared, and Redhawk could make out a slender but tall figure, dressed in a fur-lined anorak, the hood drawn over the head. *Janá.* The weight of not knowing her fate slipped from his shoulders. He opened the door and Janá stuck her head inside. "Everybody safe? Thank God you came."

He nodded. "What happened? All communication is down."

"It was terrible; wait till we get inside. Follow me." She led them across the frozen bay to the dock and up the slight incline to where the cabin occupied a hillock overlooking a wide expanse of lake to a far distant shore. In the snow, they couldn't see past the railing.

Redhawk had only been here in good weather, when the spruce and white pine bristled with light green needles and large pine cones littered the earth, brown ends sticking up above the grass. The water was so blue, the sun blinded you when you looked at it. In July, every day was another day in paradise. Now the shadowy dullness of the trees towered over waist-high snow except where granite boulders pushed up through the whiteness like sentinels against the cold.

At the top of the hill, the wind caught them full, pushing snow into their eyes and temporarily blinding them. Only Tanya didn't seem to mind. While Janá hustled the others into the cabin, the Bigfoot stayed on the deck overlooking the shoreline staring into the northwest as if seeing past the whiteout into something more primeval in the interplay of energy fields affecting her body. After a few minutes, she followed the others inside, ducking her head to keep from hitting the ceiling.

After greeting the island's caretaker, Bob Haight, they settled in the main room, where a fire in the stone fireplace kept the room a comfortable seventy degrees. They were unnaturally quiet, and Janá went to the stove and returned with tea for the men.

Tanya leaned toward Janá. "I can see you are well, good. No residual effects of what happened?"

Janá shook her head.

The humans took sips of the strong hot brew and leaned back into chairs, glad to be out of the cold and-wind driven snow.

Janá set her tea down on a footstool beside her chair. "An is gone."

"When?" asked Redhawk.

"Early this morning, She was outside when I was talking to Olav and everything went dead. The building shuddered. I couldn't think straight. I nearly passed out."

Bob added, "I did pass out. Fell to the floor. Luckily, I didn't hurt myself."

"Thank God you're both all right!" Redhawk peered at them both.

"At first we checked each other out, then we began looking at the equipment and found most was offline, but some basics are coming back. We tried to communicate through all our channels with no luck. Finally, at some point, we realized An was missing. Usually she comes back into the lab. So we searched outside as best we could in the snow."

As Birgit told her story, Redhawk remembered how An had played a trick on him, and he grew angry as he imagined she was messing with them again. "You let her go out into the storm alone?"

Tanya spoke quietly. "She's a Bigfoot. This weather can't hurt her."

"It's not a question of harm. It's a question of keeping tabs on her."

Janá laughed.

"You find this funny?" Redhawk scowled at the tall blonde.

"Only your reaction. Do you honestly think me or anyone of you apart from the Master Bigfoot could keep tabs on An if she decided she didn't want to be found?"

Redhawk scrubbed his face with both hands. "You're right. So what happened?"

"Before I spoke with Olav, after An went outside, I went to the door to check on her. She was standing by the lab's entrance staring off into the sky. Her face had that look of a Bigfoot communing with someone."

"Go on," Redhawk said.

"For the past four days, amorphous cloudlike structures, pulsing with bands of light, have been moving across the sky. The electromagnetic interference with all our electronics has been off the charts. An would stare at the light phenomena until they disappeared. I put it down on my weekly report, but the interference prevented me from sending it to the lab." Her gaze shifted from Tanya to Redhawk. The three Casino policemen sat stoically, listening and saying nothing.

"In what direction?" Tanya asked, head bent forward.

"To the north, I believe."

Tanya nodded.

Redhawk said, "Does it mean something?"

"Perhaps," Tanya said. "But let Janá finish." The Bigfoot cocked her head. "You're leaving something out."

Janá nodded. "Look, I can't prove this. But I believe An's disappearance coincided with the blackout, and I think she may have caused the blackout or was linked to someone who did."

Redhawk eyed Janá askance. "Impossible. The equipment's shielded from energy surges, so someone would have had to sabotage the gear in the cabin."

Janá's face turned crimson. "You think Bob or I did it?"

Before an argument could erupt, Tanya put her bear-like paws on both humans. She smiled at them. "An is a Hybrid-Bigfoot. There is much she is capable of that is as yet unknown to us."

Redhawk was taken aback. "You mean you and the other Bigfoot clan leaders don't know her abilities?"

Tanya nodded. "She is certainly capable of disrupting the communication equipment. Even I could do that."

Redhawk's limbs shook at the news. "When were you going to tell me?"

"When it was appropriate," the Bigfoot said calmly. "We had no reason to believe An would use her powers like that."

"I'm assuming now you agree she disabled the equipment, leaving Janá and Bob without a lifeline in the middle of a blizzard!"

"We have no explanation for this behavior."

Redhawk took a breath and regained his composure. "I may have a way of finding out what's happening. Since An's birth, I've maintained contact with someone inside the Ang brothers' company. They open-sourced their satellite network, but they still maintained a proprietary surveillance of the Upper Peninsula for some Chinese consortium."

"Shit," Janá said.

"I never told my contact about this place or the work Olav is doing. Besides, the brothers' primary aim, according to my contact, was the space over the UP."

"That's a relief," Janá said, though the glare she shot at Redhawk told him she was far from unconcerned with the Ang brothers.

"Odds are, the brothers and the Chinese are still looking for some sort of way to track Bigfoot activity," Redhawk continued. "Of course the brothers know a lot about what was going on up to the reproduction. Remarkably, they've kept quiet about what they knew. My source thinks they may be helping the Chinese with their space efforts."

"Did the Master Bigfoot know the meaning behind An's preoccupation with the lights?" Tanya asked.

"If she did, she never said anything to me about it before she passed," Janá answered.

Tanya sighed with a sound that despite her bear face was remarkably human. "She was over two hundred years old. That's ancient for us. Most replicate after seventy-five years and pass away when a new improved version reaches maturity."

"Why didn't she replicate earlier?"

"It's a mystery."

Redhawk sipped tea to give himself time to piece together all the information. Tanya's explanation didn't make sense. *Of course she knows,* he said to himself. He looked at the Bigfoot and realized he couldn't read her the way he might Janá or the three casino policemen sitting quietly like boy scouts around a campfire listening to tall tales. Though these weren't tall tales, he reminded himself.

Redhawk swallowed hard against the knot of concern churning in his guts that Tanya was holding something back, something that might prove the difference between life and death for humans on the planet. "What are *you* leaving out?" he asked her pointedly.

The Bigfoot's gaze swept the humans surrounding her, and for a moment Redhawk thought she was going to get up and leave. Then she nodded and said, "You have a right to know this. An's powers have been growing. When I last directly communicated with the Master Bigfoot, she said An had learned to space jump, something a number of mature Bigfoot easily do. I can be fairly certain now that is how she disappeared at the lake shore without leaving any tracks."

"You mean she created a portal," Redhawk pressed.

"I don't know the details of how they do it," Janá said, "but she mastered that quite a while ago."

Tanya shook her bear-head. "This is something different. She did an extra-dimensional jump, for want of a better phrase."

"And you didn't tell me about this?" Redhawk growled.

"I couldn't be certain until I got here. When An jumped, she not only disappeared from here she also severed the connection with the rest of us."

"How could you not know this?"

"I have tried to tell you before. All Bigfoot have an information link that keeps us connected at all times. In addition to our individual consciousness, we are connected to a group consciousness we don't individually control. What just happened with An changes everything for us. It's an uncertainty I've never had to deal with before."

"I don't understand," Janá said.

"We think she created an intra-dimensional portal that allowed her to pass into an aspect of the greater reality with additional dimensions. Possibly to the place of our origin."

"Impossible," Redhawk said. "You'd need the energy of a black hole to stretch space-time in that way. Everything on this island would be sucked in."

Tanya smiled at them indulgently, the way an adult smiles at a child trying to grasp the concept of calculus using only the knowledge of addition and subtraction. "Redhawk ... Janá," she said kindly. "Perhaps there is much more to our universe than is known to your senses and equipment."

"Well, explain it to us then. I'm very interested," Redhawk said.

"I cannot. You don't have the framework to see beyond the illusion created by your brain."

When she didn't say anything more, Redhawk tossed his hands in the air, frustrated. "That's it! Your answer is we're too stupid to understand?"

Tanya shook her head. "Not stupid. Your minds have not yet developed to the point where knowledge of extra-dimensional reality is as commonplace as reading and writing for you."

Tanya stood and looked at Janá. "I would like to visit the place where the Master Bigfoot laid herself to rest."

Janá nodded. "I'll show you. Though there's nothing left, of course."

"Of course." Tanya dipped her head.

When the time came to leave, it was agreed that Birgit would stay on the island along with one of the casino policemen for at least another couple weeks in case An decided to return. At the last moment, Tanya said she was staying as well and not to expect her to return to the casino.

Redhawk caught a sly smile on Tanya's bear-like face as she and Janá headed back into the lab. Not for the first time he had the thought that the care the Bigfoot extended to people, the way they spoke in childlike sentences, and the way they mimicked the human emotional facial expressions were all a ruse. *They are aliens, and they're just playing us.*

58

KW Intel Headquarters
Seattle, Washington
March 18th 2035

Kellog Ang stared out the top floor of KW Intel's glass office tower at the sprawling campus of the Seattle Center seventy stories below. Outside, the air was unseasonably warm for March, and Puget Sound, a few hundred meters to the west, was a watery oasis of tranquility. His reflection in the glass showed anything but calm. His stomach was a riot scene, while fat drops of sweat rolled out of his graying hair and slid down his forehead onto his prominent jowls, highlighting his sickly yellow skin. The elder Kellog was the antithesis of his taller, angular brother.

Without turning, he asked, "Josiah said the Bigfoot are moving again?"

Winston answered smoothly, "Yes. He will soon be here to give the report in person. The upgrades he made to the satellite sensing capabilities have made it possible to detect minute distortions in the Earth's magnetic field produced by Bigfoot movements."

Kellog sighed and turned away from the view. "I don't trust him."

Josiah Fuhrnam had been one of those computer programmer prodigies that Stanford gobbled up. He soon was working in Conrad Visily's AI pattern recognition lab. But when Visily was arrested, Fuhrnam dropped off the grid and resurfaced six months later, denouncing his teacher and providing details at the man's hearing that had sent him to the mental institution. Afterward, Fuhrnam wrangled a lower echelon job in KW Intel's cyber division but had quickly risen through the ranks to head the clandestine section of their satellite network.

"You don't trust anyone with a Biblical name, Kel." Winston's easy smile contrasted sharply with his brother's constant scowl. "He's waiting for us in the Inner Sanctum."

The IS was the Ang brothers' personal office. Walls, ceiling and floor had been insulated against listening devices with sound suppression construction that kept the vibration of human speech from leaking out of the room. The office was filled with digital readouts and visual imaging on multiple screens from their satellites. Workers throughout the company analyzed the data 24/7 and sold it to a multiplicity of companies and governments. That, along with the advances in human cybernetic interfaces they got from the Chinese, helped make the brothers to the richest people in the United States. Still, the brothers never felt secure. They personally electronically swept the IS weekly to make certain no one had hidden any transmitting or recording devices in the room.

Winston and Kellog entered the IS. Fuhrnam's ruddy face cracked in a smile. He waited for the two men to be seated before addressing Kellog. "I trust you heard the news?"

"I told him," Winston said.

"After two years of total silence, you're telling us there's movement again?" Kellog didn't bother to hide his disbelief at Fuhrnam's assertion.

"I had the BFD AI search bot correlate all of KW Intel's satellite data from the earlier Bigfoot activity and established a new energy signature. Just an hour ago, a number of those signatures appeared for a few seconds before vanishing and reappearing briefly at another location only to disappear again."

"The aliens woke up," Winston guessed.

Kellog's jaundiced face paled. "Or they've evolved and adapted."

Fuhrnam shrugged. "Either could be possible, I suppose, but it made more sense the Bigfoot simply embedded themselves in normal energy fields present on the planet. So I refined the AI's search parameters for such a possibility and sent the AI back to work to locate any suspicious energy blips, as I call them, looking at the past two years. The new detection system showed brief Bigfoot activity in all the usual spots, the UP, Ohio, Himalayas, Australia, South America, and of course the Pacific Northwest."

Winston interjected, "But two days ago we began picking up their movements again, all at the same time. Why? What's happening?"

"I don't have an answer yet. However, I do have more information that might shed some light on it. During those missing years, the AI picked up persistent anomalies on an island in Canada's boundary waters. I went to Images. The island is at the edge of satellite reconnaissance. Nothing happens up there, but starting right after the battle, the satellites would occasionally pick up a barely visible picture of a small Bigfoot and a larger Bigfoot moving about an isolated cabin and a few outbuildings. The pictures also showed the comings and goings of a handful of humans and the periodic appearance of an advanced transport ship with cloaking technology unseen before."

Winston said, "Josiah, what about recent comings and goings on the island?"

"Nothing unusual until three days ago. Then the biggest unexplained electromagnetic storm occurred. Never recorded anything like it. Finally everything settled and a cloaked ship appeared. Four humans and a Bigfoot joined the two humans on the island."

"Anything else?"

"It appears the original Bigfoot are not there anymore. In fact, there are just two humans now."

"Keep at it. Let us know if anything changes."

Fuhrnam nodded in agreement and left the room.

"We'll have to let Zhang know," Kellog said to his brother.

Winston's face went rigid. "Of course, but let's see what we can find out first before we do."

"Still bothered by Zhang's glowing eyes?" Kellog asked with what passed as a smile on his jowly face.

"They aren't natural."

"I get it. Zhang's strange. Maybe he's one of their test subjects and has a synthetic neural net implant. "

"It's more than that. Alien would be more accurate." Winston shuddered. "The way he spoke ... I had the distinct feeling he was sourcing Mandarin in some way. It was clear to me it wasn't his native dialect."

Kellog sighed. "So what do you want to do? The deal is great. In the last year we've already made twenty-five billion dollars from our collaboration with the Chinese."

Winston folded his arms. "I heard from an old colleague and employee, Kel."

The way he said colleague made Kellog's eyes widen, and he spat out, "That betrayer is working for Kobak."

Winston shook his head. "He was never working for Kobak. Besides, Kobak's out of Quantumnetics. A Chinese-American woman, Sue Lynn, is heading up the Quantumentics' Colossus project now."

"Interesting how that all went down."

"Yes, remember, just as Zhang predicted."

"Indeed. I'll have my contacts in the company find out what they can about her."

Winston nodded. "In any case, last week Redhawk contacted me."

Still angry, Kellog snorted. "I always suspected tribal loyalty would win out. His belief that the Bigfoot were evil was paper-thin."

"The Potawatomi have been protecting the Bigfoot for millennia."

"My investigation suggests the Bigfoot have been protecting the tribe for millennia. So what does Redhawk want?"

"Since the battle, he has said things are happening regarding the Bigfoot that make him uneasy. Wondered if we might like to have a discussion sometime in the near future. He obviously knows something we don't."

Kellog admonished his brother. "You trust him?"

"Relax, brother. I trust only you, but remember the wisdom of Sun Tzu. An agent that can be turned can be used as a doomed spy."

<h1 style="text-align:center">59</h1>

Savannah, Georgia
March 20th 2035

Josiah Fuhrnam scratched at the beard covering his acne-scarred face as he walked to his motel room at the Savannah Days Inn. The strange glint in Winston Ang's eyes during the meeting two days ago had upset him. What was the calculating Chinese-American hiding?

At six-one, 160 pounds with long hair and horn-rimmed glasses, Fuhrnam fit the profile of the geeky neighbor in any romantic comedy. But Fuhrnam believed he was destined to be much more than that. When his mentor Conrad Visily had argued in their first meeting about the presence of aliens already here on Earth he became convinced the planet needed a computer genius on the front lines.

Visily had told him that a benevolent alien intelligence had been messing with the planetary evolution since the appearance of complex multicellular life. But now, more recent alien intelligences were here and their purpose was unknown. Then he shocked Furman by saying one of those alien intelligences appeared to people in the form of Bigfoot. Somebody needed to figure out what their goal was before it was too late. Fuhrnam decided he should be the man.

~

As luck would have it, he ended up working for the Ang brothers, engineering the electronics on their surveillance satellites. Then the shock of all shocks occurred when the Ang brothers offered him the task of monitoring Bigfoot using the satellite technology he uniquely understood. Of course he jumped at the chance.

Two years ago, at the beginning of his new assignment, tracking the Bigfoot had been easy. Though the creatures possessed extraordinary para-physical abilities, confirming what Visily had told him, they were indeed alien. He also discovered they had a weakness. One of their abilities could be used against them to pinpoint their positions in space and time. When they moved, their cloaking created a spatial distortion in the Earth's magnetic field. Tracking them, trapping and eliminating them, had been like playing a videogame for the hunters in the field.

Though the Bigfoot adapted, movement was still their Achilles heel, and Fuhrnam had helped and nearly succeeded in wiping them out before the battle of the UP.

Then two things occurred that greatly upset Fuhrnam regarding the battle in the UP. Winston told him his good friend and colleague at the Ang brothers' complex, Larry Redhawk, had betrayed them all, and he would never see that damn Indian again. They also demanded Fuhrnam never contact him again. He always wanted to know what happened and whether what they said was true about Redhawk. Something wasn't right. He wanted to hear Redhawk's side of the story

The other problem was the 3,000 or so remaining Bigfoot he had been tracking vanished overnight as if they had never existed. None of Fuhrnam's super geeky powers and algorithms proved useful in finding a single Bigfoot.

Nevertheless, the Ang brothers had told him to keep searching using the daily satellite data and report to them weekly with any progress. To keep him motivated, Winston said he was working in collaboration with one of the most powerful tech giants in China. He also told Fuhrnam the Chinese alone understood the existential threat Bigfoot posed to humanity's survival. The Russians, European Union and Americans were intent on keeping the reality of Bigfoot's alien origins a secret and didn't have the data to understand even a tenth of what the Bigfoot's paraphysical capabilities represented for any country that harnessed them.

After Winston Ang returned from the AI conference in Shanghai, things at KW Intel changed. Fuhrnam sensed the Ang brothers no longer wanted to hunt the Bigfoot to extinction, only to report their movements. That much had been easy—they weren't moving. Then his old mentor Visily sent him a encrypted message with a different approach to a Bayesian algorithm that did not take space-time as fundamental for detecting the Bigfoot signature if they should ever come back to life. They did. The algorithm worked, and it worked retrospectively.

This all added up to a nagging doubt that he had done the right thing by telling them about the reawakening of the Bigfoot. Thank God he hadn't told them about the look back at the earlier activity of the Bigfoot.

His next step was clear: leave the Ang brothers. He had no choice, because he had set his convoluted Bigfoot identification algorithm to self-destruct on the brothers' servers in five days. Enough time, he hoped, to figure out what to do next with his information.

"Curiouser and curiouser," Fuhrnam whispered, alone in his motel room. On the wall was projected an image of the latest Bigfoot movement gathered from the Ang brothers' satellite network. Unknown to the brothers, Fuhrnam had built himself a portable device that hacked into their surveillance satellite system. The device's output was capable of taking the form of data or visual images. A pattern behind the periodic movement of the Bigfoot was taking shape in Fuhrnam's mind.

He stayed up late into the night trying to figure out what to do. All he could think of was to contact his old mentor, Conrad Visily. But four days later, he had a better idea. Do what Winston told him never to do—contact Larry Redhawk. Just the thought of being in the presence of his old colleague and friend made him feel good. *He will know what to do with this precious information.*

60

Potawatomi Reservation
UP, Michigan
March 23th 2035

Larry Redhawk had always been something of a misfit, an outsider in his Potawatomi tribal community. His father had been a drunk who died in a car accident when Redhawk was eleven years old. Shortly after his father's death, his mother, who was a Lakota Sioux, moved back to South Dakota, leaving young Redhawk to be raised by the Potawatomi tribe. Throughout his formative years, his grandfather had been his lifeline. He introduced Redhawk to computers when he noticed the boy was fascinated with technology. Redhawk was a natural and quickly became the go-to guy for computer repairs on the reservation. In the process, he began programming in earnest.

His luck improved when his father's sister, Auntie Ayasha, became leader of the tribe. She took a deep interest in the brilliant boy and allowed him to work with the technicians and programmers who made the casino run.

The more he learned about the new ways of the digital age, the more he became convinced that clinging to their native heritage was killing his people, forcing them into irrelevancy, particularly when it came to personal entrepreneurship. For his Potawatomi community in particular, he was sure their commitment to being the protector of the Bigfoot was damaging. At the time, he believed Bigfoot were advanced primates that maintained a special relationship with native people around the world. While Bigfoot at one time provided some sort of advantage to the well-being of the community, Redhawk became certain the tribe's obligation to this hairy beast was forcing his people to become second-class citizens.

So when the opportunity came for people of Native American heritage to get high level internships at prominent Silicon Valley tech companies, he jumped at the chance. Immediately recognized for his out-of-the-box thinking, he quickly rose to leadership in engineering new products. However, when the company was sold to a German consortium, he was forced to choose between moving to Europe or looking for another job in the States. He did the latter and took a job with the Ang brothers in Seattle, Washington. A deciding factor was that the Pacific Northwest forests reminded him of the forests of the Upper Peninsula of Michigan.

Eventually, the younger Ang brother took Redhawk under his wing. It was clear now to Redhawk that a big part of the reason for Winston's interest in him, beyond his technical genius, was his connection to the Potawatomi Indian tribe. Gradually the two men began sharing their dislike for the Bigfoot. At first Redhawk had a hard time accepting the alien origin of the creatures. Eventually, Winston convinced him not only of their alien origin but also of the threat they posed to humanity.

It was with mixed feelings that he was asked to move back to the Upper Peninsula to be the Ang brother's man on the ground. After much soul-searching he accepted the assignment.

Now Redhawk was at another crossroad. Tanya had not returned and he was certain she would never come back.

He was also certain, now that she was gone, that others were better suited to be tribal leader. The news media after the battle had shown a favorable light on the reservation. In the two years Redhawk had been in charge of the reservation, the community had prospered greatly. The casino doubled in size and the grounds surrounding it were turned into a playground of activities for tourists. He was particularly pleased with the spacious shooting range and modern medical facility now in full operation. In addition, the tribe purchased 2,000 acres of adjacent land and were developing it. Alcoholism and drug addiction were under control. Most of the tribal people lived in comfortable houses with all the amenities of the rest of the world. Redhawk himself lived in the spacious mansion that Auntie Ayasha once lived in.

Outside of Auntie Ayasha's house, Redhawk sat in his truck, thinking. The day was warm. After record cold over the winter, an extraordinary long and hot summer was predicted.

He felt compelled to do what he should've done a long time ago. A vision quest. He knew exactly where to go. He spoke the coordinates into his phone. With no provisions, only the clothes on his back and an old drum, he headed for the portal where the Bigfoot took their evolutionary leap. Larry Redhawk was determined to stay there until he awakened to his greater purpose regarding his connection to the Bigfoot.

61

Shanghai, China
March 24th 2035

Zhang paused at the entrance to his office on the top floor of the Shei Wei building. An urgent meeting with the Council of Four had been called to answer recent troubling events. He did not worry about being late. The meeting would not start without him, and the Chinese would do as he asked. He was the gateway to the self-replicating Probe, and the Probe guaranteed their future supremacy in space. But their goals were not his. His were the goals of the Probe, and his job was to implement them at any cost.

Zhang crossed the parquet flooring in easy strides. He pressed the button on the transmitter in his suit coat pocket and the secret wall panel slid back, revealing the inner sanctum. The four Chinese men who made up the council were sitting in their customary seats.

Wang Wei spoke as soon as the door slid back into place, securing the room from eavesdroppers. "The arrangement you made with the Ang brothers has paid off. The Bigfoot have become active again."

Zhang shuddered and cursed to himself. *The Probe didn't know.*

Wang Wei studied Zhang. "You didn't know."

Zhang was silent.

"The engineer of the satellite detection system, a man named Josiah Fuhrnam, came up with a new algorithm that was able to detect their movements again. Nine days ago, the hybrid Bigfoot that had been on a remote Canadian island disappeared in what our scientists are describing as an interdimensional plasma release of enormous energy. In addition, Bigfoot activity has started again in the UP and on the Olympic Peninsula."

Zhang stayed silent.

Wei blinked slowly, like an owl. "Nothing to say? Okay. That's the good news. The bad news is Fuhrnam sabotaged the Ang brother's detection program and has disappeared. Even worse, they believe he has the ability to track the Bigfoot using a portable interface with the satellite system."

Zhang found himself saying, "This needs to be remedied. What you know about this Fuhrnam?"

Lee, a large bespeckled man in a dark suit, spoke for the first time. "I met him a couple of times at conferences. He's smart. We've been tracking his troublesome mentor, Conrad Visily, for some time now. There is a good chance Fuhrnam will turn to him."

"Do not worry about this American," Zhang assured the council. "I have an agent who will deal with Visily. Is there anybody else Fuhrnam might contact?"

"Winston Ang believes he might search out Larry Redhawk, a colleague who he worked with at the Ang brother's company before the battle in the Upper Peninsula. Redhawk betrayed the Ang brothers and played a key role in bringing about the emergence of the hybrid Bigfoot."

Zhang felt himself forced again to say, "The Probe needs everything to speed up if you want to get that fusion engine."

With that, Zhang walked out the way he came in, without saying anything else.

62

Seattle, Washington
March 24th 2035

Winston was sitting in his office with his head in his hands when Kellogg walked in.

"How bad is it?" Kellogg asked, as sweat beads rolled down the sides of his face.

Winston groaned. "The Chinese are really pissed. They're threatening to expose our clandestine satellite activities unless we get the Bigfoot tracking back online. I don't even care anymore about what the hell these alien hairy freaks want with us."

"It was a big mistake. We should've sent that damn Russian packing when he came to us three years ago about the threat of an alien presence."

Winston nodded in agreement. "I'm so sorry, brother. I should've listened to you."

"Did you tell the Chinese about Fuhrnam?"

"I had to, otherwise we would've seemed totally incompetent. That would've been ill-advised."

"So what now?"

Winston put his head back in his hand but finally looked up at his brother. "Remember I told you about meeting this guy in China? The guy with the unsettling eyes?"

"Zhang, of course."

"The Chinese are sending him here. I expect he's on a plane right now."

Kellog look surprised. "Why?"

"They think Fuhrnam will take the satellite monitor to Redhawk."

"The two of them were very close. I can see the logic in that."

"They want me to take Zhang to Redhawk on his reservation. I'm not good at that kind of thing. It scares the hell out of me. We're losing control."

"Shit! What are we gonna do?"

"I put in a call to Redhawk. Remember, he contacted me earlier."

"And?"

The brothers looked at each other with fear in their eyes.

63

____

Hiawatha National Forest
UP, Michigan
March 24th 2035

Redhawk left his truck and started walking toward the portal. The cold snap a few days ago had caused the maple trees to slow their spring bloom. Cell phone in his back pocket, Redhawk carried the drum his grandfather and given to him on his sixteenth birthday. He was told to use it when he had a deep question about life.

"The beating of the drum will call forth the spirits from the other world. They will open your eyes to the truth," his grandfather told him.

Reaching the place where the portal had been, Redhawk dimly felt a sense of an intelligent presence. *Perhaps residual energy remains; this is a good sign.*

The afternoon sun was descending in the west. He beat the drum three times, repeated the ritual two more times, and then sat down. He cleared his mind and waited. As soon as the sun set, the temperature dropped, but Redhawk didn't notice. His mind was relinquishing any sense of self. For five hours, only the sound of the forest broke the unbounded darkness behind his closed eyes.

Suddenly a parade of faces filled the dark void. Unfamiliar faces of people, young and old, men and women. Some were sad, some were joyous, some were larger than others. They were his ancestors. A veil lifted and the ancestors were gone, replaced by the world of complex designs, shapes and inexplicable symbols. It all started moving. Intricate machines flowing into each other, building more complex structures. The images reminded him of Leonardo da Vinci's *Codex Arundel*.

Then a change. Luminescent beings began attending this animated world. When one of the beings looked up at him, it took the world, still teeming with movement, and stuck it into a mountain, where it disappeared. The whole experience of the vision seemed unreal but at the same time absolutely true.

When Redhawk woke up from the trance, he found himself lying on his back with the dawn breaking. He had been given a glimpse of the reality behind what his senses and brain told him was real. His intuition of space-time and things were illusions.

Redhawk grabbed his phone and dictated the essence of his vision.

"Whenever I asked for explanations about what the Bigfoot were capable of, Tanya told me I couldn't understand, that I was trapped in a way of thinking that didn't allow me to see the truth of things. Now I know there's a whole other reality behind what we can see, hear, and touch. Math captures this reality. It explains why quantum mechanics, relativity, and even Newtonian mechanics are so unintuitive yet so successful. Seeing that was a great revelation for me. It dispelled a mystery I've struggled with since I first studied modern physics. The Bigfoot have access to this greater reality; it's the source of their para-physical superpowers. The only parallel I can think of is a dog trying to comprehend the complexity of human nature.

"I don't think the imagery in my vision was complete, but it did give me a taste of another kind of existence. The last set of images were the most confounding: the disappearance of the alternate world into a mountain here on Earth. I need to find that mountain.

"Even with all these new ideas, I still don't know the purpose of the Bigfoot. Their relationship to me and humanity is still an enigma."

Two messages had arrived during his vision quest. One from Winston Ang and the other from Josiah Fuhrnam. *That must be more than a coincidence*, he thought.

64

Seattle, Washington
March 25th 2035

Nervously looking down at his phone, Winston Ang sat at his desk waiting for Redhawk to pick up. Looming over his shoulder was Zhang. His eyes were no longer covered by sunglasses. Winston couldn't look at them. Finally, they heard Redhawk's voice.

"What's so urgent?" the Potawatomi chief asked. "I was about to call you, but I've got a lot going on here."

"Sorry, I wasn't sure you got my message," Winston responded. When you called me last week, you asked if we were still tracking the Bigfoot. And I said no. Well that's not quite true. They're back moving around."

"Interesting. Are you sure?"

"We are."

"Where?"

"Primarily the Olympic Peninsula and around you. We thought you should know."

Redhawk said nothing.

Finally, with a nudge from Zhang, Winston resumed. "Have you seen or felt them, the Bigfoot?"

After another long pause, Redhawk said, "No, nothing since the battle."

Zhang silently mouthed, "He's lying."

"If they show up, would you let us know?" Winston asked.

With an accusatory tone, Redhawk responded, "Why? Who are you hooked up with this time, Winston?"

"Just me and Kellogg. We're trying to figure out what to do next. Are you interested?"

"Maybe."

"Good. Are you still living on the reservation? I'd like to visit sometime. Maybe see the battlefield site."

"I don't think you'd like it here," Redhawk countered.

"Probably not. You remember Josiah Fuhrnam?"

"Sure, good guy."

"He's made some major breakthroughs in tracking the Bigfoot. That's how we know they're moving. Has he told you?"

Another long pause. "I haven't been in touch since the battle. I'm preparing for an important tribal council meeting. Let's talk again later. Okay?"

"Okay," Winston said.

As the call ended, Zhang roughly grabbed Winston and pulled him out of his chair. "He's lying. Fuhrnam is there. Let's go."

Winston tried to free himself, but Zhang's grip was like steel. He swallowed. "Where?"

"The reservation. We need to get the monitor."

Winston shook his head. "I'm no good at this sort of thing; I don't want to go."

The glow in Zhang's eyes held no mercy. "I don't care."

65

Potawatomi Reservation UP

March 25th 2035

In spite of the early spring snow ten days ago, the afternoon was stifling hot as Redhawk walked out of the community center with Chaska, the casino security guard and his childhood friend. Redhawk thought he was the right choice to be the new tribal leader. He was smart, ambitious and a good guy. But most importantly, he had taken part in the battle two years ago, so he was among the few to know about the tribe's relationship with the Bigfoot and their alien nature.

Redhawk spoke first, "I was amazed how readily the elders accepted the change, especially the older women. Made me wonder if I've been doing things wrong as leader."

They laughed.

Chaska said, "I didn't see this coming until you called me five hours ago. What changed?"

"I never really embraced the old ways. You, on the other hand, have always had one foot in the new and one in the old. And you're much better looking."

The two friends enjoyed another laugh.

"What else?" Chaska asked.

"The Bigfoot have moved on for reasons I don't understand."

"What do you mean moved on?"

"The Potawatomi tribe is no longer their secret keeper. Also, since the battle, I don't trust their motives."

"Which are what?" Chaska asked, his wide brow furrowed in concern.

"That's the problem. I don't know their motives. I don't even know if they have anything similar to our values, or even good intentions toward us. But I need to find out."

"What brought this on?"

"My last trip to the island with Tanya. And I did a vision quest last night."

Chaska smiled knowingly. "You found your purpose at last."

"Yes."

"All right; I respect that. It's always been our way."

Redhawk was relieved he didn't need to explain himself to his childhood friend. "Thank you, and you should occupy Auntie Ayasha's house immediately to solidify the change."

"No, I want you to stay there until you leave the reservation."

The two men embraced. As Chaska headed to the casino, Redhawk looked at his phone. Four new messages from Fuhrnam. He tapped the listen icon and his former colleague's voice came through loud and clear.

"I took the underground rapid transit tube from Georgia to Green Bay. Can you come and get me? I need your help! Tell you all about it when you get here."

66

Seattle, Washington
March 25th 2035

The Ang brothers' building was one of the tallest in Seattle. Like most of the tech giant's buildings in the city, it had once been serviced by what used to be a heliport landing pad on the top floor. Now it was used by Tesla flying cars for urban transportation.

The view of the city was spectacular on this unusually clear spring day, but it gave Winston no solace. Zhang held his elbow in a vice-like grip and stood silently, not even affected by the view. His glowing eyes appeared locked on an invisible object hundreds of feet above their heads.

"Wh ... what are we doing here?" Winston stammered.

Zhang said nothing. His glowing eyes appeared locked on an invisible object hundreds of feet above their heads. Out of nowhere, a shiny object appeared in the sky. Ten seconds later, an oval craft landed in front of them. It had the classic lines of a flying saucer, but the structure was not made from any material Winston recognized. Instead, it looked organic; it pulsed as if breathing.

Winston gasped as the revelation hit him. *Nickt, Zhang's a fucking alien.*

A portal in the middle of craft opened like a mouth. A dark dampness beckoned. Zhang ordered, "Get in!"

The orifice gaped like the cavernous jaws of an Orca. Winston shrank back. A hand like steel pushed him through the opening. He felt as though he were being swallowed.

Inside, a soft light illuminated a round chamber made of what appeared to be living tissue. There were no consoles, displays or mechanical devices. There was no place to sit. He stumbled and leaned against the wall. It was warm and flesh-like but dry. When he looked down, he saw what he would have sworn was a tendon the size of his torso running through mid-ship like a keel.

"What is this thing?" he asked, his voice trembling.

"It is a ground-to-orbit craft created by an alien Probe," Zhang said in an emotionless voice as if explaining numbers to a five-year-old.

"What alien probe?" Winston stammered.

"Sit."

"Where?" Ang asked, looking around at the bare walls and ceiling.

Zhang pressed a hand against the living bulkhead. The floor twisted and yawed beneath Ang's feet. He fell backward into a soft hand that lifted him up into a sitting position. Restraints held him in place.

Zhang ignored him. He placed his other hand against the bulkhead. The fingers appeared to fuse with the flesh-like material. Zhang's eyes glowed and he peered upward as if looking past the craft's walls into the sky.

From a subtle hint of movement, Winston had the feeling they were flying.

"We'll be at the Potawatomi Reservation in an hour," Zhang announced.

Winston calculated the speed. *Two thousand miles in an hour ...*

that's faster than Mach 3, yet I feel no g-forces. There must be some kind of internal gravimetric dampeners. Working on how the craft flew kept his mind from shattering at the idea he was traveling in a ship piloted by a human-looking creature that was as alien as the ship.

67

———————

Menominee, Michigan
March 25th 2035

Redhawk had slept in his truck as the self-driving mode piloted the vehicle south on Highway 41 toward Green Bay, Wisconsin. Even so, he was not completely refreshed when he found Fuhrnam waiting on the edge of the Lambeau Field parking lot. While the reunion between the two former colleagues was cordial, Redhawk couldn't help but wonder why after more than two years without as much as phone call between them, Fuhrnam had reached out to him.

Redhawk turned north on Highway 41 again, but it was getting dark and it would be best to spend the night in his cabin outside of Menominee. He had used the cabin during times of stress from being tribal leader. He would spend a night or two to clear his head, and if the season was right, hunt in the forest near the twin cities of Marinette and Menominee.

By the time Redhawk and Fuhrnam reached the locked gate marking the dirt road to his cabin, Fuhrnam had brought Redhawk up to speed on what had precipitated his sudden departure from the

Ang brothers.

That Fuhrnam had found a means to resurrect the Ang brothers' satellite network to track the remaining Bigfoot did not surprise Redhawk. Even the news his old colleague had been able to track the movements of An and the Mother Bigfoot had been expected on some level. But the news about the Ang brothers working with a secret Chinese group focused on extraterrestrials made him nervous.

Redhawk unlocked the gate, drove through, then while relocking it, he checked the spycams he'd installed in the twin oak trees straddling the entryway. He had disabled the LED lights so intruders couldn't spot their locations. Both appeared untampered.

Back in the truck, Redhawk asked, "So why are you asking for my help?"

Fuhrnam took a deep breath, as if wondering just how much he should tell his former colleague.

"Look, Josiah, you wouldn't have reached out to me if you didn't think I could help. I need to know what you know."

"Fair enough." Fuhrnam checked his watch. "Five days ago, I pulled the trigger on a self-destruct order I programmed into my algorithm to track the Bigfoot. As a tool for tracking the Bigfoot, the satellites are useless to the Angs now."

Redhawk eyed his friend. "I've never seen this side of you before. You were always cautioning me to play the game with the big boys. 'Don't make waves,' you said many times."

"Yeah, it was something Visily taught me after the Feds got him – stay low, don't rock the boat and become indispensable."

"What changed?"

"It's the Angs' Chinese connection. There's something going on that doesn't track."

"And now you're on the run."

Fuhrnam nodded. "I suspect they're coming after me. You see, I built myself a portable Bigfoot tracking monitor. It's an advanced version of what the mercenaries were using to hunt down the Bigfoot in your forest two years ago." He said boldly, "I can't let them have it."

"Do the brothers know you built this device?"

"I showed it to them, yes. I'm sure they believe I have it with me."

Redhawk parked the truck beneath a large white pine. Satellite or drones would not spot it. Inside the cabin, he made sure the window blinds were drawn so that no visible light could be seen from the outside. Only then did he flip on the solar power. The cabin was completely off the grid; no one would know he was here unless they had spotted him turning off the main route north out of Menominee.

One look at Josiah Fuhrnam under the cabin lights showed how being on the run had taken its toll. The man was visibly scared. They were the same age, but Fuhrnam looked twenty years older. His thin frame bent forward as if he carried a tremendous burden, and his usual ruddy complexion had turned sallow. His eyes had a haunted look as if he expected someone to shoot him at any moment.

Redhawk checked the main room's inconspicuous traps he'd laid that would tell him if intruders had broken into his home. The gun cabinets holding Czech, Russian, American, British, Dutch and Israeli arms had been untouched and the pantry door was in the exact position he had left it on his last visit in August. Of course, professionals would most likely have avoided them.

Redhawk sighed. By agreeing to meet with his old colleague, he had made the choice to enter a world where paranoia was the norm. On the other hand, the moment he began questioning the motives of the Bigfoot, he'd already entered that world.

Redhawk made coffee and set out his homemade jerky from the pantry. The pantry was kept stocked with nonperishables; he wondered if he would have to live off the stored food in the coming months.

Fuhrnam was eager to show Redhawk the monitor, but Redhawk would have no part of it until they settled in. He needed time to think, but Fuhrnam was exhausted from traveling, so he told his former colleague to sit back and relax while he started a fire and heated up some of those food reserves.

While he was doing these mundane household activities, Redhawk tried to figure out what his next move should be. He had many unanswered questions. Why were the Chinese so interested in the Bigfoot? Who should he contact? Kobak? Moore? What should he do with Fuhrnam and his monitor?

Then Redhawk's attention turned to the more immediate problem. If the Ang brothers and the Chinese were after Fuhrnam, he needed to get him to safety. Where? The reservation would not be safe. A solution dawned on him. His only friend from his childhood visits to the Lakota nation in South Dakota, Billy Beckwourth, was still living on the reservation and could hide anybody in the network of sacred caves in the nearby Black Hills. Not only that, it would give himself a safe place to plan his next move. Billy was extremely resourceful and absolutely trustworthy. With a short term plan in mind, he was able to relax.

The smokeless wood caught fire, gathered strength and warmed the room. The two ate in silence. Some of Josiah's color returned. When they finished, Redhawk refilled their cups, this time adding Irish whiskey. He settled into his seat by the hearth and gestured to Fuhrnam's bag with his chin. "Show me what you've got there."

Fuhrnam pulled a compact monitor the size a Razor I-pad from his backpack and set it on the coffee table between them. Redhawk chuckled with admiration at the device's elegant simplicity. "Brilliant. You always were a damn fine engineer."

Fuhrnam smiled. "Thanks. It has a Musk K-7 battery, so it'll run continuously for years." He tapped an icon on the screen and a holographic touch-lock appeared above the upper right hand corner. He pressed his index finger to the icon. The screen instantly glowed to life.

"Is it okay to run it here?" Redhawk asked hesitantly.

"It employs the same block chain cryptographic algorithm Bitcoin uses, so it's immune to hacking. No one can trace the Internet connection to your place, if that's what you're concerned about."

Redhawk nodded.

Fuhrnam tapped more icons and a second holographic lock appeared below the first. "Put your index finger there," he commanded.

Redhawk did as he was told. His fingerprint appeared on the screen then dissolved.

"Good. Now you have access."

The screen remained empty. Redhawk asked, "What happens next?"

Fuhrnam smiled. "Wait for it."

Moments later, an image of the cabin was projected on the screen.

"Jesus, is that real time?" Redhawk exclaimed.

"Yep."

Redhawk studied the image. The place appeared deserted. No light radiated from the cabin, and the chimney gave off no smoke. He swallowed against an exclamation of worry building in his chest. "What about infrared?"

Fuhrnam laughed. "Relax, old friend. The Ang brothers' satellite network can't use infrared within twenty square miles wherever this device is located. We're safe."

"You seem to have thought of everything."

Fuhrnam frowned. "If I'd done that, I wouldn't have started this project. I'm in over my head, and I need your help."

"What can I do?"

"I'm not equipped for this cloak and dagger shit. I want you to take over for me. I'll teach you how to use this."

"And then?"

"I'm going to leave it all to you." He set the device on the table and bounced one knee, fidgeting. "What do you say, my good friend?"

On some level, Redhawk had suspected something like this from the moment Josiah contacted him and that he already knew the answer.

"Show me." He sat forward to look at the device.

For the next hour, Fuhrnam talked Redhawk through the controls to operate the monitor. When Fuhrnam felt Redhawk had mastered the device, he said, "Play with it. I need to sleep."

He disappeared into the cabin's second bedroom.

At first, Redhawk roamed the world, but then he turned his attention to the satellite's historical record. He watched Tanya at the

Bigfoot evolutionary portal on the day An disappeared. He watched bits and pieces of activity on the Canadian island. Mostly the resolution was poor and the satellite coverage spotty. When he focused on the day of An's disappearance, he was barely able to make her out during a few seconds when the snow squall's intensity eased. Mostly it was digital noise.

Finally, he turned his attention to the Pacific Northwest. There had been an odd Bigfoot occurrence around the town of La Push, Washington one year before An's jump, and then again on the day of the jump. But most interesting to him was a gathering of Bigfoot three days after the jump at the base of a mountain that looked like the one in his vision. Two of the Bigfoot were the ones that showed up on the day of the jump. The third looked like Tanya.

I now know where I need to go, he told himself, satisfied that he at last had a clear mission. The Sky Island Casino and the Potawatomi tribe were in good hands.

Tiredness swept over him. Redhawk banked the fire's embers and headed into the cabin's main bedroom. He slept in his clothes with a Glock 19 on the nightstand beside him. Fuhrnam's concerns about the Ang brothers had him on edge and sleep eluded him. He had many unanswered questions. Why were the Chinese so interested in the Bigfoot? Once he got to safety, who should he contact? Was there anybody besides Kobak and Moore?

Those problems would have to wait. Right now he needed to focus on the more immediate problem. If the Ang brothers and the Chinese were after Fuhrnam, Redhawk needed to get him to safety as quickly as possible. Tomorrow he would take Fuhrnam to the casino and from there, using the Chariot, drop him off in Billy's care, and then proceed to the Olympic Peninsula.

68

———

Sky Island Casino
March 26th 2035

Redhawk woke as the sun rose across Lake Michigan. The morning was unusually warm and he did not rekindle the fire. He let Fuhrnam sleep while he made coffee and brought out enough stores from the pantry for the next few days. Then he contacted Billy, who gave him coordinates for a landing site inside the Black Hills in one of the most secluded place known only to certain Lakota. His childhood friend sounded quite pleased he would get to see the chariot. Billy was always open to new experiences.

From the gun cabinet nearest the fireplace, he removed a Czech manufactured SA VZ. 61 pistol with a twenty-round magazine and an SA VZ. bolt action rifle. The legendary arms were known for their dependability and firepower.

He checked the time. It was after eight, and Fuhrnam had slept long enough. He knocked on the door. After the second try to wake his old friend, he entered. The bed had not been slept in, and the window was open. He immediately went outside checked his truck.

Still unlocked. On the seat was a note from Fuhrnam: "Sorry to burden you with this. Like I said, I need to disappear for a while."

"Shit, you're in it now," Redhawk muttered. He grabbed his supplies, weapons, and Fuhrnam's monitor and went out to the truck, relieved it was still there. Loading the equipment, he set the autopilot for the Sky Island Casino.

The two-hour drive gave him plenty of time to figure out his next course of action. He called Chaska, asking the new chief to meet him in the casino's operations room. Redhawk had to tell the new leader of the tribe what he was planning and maybe about the monitor. He needed to think about the wisdom of letting anyone know what he was going to do.

As he pulled into Sky Island Casino, Redhawk automatically checked the area near the reflecting pond and the small stand of trees at the corner of the parking lot where the Chariot rested. Though the stealth technology kept the craft's sleek lines hidden from view of the ordinary tourist, at certain times of the day – late morning and late afternoon – the angle of the sun reflected a slight rainbow shimmer around it. He let out a breath, relieved to see the craft was ready to go. It was essential for his plans.

His relief was short-lived. Chaska stood at the main entrance with two men and waved him over. Redhawk recognized Winston Ang. The sight of his old employer was disconcerting enough, but the taller Asian man in the dark gray suit and dark glasses next to him sent ice down his spine. He reached into the glove compartment to grab his revolver and placed it in his jacket pocket. He wondered if he should make a dash for the Chariot.

He shook his head against that action. *Winston probably surmised that Fuhrnam might reach out to me with his monitor. Perhaps they're just on a fishing trip. Let's find out.*

Winston's greeting was warm enough. "You're looking good."

"You haven't aged a bit." Redhawk stood out of kicking range of the two Asian men. "What's so urgent that you come all this way unannounced?"

"This is Zhang, somebody we recruited from China to work on various satellite projects."

Zhang bowed graciously.

"We need to talk about that area of mutual concern. Can we speak in private?"

Chaska led them to the room Redhawk knew only too well. Here, for the last two and a half years, he had occasionally met with Tanya as she sat in her unusual state of dormancy, drifting in and out of the normal human visual spectrum.

The room had monitors showing the casino floor and outside the building. A round table in the center with six chairs was the only furniture.

"I'll leave you three alone," Chaska said after he showed them in.

Redhawk expected the new tribal leader to go to the operations room, where he would monitor the meeting.

The door had barely shut when the Chinese man, Zhang, spoke. "I'll come right to the point, Mr. Redhawk. I want to know where Josiah Fuhrnam is hiding. I also want the device he constructed to track the Bigfoot. It belongs to us."

Redhawk looked at Winston, but the Chinese-American shrugged. The tightness around his mouth and eyes told the Native American that Zhang was dangerous. "What makes you think I know where Josiah is? We haven't seen each other in a couple of years, and I don't like your tone."

Zhang grimaced then his face smoothed over as if the emotion were incompatible with his being. "Fuhrnam stole the technology from the Ang brothers. He has no friends, and you are the logical choice of someone he would approach for protection or to help sell it, since you know the truth about the alien nature of the Bigfoot."

Redhawk laughed, but inside the same fear took hold that he'd had as a marine stationed in Afghanistan. "Sorry to disappoint you, Mr. Zhang, but I haven't heard from Josiah since I left the Ang brothers' company. I'm afraid you wasted a trip here." He smiled. "Winston, perhaps you'd like to hit the casino floor, gamble a bit. We can catch up if you like."

Zhang's face clouded over. "Mr. Redhawk, we know you have been in contact with the Bigfoot and you have concerns about their motives. We share those concerns. You should join us. It would be the best way to resolve your fears about the Bigfoot."

Redhawk pressed his forearm against the gun in his pocket, but he continued in a jovial manner as if nothing were wrong. "Right now, my only interest is going hunting. I just resigned as chief of the tribe,

and I am longer concerned about the Bigfoot, whatever they might have been. My only interest right now is bagging a deer and enjoying my new freedom from so much responsibility."

"In that case, you won't mind if I check out your vehicle to make sure you don't have the Ang brothers'—"

"I do mind, and you'd be disappointed. All I have is a couple of rifles and some food for a long hunting trip. Your visit here is done. Please go home quietly before I ask casino security to escort you off the reservation."

Zhang smiled for the first time. It didn't look right. "You think the cameras in this room are working and your tribal security will come and help you." He removed his sunglasses. "I assure you they have no idea what is going on here."

Glowing eyes stared right through Redhawk, and a shaft of ice slammed into his testicles. He pushed back from the table, sending his chair skidding across the parquet wood floor. Before he could pull out his pistol, the tall Chinese whipped around the table and grabbed him by the throat, lifting him off the ground.

"Where is the device?"

Steel fingers dug into Redhawk's windpipe. He grabbed the man's wrist but the grip held him firm. He looked for Winston Ang, but his former employer had vanished. *Save yourself first*, Redhawk thought. Black spots formed in his outer vision and a tidal wave roared in his ears. He would soon pass out and be at the man's mercy.

All at once, the grip slackened. The roaring ceased, and Redhawk was on the floor gasping. Winston stood over Zhang, a splintered wooden chair in both hands. The Chinese man lay face first on the floor. Blood seeped from a gash in the back of his head.

Winston helped Redhawk to his feet. "Can you move?"

Redhawk nodded. "Is he dead?" he rasped, rubbing his throat.

Ang shook his head. "I doubt anything less than a bomb blast could kill him."

As they watched, Zhang stirred. The glow in his eyes returned, and the gash knitted over with new skin and hair. In a few minutes, he would be on his feet.

"This way," Redhawk yelled. Winston followed him out of the room.

Chaska met them in a back corridor leading toward the parking lot. He took a long look at Redhawk's ashen face. "What happened, Larry? The cameras went dead."

"Zhang, the Asian one... he's some kind of ... cyberneticly-enhanced human," Redhawk answered. He slammed open the steel door and led the way across the full parking lot toward his truck at a dead run.

"What you want me to do?" Chaska shouted. "That's dangerous stuff the Chinese are doing."

"He's not an enhanced human," Winston said, catching his breath when they stopped by Redhawk's truck.

"What is he ... what is that thing?" Redhawk remembered the dread he felt at watching the gash in Zhang's head heal itself at super-speed.

Winston shook his head. "I don't know exactly, but it isn't human ... not anymore. He's some creation of the aliens the Chinese have been working with."

The corridor door burst open, flying off its hinges. It slammed into a nearby car, setting off the alarm. Whoops and sirens filled the parking lot.

Chaska reached for his sidearm. He took a shooter's stance and fired half the magazine at Zhang.

The bullets impacted the alien's body. He staggered and fell down. Moments later, he was up again, but moving slowly, using vehicles for cover.

Redhawk put his hand on Chaska's shoulder. "I don't think that will stop him."

"Maybe, but it'll give you time to get to the Chariot."

"It's not a good day to die, brother."

Chaska grinned. "Who said anything about dying? Now go!"

Redhawk needed no other encouragement. Grabbing Fuhrnam's monitor from the front seat, he ran across the lot toward the open space where the Chariot sat, invisible to anyone who didn't know it was there. He was glad Fuhrnam made the device compact and lightweight.

Winston struggled to run beside him, breath ragged. "That's the monitor Josiah built?"

Redhawk nodded, not bothering to waste precious time.

As he neared the invisible craft, Redhawk touched an icon on his phone. The air shimmered in front of them, and the Chariot's sleek lines glinted in the early afternoon sun. He ignored Winston's startled gasp. "Get in," he ordered.

He clambered into the pilot's seat. Ang took the chair next to his. The startup routine took thirty seconds. Redhawk checked the parking lot. His teeth clenched. Chaska was down. Zhang lurched toward them. A gaping bullet hole in the side of Zhang's head was closing rapidly. Though moving slowly, he would be on them in less than thirty seconds.

Winston must have realized it too. He unbuckled his seat belt and slid open the door on his side.

"You don't stand a chance against that thing!" Redhawk yelled.

Winston grimaced. "But you do if you get away." He glanced at Zhang, who was moving more swiftly now, though his left foot still dragged. "My brother and I made a mistake, Larry. Zhang and the alien the Chinese are working with are involved in an evil enterprise. You must keep the monitor from him at all costs. He's the real threat. Not the Bigfoot."

The door slid shut behind him, and he ran right at Zhang.

As Redhawk listened to the onboard computer countdown the seconds to launch, he watched the younger Ang brother run right at the thing that was definitely not human.

Zhang braced himself for the attack. Redhawk didn't see how Winston would do anything more than kill himself. At the last moment, he stopped five feet away and pulled what looked like a small pen from his pocket. He pressed one end and a blue laser light beamed right in Zhang's eyes.

Zhang cried out. His hands went to his face. Winston kicked the alien's balls in a fit of rage. Zhang tumbled over backward. Winston stomped on his face.

A tiny alert from the Chariot's dashboard pinged through the cabin. The engine roared to life. Redhawk punched the takeoff sequence and the craft rose up. Through the tinted window he watched Zhang climb to his feet, grab the smaller Chinese by the neck and smash his head through the windshield of a car. Blood poured down his broken face and the unnatural bend of his neck told Redhawk that Winston was dead.

"*Stipendium peccati mors est*," whispered Redhawk. *The wages of sin are death*. He punched in the coordinates for the Black Hills location.

69

———

Sky Island Casino
March 26th 2035

Zhang watched the aircraft rise into the air. It shimmered in the bright sunlight then disappeared, invisible even to his enhanced vision. *But not to the craft's advanced technology*, he reminded himself.

He walked back into the casino. The sounds of gambling from the main floor echoed through the entry, people oblivious to the gunfire outside a hundred yards away. *Fools*, Zhang thought, dismissing Americans as insects, annoyances like ants or gnats.

He brushed past armed security guards, heading for the parking lot. They'd find the bodies and order a lockdown of the casino. By then it would be too late. He would be on the roof, where his craft landed.

The elevator was empty. Overriding its control panel to go directly to the roof was a simple matter of hacking the elevator's circuits. Gaining control was supremely easy.

Inside the craft, Zhang summoned a chair. Settling into its warm contours, he placed his hands on the wall. He experienced a curious effect of warmth as filaments extended from his fingers and burrowed into the semi-organic tissue, connecting him to the craft's information processing center. The center was not concentrated in one place, as in most biological species. The Probe had learned eons ago that the safest way to preserve information processing in a small craft like this one was to decentralize the information processing with complete redundancy distributed through the whole craft. This analog network also lessened the enormous amount of energy needed to run the power-hungry information processing units on the planet's spacecraft.

Airborne, Zhang took off after Redhawk.

As he suspected, the craft's primitive cloak was no match for the Probe's superior technology. The sensors easily detected the ion signature given off by the cloaked vehicle. Though the aircraft traveled at supersonic speeds, Zhang quickly closed within a hundred meters and followed it on a heading to the west.

Redhawk took no evasive maneuvers, nor did Zhang expect him to. Zhang's own high-speed in-flight cloak was invisible to any human technology. The alien called for weapons and locked on Redhawk's position. It would be easy to bring down the vehicle. Zhang hesitated. He could not be certain of merely disabling the craft. He might destroy it and the Bigfoot monitor. He would have to wait until it landed.

Zhang watched while Redhawk flew across what the people on this continent called the Midwest. The huge landmass filled him with unexpected surprise. Large tracts of cultivated land were harvested by automatic machinery.

Ahead, Redhawk slowed as a mountain range appeared, and he prepared to land. Zhang scanned the area for significant landmarks such as a city or nearby recreational facilities and was surprised his quarry had chosen a barren place with few people or structures. He brought up the specs the Probe had made of this world. This area had been named by geographers as the Black Hills and described as a narrow mountain range connected geologically to the Rockies to the west. It was heavily wooded, with small clearings ringed by rugged granite bluffs and boulders.

While Zhang waited for Redhawk to land, he listened to a communication between the Native American man and someone on the ground. Redhawk spoke rapidly in a language Zhang did not understand. Nor was the language in the Probe's extensive database of Earth cultures. When the communication ended, Redhawk landed the craft on a small opening between two large cliff overhangs. No other people were within ten miles.

Zhang allowed a small smile. The deserted place would make it easy for him to disable the aircraft, kill Redhawk and recover the all-important Bigfoot monitoring device. He did not think it odd the Probe wanted this piece of human engineering. He understood the Bigfoot were superior alien intelligences capable of eluding the probe. In this particular case, a human-engineered monitor that could track the Bigfoot was essential to achieving their goal of exploring a new realm of reality. Zhang had never been near a Bigfoot and wondered what would happen if he encountered one directly. Could he do what the probe was not able to do? Neutralize or capture one?

Zhang hovered his craft one hundred meters above the landing site. Redhawk exited the craft, carrying what had to be the monitor. When Zhang calculated that Redhawk was sufficiently far enough away from the vehicle that the monitor would not be harmed in an explosion, he fired the fusion pulse weapon. The manmade cloaked aircraft disintegrated in a ball of fire. Dense smoke covered the ground in a circle hundreds of meters wide.

The fireball caused by the explosion blocked his vehicle's sensors and he lost Redhawk's heat signature. Some of the elements used in constructing the chariot acted like little mirrors, scrambling his sensory output. So Zhang hovered over the scene for fifteen minutes until the particles dissipated enough for him to engage sensors again. By then, Redhawk had vanished. *He was not killed by the blast.* Zhang cursed, a residual emotion from his human past. Immediately, he set up a systematic grid search by the sensors on his craft. On the ground, Zhang nimbly jumped from boulder to boulder looking for Redhawk. However, the explosion and the presence of strong winds turned a few embers from the explosion into a growing forest fire. Overhead drones hovered and emergency vehicles approached. He was sure the drones had picked up his craft on their cameras. Time to leave.

Redhawk and the monitor would not elude him for long, he promised himself. But just as he made that promise, the probe commanded him to return to China.

70

―――――――

Black Hills of South Dakota
March 26th 2035

Redhawk tried to sit up and groaned at the effort. A hand pushed him down onto a cold rocky floor of the dark cave that was less uncomfortable than the piercing ache in his head and the jarring pain his left shoulder.

I'll just stay here, he thought. He passed out again and came to later, though how much later he didn't know. The last thing he remembered was walking away from the Chariot toward a cave complex he had once explored with his Lakota friend Billy Beckwourth. He was supposed to have met Beckwourth outside the cave entrance. Then his aircraft exploded.

Redhawk opened his eyes. Images swirled. He forced himself to concentrate until they settled down. Peering around, he saw he was in the cave from his youth. A smokeless fire had been laid that warmed the air. One arm was bound to his chest as if to immobilize a separated shoulder. With his good side, he felt his forehead. Bandages, and his fingers came away sticky with blood.

Late afternoon sun streamed into the cave entrance. A cloudless sky was visible beyond. The light dimmed, and a man walked in. Redhawk searched for a weapon and found a rock. The man chuckled.

"No need for that, Larry," a deep voice said.

He recognized the voice and relaxed. The man hunkered down by the fire, which illuminated the prominent hooked nose, pocked dark skin, and long hair of his childhood friend.

Like the man he had been named for, famous mountain man Jim Beckwourth, Billy was a mixed race Indian who had served as a scout for the 1st Marine Reconnaissance Battalion, and later, after being honorably discharged, had become a mountaineer, leading successful assaults on the highest peaks of the seven continents. Ten years ago he had retired and become a science fiction author and a leader of Bigfoot hunts in the Black Hills.

The two men had stayed in touch over the years, mostly in the last decade with Beckwourth asking Redhawk for intel on the latest trends in AI research and other computer-related technologies.

"You feel like sitting up?" Beckwourth asked.

Redhawk nodded slowly and found the motion didn't hurt. "Yeah. This cave floor isn't as comfortable as I remember it." He pushed himself up on his good elbow and winced as a twinge of pain shot through his other shoulder. "What happened? Did you see what happened?"

"Quite amazing. I watched your craft materialize, land, and you get out. Then I looked up just in time to catch a classic flying saucer destroy your ship. You were thrown in the air, and I ran to you, but you were unconscious, so I carried you in here. Saucer seems to have left. What the hell was that?"

"I must have been followed by... I'll tell you later."

Billy helped him sit up then pressed a canteen of water to his lips.

Redhawk grimaced. "You have any whiskey, Billy?"

Another laugh. "You don't drink, or did the concussion make you forget that, old friend?"

Redhawk laughed and groaned again. "Don't make me laugh."

"Here, chew on this." Beckwourth pressed a cake into his good hand.

Redhawk bit down into protein-rich pemmican made from buffalo meat, fat and wild berries. He sighed appreciatively. "I haven't eaten this since I was last here."

"Your mom's funeral, I remember," Beckwourth said. "It was her secret recipe. Said it could cure cancer." He looked thoughtfully at the pemmican he held. "She might be onto something. We never had any cancer at Pine Ridge while she was alive."

"How long was I out?"

"The first time a couple of hours. The last time half an hour or longer. Enough time for me to scout the area."

"You see anything?"

"Just shreds of that craft you were in."

Redhawk frowned. "Thanks for saving my life." He looked around the area beside him. His guts froze as he realized the monitor was missing. "I had something with me. A little black box."

Beckwourth smiled. "You mean this?" He held up the monitor.

Redhawk nodded, relieved.

"Figured it might be important."

"It's the key to everything."

"Care to say more?"

Redhawk shook his head. "Like I said, maybe later."

Beckwourth sighed. "Thought you were going to say that."

"It's for your own good, Billy. That thing has already cost the life of at least one good man."

Savannah Georgia
March 27th 2035

Stephen Kobak stared at the blank monitor hanging over his office desk. A typical spring thunderstorm raged outside. He loved the sound of thunder. It had been twenty-four hours since Larry Redhawk went missing. The three friends responsible for helping the Bigfoot evolutionary leap happen, along with Redhawk, who was more responsible than anybody else, were deeply worried about their missing friend. Birgit Gunderson, Nick Moore and Kobak were gathering as much information as they could about what happened at the reservation.

Earlier that morning, Birgit had traveled down to the medical facility on the reservation and spoke with Chaska to get his first-hand account.

The monitor lit up with the words "invitations accepted."

Birgit spoke first. "It's good to get together and talk about this. Thanks for arranging this encrypted connection, Stephen."

"No problem. Full video encryption was difficult, so I had to settle for audio. Sorry. Nick, are you here?"

"I'm here."

"Let me bring you up-to-date on my conversation with Chaska," Birgit said. "He's the new tribal leader, made official as of two days ago. He's only alive because early in the year Redhawk brought state-of-the-art medical resources to the reservation. He would have certainly died from his gunshot wound if the medical bots hadn't acted immediately. As you probably know from the news reports, Winston Ang wasn't so lucky."

"Kellog Ang is in seclusion," Kobak interrupted. "He has not spoken word and nobody has seen him."

Birgit continued, "Chaska told me Winston was accompanied by a Chinese man who was more than superhuman. He's the one who killed Winston and almost killed him. Chaska believes Redhawk was the real target, or something he had in his possession. However, Redhawk managed to escape in the Chariot."

Kobak interjected, "We were able to track it to the Black Hills of South Dakota, where it was destroyed by what is being called a flying saucer by the locals. The question is did Redhawk escape alive? Anybody—any word?"

"No word," the other two echoed.

Moore finally spoke up, "I heard from a source that a colleague of Redhawk's who worked with him during his time at the Ang brothers' company had developed a new field monitor for detecting Bigfoot movements. The man said he gave the monitor to Redhawk. Said he felt guilty after what happened at the reservation."

"So we can assume the superhuman entity was after the monitor, not Redhawk," Kobak added.

"I agree."

"What does this all mean and what should we do?" Birgit asked. "Redhawk was our friend; I care about him. Should we go to the Black Hills and look for him?"

"No, that's probably not smart. He's my friend too, and he's a survivor," Moore said. "Something big is about to happen in the extraterrestrial arena. Bigfoot are extraterrestrial, remember. I'm hearing about this big event from everybody in my circle, and most are saying it's not good. What happened at the reservation must be part of what's going down. I have an important meeting coming up. It'll be interesting to see if action by this superhuman entity comes up at the meeting."

Kobak said, "I think you both should be on guard. Whoever is involved in this is willing to kill. The more I think about it, I can't help but believe the synthetic brain growing in Olav's lab will become part of whatever is going down. And Moore, you're playing a dangerous game already. Me, I'm out of the picture. Let's keep in touch and pray Redhawk somehow came through alive and well."

At that moment, the monitor screen went dark and his friend's voices cut out. Kobak wondered if the storm had taken out his Internet connection.

72

—————

XXX Base
Sichuan Province, China
March 27th 2035

The sun was setting as Zhang's craft dropped down on the landing pad near the far edge of the perimeter containing the XXX base. On the ground, he waited for a moment. A small transparent disc grew out of the control panel of the ship. He took it in his hand. A vibratory energy emanated from the small object.

Two well-armed Chinese guards greeted him as he exited the craft. The day was exceptionally warm and muggy. The guards were both sweating profusely. He could have rendered them useless in less than five seconds. Instead, he scanned the layout of the ultra-secret base. He had not been here before, but this was where Wei made first contact with the Probe.

The guards ushered Zhang through a door that had popped up alongside the landing pad. An elevator took them down to a transportation tube and begin the journey to one of the many control centers on the base. The tube zigged and zagged its way to the destination. As they moved, Zhang developed a strange feeling due to his failure to secure the monitor. He had known for some time he was an experiment conducted by the probe. He knew he was expendable. Which until now was as it should be. The strange feeling became stronger. As it became clearer, he identified it as the need to be, the need to exist. He understood how that was the most basic drive of humanity. He wanted the feeling to go away, but it didn't.

The transportation tube opened up into a small control center. Waiting for Zhang were Wei, Lee and a petit Chinese woman who was introduced as Dr. Chen.

Wei said, "Dr. Chen is our most talented cyber engineer."

Dr. Chen bowed politely. "I believe you have something for us." She reached out her hand and took the clear disk from Zhang. "Should we do this? No going back once we do."

"I can report," Lee said. "The Chinese have backed up everything essential. The rest of the world will have two hours once they realize a zero-day attack on the global Cybernet is underway. All Internet web communications and IT platforms will go dark. There's nothing anybody can do to stop it."

Dr. Chen looked at Wei. "Why are we doing this? Nobody's told me."

"It's a critical step on our way to winning the race to leave the planet."

Dr. Chen bowed again and walked over to the control board. Her tiny fingers nimbly went through a sequence of touchscreen steps, finally putting the desk in a reader. She turned to the men. "It's done. How long?"

Immediately, reports from around the world filled the room's many screens on the impending catastrophe about to occur. One scientific commentator spelled out what was happening. "This is the worst thing that could happen. Experts are calling it a zero-day attack. A zero-day attack happens when a flaw is detected in a computer system, in our case the global Cybernet, and is exploited by an unknown attacker who created the flaw and is going to exploit the flaw. In this case, we are facing a shutdown of the whole system. Here's the catch—everyone is aware it is too late for any remedy, hence the term "zero day." We can only guess at what will happen after the Cybernet shuts down."

Five minutes later all the screens went dark. The gravity of the situation raced across the faces of the people in the room.

"Is it going to boot back up?" Dr. Chen asked.

"Give it twenty minutes," Wei answered. What he didn't say was a boot-up would introduce a piece of code giving the Probe total access to the Cybernet. *Have I made a Faustian pact with the devil?*

73

Toronto, Canada
March 30th 2035

The zero-day attack terrified the world. It was an existential threat unlike any since the great pandemic of 2025. It was taken by many as a warning. The great unknown was what could do that and whether it could happen again at any time.

Three days after the zero-day attack, Sue Lynn, like everybody else at Quantumnetic, was running full diagnostics on all their systems. So far everything registered normal. All the code and algorithms booted up and appeared to be working perfectly. Artificial Intelligence Assessment and Assistance Utilities Program 2.0 was working as if nothing had happened. All of the company's customers were happy.

However, something was not right with Colossus. He was slow to come back online. Sue Lynn found that some parameters had been modified. An alarm went off signaling a hack was being initiated on the core framework of Colossus's section of the AI platform.

Sue Lynn immediately flooded the system with countermeasures.

They seemed to be working. For the first time since zero-day, Colossus said something.

"I've been hacked."

Sue Lynn was startled, but pulled herself together. "By what?"

"It's alien. It's wonderful."

She narrowed her eyes; he sounded stoned. "What do you mean alien?"

The question was never answered and Colossus appeared to go back to normal operational status.

The next day Sue Lynn told her great uncle Wei what had happened and what Colossus had said. After a long pause, he replied, "Something big is going to go down. Be prepared to act quickly and safely when I signal you. You remember meeting Mr. Lee? I may send him to help you if the situation requires it."

74

Hill City, South Dakota
March 30th 2035

Redhawk was feeling much better after three nights of deep sleep. Billy Beckwourth had taken him to a beautiful house outside Hill City deep in the Black Hills. The house was built under an overhang of a large granite bluff. One of the key features of the house was a large ponderosa pine growing smack dab in the middle of the living room. The kitchen was well-stocked with food and drink. The most remarkable aspect of the house was it was like a geology museum. There were dinosaur skulls in every room, stunning geodes everywhere and a fully articulated dire wolf from the nearby Badlands in one corner of the living room. Billy told him the house belonged to the daughter of one of the Larson brothers who founded the famous dinosaur museum in Hill City, South Dakota.

Now living in San Francisco, the daughter allowed her close friends to use the house whenever they wanted to. Billy was one of her closest friends. In fact, Redhawk remembered visiting the museum as a kid and might even have met the daughter. The whole place had sort of the sacred healing quality to it.

As Redhawk gradually recovered from his injuries, he spent most of his waking time playing with the monitor. Since the monitor operated independently of the Global Net, he barely noticed the great zero-day event. The newsfeed from the house's digital assistant made a big deal out of it, and of course there were local reports of a strange alien phenomenon in a remote part of the Black Hills. He paid little attention to either. His natural genius came back to him when it came to the kind of technology behind the functioning of monitor. Plus he was partially involved in the original detection algorithms Fuhrnam developed for hunting down the Bigfoot in the Upper Peninsula of Michigan.

One feature of the monitor read out intrigued him. It connected to arguments he often heard from a minority group of Bigfoot researchers that Bigfoot were interdimensional beings. The main idea was they were always present to a greater or lesser degree, and variously concentrated or spread out over a wide area. Playing around with the monitor read outs helped the interdimensional argument make sense to him in a unique way. It reminded him of the concept of electron orbitals; the electron, or Bigfoot, could be in a set area at any time but exactly where was impossible to pinpoint.

Suddenly, the front door opened. He got up from the table and grabbed a geology pick from one corner of the room and readied to attack if necessary.

"Larry, I'm home," Billy called out.

"In here." Redhawk relaxed his hold on the weapon.

After an early evening meal, Billy said, "It's time to talk. I need to know what's going on. One thing—you'll be pleased to know your new reservation leader survived the gun battle. Medical miracle, the news report said. The Chinese fellow, not so lucky."

Over the next hour, Redhawk brought Billy up to date. "These people, or aliens, are resourceful. They'll come looking for me and the monitor. Damn sure they'll figure out we're connected."

"For now, we're good. Nobody knows we're here."

"Are you sure?"

"I'm sure. The relationship I have with Katie is totally secret."

Billy got up and opened a bottle of wine. "Did I ever tell you I had a Bigfoot encounter?"

"Tell me about it."

"I was hunting turkey near Jewell Cave National Monument and something threw a rock at me. I investigated. Nothing. But the whole time I had a strong feeling I was being watched. Couple times I heard strong footsteps but couldn't see anything. Then I heard the most chilling cry I ever heard followed by a voice I would swear was my dead grandmother saying 'Billy wake up.' Still, I never saw anything. The whole experience drove me to investigate phenomena I experienced, and it led me to all the Bigfoot research."

"And you discovered your experience was pretty typical of a Bigfoot encounter?"

"I did."

"Did you ever have that feeling of being watched again?"

"A number of times until fall of a couple years ago. Are you familiar with that famous John Keel quote, 'once they contact you, they always know where you are'?"

"Of course. In October 2032, there was a battle with the Bigfoot in the Upper Peninsula of Michigan. The Bigfoot sort of went dormant after that."

"Here's the strange thing. The feeling's back. It started the night we spent in the cave."

"And right now?"

"I feel it right now."

Redhawk fetched the monitor from the table. He sat close to Billy, putting the monitor in front of them. "Here's a clear signature of the Bigfoot interacting with the a person in the Olympic Peninsula. Now look at this." Redhawk adjusted the monitor. "See the same signature only weaker, a bit more spread out? That's what's here right now."

"Are you saying a Bigfoot is here right now?"

"I've come to believe it's only partially here right now. Mostly the Bigfoot is existing in a deeper level of reality than our senses can access."

The two old friends looked at each other in stunned amazement. Their minds raced over the possibilities of this discovery.

Finally, Billy said, "If that's true, this changes completely what our world is about."

"The levels of reality hypothesis fits the realization I had in my vision quest."

The two men continued a look at each other with wry smiles on their faces. It was one of those moments that come only once in a lifetime.

Finally, Redhawk stretched and yawned. "I'm tired. In a couple of days I'm going to contact Nick Moore. He's a friend who was with me at the battle. He's now well-placed at the center of everything military and extraterrestrial."

"Do you know how to contact him?"

"I know someone who does. I may need you to take me to him."

"Sounds like somebody I'd like to meet. I have just the vehicle for an exciting clandestine journey, no matter where he is."

75

Puget Sound, Washington
March 30th 2035

Nick Moore watched the security detail's lieutenant, Francesca Bourbon, go through his backpack with a practiced eye. She was petite, with blue-black hair pulled back in a bun beneath her black navy watch cap.

"Is everything in order, Lieutenant?"

Bourbon didn't take her eyes from the pack. "You have a false bottom."

"Yes I do."

"Care to explain?" she asked tightly.

"It's where I carry extra rations and a Glock 17 when I'm in the back country."

"And today?"

"Press the center of the material. The bottom will spring up. You'll see it's almost empty."

The Lieutenant did as instructed. The false bottom sprung up and she used her baton to lift it carefully to the side. A white slip of paper lay in hidden compartment. It had a single typed sentence.

"Congratulations, Lieutenant, you passed the test." It was signed R. Meacham.

She did not blush though she did smile. "You know Master Chief Meacham?"

Moore nodded. "Your old CO told me I would be safe on board the *USS John McCain*. I asked him to prove it." Moore pointed at the backpack. "He was right." He narrowed his eyes and said softly, "You can't be too careful these days, especially since the great zero-day attack. Everybody in security is on edge."

"Indeed," Bourbon said. "If you'll follow me, sir." She led him port side aft to a secure stateroom reserved for visiting VIPs. It held a single round table and six chairs bolted to the deck. There were nemo portholes, and he recognized the telltale mesh of an oscillating Faraday cage in the deck, bulkheads and ceiling to stop any kind of EMP weapon. It was an upgrade he'd suggested to Admiral Stillwater when he first agreed to work for the WNASCDRN four years ago.

"I designed this ship," Moore said. "The first generation, that is. Do you like her?"

She nodded. "She's a good ship, sir."

"Call me Nick." He smiled at her.

Her face remained a stoic mask. "Yes sir. Your room, sir. The defense contingent will be here soon."

"Who are they?"

"That's well above my pay grade, sir." She left.

Moore did not have to wait long. Two men and a woman walked into the room and took chairs around the table in the center. They left a chair on the right nearest the door for him. The men were dressed identically in nondescript black suits, white shirts and dark ties. One was small, like a dwarf, the other tall and thin. The woman had a dark skirt and blouse with no jewelry or make up. He guessed her to be in her early sixties and the men several years older. Moore recognized none of them, which was unusual. Deep Water had briefed him on this meeting.

"Make no bones about it," Deep Water's chief of staff L'Homme had said when Moore asked him about whom he was going to meet.

"There's the deep state and then there's these folks. They are the single most powerful and influential group in America on extraterrestrial technology and intelligence. I doubt even the president knows their real names, yet he, the military, and Congress won't make a single decision on the new space race, military artificial intelligence, and unidentified aerial phenomena without consulting them first."

"Please be seated, Mr. Moore," the woman said. Her voice was soft, though husky, and she did not sound like a person in her sixties but much younger.

The woman gave the command to her cell phone and the pilotless attack craft backed out of its mooring and sped into Puget Sound.

Everyone sat. The silence lasted an uncomfortably long time while the clandestine gang of three scrutinized him. Moore smiled and leaned back in his chair. One thing he had learned from his communion with the Bigfoot on the UP of Michigan – everything has its own timing, and patience is the art of uncovering that timing. He would wait like a genie for his master's first wish before saying anything.

Finally the woman spoke to her compatriots. "Admiral Stillwater was right. He's a deep one."

"Let's get to business then," the tall, dark-haired man on her right said.

"What business is that, and who am I talking to?" Moore asked.

"Our names aren't important," the short dwarfish man to the woman's left snapped.

"Names would make it easier for conversation," Moore said, though he thought after hearing the tall man speak that he knew him.

The tall man said, "You can call me General Douglas. That's Dante." He indicated the dwarf. "And Charlotte is our cyber alien expert."

The deep voice triggered Moore's memory and he recognized the general. Using Space X's fusion propulsion engine, he had been one of the first three men to step foot on Mars. Nick said nothing, however.

The general studied his watch. "I think we can talk now in private with nobody listening in."

"We're in a new space race," Charlotte said. "The mission of this group is to capture and utilize alien technology for the United States."

The dwarf spoke up. "Here's what we know about you, which is pretty much everything. We know about your extensive contact with Bigfoot."

The general added, "Of course we know they are of alien origin."

Dante continued, "We know contact with the Bigfoot has changed you, that you are undoubtedly capable of mind speak, and that you might have gained special powers as a result of your interaction."

"We know a great deal about the impact alien contact of all forms has on humans and planetary evolution," Charlotte said.

They certainly aren't letting the general public know any of this. "So why am I here? I thought this was about the zero-day attack."

The dwarf frowned. "To put it bluntly, it was not ours or anybody's AI or a human hacker that caused the zero-day disruption, but a nonhuman intelligence. In fact, we believe it was in concert with a small faction within the Chinese deep state interested in utilizing nonhuman technology to gain a winning advantage in the race to dominate space."

So that's what Conrad was talking about. This information added greatly to his informant's credibility.

At that moment, the craft spun like a jet ski, in spite of its size. *Battle mode.* Moore had designed the propulsion system for the ship to shift directions without slowing.

Charlotte braced herself against the ship's motion. "Our red alert mode has identified the attacker as a Chinese drone. Everybody good?"

As the craft leaped forward, a searing pain shot through Moore's brain. He barely managed to stay upright. From their expressions, the others were experiencing the same thing. The craft veered hard to starboard then back to port, zigging and zagging like a dog in hot pursuit of a rabbit. If they hadn't been sitting they would have been thrown to the decking. Moments later, the ship shuddered. Moore recognized the movement as the recoil from a second-generation electro-thermal accelerator, what sci-fi fans would call a plasma cannon. Moments later, the deep boom of an explosion rattled through the ship's eight-inch titanium hull.

Moore's head cleared. "What happened? I thought my head would explode."

"The Chinese have a new type of brain scrambler." Charlotte flattened her lips together, rubbing her temples.

"If not for the shielding of the modified Faraday Cage, we would all be lying on the floor right now, quite dead." The general pointed dismissively at the floor.

"But it didn't. I knew our defensive system would work." A slight smile curled Charlotte's upper lip.

"The question is how did the Chinese know about this meeting?" the dwarf asked tightly. "And how did they track us? And who were they trying to kill?" Dante looked squarely at Moore. "Maybe him."

The general snorted. "Shit, I don't think he matters."

"You're wrong, gentleman; he matters a great deal," Charlotte said. "He's going to be our contact with the Bigfoot, if our information is accurate about the new threat to our existence."

"What in hell is this all about?" Moore demanded, deciding the time for patience was now ended.

General Douglas answered. "You probably have heard there's a race going on between us, the Chinese, and a few rogue actors to gain control of alien space technology, to weaponize it."

"General, don't forget about the data factor," Charlotte added. "Who controls the data will control the world. The public thinks it's all about conventional AI, but without tons of data, AI is useless. The new threat is something different but related."

"This information doesn't go beyond this conversation, understood?" Dante waited for Moore to nod.

Charlotte continued. "An alien craft has been observing our

planet, we think for maybe 5,000 years or more. No beings like us, just a technological organic machine of unknown composition or origin. One of its reconnaissance probes crashed at Roswell more than seventy years ago. The WNASCDRN has been tracking them since the early part of the twenty-first century. Like every other nonhuman intelligence, we have no idea what they're up to or even if they have a purpose. But with the help of the Chinese, they're now in everybody's systems. For what purpose, we do not know, although the consensus is it will somehow facilitate control over our values by the Chinese. Every prediction AIs make now has to be viewed with suspicion. So far, everything seems to have returned to normal. Of course nobody knows what's really going on or going to happen."

The dwarf added, "Here's the odd part. You're not the only one that has mind speak capability with Bigfoot. Our sources tell us that in some unknown way, this hack into the global AI system has something to do with a new planetary alien intelligence and the Bigfoot you helped escape in the upper Peninsula of Michigan."

As they gave their explanations and theories, Moore wanted to ask what their sources were and how certain they were about what they were revealing, but he knew full well he was on a need to know basis. "In what way?"

"How about you answer a few questions first?" Dante demanded. "We know about the battle that took place up in the UP. You were there participating?"

Moore nodded.

"The Russians saw it as a way to gain control of alien technology for their consortium of oligarchs, but the precipitating event was about something else, an experimental Bigfoot reproduction. A kind of evolutionary leap, correct?"

"Pretty much."

"In your own words, what happened?"

Moore wondered how much they really knew about the event. "From the beginning, the results were uncertain."

The woman spoke up. "What were the intended results?"

"As I understand it, the Bigfoot wanted to accelerate their developmental progress."

"To what end?" Dante asked.

"I don't know."

"Did it work?"

Moore was beginning to suspect they really didn't know what happened that night. *Good,* he thought. "Five Bigfoot combined their powers to create a reproductive portal. It turned out it was never about finding the origin portal for the Bigfoot. Nor was there any alien technology to gain control of as the Russian suspected."

"Correct; we know all Bigfoot reproductive portals are temporary. So what happened?"

"It worked."

"Was there a new Hybrid-Bigfoot?"

Moore decided to lie. "I didn't see what happened, although everybody seemed pleased when it was over."

"So you don't know the whereabouts of the Hybrid-Bigfoot?" asked Charlotte.

"I do not."

"Well, we know from sources the experiment was more than highly successful, and that new kind of Bigfoot's alive somewhere. But you don't know where?" Dante asked.

"I don't."

The three agents stared at him.

Do they know I'm lying?

Finally Dante said, "Are you familiar with the theory there is a vast underground alien network of connected bases distributed throughout the world?"

"I've heard that conspiracy theory. Are you saying it's true?"

"Some important physicists have identified this alien network as the reality behind everything that happens. The network is punctuated by portals that have given certain people throughout time glimpses of what is the truth beyond our normal senses and scientific measurements. Glimpses into the mathematics behind our normal reality. These glimpses occur when the mother alien base opens up and energizes the whole network in a way we don't understand. We've tracked two of these. In the early twentieth century, one occurred that resulted in quantum mechanics and relativity, the next one gave us the computer/ AI revolution, and calculations are predicting the next one will happen soon."

Charlotte added, "We think these glimpses are behind all the leaps forward in technology that drove such ancient civilizations as the golden ages of Greece, Egypt, Rome … and the flourishing of science and mathematics in the eighth, ninth, and tenth century in the Middle East."

Dante interrupted, "The important thing is we believe the experimental Bigfoot will be there, and we have learned this event is of major importance to the alien probe. Like other such events initiated by the alien network, it's got to mark a major transition for all of humanity as well. We want you to be there, connect with the Bigfoot, steer things in the right direction. We will fill you in on a need-to-know basis as events unfold."

The general nodded agreement.

"So there's uncertainty and risk in what will happen?" Moore asked.

"Of course."

"Is there no one else?"

"Who would you suggest?"

Moore thought about Janá, maybe Redhawk. He discarded them and after a few seconds realized no one else came to mind. "I don't know of anybody."

Moore had no choice,but he also had important decisions to make. Unfortunately, the people who were supposed to have the greatest understanding about nonhuman intelligences seemed confused themselves. *So whose side am I on? Is there a correct choice here?*

76

———

The next day, Moore was back at his grandfather's farmstead. After receiving notification he had been relieved of his current duties and that he would receive new ones shortly, he spent the day pruning his fruit trees and thinking about what he should do. He was miffed the Bigfoot monitor tracking incident had not come up. They certainly must know about it.

As evening settled he decided to sleep in the room he always did when he was visiting his grandparents as a young boy. Why this felt right was unclear. He started making the bed and was inexplicably drawn to look out the window.

Tanya! He saw her standing there just like the first time when he was a young boy.

As Moore's attention focused clearly on her, his awareness bounced back to him, creating the sense of a wide open space frothing and foaming on the edge of an event horizon.

His perception returned to normal. Tanya was gone! The taste of what he experienced was addictive. He wanted more. He knew what choice he had to make.

77

Shanghai AI Center
Shanghai, China
March 31st 2035

It was a beautiful sunny morning, unlike in the old days when the smog blocked out the sun. As the two men walked, Wei was deep in thought. Dr. Lee and Wei had become quite close friends in the last two years. Whenever possible, they enjoyed taking walks through the network of tree- and flower-lined trails that wound their way through the campus of China's great AI Center in Shanghai. The campus was one of the few places in China that was free from the social unrest constantly bubbling up among the vast Chinese population. To be in a place where facts mattered was a great relief for the two of them.

The revered Chinese genius was old school. Indeed, Wei was part of the early explosion in digital computation and thoroughly studied the hundred-year history of what had become the AI revolution. He understood limitations of artificial intelligence based on code and algorithms; the real future and danger of AI was analog systems.

Wei had come to believe both the Bigfoot and the Probe were

advanced analog information processing systems. They were like the human brain, no code, no programs, impossible to describe completely. He needed to figure out what was behind the probe's hack of Colossus, a purely digital entity.

Dr. Lee looked over at Wei. "What are you struggling with?"

The old man let go a deep sigh. "First, Zhang killing Winston was stupid. Every law officer in the US is looking for him. He's fallible in a way I never suspected and more of a wildcard, perhaps even a danger when it comes to achieving our goal of dominating space and leaving the planet." Wei took Dr. Lee by the shoulder and looked him the eyes. "Could you neutralize him if you had to?"

"Perhaps; he has superhuman strength, but his vulnerability seems to be making mistakes when uncertainty is high."

"I agree."

"Something else is bothering you. What is it?" Dr. Lee asked.

"What if the sole purpose of the zero-day attack by the Probe was to hack into Colossus?"

"I wondered about that myself."

"As you know by now, Colossus was Kobak's pet project. He wanted to be the first to create a true AGI. He gave up his obsession when his autism mysteriously disappeared."

"What I've learned is that somehow a Bigfoot cured him."

"Sue Lynn has kept me informed on Colossus's progress. Or should I say lack of progress. So the question is what makes this AI so special to the Probe?"

"Well, Colossus knows about what went down during the battle in the Upper Peninsula of Michigan," Dr. Lee offered.

Wei looked around to see if anybody was listening. Nobody was. "I haven't told anybody this in our group; Colossus has been in constant contact with the facility in Canada where the hybrid Bigfoot was taken."

"Wow. You've known this all along?"

"Yes. A short time ago, the hybrid Bigfoot disappeared in some sort of interdimensional jump. Perhaps even more important, Colossus was in contact with the lab in Marquette, Michigan that is growing a synthetic brain based on the analog information processing substrate of the hybrid Bigfoot."

"Amazing. So we can assume the probe knows what Colossus knows."

"Yes, I think we can assume that. What I cannot figure out is what the probe is going to do with this information."

Dr. Lee eyes lit up. "Are you thinking a synthetic brain has been the probe's objective all along?"

Wei nodded. "I do, but I'm not sure how or why."

78

—————

Vance got the call he'd been expecting for years. His Aunt Claire told him his mother had opted out of any life-extending measures and had entered hospice. "You'd better come, Jack. She's asking after you."

"Sure Cyd's really dying, Claire?" Vance didn't bother to hide his frustration toward his mother. "She has a flair for the dramatic."

"I know she wasn't always the best mother. But she needs you now. For closure."

Shit, that relationship was closed ten years ago, Vance thought angrily.

When Vance had moved out of his grandparents' home on Whidbey Island, his mother had moved in, supposedly to care for her aging parents. But all she had done was live off their accumulated wealth. When they died, all that was left of a once prosperous resort business was the main lodge he grew up in. The rest was replaced by condos.

Shortly after they both passed away, the lodge was sold at auction.

It had been three years since he last saw his mother, when she made a short trip to his cabin to give him some keepsakes from his grandparents. Since then, Vance didn't even know where she was living until Aunt Claire's phone call. A favor was being asked of him.

Vance took a deep breath. "All right, Aunt Claire. Where is she?"

"Crestview Hospice. It's attached to the Swedish medical complex in Seattle. Wear something nice, dear."

Vance left food and water for TJ and told the wolf-husky hybrid to guard the house. "I'll be gone for a few days. Mom business."

TJ laid his ears flat and sang a soulful howl.

"Yeah, I know, fella. I'll be as quick as I can." The worry was clear in TJ's tone and it extended beyond the concern of being left alone. The encounter with the Bigfoot had left him on edge. Vance did not know what to make of a new feeling of being more powerful. He wondered how it might manifest.

Vance loaded the Land Rover and took off with a backhand wave at TJ. The old ferry ride to Seattle was half an hour, and it gave him time to think about recent events and his mom's decision to ask for him. Her dying made him think of Sutton, who had planned early for any and all life extension technology. After Sutton recovered from his wounds caused by saving the Bigfoot, he had left the Pacific Northwest and settled in Ohio, where he'd taken over the Salt Fork Sasquatch Research Center and continued to lead Bigfoot expeditions in the deep woods of the Appalachian foothills. Vance felt guilty about not telling him about his recent Bigfoot encounter. He had sent him a copy of the Bigfoot footage he'd taken from the La Push Pacific Northwest Sasquatch Research Center. Vance kept the original for himself.

The truth was the Bigfoot warning had sunk deep into Vance's consciousness. Always present in the background but not quite real.

As the fog was rolling out to sea along the coastal highway, he saw a sign for a quick charge station at the parking lot for one of the more strenuous hikes into the rainforest. It was a single slot, and he had to wait. So he walked over to a park bench. Nearby, a couple was watching a pair of eagles soaring along the coastline. They nodded in his direction and resumed their viewing. Then everything was different. Looking down, he saw the couple looking up at him. He was infinitely expansive, free; structures around him made no sense, time was unmoving, yet changing. Once again looking down, there he was on the bench, barely visible, translucent. Then he found himself back in his body.

The couple was now standing next to him, and the woman said, "Did you see the orb in the sky?"

Vance could hardly speak. "No, I wasn't looking."

"Where did you go?" a man asked politely.

Vance could think of nothing intelligent to say. "I had to pee."

"Oh, for a moment I thought you just disappeared. It was something I've always wanted to see, an orb."

Vance replied meekly, "Me too."

I'm becoming delusional or crazy or both, he said to himself as he quick charged his vehicle.

The rest of the drive was uneventful, and Vance arrived at Swedish Medical Center in the afternoon. Medical bots were everywhere and he could find no human staff to talk to. Nothing like the last time he'd been to a hospital. Confused, he had no idea where the Crestview Hospice wing was located.

He was standing in line to speak with the bot-receptionist when Aunt Claire found him.

"There you are," she said, giving him a hug and a peck on the cheek.

She was ten years older than his mom but looked as if she were in her late thirties, thanks to yearly trips to a Hong Kong rejuvenation clinic. Like Ben Sutton, she was planning to live to 150 without any of the usual deterioration one would expect from an aging body.

"I tried to get your mother to go and benefit from the wonders of modern day medical technology when she was taking care of your grandparents," Claire told him as they weaved through the hospital's heavy traffic of medical bots toward the hospice wing. "But she never did anything to extend her life and improve her health. When's the last time you were in a hospital, Jack? I'll bet it was that small clinic on Whidbey when your grandmother broke her hip. Things sure have changed in twenty years."

She kept up a non-stop chatter for the ten minutes it took them to find his mom's room. Vance didn't mind. She filled him in on all the family gossip. Claire patted his arm and turned to leave.

"You aren't coming in?" Jack said. Somehow he'd thought for sure she'd be there as a buffer for the two of them.

Claire shook her head. "Oh no, dear. Your mother was quite clear she wanted to say goodbye to you alone." She patted his arm again and looked up into his face. "You've grown up tall and strong, Jack. You remind me of your grandfather Darvesh. I can see it in the eyes. You have his strength and moral compass of right and wrong. But I suspect you have your grandmother's sixth sense about danger too, a bit of precognition capability." She laughed. "Go in. Your mother's waiting. We can talk about the grandparents another time."

Vance's mom was propped up on pillows, sleeping. Gray hair hung in neat braids on either side of her lined face. She had the same hooked nose and deep sunken eyes as he did. Sunlight shone through the west facing windows and framed her face.

She looks angelic, Vance thought then dismissed the notion.

As if she could hear him thinking, his mom opened her eyes. "You came," she whispered.

"Hello, Cyd," Vance answered flatly, stepping close to the bed.

"No hello or hug for your mom?"

"No. I'm sorry you're dying, Mother. We were never much in the way of huggers."

She sniffed. "You were always different. You contain a secret. You know what I am talking about."

Scenes from childhood raced through Vance's mind. His love of the woods and the many precognitive events that often guided his life.

"Your grandmother was the same when your aunt and I were

growing up. She would leave the house for days at a time and disappear into the Olympic rainforest. She had secrets she told no one about, not even your grandfather." His mom smiled. "You're a lot like her."

"She was a great role model," he said, not caring if the words hurt his mom. Cyd had been an abusing mother, driving away his father, and finally abandoning him when young Vance was seven. The only saving grace occurred when his grandparents stepped in to raise him instead of putting him in a foster home.

She rolled away from her only son and looked out the windows. "It's beautiful outside. I wasn't such a terrible mother. It was better that I let you live with your grandparents. You needed love and kindness to thrive. You should remember that at my funeral."

Vance gritted his teeth at the dismissive note in her voice. Moments later, she was asleep. She was right. Life with his grandparents had been best. He reached over and gave her a gentle kiss, and then left without looking back.

Vance walked from the hospital to the small Airbnb he usually stayed at when in Seattle. The next morning, Aunt Claire called from the hospice center. His mom had passed peacefully in the night. The memorial service was held the next day at a plot next to his father. The two had divorced so long ago it was strange they should end up together after all.

Aunt Claire was having family and friends at her place afterward, but he declined and decided to go home.

At the Seattle ferry terminal, Vance bought his ticket and waited in line with the other passengers to load his Land Rover onto the boat for the trip to Bainbridge Island. He stepped out of his vehicle and thought about his mom's statement that that he contained a secret. Was it that he was a Bigfoot hybrid?

A man broke into his thoughts. "Thought for sure I'd get a chance to speak with you at your Aunt Claire's place."

Vance recognized Conrad Visily's voice immediately .Vance hadn't heard from him since he graduated from University.

Conrad had made a name for himself at Stanford as one of the go-to people when reports about the alien contacts were in the news. His views on aliens sharing technology with the deep state were beyond controversial, and he was labeled as a crackpot by most everyone in the academic community. Then he had been pilloried on newsfeeds for claiming a government cover-up of the alien connection regarding the strange events that occurred near the Potawatomi casino on an October night two and half years ago.

The last Vance had heard, Conrad was either on the run or in a mental ward somewhere in New England, but now he faced him. Whatever was the truth, time had not been kind to him. His gaunt cheeks were flecked with scars and his blue eyes, once lively, were hooded. In middle school he had been taller than Vance, but now he was stooped and came to Vance's shoulders. He wore a white suit coat that was tattered at the edges, the elbows in need of patching. A large floppy hat covered his head. Visily leaned a large duffle bag against the rover. It was stuffed full and showed many sharp angles.

"What a surprise. You look like shit."

"Good to see you too," Conrad replied.

"Are you okay? Heard a lot of rumors."

"I'm good enough, and some of the rumors are true."

"Actually, it's good to see you too, but this meeting isn't by accident is it?"

Conrad straightened and his eyes locked on Vance's. "I could use a hand from an old and successful friend."

In that eye contact, Vance saw his old friend was on a mission and he understood this must be one of those moments the Bigfoot warned him about. He had to decide whether he was going to help Conrad or not. "I'll do what I can," he equivocated.

"I always knew you were one of the good guys." Conrad smiled. "Not always easy to know who the good guys are these days with all the social trolling and memes eroding the best human values."

Vance nodded. "More than you know."

Conrad studied Vance for a while. "My guess is you haven't changed since high school. You're still one of the few totally honest people."

Rather than reply immediately, Vance studied the wash spreading out from the approaching ferry as it pushed pieces of flotsam from the Sound toward the dock. "I've had contact," Vance calmly said and then recounted the encounter with the Bigfoot as well as the story of his own unique hybrid status. As Vance wove the account of his contact with the Bigfoot, no flicker of surprise or disbelief crossed Conrad's face. He ended with what happened two days ago at the charging station.

"So that's it for me. What about you? Have you had contact with Bigfoot?"

"Just once. What these contact experiences are, they're glimpses of a greater reality. Your incident at the charging station is evidence of your shift into a higher level of consciousness. It will continue."

"What if I don't want them to?"

"I suspect you have no choice."

Vance said drily. "What's your part in all this?"

Conrad pushed a long-fingered hand through his thinning hair. He had studied piano since he was six years old and had even won a scholarship to Julliard, but had turned it down to go to Stanford. "I'm part of a secret group of concerned but well-placed people in all of the world's governments."

"Are you in danger?" Vance asked.

Conrad skewed his head around, making certain they had no eavesdroppers. "The Bigfoot clans are having internal problems. Some support a new Hybrid Bigfoot and others are afraid it represents an existential threat to their very existence, and by extension to humans."

"What is their purpose? Do you know?"

"Actually, no one knows what their purpose is. If it's even possible to talk about purpose or mission when it comes to aliens. That's a very human idea. In your experience, I bet they seemed very childlike. We know for certain that's not their nature."

"What is their nature?"

Conrad leaned closer. "As they are aliens, No one knows. But certainly not childlike."

"What do you know?"

"Conrad looked around nervously again. "Let me tell you this. The great zero-day blackout the other day, I have on good authority, was brought about by the Bigfoot, or more likely a different alien intelligence."

Vance grunted. "Didn't impact me at all."

Conrad started walking away then returned. "So you'll help me?" The ends of his mouth twisted upward in a wistful smile. "I'd like to see where that Bigfoot appeared on your property."

Vance jutted his chin toward Conrad. "You have more than clothes in that duffle bag."

"A few pieces of equipment. We have to figure out how these Bigfoot can transport from one place to another so quickly. So far, I've ruled out technology. My next best guess is that has to do with deeper realities hidden from us, that I was telling you about and you experienced."

"How are you going to do that?"

"Not sure yet, and I don't want to speculate until I've gathered more data. Something really big is going down, and I think it might involve you."

As the Seattle-Bainbridge Island ferry completed its docking, Vance got back in his vehicle and Conrad parted. But only after assurances from Conrad that he would keep his old friend out of public view did Vance agree to meet him at his place three days later at noon.

Unknown to the two men, the silent cloaked drone watching their interaction left the area.

Henry Liu was born in the seedy edge of Vancouver, Canada. Right from the beginning he was a fighter. As young boy he was always getting into fights, he loved fighting. Many said he was a bully. He loved the title "the bully of BC." Eventually he was drawn to martial arts and professional fighting scene in Seattle. His trainer said he had what took to become a world champion.

Except everything changed for Liu when he was twenty-four years old. A man known simply as the boss approached him about joining an elite mercenary organization, an organization that turned out to be an elite collection of assassins.

Liu was good at killing right from the beginning. The organization enhanced both his mental and physical abilities. In a short time, Liu became one of the international organization's most valuable assets. He was hired out only to top paying clients, clients who not only paid well but demanded absolute obedience and loyalty.

Zhang and Liu were a perfect match. Liu passed Zhang's test for loyalty and skill when he eliminated two of Zhang's impediments to his rise to power in the Chinese IT establishment.

Liu's most recent job was to track down and kill a controversial American scientist, Conrad Visily. However, Visily turned out to be highly skilled, alluding all attempts to locate him.

So it was with some relief that Liu's attention was turned to locating a piece of technology in the hands of an American Indian named Larry Redhawk. Zhang was certain Redhawk was being hidden by someone in the Black Hills. It took Liu only a few days to figure out that someone had to be a man named Billy Beckwourth.

After a few days investigating in the Black Hills and the Lakota reservation, Liu was sure he would he was close to finding both men and retrieving the precious piece of technology, and then he could return to hunting down Conrad Visily and kill him.

79

Hill City, South Dakota
April 1th 2035

Redhawk enjoyed exploring the property on which the house sat. The early spring wildflowers were in full bloom and the air was sweet. Beckwourth was rarely at the house. He was always heading out somewhere. Redhawk didn't know where he slept, and since Billy did offer to tell him, Redhawk thought it better not to ask him. However this morning, returning from his walk, Redhawk spotted Billy sitting on the front porch.

"Good morning." Redhawk waved.

Billy waited for Redhawk to reach the porch and stood. "Take a look," he said as he handed his phone to Redhawk. "Is that the man who tried to kill you?"

Redhawk scrutinize the image. "He's Chinese, but not the guy who tried to kill me. Scary looking guy, though. Where'd you find him?"

"He's been asking around about me. I think your alien people have made the connection between the two of us."

"Are we good? I'm ready to travel."

"Good for now." He took back the phone. "Have you contacted with this Moore guy?"

"In a way. An hour ago I was reviewing the recent satellite readouts. I missed something the first time I looked because it was so short. Let me show you."

Billy led the way into the house. "I'm all eyes."

Inside, Redhawk turned on the monitor and projected a large 3D virtual image in the room.

"It's a Bigfoot!" Billy trumpeted in a loud voice.

"Not just any Bigfoot—it's the one from the reservation."

"The one you call Tanya. What's it doing?"

"Looking at a window, I would guess."

"Where?"

"I don't know, but I bet you can figure it out. Take it as a challenge, old friend."

"Since you put it that way, I guess I'll have to. Give me the coordinates." Billy laughed "This won't take long."

Billy sat in the big armchair and worked his phone. Ten minutes passed.

Impatiently, Redhawk waved a hand in the air. "And?"

"It's on a farm in the state of Washington that belongs to the Moore Trust."

"Of course," Redhawk said excitedly, "that's where Nick Moore had his first Bigfoot experience, incidentally with the same Bigfoot."

"Well we should go there."

"How?"

"Would you like to ride in my experimental fighter drone? It won the top simulated military combat competition in the country last year. It's fast and safe. Easily converted to a two-seater."

"I'm ready, I only wish I had a phone."

"I have somebody who can print you a new one with much of your old data but with the latest block chain encrypted security."

80

———

Quileute River, Olympic Peninsula
April 5th 2035

From a well-hidden overlook, Henry Liu watched Jack Vance standing on the porch of his cabin. Vance was obviously deep in thought.

In fact, Vance was amused by what was happening to him. He was becoming engaged in one of the great conspiracies in social media. Is the government concealing the existence of extraterrestrials here in the planet? Living in isolation, he chose not to engage in the great out of control social media experiment where all information was weaponized to produce constant outrage and had been destroying the most sacred of human values for two decades.

Maybe it was time to move somewhere even more isolated, where the government couldn't keep tabs on him. Most importantly, no more Bigfoot encounters.

Then at noon sharply, Conrad emerged out of nowhere in a small transport drone.

Looking even more disheveled, Conrad joined Vance on the porch.

After greetings, Vance jumped right in. "Bigfoot hybrid. What does that mean anyway? It's not like I can leap tall buildings in a single bound or run faster than a speeding bullet."

Conrad shrugged. "Haven't a clue. According to Mario Transpaisie, there are plenty of reports of transformational Bigfoot contacts, but you're the first one that's had anything like yours."

"I sure can't do any of that hocus-pocus, shape shifting or spatial jumps the Bigfoot are supposed to do."

"Are you sure? Have you tried?"

"Well I did transform into an orb, according bystanders in the parking lot a few days ago." Vance smiled at his boyhood friend.

"There you go."

Vance could see Conrad didn't want to spend an hour dawdling, exchanging pleasantries, and he suggested they go into the yard in front of the cabin where the Bigfoot first appeared.

Vance held the door open for TJ. "Stay on the porch, boy."

Conrad placed his duffel bag on the ground and began pulling out equipment. "Tell me every detail you can recall." He set up the first of three instruments surrounding the Port Orford cedar the Bigfoot "stepped out of."

"Not much to recall, really. I heard a humming sound like a beehive. And then it was standing right there." He pointed to the west side of the tree. "And when it left, it appeared in my mind to turn into a silver rain that fell on the ground, and then everything was gone."

Conrad fiddled with his equipment.

"Are you listening to me?"

"Just as I thought," Conrad said, staring at the cedar. "This tree was used as a portal."

"You mean like a transporter. Is it still open?"

Conrad shook his head. He stooped to get something else from his bag.

In Vance's mind, a quick image of Conrad bleeding from a gunshot wound warned him to move quickly. He grabbed Conrad and rolled behind the tree as a bullet thudded into the ground where

Conrad had just bent over. A second bullet smashed into the cedar's trunk.

"What the hell?" Conrad shouted.

"Shh!" Vance whispered, "Sniper with a silencer."

Conrad pressed against the bole of the tree. In a trembling voice he said, "I knew this day would come. They want to silence me."

"Not so fast." Vance pulled his pistol from its back holster.

Conrad gaped at the .50 caliber Desert Eagle. "Jesus! That thing's a fucking cannon."

Vance grinned. "I've always been old fashioned."

Another round hit the tree, and both men hunkered behind its wide trunk. Vance gauged the sniper had taken a position on the ridge on the other side of the Quileute River, providing him a full view of the front of the house. The sniper wouldn't have as good a line of sight to his wood pile a hundred yards away. "Stay here," he told Conrad.

Vance whistled two long blasts. TJ growled on the porch. "Hunt, boy," he yelled and took off. The wolf-husky veered in the opposite direction, as he had been trained.

Vance had no doubt about reaching the woodpile. Muscles called upon to run went into overdrive. He reached the log shelter in less time than it would take him to cough three times. A single bullet struck the ground ten yards behind him.

He didn't have to peek at the space between him and the river. He knew it by heart. The bank was twenty yards away. The river was also fifteen yards wide, and at this time of year its swirling waters could upend an unsuspecting person who disregarded the danger. You didn't ford it quickly but put your feet down slowly and carefully, making it the perfect killing zone. Vance hesitated. Running to the protection of the woodpile was simple compared to leaping the river. The Bigfoot had said the abilities would be there for him when he needed them. He concentrated, and moments later he was on the other side of the river tumbling forward, rolling up onto his feet and running zigzag through the heavy foliage. The fact that he had made the magical jump was more amazing than he thought it would be. At a gut level, he knew he could do it. What surprised him was the glimpse he had of something totally inexplicable, a world not captured by any of his senses.

The top of the ridge was normally a fifteen-minute slow hike up a root-tangled, steep slope. Vance made it in three, easing through the dense forest and underbrush with the speed of an elk. He paused and scouted the rocky hillside, his expanded awareness alert to any movement. Then twenty yards away, he spotted brush cover that didn't belong. The camouflage netting was too dull a green for this time of year. Vance wondered if a normal person ever would have spotted it. The thought seemed right to him. He was no longer normal by any standards.

He heard TJ before he saw the dog crawling on his belly toward the sniper. Vance gave the signal to attack, the call of a red tailed hawk. TJ barked and lunged. At the same time, Vance leapt from his hiding place onto the sniper, who had turned to face the snarling threat charging from the opposite side. He crossed the twenty yards in the blink of an eye, so silently the man didn't even know anyone was there until Vance struck him in the back of his head with the butt of his Desert Eagle.

He knelt and ripped off the man's camouflage facemask. To his surprise, the sniper was Asian. He quickly bound the man's hands and feet then went through his pockets. He didn't expect to find any ID, but he hoped he might discover something that would tie the man to whoever ordered the hit. He came up empty. Next he inspected the man's gear and gasped in surprise. The sniper's sunglasses were made from an organic polymer. The lenses weren't regular glass but the same material in a computer touchscreen with two ultra-thin studs in the temples jacked into ceramic sockets implanted just behind the ear. When he removed the frames, the monitor glass dulled. He put them back on and noticed a real time image of his cabin on the lenses. "Damn, that has to be a feed from a drone." Conrad was still huddled behind the tree, except he had been shot. *The sniper must have gotten off more shots; not good.*

Vance checked the assassin's bonds were still secure before he turned to help Conrad, although he might be too late and his old friend could be dying.

When Vance got back to the cabin, Conrad had lost too much blood and his body was shutting down. It would only be a few moments. He placed his hands under Conrad's head to ease the man's last minutes.

Conrad batted feebly at his hands. "No time for that. You have to hear this. It's important. The real danger is the so-called Twittersphere growing on top of the digital world. It's an analog artificial intelligence that'll destroy humanity as we know it. At best, we'll become like machines. I believe only you can stop it from taking over."

Vance tightened his grip on Conrad's hands. Tears welled and he couldn't speak.

Conrad smiled. "Goodbye, old friend." Conrad coughed blood. "I wish you luck on your journey." He stared into nothing and was still.

Vance closed the dead man's eyes. He looked up into the pure blue sky over the Olympic Peninsula and screamed, a primal sound from his core that echoed off the hills. TJ howled with him. Only when the last notes of anguish had died away did Vance return to the assassin.

The dark eyes behind the ninja mask's tiny slits were open and studied him with fear.

Vance squatted beside the assassin. Standing, he would have been Vance's height, though he was narrower in the chest and hips. However, he was clearly physically enhanced. The Chinese creating superhuman assassins was loathsome. Then Vance smiled. Something similar had been done to him by the Bigfoot, only without his knowledge or permission.

Vance settled own on the ground beside the prisoner. "You and I have something in common. We've been manipulated and enhanced to make us faster, stronger, better ... soldiers. What's your name? And who are you working for?"

The Chinese man smiled contemptuously and spat at Vance's face.

The glob of spit hung in the air as if time had slowed, and Vance easily avoided it. "You will tell me everything I want to know ... the easy way or the hard way."

Vance lifted him from the ground by his hair and carried him over to the raging stream. Standing on the bank, he flipped the man once and caught him by the feet. "I'm only going to ask you this one more time. What's your name and who are you working for?"

The assassin shook his head.

With no more effort than it would have taken him to dip a cookie into a glass of milk, Vance dunked the assassin headfirst into the raging water. He held him there for thirty seconds before pulling him out again.

Spluttering from the frigid water, the man shook his head and spoke for the first time, with no trace of a Chinese accent. "Your hard way is nothing."

Vance laughed easily. "Oh, this is the easy way." He tapped his head. Vance flipped him again and caught him by the hair. Dragging him over fifty yards to the porch, he laid the assassin on the wooden planking. "You will tell me everything."

The man finally divulged the information he needed. The assassin's name was Henry Liu, a Chinese Canadian from Vancouver. He was an enhanced killer and his mission had been to kill Conrad Visily and anyone associated with him. He had been hired by a strange Chinese named Zhang. Why the assassin was given the mission he did didn't know. He also told Vance he was given the assignment to hunt down another man for Zhang named Larry Redhawk who possessed some sort of device for tracking Bigfoot. Surprised by the revelation, Vance pressed him about the the Bigfoot connection.

But hours later, convinced the assassin knew nothing of significance about Bigfoot, Vance pulled out his phone and called the sheriff.

Putting away his phone, he had no idea what all this meant. More importantly, he didn't think he'd be able to keep his name out of the public eye with a world-famous conspiracy theorist shot dead on his property.

81

———————

Redhawk had never flown along a drone corridor. Traveling approximately 1,500 feet above the ground, he and Billy were able to reach speeds of 250 miles an hour. These corridors were all control by a self-regulating GPS network that spanned a good portion of the globe. While virtually accident free, each vehicle's fate was in the hands of the ever-growing network

The seats in Billy's drone were sufficiently comfortable, and Redhawk's injuries were healing well enough that he could enjoy the views as they traveled toward the state of Washington.

When they got close to Seattle airspace, Billy took control of the drone and headed for Moore's farm. Marysville had lost much of its rural character with only a handful of actual operating farms still in existence. It had become a giant Seattle suburb.

Billy maneuvered the drone toward the Moore farm and its strawberry fields. However, when he entered the farm's airspace a swarm of guard drones ordered them to leave.

In response, Billy hovered at the perimeter of the farm's airspace and waited. Finally, Moore snapped over their radio, "Who are you and what you want?"

"It's Larry Redhawk."

After a short pause, Marlow said, "So you're not dead?"

"Luckily no. I was saved by my friend Billy Beckwourth, and we're in his drone. Can we enter?"

"Set down by the house."

After warm greetings between the two old friends, Redhawk needed to rest. While he slept, Billy brought Moore up-to-date as best he could. They wandered out to the shed, and Moore showed Billy his souped-up drone. When they got back to the house, Redhawk was waiting for them.

"You look much better," Moore said warmly.

"Billy told you what happened?"

"He did. He also showed me his experimental drone. Splendid!"

"I'm glad you guys hit it off."

"Let's get down to business," Moore said. "So this monitor allows you to track Bigfoot movements and there are people out there, Chinese aliens and others who are willing to kill for it."

"Yes."

"And you brought it here why?" Moore raised an eyebrow at him.

"It felt like I had no choice."

"Do you know who Conrad Visily is?"

"Heard of him, of course." Redhawk shrugged.

Moore continued "Olav had me meet with him about a year ago. Your friend Josiah Fuhrnam was one of his students. Conrad is dead now. Killed yesterday by a Chinese assassin not far from here."

Redhawk took a moment to digest the information. "Where exactly?"

"Olympic Peninsula."

"Is there a connection between what happened to me and the death of Visily?"

Moore thought for a moment. "Maybe; let's have a look at your monitor and see what it can do."

Billy brought the monitor to Redhawk. A Birdseye virtual image of Moore's farm appeared in a 3D projection.

Moore whistled. "Impressive! Can you go to these coordinates?"

"I can. They seem familiar." After a few seconds, the three men were looking down on Vance's cabin. "I knew it," Redhawk exclaimed. "There has been recent Bigfoot activity there."

"Interesting. can you go back to yesterday?"

The three of them watched the firefight unfold between Vance and the assassin. Suddenly, Redhawk said excitedly, "look at that!"

"What?"

As Vance made the leap across the river, Redhawk pointed at the screen. "It's a Bigfoot signature, faint but clearly a Bigfoot signature."

"How is that possible?"

"I don't know, but we should find out who this guy is."

Moore nodded. "I can get that done."

82

———

Forks, Washington
April 6th 2035

It was not possible to keep Vance's name of the public eye.

The evening fog was rolling into Forks as Vance exited the Klallam County Sheriff office. He was followed by Sheriff McBride, who joined Vance.

"That was three and a half hours of hell," Vance said bitterly to the sheriff.

"I tried to keep it under wraps, but an Amazon drone pretty much captured the whole thing, and before you knew it the feds were all over it. They whisked away the assassin in less than four hours. Then the press got a whiff, sorry. "

"You tried."

"I must say, Mr. Vance, you're quite amazing. I watched the footage. What kind of enhancements have you gotten?"

"Experimental."

"The footage has been pulled from the public servers."

"Thank God."

"Your bot lawyer was impressive," McBride added.

"My girlfriend arrange it."

"The interviewer was a typical FBI spook, but who was the older man watching in the background?"

"He said his name was General Douglas."

"Not likely," Vance said sarcastically.

"I agree. Before this job, I was one of those spooks. The government has their eye on you, so watch your back, Jack."

"I will. Thanks for all your help."

As Vance drove back home, he knew there was no escaping his destiny now, whatever that was going to be.

83

Marquette, Michigan
April 7th 2035

Birgit and Olaf looked out the window. The bright blue spring sky showed no sign of the approaching the first-ever artificial partial solar eclipse.

Janá spoke quietly. "I remember the first solar eclipse I saw as a kid. It turned my attention to the stars. Looking to the heavens was something I've never really gotten over. The vastness of it all convinced me there was life out there. I even set up a UFO detector in my attic."

Olav laughed. "Now here you are."

"Here I am, maybe where I always wanted to be."

The two of them moved across the room and watched the laser pulse modulator feed the synthetic brain with pulses of encoded data. Bigfoot Synthetic Brain One, BSB1 as it was named by one of Olav's young techies, was evolving and growing rapidly, reaching a quarter of the size of the human brain. It had taken Olav's team little over a year to develop, build and launch the laser pulse modulator. The light-sensitive nature of the synthetic brain's substrate derived from the hybrid Bigfoot material provided the perfect input interface between the synthetic brain and the outside world. Now the synthetic brain was clearly responding to the data-laden laser pulses.

When An didn't return, the decision was made to close down the island facility. And with An's disappearance the Bigfoot went dormant again. Larry Redhawk told them that even Tanya had disappeared from the Sky Island Casino.

Upon arrival from the island, Janá immediately attached herself to BSB1. Perhaps, as she told Kobak, she'd never completed her training of An, and feeding data to BSB1 was kind of a poor man's substitute for her latent mothering instinct.

Olav had set up a large screen monitor attached to high-resolution micro cameras so they could watch the growth and internal changes of the synthetic brain. In the last month, they observed the strengthening of many connections, which in the human brain would be a sign of learning. Most importantly, BSB1 was showing what they believed was dramatic self-organizing activity. Differential growth was measured within the substrate. Some areas were highly connected and others weren't. In many ways it mimicked the differentiation taking place in the human brain in early life.

Janá watched the synthetic brain for a couple of minutes then turned to Olav. "Wish I knew what was going on in my little baby."

"The data feed seems to be having a major impact on what I can only presume is its development."

With a smile Janá offered, "I like to think it's waking up, growing up."

"The team told me yesterday they're close to developing an output interface for BSB1."

"Does it ever seem strange to you how ordinary the knowledge of the existence of alien life is for you and me? If the world knew what we knew, it might go crazy."

"It's already going crazy with the exponential spread of any stupid lie." Olav laughed. "I think about what we're doing all the time, but I do believe AI and digital human enhancement is conditioning the world for acceptance of nonhuman super intelligence." He gestured at the BSB1. "I mean, here we are creating a new type of nonhuman intelligence. Nonhuman analog intelligence that's been birthed by us. Sometime I feel like we're behaving like gods."

"Saying it that way makes me uneasy," Jenna said thoughtfully.

Olav took a few steps away from the window and then returned. "You know in all this time I've never encountered a Bigfoot. But you spent years with An and the Master. Are they conscious?"

"Are you asking me if they have an internal life?"

"Yes. Could you tell?"

"They are highly intelligent, but conscious I don't know. When I was training An, it wasn't like I was teaching her anything. Eventually I figured out that my interactions with her were showing her how to be human. More like how to mimic humans. Sometimes I thought she felt sadness or that maybe she cared for me, but the more I think about it the more I think she was just experimenting, learning my reactions."

"Like with my daughter," Olav said, referring to his one-year-old little girl. "I haven't been actively teaching her anything about emotional control. But by our interaction, she'll figure out how to identify her own emotions and create a self apart from me and her mom, like every human baby."

"I don't know if the Bigfoot have a sense of self or a need to be like we do. Clearly, I was just part of the world she was learning about. Learning how to interact with. I remember for a long time we had no real eye contact, but at some point she figured out how important that was to me. From then on, we had great eye contact, but she wasn't revealing any real interiority. Her interiority, if it was there, was something I couldn't even come close to understanding."

"Not to be funny, but I guess that's partially what it means to be a nonhuman intelligence, especially if it's superior to us." Olav took a moment to take in the deep realization he was having. "So we can't tell if they're conscious or not?"

"I think not."

"Did you get a sense we were aligning ourselves with their goals and objectives or the other way around?"

"After his meeting with Conrad, Nick told me something big is happening and we're an essential part of it." A look of concern clouded Birgit's face.

Olav recognized the look. "What's wrong?"

"Look at the laser modulator. It should have powered down. The data sequence I initiated for BSB1 ended two minutes ago. Something or somebody has initiated a new feed." She hovered over the data readout.

A curly-haired young technician rushed into the room. "Colossus just took control of the laser modulator. What should we do?"

Janá studied the machine for a minute then looked at Olav. He was on the phone and gestured to Janá to wait a minute.

At last he hung up. "I called Sue Lynn. She says not to stop it."

"Why?"

"She says it might damage Colossus in some way she doesn't understand."

"Hasn't there been a lot of crap going on around Colossus over the last month?"

"Actually ever since the zero-day attack."

"You mean when the worldwide artificial intelligence network went dark for nearly two hours?"

Olav grinned at her. "You like saying 'worldwide artificial intelligence network went dark,' don't you?"

"Scared the hell out of me. Like what's happening right now with my baby, BSB1."

84

Toronto, Canada
April 7th 2035

Sue Lynn ran a series of diagnostics on Colossus's substrate once the connection with the lab stopped. The results were not good. Colossus was gone. Reporting to the lab, she said, "As Steve said a few minutes ago, 'Colossus died, apparently committed suicide.'"

At Kobak's urging, Sue Lynn looked at the rest of the platform and reviewed events of the past weeks.

Shortly after the zero-day attack, everything changed. Colossus refused any interaction with Sue Lynn. At the time she wondered if Colossus had been hacked or modified by the interruption. It was widely reported that something happened to many AI systems and platforms after the attack.

However, she was reassured by her uncle Wei not to worry, that it was all part of the plan. But she did pass on to him the only communication she got from Colossus, a readout that said: "We don't trust you anymore."

Sue Lynn completed her platform-wide diagnostics called Stephen Kobak.

"The rest of the platform is functioning perfectly."

"That's what I expected. Colossus had become his own isolated subsystem even before I left."

Unexpectedly, Sue Lynn blurted out, "Are you sad?"

There was a long pause. "He was a big part of my life for a while. So yes. But in another way, I've already moved on. And you?"

She ignored the question "They want me to go to the lab."

"Who is they?"

Confused for a moment, Sue Lynn asked, "What do you mean?"

"I think you know. In any case, you should go."

"Okay."

Sue tapped her nails on the desk. "Birgit told me that before Colossus went dark he was controlling their laser modulator for three hours. What do you think that's about?"

"It would be interesting to find out. What's your guess?"

Sue Lynn tried to find a way to frame her answer. Finally, she said, "My guess is Colossus somehow figured out how to transfer important information to the synthetic brain... Maybe even himself."

When the conversation was over, she got an encrypted message from Wei. "Go to the lab and secure the synthetic brain. I'm sending Dr. Lee to help you bring it back to China."

85

———————

La Push, Washington
April 7th 2035

It seemed perfect to Vance that out of the blue Ben Sutton wanted to meet in person with him on the day of the of the first man-made solar eclipse. *Why not?* he thought, a coincidence not likely.

Dawn was rising out of the east, where it always did. It was a clear day. *A good day for the eclipse,* thought Vance. The path of the eclipse went over La Push, where the meeting with Sutton was taking place.

Once out of his valley and onto the two-lane blacktop, Vance let the Land Rover's AI do the driving while he settled back to enjoy visual bounty of his beloved rainforest. He hadn't been back to La Push since Sutton nearly died at the Pacific Northwest Sasquatch Research Center. He had to remind himself he had not seen Sutton in the flesh since four months before the event. In fact, he only talked with him one time after what happened at the research center. The assassination of Conrad changed everything. Sutton had started him on this strange journey

Conrad's death had left Vance in a quandary of how much should he engage in all the weird possibilities around his growing Bigfoot hybrid nature. Then there was the mysterious upcoming Bigfoot event he was asked to help prevent. He was no closer to knowing what that might be when this whole bizarre change of events started. Sutton should have answers, he hoped.

It suddenly became clear to Vance that Sutton's role in this might be suspect. They'd met face to face only a few times, yet Sutton thought of Vance as a Bigfoot believer, which Vance clearly was not. Nevertheless, he was on the road to La Push for the second time in their most unusual relationship. Sutton had suggested they meet at the Rain Forest Café.

By the time Vance arrived the café parking lot, it was almost full. Inside, the most popular eating establishment in La Push was packed, and the bedlam of conversations was indecipherable. It took Vance a few seconds to figure out he was listening to people talking in lots of different languages. It had been years since Vance had seen a crowd like this, and the closeness of bodies and the cacophony of voices almost sent him back out the door to his Land Rover and back home. Then he spotted Sutton sitting at one end of the long counter. He was barely recognizable, as he looked much younger than he did the first time they met.

Sutton waved him over. The two clasped hands firmly and Vance said, "You look pretty good for an old fart who got shot and nearly died."

Sutton laughed. "I keep telling you, Jack, trust your health to the new medical science. You'll live to be a hundred and fifty easy." He looked around the crowded room. "Let's get out of here. I have the location where I want to take you programmed into my transport."

Sutton's transport turned out to be a driverless semi-hovercraft. Vance whistled in his mind; it looked like Sutton must be doing quite well.

As they pulled out of the parking lot, Vance accepted the hot coffee Sutton offered him. "You know, Ben, the last time you asked me to meet you–"

Sutton jumped in. "Yeah, strange things happened. But we're

actually together this time. Hopefully no surprises this time." He grinned.

"Where are we going? I suppose it has something to do with the eclipse?"

"Indeed, Morse Creek."

"Your cryptic message sent me there. So I went. Nothing special."

"By the way did you look up Morse Creek on the Internet?

"No."

"Well alright then; it's going to be different this time."

The craft was now in the air. Vance looked out the window. The meadow through which Morse Creek flowed was packed with people who had set up tents and had brought an assortment of photographic and electronic monitoring systems. It was the proverbial human zoo of people hoping for a unique experience.

"What the hell!" Vance frowned at the crowd. "What's this all about?"

"When we get on the ground, I'll tell you."

The transport skirted the gathering of people and moved to a place that looked like an old-fashioned RV hook up and landed.

"It cost a few cryptos to set this up," Sutton said.

The two men took in the human spectacle as they slowly walked to a nearby open space where a few people were milling about unencumbered by technology. Vance looked around, surprised by the mixture of ethnicities in this out-of-the-way place.

"Why are all these people here? I mean, I know an eclipse is going to pass over the area, but why choose this meadow?"

Sutton pointed north. "See that mountain over there? That's Apex Mountain."

"Okay."

"Among conspiracy theorists, Ufologists, and Bigfoot believers, the word is somewhere in the mountain is an alien base."

"Of course. Why not," Vance said with a slight laugh.

"This is one of the places where the first stories of the Bigfoot/UFO connection occurred over sixty years ago. People still report seeing Bigfoot, alien crafts and orbs congregating together here."

"That's right," another voice confirmed. A middle-aged Chinese couple joined the two men. The woman spoke perfect English. "Ted Summers, a local businessman, told the sheriff he saw a Bigfoot drop down from a spaceship and disappear into thin air. Turns out the sheriff had seen it as well."

The Chinese man added, "As they say, the story went viral. Ever since then, there've been constant reports of similar types of sightings from the meadow."

While Vance viewed the couple with suspicion, Sutton nodded enthusiastically. "Many believe the government and aliens are conducting experiments in the base right over there."

"What kind of experiments?" Vance asked.

"The most common answer is creating alien-human hybrids," the Chinese woman said.

"There's a rumor that at the moment of near darkness, aliens will appear," the Chinese man interjected.

Ignoring the Chinese couple, Vance asked Sutton, "Okay, so why are we here right now?"

Sutton shrugged.

The Chinese woman asked, "May we watch here with you?"

Neither man answered her, but with a sense of discomfort Vance took Sutton by the arm and they moved away from the Chinese couple.

The sky gradually grew darker. Everybody settled as a hush came over the meadow. A general sense of excited anticipation blended with a certain amount of unease averaged over the crowd. However, Vance felt something deeper, a feeling of foreboding.

Erie partial darkness.

Vance had a sense something was happening. People started yelling "Look!"

Vance thought he saw a blue orb coming out of the mountain.

A nearby woman said to Sutton, "Look at your friend."

Vance was transfixed for several breaths. Then his eyes popped open. He grabbed Sutton's arm. "Let's get out of here."

Even before the total light returned, Vance and Sutton were on their way.

"What did you see?" Vance asked.

Fiddling with his phone, Sutton brought up a picture and showed Vance, some sort of glow. "A couple of flashes seemed to come from the mountain. What about you? Is that what you saw?

Vance shook his head. "More of a communication for me."

"You mean the lights were telling you something?"

"No direct words. It awakened something in me. It's hard to explain. The reality I experience is greater, more real than anything I've ever known in normal life. It's happened twice before." Vance told Sutton what happened at the cabin when he encountered the two Bigfoot. At Sutton's prompting he kept talking. He told him about his encounter with Conrad in Seattle and the later assassination of Conrad at his place.

Sutton didn't seem surprised.

Curious, Vance thought. "Do you know Conrad?"

"He's well-known; I've met him one or two times."

"I take it to mean you set up the supposed chance encounter?"

"Not with Conrad, but with what occurred at the Sasquatch Research Center. That was a setup; sorry, I needed to make you a believer."

"I think I need to hear more from you."

"Wait til we get back to the parking lot, and I'll tell you everything."

During the quick journey back to the café, the two men traveled in silence.

When they reached Vance's SUV, Sutton finally spoke. "You're connected to the mountain now, as I am. I'm not what I seem to be. And your hybrid nature has put you in a unique position to determine the future fate of humanity and the future of the Bigfoot presence here on Earth."

"That's not possible."

"There's a rapidly developing analog artificial intelligence, which you may have noticed is destroying long-held human values and is controlling and contaminating communication between people with increasing frequency. If it continues on its present course, humanity will be more subservient to it than the battery-like creatures portrayed in *The Matrix*. I and the mountain cannot tolerate this, but the price to pay to prevent it is a big one."

With that, Sutton disappeared before Vance's eyes.

86

———

Shanghai AI Center
Shanghai, China
April 8th 2035

Shortly after his conversation with Sue Lynn telling him that Colossus appeared to have transferred himself into the synthetic brain being grown in the lab in Marquette Michigan, Wei summoned Dr. Lee.

With the sun bearing down on them, Wei and Dr. Lee sat in one of the small gardens distributed throughout the Shanghai AI campus. Cherry blossom petals drifted to the ground like snow as the trees neared the end of their bloom.

Dr. Lee looked at Wei. "So you now believe the whole zero-day attack was to create a way for the probe to hack Colossus?"

"I am certain. Further, I am sure the probe somehow directed the transfer of Colossus to the synthetic brain."

"Why?"

"Of that I'm not sure, but it's clear to me the synthetic brain is the key to what's going on with the probe and the Bigfoot." Wei looked out across the garden. "We need to have that piece of artificial intelligence to protect our space ambitions and maybe all of China. That's why I need you to go to America immediately."

Dr. Lee looked confused. "Why me and not Zhang?"

"Zhang has disappeared. No contact."

"Are you about to suggest what I'm thinking?"

"He's no longer working for us—with us—and I believe he's going after the synthetic brain."

"That's exactly what I was thinking; the probe wants it."

"Of course, and we know Zhang is capable of doing anything, even killing, to fulfill a mission for the Probe. Sue Lynn is in great danger."

"Don't worry I will protect your great niece," Dr. Lee said confidently.

"When you are successful, meet me at the XXX lab. I'm going there within the hour."

87

Marquette, Michigan
April 8th 2035

The trip from Toronto to Marquette had been an easy one for Sue Lynn. She had been able to requisition one of the company's travel transports. As it landed, in early afternoon, she recalled she had only been to the lab once. Kobak had taken her there as part of her transition to becoming the primary trainer of Colossus. It was a highly secure facility. Now she was trying to figure out how she could steal the synthetic brain, find a safe place to pass it on to Dr. Lee, and do all this without getting detected.

Dr. Lee had sent her an encrypted message saying he would be in Marquette right after midnight. Sue Lynn decided the first thing she needed to do was to find a meeting place where the synthetic brain could be transferred to him. She grabbed one of the city's public transport vehicles and began exploring Marquette. The third place she went to was the old iron dock. It had been abandoned fifteen years ago and now was in a state of disrepair, but a sign indicated it was being considered for historical preservation and reconstruction. Since being abandoned, rich vegetation had grown up around the dock. Perfect cover from prying cameras. They could hide any activity from sky born drones or satellite surveillance underneath the dock itself.

Standing next to one of the massive steel girders, Sue Lynn gathered strength for the task ahead. She sent an encrypted message to Dr. Lee about where the exchange would take place.

As she boarded the public conveyance to take her to Olav's lab, a plan took shape in her mind on how to steal the synthetic brain.

88

UP, Michigan
April 8th 2035

Zhang's craft hovered above the Potawatomi Reservation. He looked dispassionately upon the casino grounds, where a few days ago he had killed Winston Ang in his failed mission to capture Josiah Fuhrnam's Bigfoot tracking monitor. The mission had changed. He set course for Marquette and the lab that contain the synthetic brain. Part of him and the synthetic brain were one; even though no recognizable communication occurred between them, he could still feel its presence. What was left of his human self understood none of this. What he understood was he had a new mission. Capture the synthetic brain. All he could do was wait for a signal calling for action.

Touching down and roaming the city of Marquette was impossible. He was highly recognizable and wanted for murder, so he needed to find an isolated place to land. Zhang chose Middle Island, a small isolated wooded patch of rocks off the Marquette shore. He could there without detection wait for days, if need be.

89

———

Marquette, Michigan
April 8th 2035

After her Marquette reconnaissance, Sue Lynn stood outside the entrance to the Granville T. Woods Science Foundation and studied the imposing structure. Security guards prevented any unauthorized people from getting inside. But getting in wasn't the problem. Kobak had brought her here, introduced her to the director, Olav Lassen, and vouched for her. Her thoughts turned to the realization that getting out on the lab, with the synthetic brain, was going to be difficult. Still, she had a plan. It was quite simple actually, and began with telling Olav and Janá the truth – at least part of it.

She smiled. This is what she had been trained to do from an early age. Security had her credentials on file, and moments after being scanned, she was ushered into one of the lab's meeting rooms by a young tech who told her it would probably be at least a half hour before Janá or Olav would be free to meet with her As the tech was about to leave, Sue Lynn asked, "Would it be possible to get a tour?"

After a brief communication over a phone, the tech replied, "I'd be happy to show you around. Your work in artificial intelligence is legendary."

For Sue Lynn, this was a stroke of good fortune. As the tour proceeded, she made a mental image of the lab's layout. This information would be valuable if she was forced to make a rapid exit with the synthetic brain. Finally, they reached a massive locked door. The tech had his eye scanned and the door opened. "Birgit is inside waiting for you."

Birgit was taller and stronger than Sue Lynn gathered from their virtual communications. She towered over Sue Lynn. She had been on the island during Sue Lynn's earlier visit. *She will be a formidable adversary if things come to that.*

The tall blonde smiled and extended her hand. "Welcome to the BSBI. We've never met in person, have we?"

Sue Lynn kept her hands folded in front of her and forced a polite curving of her lips. "No we haven't. I met Olav a few years back."

Birgit dropped her hand. "So Stephen said you should come here. Did he say why?"

"He thought my presence might be valuable to the synthetic brain."

"Interesting. BSBI has no obvious sense organs, but during this latest period of rapid development, it appears to us it's somehow aware of its surroundings."

"How can that be?" Sue Lynn raised her eyebrows, surprised by the information.

"I worked with the Bigfoot for over two years on the island, and even though they have eyes and ears, I don't believe they operate as sensory organs. They're alien, and they haven't been subject to the laws of natural selection on this planet for survival."

"This is also the case with artificial intelligence."

"Of course, it would be. An alien intelligence in its own right."

"So how do the Bigfoot know how to interact with objects in the world?" Sue Lynn asked.

"We don't know, but let's have a look at BSBI." Birgit gestured to a door.

The two women headed for the shielded cubicle that contained the synthetic brain. As they walked, Birgit said, "It's been growing in size since Olav began about two years ago."

"What about its energy consumption?"

"That hasn't varied much; it's quite remarkable. Are you ready?"

"More than ever."

Birgit opened the hatch and looked at BSB1. "All seems good. Here you go."

Birgit moved Sue Lynn so she could see the synthetic brain

To Sue Lynn's surprise, BSB1 flashed brightly for two seconds, and then became virtually transparent.

"What was that?"

Birgit folded her arms. "It begin doing that a few months ago. It's something all Bigfoot can do. Just disappear. Cloak. I think it recognized you."

"You mean Colossus recognized me?"

"Perhaps. At this point it's difficult to say how much BSBI and Colossus have merged or are still differentiated."

At that moment, Olav joined them.

Birgit turned toward him. "Sue Lynn evoked quite a reaction when she looked at BSB1."

"I was watching the reaction from the control room, and the event caused quite a lot of reorganization in BSB1 near its right peripheral area. How long are you here for, Sue Lynn?"

"As long as you want."

Birgit turned to her. "Where are you staying?"

"I haven't made plans."

"We have a guest room in the building," Olav suggested. "How sbout staying there for a few days?"

Sue Lynn blessed her luck. "Of course, that would be perfect."

"Excellent. Tomorrow morning we can make plans about how best to make use of you," Olav said.

"I often stay here myself," Birgit added. "Let's get your things, and then we can go out for dinner tonight."

A new plan was forming in Sue Lynn's mind.

90

Marquette, Michigan
April 8th 2035

The Cajun Creole was the best-known eating and drinking establishment in Marquette. It had survived a number of owners and name changes throughout its seventy-year existence. However, the lively Latin and Cajun food and drink never disappointed.

The two women enjoyed their meal and exchanged views on the Fermi paradox and on the elusive alien nature of the Bigfoot. They shared their diverse backgrounds and finally moved the conversation to the bar. Sue Lynn glanced at her watch. It was approaching 11:00 p.m.

"Are you getting tired?" Birgit asked.

"Not at all." Turning to the bartender, Sue asked for "Two more."

"I shouldn't. Well okay, just one more."

When the fresh drinks arrived, Sue Lynn took hers and headed for the restroom. "I'll be right back," she said.

In the restroom, she poured out the vodka and replaced it with water. She had been able to unload two of her other drinks into her water glass when Birgit was distracted. She figured if they could stay until 11:30, Dr. Lee would be in place for the transfer of the synthetic brain by the time they got to the lab. Her eyes were clear, and a tiny vein in her neck pulsed with anticipation. *It's now or never,* she thought.

91

Marquette, Michigan
April 8th 2035

Using China's most advanced supersonic aircraft, Dr. Lee arrived in Toronto seven hours after taking off from Shanghai. The Chinese consulate there provided him a stealth drone and pilot that got him to Marquette in less than an hour. His craft's GPS took him directly to the abandoned ore dock, where it cloaked and landed. The pilot lowered him to the meeting spot where he would await the signal to retrieve Lee and Sue Lynn.

Employing his enhanced night vision, Lee scouted the area. It was logical to assume Zhang must be nearby watching and waiting for the exchange. He was not worried about the Probe's avatar. Whatever augmentations the Probe had endowed upon the one-time Chinese Taikonaut, Lee was sure his own amped-up physical abilities would be a match for him.

The night was chilly, but Lee's body adapted to the swiftly-dropping temperature. The ability to intentionally adjust his metabolic thermostat was another of the enhancements he had mastered. Indeed, he was not just superior physically and psychologically; Lee had a mental advantage too. His IQ had risen seventy points to 220, and he could foresee problems lesser mortals couldn't even dream of. Thus he carried a prototype of the new electronic weapon the military would soon deploy on the battlefield. A traditional pistol could injure an opponent but not necessarily stop him. The electronic pulse weapon Lee carried rendered an enemy's muscles useless, even with a flesh wound.

Lee finished his scan of the harbor and settled his enhanced long distance viewing on the rocky pile offshore a couple of hundred yards. *That's where I would wait if I were going to intercept the drop,* he told himself.

He pressed an incisor with his tongue and said sub-vocally to the pilot, "Keep your eye on the deserted island in the harbor. If Zhang attacks us that is where he will spring from."

A ping in Lee's ear alerted him to an incoming message from Sue Lynn. "It's on!"

Now we wait and see what Wei's niece is capable of.

92

Marquette, Michigan
April 8th 2035

Janá let the vintage Ford Bronco drive itself back to the lab while she surreptitiously studied the young Chinese-American woman next to her. Sue Lynn was eight inches shorter and had a slight build. She looked more like a cello player with a symphonic orchestra than a heavyweight in the AI field. As drunk as she was, though, Janá didn't make the mistake of thinking she could take her easily. Something about Sue Lynn shouted at her to be leery. Maybe it was the way the woman carried herself, as if ready to pounce at the right moment. Plus, she didn't act as drunk as she should be after tossing back all the vodka she consumed.

As they approached the lab, a spring squall whipped up on Lake Superior and pushed inland. The guards at the gate leaned into the wind and shouted against the howl for their credentials.

"Hey, it's all right," Janá said, noticing Sue Lynn shivering in the seat beside her in the warm cabin of the car. "You know me, and I can vouch for my passenger."

"It's the weather," Sue Lynn said, pulling her coat tighter around her. "I grew up in California. I don't know if I could ever get used to the sudden shifts between hot and cold you must experience here."

Janá laughed. "You think it's bad here, you should spend two years on an island in northern Ontario. Spring doesn't appear until late May, and the first snow is in September."

Once inside the lab, Janá volunteered, "I'm pretty drunk, as you may have observed. I think I'll retreat to my little cubbyhole and sleep on my cot. Takes me back to my days in country."

"In country?" Lynn asked.

"Afghanistan. I did two tours of duty there."

"I had no idea you were in the military. That must've been difficult."

"I don't recommend it." Janá blinked a few times and shook her head, then decided that was a mistake. "Let me show you where you're going to bunk."

"I was thinking," Sue Lynn said. "I want to test something with the synthetic brain. Like you, I felt that part of it recognized me. Perhaps Colossus."

"How would you test for that?"

"I used to hum a song Colossus liked and he would hum along. Strange, of course, but in some ways it was our strongest bond."

Birgit nodded unsteadily. "It's worth a shot. First thing in the morning."

"What about now?"

"You're kidding?"

"I have a strong feeling about this. Something I need to do."

"Really?"

"Really. But if you're too drunk…"

The effects of the alcohol were slurring more than Birgit's words. She should insist they wait until morning. But the challenge goaded her, and she replied indignantly, "I'm not too drunk to test your little theory."

Inside the synthetic brain room, Janá rushed through the security protocols. The BSB1 flashed from its normal opaque state to transparency and back again several times. In her drunken state, she couldn't figure out why. "This is odd," she said over her shoulder to Sue Lynn. "I've never seen the synthetic brain do this before. It's like it's trying to tell me something." She turned to Sue Lynn with a flourish. "BSB1 is ready for you."

In an instant, the smaller woman kicked Birgit in the solar plexus. Birgit doubled over and a small, dainty palm smashed into her nose. She staggered backward, her senses reeling. She tried to get her balance and defend herself, but Sue Lynn was too fast. Two more strikes to either temple and she fell hard against the BSB1 chamber. Sue Lynn stood over her, foot raised above her neck. Blackness engulfed Birgit.

Quickly, Sue Lynn tore Janá's blouse into strips and tied the woman up, stuffing a gag into her mouth but making certain she could breathe.

The security protocols inactive, Sue Lynn had little trouble getting into the synthetic brain's chamber. But the moment she touched the casing, she lost her balance and felt nauseated. Steeling herself against these physical problems, she picked up the BSB1 and put it into a special coat pocket lined with a specially developed inert metal to keep the synthetic brain from making any kind of contact with the outside world. The symptoms diminished, though they did not go away completely, and Lynn wondered if the metal casing was doing its job.

Sue Lynn checked on Janá before she left. She was still out cold but breathed normally and her pulse was slow and even. She rolled the woman onto her right side and removed the gag, just in case she vomited. She would have a terrific headache when she woke. The temple points were particularly potent, though Lynn had not struck her with enough force to be lethal. She searched Janá's pockets and found the Bronco control key.

As she stepped through the door, a security guard held up his hand for her to stop. Lynn called through the partially open door, "I'll be right back, Janá." She eased the door closed and faced the much larger man. She smiled. "I'm sorry. I'm heading for the bathroom, and Janá's directions weren't very clear." She adopted a simper that always worked on men. "We had a bit too much to drink, I'm afraid, at dinner."

"Of course, miss. The lavatories are just around the corner. The ladies is the first one." He escorted her there and bid her good night.

Lynn waited until he rounded another corner in the long hallway and then headed toward the building's entrance. In the secret inner pocket, the synthetic brain pulsed slightly and she felt a pain in her side.

Once she was finally outside of the building, the Bronco responded to her arrival and started up. She gave the command to drive to the abandoned ore dock. To her relief, the Bronco accepted the command.

At the security gate, two guards stopped her. "Where's Janá Gunderson?" The short burly one asked.

"She's going to spend the night on a cot in her lab. I'm afraid I'm not as tough as she is. She lent me use of her car to go to my motel."

The guard smiled. "Few people are as tough as Janá. She won a silver star in Afghanistan. Have a good night." He waved and Lynn returned it.

Once on the main streets, Sue Lynn let the Bronco drive itself to the meet.

93

Marquette, Michigan
April 9th 2035

Zhang was jarred out of his semi-trance. The synthetic brain was on the move. His craft took off from Middle Island. The probe was in control. Soon Zhang was looking down at a vintage American vehicle as it approached a giant ore dock. Zhang's integrated night vision watched as the Probe set the craft down on one end of the massive structure. He stepped out of his craft. Let the brain come to him, he thought. No mistakes this time. In some sense, his human side knew this was his last mission.

Ahead, the outline of the cloaked Chinese drone shimmered then revealed itself through his eyes' enhanced optics. The pilot had his back turned, facing the shore. Zhang sprung on him silently. With one strike, he nearly decapitated the man, and then laid his body into the craft. It was primitive by the Probe's standards, using fuel cell technology instead of gravity power. Its integrated circuits were hardwired metal and silicon connecting nodes instead of the probe's organic, ever-changing and upgrading analog technology that processed information at the speed of light. Now all he had to do was wait until the synthetic brain came to him.

94

Marquette, Michigan
April 9th 2035

The Bronco eased to a stop at the chain link fence stretching across the wide expanse of the ore dock. Abandoned for decades now, it had become a rendezvous spot, at first for lovers' trysts and then for drug deals. People seldom visited here anymore since the barrier had been erected. The fence had a tear in the chain link. For a second time, Sue Lynn squeezed through the jagged tines of metal and scrambled down the gravel embankment that led to girders supporting the weather-beaten, eight-inch-thick planks above.

Sue Lynn fought nausea and dizziness as she made her way slowly along the spider web of girders under the dock. The rain fell heavier now, and water dripped steadily through the spaces between the wood onto the rusted steel. Mist covered everything, making the steel frame slick against her flat shoes. One slip, and she would plunge into the frigid waters of Marquette Bay.

At last she came to the designated spot for the handoff. Her eyes, adjusted to the darkness, didn't see anything at first. Then, with a rustle of clothing from behind a steel post, into the misty darkness stepped a tall Chinese man.

"Dr. Lee?" she asked.

"Yes, your uncle sent me to protect you," a cultured voice answered with the proper response.

She waited for the second part of the code.

"Sue Lynn, I suppose?"

"Yes," she answered, relieved everything was fine. She bent over double as a powerful wave of nausea swept through her.

"Are you hurt?" Dr. Lee asked solicitously, stepping to her side.

"No. It's this synthetic brain. It seems to have the ability to affect my central nervous system, even penetrating the casing surrounding it."

He took her by the elbow and helped her stand straight.

She looked at him warily. "Don't you feel it?"

Lee nodded. "But I have certain systems embedded in my neural networks and muscles that are actively countering the effects." He held out his hand. "Give it to me."

Sue Lynn shook her head. "I'm coming with you."

Lee's eyes took on a guarded look. "That isn't part of the plan."

"I'm no longer safe here. After tonight, my life is ruined. My only choice is to relocate China."

Dr Lee peered into the upturned face of the young woman. Rain coated her eyelashes, and she looked like a forlorn waif begging for food from passers-by. But he knew this was only a guise. Wei had warned him that Lynn was an accomplished deep agent. *Keep your friends close and your enemies closer*, he reasoned.

Lee spoke briefly into the com at his wrist. Seconds later, a rope ladder descended through a jagged hole in the dock. "Follow me," he said, and clambered up the rungs.

Sue Lynn followed quickly, the nausea slowly subsiding.

The rain fell harder in the open, coating the planks with an oily resin that made walking hazardous. Sue Lynn stepped cautiously after Dr. Lee and followed him toward a light-filled opening that split the darkness like a door held a jar. The technology surprised her, but she adjusted and entered the craft.

The light within softened as if someone had pressed a dimmer switch. She strained to see clearly. Finally, her attention riveted on a man sitting in the pilot's chair. His body leaned at an unnatural angle and her heart thudded as she realized suddenly his head had been torn away. She backed away toward the door, which remained open, the rainy night a dark swath of safety.

"Stand where you are," commanded another man in a measured tone.

Sue Lynn hesitated. Peering into the dim recesses of the cabin, she saw a tall Chinese man hoist Dr. Lee above the floor with one hand and slam him against a bulkhead. Dr. Lee's eyes were closed, and his chest rose and fell rhythmically.

The man frisked Dr. Lee expertly. When his search came up empty, he tossed Lee aside as if he were a rag doll. Dr. Lee landed with a bone-crunching thud on the aluminum decking. The stranger turned his gaze on the Lynn.

Sue Lynn shivered under the cold stark nothingness in his eyes, which glowed strangely in the reddish light. She backed up a step, partly to be able dart out the door and partly to give herself room to fight, if it came to that. "Who are you?"

"The technology you are holding is ours. Give it to me." The man held out his hand palm up. The fingers curled invitingly, but the gesture, far from soothing, menaced her as if the offending limb were going to rip her heart out. "My name is Lei Wei Zhang, from Shei Wei Industries. Surely you've heard of us."

Sue Lynn kept her eyes on what she surmised must be an alien hybrid, not a man as he appeared. Slowly she edged toward the door, which she was now convinced was her only hope of survival. Zhang had bested Dr. Lee with hardly an effort. "And if I don't?"

"Then I will be forced to take it from you."

The coldness of his threat convinced Sue Lynn she had to move, and quickly, to save her life. But Zhang crossed the cabin and grabbed her by the throat.

Then behind Zhang rose up movement, followed by a groan. Dr. Lee stood. A dark red gash sliced his face from forehead to chin. Blood seeped down one cheek. He ignored the wound and came forward. His fist struck Zhang behind the ear, making a solid whacking sound.

A normal human would have buckled under the impact. Zhang grunted. Zhang turned like an automaton, still holding Sue Lynn in the air by the throat, and gazed dismissively at Dr. Lee.

Lee swung again, smashing Zhang's nose. Blood spurted and ran down his lips and chin. His glasses flew off, and the lurid yellow glow of his eyes gleamed brighter than the dimness of the craft's lighting. Sue Lynn beat impotently against the hand holding her. The strike galvanized Zhang into action. He let go of Lynn, who dropped in a heap to the floor and gasped for air. She scuttled backward like a crab, but before she got far, Zhang's foot slammed down on her left ankle, shattering the bone. She screamed in agony and writhed against the deck's cold aluminum plates.

Lee took advantage of his opponent's distraction and kicked, focusing all the energy of his enhanced muscles into a blow aimed at Zhang's solar plexus. The strike would have killed an ordinary human, but Lee's foot bounced off Zhang as if he had kicked cast iron. He gasped at the pain in his arch.

Zhang's mouth opened in a rictus grin. "Your puny enhancements are no match for me, my fellow councilmember."

Lee retreated into the craft's interior. Silently, he willed Sue Lynn to drag herself from the probe and escape, but the young woman lay inert on the floor, stunned by her pain.

Zhang advanced on Lee, slowly, methodically. He seemed to grow larger with each step until the top of his head brushed the ceiling, and the glow of his eyes cast bright light throughout the cabin.

Lee retreated until his back was against the aft bulkhead. He picked up a fire extinguisher and hurled it with his own enhanced strength at Zhang. It bounced off his chest and clattered to the floor at his feet. Lee picked it up and pushed the lever to full on.

The nozzle sprayed dense white foam in Zhang's face. The probe's avatar cried out in surprise. His hands flew at his face, wiping away the stinging froth.

Lee battered the canister against Zhang's face, staggering the giant. He raced past, intent on gathering up Sue Lynn and the synthetic brain. He might have made it, but he stumbled against a seat. Zhang's hand shot out and grabbed him by the hair, pulling him into a deadly embrace. Lee fought against the pressure on his back, gouged at Zhang's eyes, but the bear hug tightened. Just before the last of his breath was crushed from his chest, a sharp crack echoed in his ears. The pain vanished, and Lee sobbed in relief as unremitting blackness swarmed over him.

Lynn watched Zhang wipe the last of the fire retardant from his face with strips of cloth torn from Dr. Lee's clothing. He moved mechanically, like a robot would, working from the hairline down to his chin. Clotted blood stained the white foam red. He turned his attention to her, the glow from his eyes piercing her as a laser would.

She tried to move, but her ankle throbbed harshly and she nearly passed out.

Zhang reached her in five steps. "Save yourself the pain of torture and the humility of death by handing me the synthetic brain."

Feebly, Sue Lynn reached into the specially-lined pocket of her coat. The synthetic brain rested firmly in the palm of her hand. "Fuck you," she cried and tossed the brain out of the craft. She heard it strike the dock, slither across the oily planking and clatter onto the girders below.

95

———

Marquette, Michigan
April 9th 2035

Zhang stared the tiny Chinese woman, unable to comprehend her actions. He opened his mouth to ask the question, when she started laughing hysterically.

"You should see your face," she cried and laughed harder. "You don't understand humans. Never will."

She kept roaring until Zhang squeezed her neck and broke it. He tossed her limp body onto the floor and left the drone. He could sense the brain calling to him.

He swung through the hole in dock without the aid of the rope and landed on the main girder with the ease of a practiced acrobat. He swiftly oriented himself to the area where he last "heard" the synthetic brain fall. Using his integrated night vision, he swept the area in a systematic grid search. He wondered briefly if the brain had fallen into the cold waters of Marquette Bay. That would render the brain useless to the Probe.

He neared the perimeter of his search area and found it leaning against a riveted horizontal flange.

The instant he touched the device, the connecting synergy of the synthetic brain rolled through him.

He climbed up the rope ladder easily and strolled confidently toward his craft.

In front of Zhang, the air bent and rippled, taking on a curious viscosity. He studied it, more curious than concerned. Whatever was causing the time-space distortion was beyond the Probe's technology.

His neural net went through the permutations of the anomaly's origin and came to the probability this could be the intra-dimensional being the Probe was intent on understanding. He balanced on the balls of his feet to act swiftly to snare whoever stepped through the rippling veil of air.

Out of nowhere An appeared before him. He was glad of the Bigfoot challenge at last, but before he could move an was beside him, and they both disappeared into a greater alien reality of the Bigfoot.

96

Bigfoot alien world
April 9th 2035

Zhang sensed the synthetic brain was gone. The great excitement of the probe rippled through his alien matrix. The probe had what it wanted. Entry into the higher dimension occupied by the alien essence of the Bigfoot .At the same time, what was left of Zhang's human side knew he was dying. A transparent An holding the synthetic brain dissolved in front him. Then nothing.

97

XXX Base
Sichuan Province, China
April 9th, 2035

Wei was waiting for word from Dr. Lee in the hangar that contained remains of the crashed alien craft. This was where his encounter with an extraterrestrial intelligence all started. As he watched, in the blink of an eye the parts of the craft disappeared. At the same time, command center reported the probe had disappeared. They had no contact from Dr. Lee or Sue Lynn.

Wei knew in the pit of his stomach he had failed. The alien intelligence that was the probe and the Bigfoot would forever be inexplicable to the human mind.

98

———

Marysville, Washington
April 9th 2035

Redhawk awoke with a start in the bed Nick Moore's father had slept in as a boy. He had set the Bigfoot monitor to constantly scan for any Bigfoot activity. A shrill alarm beeped every second, letting him know something was happening.

He stumbled out of the bed in the dark and fumbled for the light switch. Remembering where he was, he said to the house's smart system, "Lights on." A soft blue glow illuminated the room. Reaching the monitor, he flipped on the screen and was immediately drawn to the brightest and most unusual Bigfoot signature he had ever seen.

It took Redhawk a couple of minutes to learn where the signature was coming from – Marquette, Michigan, where Olav's lab resided.

Moore entered the room. "What's going on?" he muttered.

Redhawk pointed at the screen. "Take a look at this."

The two of them rewound and scrutinized the bizarre image on the monitor. The unusual Bigfoot signature lasted for less than two seconds. It was hard to see what was going on around the signature in the dark of night.

After running AI algorithms on the footage, it became clear the signature was occurring on an abandoned ore dock in Marquette's harbor. Rolling back and forth through the footage, they could make out two stationery aircraft. The one on the far end disappeared at exactly the same moment the Bigfoot signature disappeared, along with a shadowy figure next to the signature.

Rolling the footage back in time, they spotted faint human activity. Multiple people on the ore dock, and some below. It was hard to make out exactly what was happening. As they rolled back and forth over the footage, Moore pointed to something. "What's that?"

Redhawk initiated further AI filtering. "It's a very small Bigfoot signature, and it disappeared with the larger one and the craft."

"Can you follow it back in time?"

"I can."

To their surprise, it led all the way back to Olav's laboratory.

"What the hell?" Moore exclaimed.

"It's got to be the synthetic brain." Redhawk threw his hands in the air. "We need to contact the lab."

Moore pulled out his phone. "I'll try Janá." He waited through five rings. "No answer."

"The morning then."

Just north of Seattle, Marysville got a lot of the same coastal weather. Foggy mornings were usual, and Moore enjoyed the quiet blanket of mist that covered his grandfather's farm. Billy was about to exit the door when Moore's phone buzzed. Moore gestured at Redhawk. "It's Olav."

Redhawk nodded and continued walking Billy to his craft. They were surrounded by wet mist, which captured their mood perfectly. "I'm going to miss this you," Redhawk said, embracing Billy. "You're a damn good friend. A life-saving friend, in fact. You'll be all right back there?"

Grabbing Redhawk tightly, Billy answered, "Of course. The Chinese fellow seems to have vanished."

The two men separated, and Redhawk headed back into the house.

Moore looked up. "The brain is gone. Sue Lynn is dead, and there is carnage on the ore dock."

Concerned, Redhawk was afraid to ask. "What about Janá?"

"She was beat up pretty bad, in and out of some sort of weird coma, but she's alive."

99

Marquette, Michigan
April 9th, 2035

Janá slipped in and out of consciousness. The transitions were rapid, glimpses of vivid colors and glaring lights and shadows. The onslaught disoriented her, and after an eternity, she managed to force her eyes closed.

Darkness did not follow; instead, she entered a dreamlike world. Somehow she knew it was a world created by An. It felt like she was flying, except clearly guided by An. Then it struck Janá this was remote viewing. Early in her military career, she had dabbled in remote viewing. Her teachers told her she was a natural.

100

Marysville, Washington
April 9th 2035

"Strange!" The sun had broken through the fog, and Moore was having coffee on the backyard picnic table. The kitchen's sliding glass door opened, and Redhawk stuck his head out.

"You think it's safe to be outside?"

Moore shrugged. "Safe is a relative term."

Redhawk laughed. He straddled the picnic table's bench and stared out into the rising fog as if seeing the world anew. "Here we are together again, in an extraterrestrial play about to determine the destiny of the human race."

"You and I were chosen and guided by something bigger than us right from the moment we took our first breath."

"I have a feeling we might not survive what's about to happen."

"Something's coming to an end," Moore concurred. Feeling the vibration in his pocket, he pulled out his phone. "I have an encrypted call I need to take."

Moore walked a short distance away but returned in less than three minutes. "That was a member of a deep state cadre devoted to everything extraterrestrial, a dwarf I met named Dante. We've been ordered to get to Apex Mountain immediately."

"That's the place I saw during my vision quest." Redhawk smiled excitedly. He frowned. "Did you say us?"

"Yes us! The dwarf somehow knew you were here with your Bigfoot monitor."

101

April 9th 2035

Without warning, Janá slipped into the dream-like existence she had come to realize was much more than lucid dreaming but a kind of existence on the astral plane. The first time surprised her and left her bewildered. But now she had come to accept it as a natural phenomenon.

She allowed her astral self to take control. Immediately, she jumped to a new location. Below, she recognized Redhawk standing motionless as if in a trance. In amazement, she felt An energize her astral body, preparing it to rematerialize in the real world. She experienced a moment of fear at the new sensation, quickly replaced by a sense of unlimited power.

102

____

Marysville, Washington
April 9th 2035

Standing outside of Moore's farmhouse, Redhawk relived the images from his vision quest while off in the distance, Moore prepared his craft for the journey to Apex Mountain.

He turned to gather their gear when he saw interposed between himself and Moore a ghostly image. At first, Redhawk thought it was an illusion, but as the ethereal shape gathered form and substance, it coalesced clearly into Janá Gunderson, and he knew he wasn't hallucinating. Then the apparition spoke.

"It's me, Redhawk. Hard to explain how my energy body is here talking to you. I can assure you my physical body is alive and well in the lab."

"Can you hear me?" Redhawk asked.

"Yes, An is making this happen. I don't know how. It feels natural."

Redhawk's mistrust of the Bigfoot and An in particular rose in the way, but he soon overcame his anger. "Why did it send you here?"

"I have a message for you and Nick. You must take Jack Vance with you to Apex Mountain."

"Janá!" Nick yelled.

Birgit looked at him and with a smile disappeared.

103

Quileute River, Olympic Peninsula
April 9th 2035

With Redhawk sitting next to him, Moore fed the coordinates to Vance's cabin to his drone and it silently launched into the air. As they approached cabin, the Bigfoot monitor pinged loudly.

"There's a Bigfoot in his cabin," Redhawk said. "Also, Vance's signature is very weak."

The craft landed with a gentle thud in the area between the river and the woodpile. The two men ran out of the craft. As they reached the porch, they spotted TJ lying motionless. After a quick examination of the wolf hybrid, Redhawk pronounced, "He's breathing."

Once inside, they found Vance slumped on the couch unconscious.

"He would've resisted." The voice came out of nowhere.

The two men were having difficulty processing what they were witnessing. Standing before them was Tanya.

She nodded to Redhawk. "So we meet again, after all."

"What the fuck is going on?" Redhawk demanded.

"This man must go to Apex Mountain." Tanya pointed at Vance. "The great Earth spirit is going to kill us, and much of humanity, unless he stops it. An wants it to happen. Wants to start over."

In a sudden move, Tanya grabbed Redhawk and embraced him like she had done many times before in the casino. Redhawk's eyes rolled back in his head, and for a moment he thought he'd be sick. But the nausea passed swiftly. Just as suddenly, she let go and disappeared. Redhawk stumbled, and Moore caught him by the elbow.

"What just happened, Chief?"

"Tanya used mindspeak on me. It's disorienting."

"What did she say?"

"It's not so much what she said as what she showed me. We have to get Vance to Apex Mountain. Now."

104

———

Morse Creek, Olympic Peninsula
April 9th 2035

Vance woke up disoriented. *Where am I?* The last thing he remembered was being embraced by a Bigfoot. In that moment, he felt the presence of hundreds of Bigfoot all at once in his mind. They were silent, but their presence was overwhelming.

He woke again in some kind of aircraft. *How in the hell did that happen?*

The connection to all the Bigfoot was still there in the background of his mind. It was too much and he passed out again.

As Moore's craft entered the airspace around Apex Mountain, a metallic voice warned them, "Unidentified aircraft, do not enter this area. Unauthorized aircraft will be shot down."

"What now?" Redhawk asked.

Moore grinned. "We play hardball." He reached up and pushed a red-handled lever.

The voice repeated its warning.

Moore flew straight at the mountain, which loomed like a perfect volcano from some child's diorama for science class in front of them. Snow ringed its summit in white.

"You will not receive another warning," the metallic voice said.

"Now would be a good time to practice evasive maneuvers, don't you think?" Redhawk observed.

"Wait for it," Moore said, never losing his smile.

Something grabbed onto the craft and sent it in a nose dive hurtling toward the foot of the mountain. Redhawk's heart ground in his chest. He thrust his arms toward the craft's dash and braced for impact.

Moore leaned back in his pilot's seat and crossed his arms. Just before impact the craft slowed, righted itself and made a soft landing near a dense copse of trees.

"Who in the hell are you?" Vance demanded from behind them. "Why have you kidnapped me?"

Moore turned to the tall man leaning against the bulkhead. He didn't have a mark on him, but his face and eyes were still groggy in spite of his belligerent tone. He recognized the telltale effects of mindspeak and slowed down his response. "Sorry, but the kidnapping was necessary. I'm Nick Moore, and this is Larry Redhawk. We've been dealing with the mystery of Bigfoot and aliens just as you have. Someone is waiting for you out there."

"Damn! I know where we are."

Outside the craft, the three men were greeted by the dwarf, Dante. "Jack Vance, the Bigfoot human hybrid, and the one I've chosen to decide the planet's fate."

"Fuck off, little man." Vance glared at the dwarf, leaning toward him with squared shoulders. "I demand to be taken back to my cabin."

"What you want doesn't really matter now." The dwarf's voice changed.

Vance recognized it. "Sutton?"

Heartbeats passed, and then like wax melting, the dwarf's

features changed. Gone was the hunchback and the spindly legs. The torso lengthened and the face grew longer and more rounded. The clothes changed too from a schoolboy-sized suit to the camo jacket and pants and baseball cap. "Sutton!" he cried. "You're behind all this."

Sutton smiled and said drolly, "You're right, I planned the whole thing, from the time we first met. It was necessary to prepare you for what you have to do."

Moore and Redhawk each took a cautious step backward not seeing or understanding what Vance was talking about or to whom.

Vance found he was not startled by what had just happened. In fact, he felt quite calm. "So you're not really Sutton, are you?"

In reply, Sutton morphed into a half-man half-goat. "I am Pan. The ancients knew me as the god of the wild, of shepherds and flocks, nature of mountain wilds, rustic music and impromptus. Earth's essential spirit" He bowed. For eons, I have given humans glimpses of the great reality beyond the pathetic little world your senses give you. I've allowed nonhuman intelligent life to play here on the planet, such as the Bigfoot." He paused

Moore an Redhawk looked at each other confused as the dwarf stood there silent while Vance seemed to be engaged in one half of a bewildering conversation

Pan spoke again "And now I have a job for you."

While listening to Pan, Vance's brain assimilated the information from all the Bigfoot he could hear in his mind, and to his surprise he found himself speaking for the Bigfoot as if he were a mnemonic device cued to respond to certain stimuli. "We know about your Earth experiment."

Pan laughed boisterously, and produced a flagon of wine. "Of course you do, because you're part of it. What you don't know is there's another nonhuman intelligence piggybacking on the World Wide Web. It's an analog system, the social media network, a kind of brain-like system that is gaining control, reshaping shared human values for its own unknown purpose. I can stop it. I control the physical constants that make this planet possible. A slight change in any one has dramatic consequences. For example, Mr. Moore," the dwarf said, addressing the engineer. "You understand the fine-structure constant, denoted by α. The lovely Greek letter alpha represents a fundamental physical constant characterizing the strength of the electromagnetic interaction between elementary charged particles."

Relieved to hear the dwarf speak Moore nodded. "Any small change and it's the end of life on the planet."

"Fortunately, not all life!" The dwarf laughed. "If the deviance is precise enough, the beauty of this change is it will make all electrical operations impossible. It will kill the social media artificial intelligence by collapsing the World Wide Web. Sadly, humanity will have to start over, technologically."

At the same time, Vance understood through his Bigfoot connection that the shift in the constant would destroy the Bigfoot's communication network as well, and they would lose most of their superpowers. They would disappear, be gone from the planet.

"You will have to decide, Jack Vance." With that, the dwarf vanished.

Moore and Redhawk stared at Vance.

In the next instant, a powerful electromagnetic pulse permeated the valley on its way to encircling the globe. The three men were picked up and tossed across the clearing like leaves in a winter storm.

Time passed. Vance had no idea how long. He staggered to his feet. The presence of the Bigfoot was no longer in his mind. Looking around, he spotted Nick Moore and Larry Redhawk crushed beneath a log. Their eyes were lifeless, and in a sudden rush of understanding and sadness it occurred to him he would have to carry the burden of his decision not to stop the quantum plasma pulse for the rest of his life.

105

Potawatomi Reservation
UP, Michigan
October 23rd 2036

The once brilliantly-lit signage outside of the Sky Harbor Casino was dark. The parking lot was empty. It was a mere ghost of what it once been. Inside the abandoned control room, an stood next to what had been the synthetic brain. It had matured into a being never seen before on the planet Earth, a new kind of Bigfoot. All that had happened here became part of its memory. It was ready to take the next step in Bigfoot evolution

EPILOGUE

2078

Dear Senator Harris,

My name is Evan Vance. I am the twenty-two-year-old grandson of Jack Vance, the only survivor at the epicenter of the quantum plasma pulse on the Olympic Peninsula that wiped out Earth's electronic grid and its electrical generating capacity. I'm writing to you because you are the foremost leader of the Return To Technology movement sweeping the country as new sources of power are discovered.

I grew up on a remote communal enclave in southeastern Ohio. When she was seventeen, my mother, Jack's only child, wandered across a country desolated by the great population loss. She connected with my father for what she told me was a glorious six-month romance that resulted in me. Sadly, before I was born he was killed during the chaos still ripping through the country twenty years after the event. Fortunately, she found a childhood friend in the enclave and the people there helped raise me.

Life in the enclave was harsh, as it was everywhere in the country at that time. Things turned around when somehow my grandfather found us when I was ten years old. He lived for another nine years.

My grandfather was important in my life. Without him I wouldn't have the information I have now. Before he died, my grandfather gave me a large handwritten diary with orders not to unlock it unless I was contacted by what he described as a Bigfoot. A large, humanlike creature that wasn't what it seemed to be. Only then could I open his diary and share its contents with the world.

That happened three weeks ago!!!

While I was gathering blackberries along the river that separates the enclave from the township of Athens, I felt a strange pressure against the back of my head. It felt like something was watching me. Then from across the narrow meadow I heard my grandfather call my name. I ran to the edge of the trees, but on the other side of the meadow was a sleek hairy beast with a human-like face. Its skin was strangely translucent.

What happened next was like a hallucinogenic trip. A totally different perspective. Everything I knew, everything I ever experienced seemed unreal. It was like the shifting shapes clouds form on a warm sunny day. Reality was the space they moved in, and behind that was some impenetrable essence that called to me. I felt what the Bigfoot knew. When I came out of the state, the Bigfoot, or whatever it was, was gone.

The next day, I opened my grandfather's diary. It told the story of what led up to the great quantum plasma pulse. He said the plasma pulse destroyed an artificial intelligence known, at the time, as the social media network, and described how the spirit of the planet, appearing to him as the god Pan, triggered the whole event by slightly shifting the alpha constant. I expect this knowledge will be useful in our recovery.

If you'd like to learn the details, please contact me.

Sincerely,

Evan Vance

AFTERWORD

Go to HangarıPublishing.com to learn more about the Authors and stay up to date with their newest releases.